Carol Ericson is a bestselling, award-winning author of more than forty books. She has an eerie fascination for true-crime stories, a love of film noir and a weakness for reality TV, all of which fuel her imagination to create her own tales of murder, mayhem and mystery. To find out more about Carol and her current projects, please visit her website at www.carolericson.com, 'where romance flirts with danger.'

Nicole Helm grew up with her nose in a book and the dream of one day becoming a writer. Luckily, after a few failed career choices, she gets to follow that dream— writing down-to-earth contemporary romance and romantic suspense. From farmers to cowboys, Midwest to the West, Nicole writes stories about people finding themselves and finding love in the process. She lives in Missouri with her husband and two sons and dreams of someday owning a barn.

Also by Carol Ericson

Evasive Action
Enemy Infiltration
Undercover Accomplice
Code Conspiracy
Delta Force Defender
Delta Force Daddy
Delta Force Die Hard
Locked, Loaded and SEALed
Alpha Bravo SEAL
Bullseye: SEAL

Also by Nicole Helm

South Dakota Showdown
Covert Complication
Backcountry Escape
Isolated Threat
Wyoming Cowboy Marine
Wyoming Cowboy Sniper
Wyoming Cowboy Ranger
Wyoming Cowboy Bodyguard
Wyoming Cowboy Justice
Wyoming Cowboy Protection

Discover more at millsandboon.co.uk

CHAIN OF CUSTODY

CAROL ERICSON

BADLANDS BEWARE

NICOLE HELM

MILLS & BOON

First Published in Great Britain 2020
by Mills & Boon, an imprint of HarperCollins*Publishers*
1 London Bridge Street, London, SE1 9GF

Chain of Custody © 2020 Carol Ericson
Badlands Beware © 2020 Nicole Helm

ISBN: 978-0-263-28038-8

0720

CHAIN OF CUSTODY

CAROL ERICSON

Chapter One

Emily held her breath as the man with the gun leaned over the playpen and ran the butt of the weapon down the front of the baby's onesie.

"Cute kid." His lips stretched into a semblance of a smile. "He yours?"

Jaycee started forward and then stopped, licking her lips.

Emily whispered to herself, "C'mon, Jaycee. Do what you do best. Lie."

Flicking her fingers in the air, Jaycee said, "It's my roommate's. I'm making her move and take the brat with her."

The bigger, beefier man in the room, who clearly didn't need a weapon for intimidation, strolled toward the window and out of Emily's view. "You sure you don't know where your boyfriend is?"

"I told you. Brett and I broke up. I don't have a clue where that loser is."

Emily squinted and brought the phone with the video flickering across the display closer to her face. Was Jaycee telling the truth this time?

Emily's client, Marcus Lanier, was sure Jaycee planned to take their baby and run off with Brett Fillmore. If Brett were in trouble with these two guys, Jaycee wouldn't be likely to hand him over.

The big man skimmed a hand over his shaved head as he stepped back into the range of the camera Emily had set up in Jaycee's apartment—without her knowledge. Once Marcus had hired her to keep an eye on his baby, Emily's first step had been to install some electronic surveillance in Jaycee's apartment. She hadn't gotten much info in the five days she'd been tracking Jaycee—until now.

Marcus Lanier, a mover and shaker in Phoenix, had suspected Jaycee of hanging out with a sketchy crowd, and these guys with their guns and veiled threats definitely qualified. Marcus had feared for his baby's safety due to Jaycee's relationship with Brett Fillmore, a low-level druggie, but these two were next-level serious.

What did they want with Brett? If they thought he was the father of this baby, what would they be willing to do?

"Wh-what do you want with Brett, anyway?" Jaycee crossed her arms and wedged her back against the playpen, blocking the baby from the intruders.

The man holstered his gun. "Don't worry about it. If you hear from him, let him know he needs to call us."

Jaycee finally asked the question Emily was dying to know. "Who's us?"

The bigger guy, the one who hadn't drawn the weapon tucked in his waistband, straightened the sunglasses he hadn't bothered to remove inside. "How many people are looking for him?"

The other man snorted. "Tell him to call us—or else."

Knots tightened in Emily's gut. Had Jaycee noticed he glanced at the baby when he said that?

"If I happen to see him, which I doubt, I'll let him know a couple of guys with guns are looking for him." Jaycee tossed her dyed blond locks over her shoulder. "I'm sure he'll get right on it."

The man with the shaved head leveled a finger at her. "You forgot the 'or else' part—and no police, or we'll be looking for you, too."

"Me and the police don't get along so well." Jaycee shrugged. "I don't think I'll have any contact with Brett, but I'll tell him if I do."

Emily blew out a long breath when the two men finally left. She'd been worried about the baby, but Jaycee must've been terrified despite her nonchalant attitude.

As soon as the door closed behind the men, Jaycee sprang into action. She ran toward the hallway and stayed out of view for a good ten minutes. She reappeared, dragging a suitcase behind her with a diaper bag slung over her shoulder.

Emily's heart rattled in her chest. Jaycee planned to leave. She'd better take the car Emily had put a tracker on, because Emily had no intention of letting that baby—or her own fat paycheck—out of her sight.

With one eye on her phone, Emily packed a bag almost as quickly as Jaycee had. She didn't have to pack baby stuff, but she had her own bag of tricks she might need on the road. She had to be prepared for anything. Jaycee might even try to slip across the border.

When the red dot on her phone indicated Jaycee was on the move, Emily grabbed a bottle of water and a half-eaten sandwich from the fridge. Holding her cell in front of her, she tossed her bag into the trunk of her car and slid behind the wheel.

She lived near enough to Jaycee's neighborhood in south Phoenix to wait it out on the street in front of her own place until she could determine Jaycee's intent. When her cell phone showed Jaycee's car heading for the 10 South, she cranked on her engine and peeled away from the curb.

Following Jaycee, Emily kept her distance—not that Jaycee would recognize her or her nondescript silver hatchback, but she might be keeping an eye out for a tail...at least she should be.

Emily checked her own rearview mirror, scanning the freeway behind her. Had the goons who'd dropped in on Jaycee believed her about the baby not being hers? Maybe they believed her about Brett. If they trusted anything that woman said, they didn't know Jaycee Lemoin very well— at least if all of Marcus Lanier's stories about her were true.

A half a sandwich, a bottle of water and about an hour and a half later, Emily watched on her phone's display as Jaycee cruised past Tucson. She flexed her fingers on the steering wheel. Did this chick really intend to cross the border?

If she did, maybe Marcus should just let her go. Maybe Jaycee and the baby could keep safe by getting lost in Mexico. But Marcus didn't want to let Jaycee go, and he wanted to keep the baby safe *from* Jaycee. Emily hadn't even informed her client of this second threat stalking his son, but it wouldn't surprise him.

Marcus knew all about the company Jaycee kept and her lifestyle, making him fear for the baby's safety. He'd hired Emily to watch out for the baby until he could prove his paternity and get his ducks in a row before making a move for custody.

This little excursion of Jaycee's would give Marcus even more ammunition.

Emily's gaze darted to her phone and the red dot heading west. Did Jaycee plan to spend the night somewhere before crossing over? Or was she waiting for nightfall before making that surreptitious journey?

Five minutes later, Emily took the same exit—to Paradiso, a small Arizona border town.

Jaycee's car had stopped, and Emily blew out a breath. She could be a lot more inconspicuous in this little hick border town than in Mexico. If Jaycee decided to stay put in Paradiso, Emily would be able to watch her and the baby better. Then Marcus could take over and do whatever he needed to do to get his son back.

Emily sucked in her bottom lip when she turned off the main road running through the town. She'd expected Jaycee to hole up at a hotel. If she were staying with a friend, surveillance would be more difficult.

As she rolled past a grove of leafy trees, Emily buzzed down her window and sniffed the air, which had a slightly sweet smell. Who knew orchards grew in the middle of the desert?

She squinted and scanned the long, empty road ahead. Jaycee must've pulled into the gates on the right. Nothing else but trees stretched on either side of the road. The house behind those gates must be set back from the street because Emily could see just the top of it.

Emily pulled into a turnoff well beyond the gates and dug in her bag for a pair of binoculars. She leaned out the car window and focused on the entrance to the property. She could research the records later for the owners and their connection to Jaycee.

She had barely settled in for her little watch party when Jaycee's car flew out of the gates, kicking up dust.

Emily pulled her head back in the car and tossed the binoculars onto the seat next to her. "Damn. On the road again."

She followed Jaycee into town and to a gas station on the edge of it. The woman hadn't made her once on the trip down and wouldn't take notice of another car fueling up.

After Jaycee got her gas, she walked into the mini-mart to pay, but she didn't have the baby with her. No wonder Marcus was concerned. That action right there screamed negligence. She'd add it to her list for Marcus's custody battle.

With her palms sweating, Emily scrambled from her car and strolled past Jaycee's at the pump. She glanced into the back seat of Jaycee's little compact and tripped, clutching a hand to her throat.

What had Jaycee done with the baby?

BORDER PATROL AGENT NASH DILLON logged off his computer and stretched his arms to the ceiling. It had been a rough few weeks after he'd come back from the rodeo in Wyoming. That headless body at the border before he'd left had ushered in a floodgate of information about a cartel's tunnels between the US and Mexico, and Border Patrol had been dealing with the fallout ever since.

As Nash locked his desk drawer, Valdez, a new agent, called out to him, "Hey, Dillon, do you have women tracking you down at work now?"

"I hope not." Nash grabbed his hat from the corner of his desk. "Someone looking for me?"

"A woman called earlier and asked if you were working today and what time you'd be off." Valdez winked. "Maybe you got a surprise waiting for you."

"God, I hope not." Nash clapped his hat onto his head. "You didn't give her any information, did you?"

Valdez's baby face sported two red spots on his cheeks. "I—I told her you were off at five."

"Valdez." Nash shook his head. "Someone needs to teach you some basics."

"Sorry. She sounded…sweet."

"They all sound sweet, Valdez—until they're not." He

leveled a finger at the green agent. "Do not ever give out information like that about anyone in this office. Got it?"

"Got it, Chief." Valdez touched his fingers to his forehead. "Let me know if she *is* sweet."

Nash fired a crumpled napkin at Valdez's grinning mug and stepped into the early summer heat of the Sonoran Desert. He shook out his sunglasses and perched them on his nose before sliding into his truck.

He hoped one of those women who followed the rodeo circuit in the Southwest hadn't tracked him down. His day hadn't put him in any mood to hang out with a woman tonight—even a sweet one.

He snorted. Not too many sweet ones around as far as he could tell.

He drove through town, grumbling under his breath about the traffic. Even Tucson drivers would scoff at his idea of traffic, but Paradiso had been growing thanks in large part to his family's groves of pecan trees. His family used to ship the pecans to be processed and packed, but some savvy business people decided to bring the processing to the pecans. The new processing plant had brought jobs, people and…traffic.

He turned onto the road that led to those pecans and his house, rolling his shoulders and blowing out a long breath. Peace, quiet and a cold beer waited for him beyond those gates.

He stopped at the front entrance to his property and picked up the mail. His tires crunched over the gravel as he made his way up the circular drive.

He threw his truck into Park and snatched his hat from the seat next to him. He exited the truck, hoisting his bag over his shoulder. He took two steps toward his porch and jerked to a halt.

A misshapen object draped with a blanket greeted him

on the second step. His hand hovered over the gun in his belt.

The last delivery to a Border Patrol agent's porch had turned out to be a severed head in a box.

Nash twisted around and scanned the entrance to his driveway through narrowed eyes. Then he glanced at the camera at the corner of his house recording everything. Whoever had dropped off this present would've been captured on video.

His nerve endings alight, he stalked to the porch. Standing on the first step, he reached out and swept the powder blue blanket from the object beneath.

The *object* blinked and yawned, and Nash stared down into the face of a baby.

Chapter Two

Nash frantically scrolled through the contacts in his cell phone until he found Jaycee Lemoin. He stabbed at the name with his forefinger. The phone rang and rang on the other end without even a voice mail pickup.

"Damn it." He threw the phone at the couch and then eyed the baby, still strapped into his car seat on the floor by the door.

He'd been afraid to even pick him up. Why in the hell would Jaycee choose him as the caretaker of her baby while she went off doing God knows what?

At the kitchen table, he smoothed out the note Jaycee had left with the baby. She promised she'd be back in a day or two and just needed him to watch little Wyatt—keep him safe.

Little Wyatt gurgled from his corner, and Nash crumpled Jaycee's note in his hand and peered over his shoulder at the baby. He couldn't even turn to his friend April for help. She and his fellow agent Clay had run off to Vegas to get married and then on to Hawaii for a honeymoon. He didn't begrudge those two their happiness, but, man, he could use April right about now.

He approached the baby, who watched him coming with wide eyes. He crouched before the car seat and niggled his finger against the bottom of Wyatt's foot. He jerked back as Wyatt kicked out his legs and waved one arm.

"At least you didn't turn out to be a severed head." Nash clapped a hand over his mouth and swore. He probably shouldn't be talking to babies about severed heads... or swearing in front of them.

And that was his problem. He had no idea how to talk to babies and no idea how to care for them. He understood why Jaycee had dropped Wyatt off with him—he'd come to that girl's rescue more times than he cared to count.

Jaycee and his younger sister had been "BFFs" in high school. Who else would Jaycee turn to in Paradiso? His sister lived in New York now, and his parents had retired to Florida, leaving the care and feeding of the pecan business in his hands. But the care and feeding of a pecan was a lot easier than the care and feeding of a baby.

"You can do this, Nash. It's just a few days." He crawled to the diaper bag Jaycee had left with the baby and dragged the zipper across the top.

Another note—this one containing instructions—lay on top of an assortment of diapers, wipes, jars of baby food and bottles. Nash shook it out and read the bulleted items.

He shoved the paper into his back pocket and rubbed his hands together. "Piece of cake."

He returned to the baby and unsnapped the harness on his car seat. "Ready to get out of there, buddy?"

Wyatt reached out both arms and Nash picked him up, holding him in the air and wiggling him back and forth. "You're a good little dude. We can do this for a few days while we wait for Mom, right?"

Wyatt gurgled and some white gunk bubbled from his lips.

Still holding him at arm's length, Nash hustled into the kitchen and yanked off a length of paper towel from the roll on the counter. He wet it under the faucet and dabbed at Wyatt's chin and his little outfit with a sheep on it.

Wyatt grabbed his finger and gave him a toothless grin, moist with drool. Between the baby and the dog...

Nash spun around and lunged for the back door. He tipped back his head and called out, "Denali!"

Clay's husky appeared at the far reaches of the backyard, where the lawn tumbled into a grove of pecan trees.

"C'mon, boy. Dinnertime."

Clay and April had left him in charge of their dog when they traipsed off to get married. He'd agreed readily enough, but that was before he knew he'd have a baby under his care. Was this some kind of test? Some conspiracy to make him responsible?

Denali scampered out of the trees and raced across the backyard, skirting the pool. When he reached Nash holding Wyatt, he circled Nash's legs, wagging his tail and sniffing the baby's feet.

Wyatt's face crumpled and his bottom lip quivered.

"It's just a dog. Denali's a good boy." Nash dipped to show Wyatt the dog, and Denali lashed his tongue right across Wyatt's face.

Bad idea.

The baby wailed, and Denali barked and pranced around on his hind legs.

So much for his nice, relaxing evening. He strapped Wyatt back into his car seat and put him on the floor of the master bedroom and shut the door while he fed Denali. He'd have to keep the two of them apart. Denali had no more practice with babies than he did.

He shooed Denali back outside, where he was only too happy to roam, and then retrieved Wyatt from the bedroom.

He sat on the couch with Wyatt in his lap and pulled

things out of the diaper bag, examining each item as if it were an object from an alien planet. They might as well have been.

Even for a few days, the baby needed baby stuff. Jaycee had reminded him in her note that a room in the guest-house had been outfitted as a nursery for the last tenants his parents had before moving to Florida. He couldn't rel-egate Wyatt to the guesthouse, but he could drag the crib, playpen and high chair over here. He shouldn't need much more than that. Jaycee had dropped her baby off with a supply of toys and bottles and diapers.

He eyed the package of diapers he'd pulled out of the bag. Surely, that had to be enough for a little baby.

After using one of those fresh diapers on the baby, Nash secured Wyatt back in his car seat and trooped over to the guesthouse, swinging the car seat by his side. He settled the baby in the corner of the nursery and surveyed the room, hands on his hips.

He'd have to take apart the crib and reassemble it if he hoped to get it through the bedroom door. The high chair and the stroller he could wheel over and the playpen in the living room looked collapsible.

On his way to the front of the house, he poked his head in the other bedroom and crossed to the far side of the bed with a spring in his step. A little bassinet with a canopy sat snugly beside the bed. Wyatt could sleep in this, saving him the trouble of moving the crib. That would be com-fortable enough for a few days. The people who'd lived here obviously had used it for their baby.

A few hours later, all the baby accoutrements in place, Nash kicked up his feet on the coffee table and flicked Denali's ear. "We did it, boy. Wyatt's fed, changed, had a bottle, sleeping. And it's only for a few days."

THREE DAYS LATER, Nash slammed down his phone after another failed attempt to reach Jaycee.

Wyatt pounded his little fist on the tray of his high chair in solidarity and Denali barked twice.

"I'm glad we're all in agreement. Your mama is a flake." Nash leveled his finger at Wyatt and snatched it back when the baby's lip trembled. Three days and he knew that sign.

Nash had considered calling Department of Child Safety, but he didn't want to get Jaycee into trouble and Wyatt would be better off with him than in the system. He'd called in sick for two days now, and he had to start thinking about making some kind of arrangement for Wyatt's care if he hoped to get back to work anytime soon. He could check with his housekeeper, but she wouldn't be here for a few days and he didn't want to lay this on her.

He reached behind Wyatt's neck and undid the Velcro on his bib. "You ready to go for a ride, big guy?"

Denali waved his tail in the air, tickling Nash's leg with his long fur.

"Not you. There's only so much I can take of the two of you at once."

He grabbed the diaper bag with all of Wyatt's stuff in it and slung it over his shoulder. He hadn't been out with him yet. He didn't need any questions from his friends or coworkers, but he had to pick up some essentials in case Jaycee planned to take a few more days of vacation or whatever the hell she was doing right now.

He secured the base of the car seat in the back seat of his truck and snapped the carrier on top. Wyatt waved his arms and kicked his legs, which indicated excitement and happiness, and Nash eased out a sigh. He didn't need a crying baby right now.

He drove into town and pulled into the parking lot of

the grocery store. He fished his crumpled list from his front pocket—formula, baby food and diapers led the necessities. He'd buy enough for the week and send Jaycee on her way with the extras.

Ducking into the back seat, he released the car seat from the base and swung it by his side as he made a beeline for a shopping cart. He secured the car seat to the cart and wheeled it in for a shopping trip like no other.

Wyatt didn't like shopping. He fussed the entire time, and after Nash made it through checkout, he rolled the cart out the front door at breakneck speed. He got halfway to the truck before the wailing started.

He swiveled his head around to make sure nobody thought he was harming Wyatt, but no one seemed to notice the crying baby.

He stationed the cart by his truck and opened the back door to get Wyatt inside. "Hold on, buddy. Almost there."

"Do you need some help?"

At the sound of the woman's voice behind him, he jerked up, hitting his head on the door frame. "Ouch!"

"I'm sorry. I didn't mean to startle you."

Nash twisted around and his gaze met a pair of green eyes, slightly turned up at the corners, like an amused cat's.

He rubbed the side of his throbbing head. "I'll live."

Wyatt had stopped crying and squirming during the conversation, allowing Nash to snap the car seat into place. He pulled his head out of the truck, taking in the rest of the person who belonged to those eyes.

The green tank top she wore coaxed a different color from her eyes, which she blinked, as a strand of red hair floated across her cheek. He had the inappropriate urge to brush that flaming lock back from her face.

Her full lips flattened into a straight line. "You might live, but it still looks like you need help."

He gritted his teeth. He'd taken care of this baby for three days with no help from anyone. Why did this woman assume he needed help just because he was a lone man with a baby?

He patted Wyatt's chubby thigh. "He's good now."

"Maybe he is, but he's facing the wrong way."

"What?" Nash's eyebrows shot up. "Facing the wrong way?"

"He's under a year old, right?"

His heart racing, Nash flicked a glance at Wyatt and back to the woman's face. Even in his current panicked state, he noticed the sprinkling of freckles across her nose. How old was Wyatt? He didn't have a clue. He must be under one if this woman assumed he was.

"Y-yes, under one."

"Well—" she reached past him, brushing her arm against his and releasing the car seat "—he needs to be facing backward."

She unlatched the base of the car seat, twirled it around and snapped it back in place, Wyatt now pointing to the rear of the truck.

"Oh, yeah, right." Nash's cheeks warmed. Why hadn't Jaycee put that detail in her instructions? Probably because she'd intended to come back before he had a reason to take Wyatt out in the truck.

Where the hell was she?

The stranger put her finger to her lips. "I won't tell your wife you messed up."

"I don't have a wife." Nash blurted out the words before they registered in his brain. He didn't owe this woman an explanation, but for some reason he didn't want her to think he was married.

"Oh." Her reddish gold eyebrows formed a V over her

nose. "I—I just assumed… Uncle? That would explain the car seat gaffe."

Nash's jaw tightened.

"I'm so sorry." She put a hand to her chest. "I don't mean to pry. I have a thing for babies. I'm a nanny."

Chapter Three

Emily held her breath for a split second as Nash Dillon's impossibly blue eyes widened.

She continued in a rush. "I specialize in babies. So, when I saw you struggling and then noticed you had the car seat facing the wrong way, my natural instincts took over."

"A nanny?"

Nash's gaze flicked over her, head to toe, and she hoped the calf-length floral skirt, the modest tank top and the flat sandals suggested responsible nanny type.

Nash glanced at the baby in the car seat, now facing the correct way, which Emily knew about from being a cop in another life.

She wiggled her fingers at little Wyatt, and he gurgled back at her through the disgusting drool on his chin.

Nash's blue eyes lit up like someone had goosed him—not like she wouldn't want to try that. "Are you working here in Paradiso?"

Emily turned down the corners of her mouth. "I'm currently unemployed. I live in Phoenix and took a trip down to Tucson to visit a friend who's in grad school there and decided to take in Tombstone and a few other sights before heading back home and looking for a new position."

The handsome Border Patrol agent studied her face. Then he uttered the words she'd been holding out for. "I might need some help for a few days, if you don't mind working on your vacation."

"I'm always interested in helping out with babies." Had she laid it on too thick? Did people actually say things like that? Crazy people.

"I'd of course need some references, and your name would be a start."

"Of course. I wouldn't work for anyone who *didn't* do a thorough check." She pulled a newly minted business card from the side pocket of the purse strapped across her body. "Emily O'Brien."

Whenever she used a fake ID, she went with a good Irish name to match her mother's side of the family and her own red hair. Best to stay as close to the truth as possible.

She held out the card pinched between two fingers. When he reached for it, she pulled it back. "And you are?"

"I'm sorry. I'm Nash Dillon. I'm a Border Patrol agent."

She tilted her head. "You said you didn't have a wife. Is the baby yours?"

"Actually, no. I'm watching him for a friend, but I expected her back sooner and I'm afraid three days of being on my own with a baby is wearing on me."

At least he'd lasted three days. She was not sure she could do it for one day, but she had a fat paycheck waiting for her on the other end of this.

"Oh." She wrinkled her nose. "Your friend didn't abandon her baby, did she?"

"Nothing like that. She dropped him off with me. We're old friends. We go way back. Happy to help."

She extended her card again, and he plucked it from her fingers. Was he in love with Jaycee? The woman had a certain appeal, if a guy liked the soft, helpless type. Billionaire tycoon Marcus Lanier obviously did, as did Brett Fillmore, low-life druggie.

"I'm staying at the Paradiso Inn. Call me once you do your due diligence and I pass muster—if you're still interested." She tapped the card still in his hand. "My website's on there, which includes testimonials and references. Please feel free to call any one of them."

She'd been busy during her downtime when Nash had been holed up with the baby. But she knew he'd have to leave the house at some point and the tracker she'd attached to his truck told her exactly where he'd gone.

He held up the card. "Thanks, Emily. I'll be in touch."

She ducked into the truck and pinched Wyatt's foot, avoiding that whole mess on his face. "Hope to see you again, little guy. What's his name?"

"Wyatt."

She patted the baby's soft head. "Be a good boy, Wyatt."

Nash closed the door of the truck and thrust out his hand. "Nice to meet you, Emily. I think you just might be a lifesaver."

First time anyone had called her that. She placed her hand in his, letting it rest there limply. She didn't want him to see her as any kind of aggressive threat.

"I hope I can help, Agent Dillon."

"Call me Nash."

"Well, enjoy that little bundle of joy, Nash. I look forward to hearing from you." She floated back to her rental car and slid behind the wheel, letting out a long breath. First contact successful.

She slumped in her seat and tapped her phone to call Marcus's private cell. He picked up on the first ring.

"What do you have for me?"

"Looks like I have an in. The guy Jaycee dumped the baby with needs a nanny because of course he does."

"So what? You're not a nanny. You're a fired cop who's trying to get your PI business off the ground."

Emily rolled her eyes. Nobody said you had to be brilliant to make a billion bucks. "Oh, but I *am* a nanny. I set up a fake ID and profile for myself. A quick background check on me, and he's going to believe I'm Mary freakin' Poppins."

Marcus snorted over the phone. "Don't screw it up, Emily, and where's Jaycee? Why'd she drop off Wyatt?"

"I lost her when she crossed the border. The GPS went out of range, but I thought it more important to stay with Wyatt."

"It is."

"Do you still want me to just watch Wyatt? I mean, if I take him and bring him to you, that's kidnapping and you'll be charged."

Marcus drew a quick breath. "I never said anything about taking Wyatt. You just watch him to make sure he's okay. I'm still working with my attorneys on this end to make a move for custody."

"And when Jaycee comes back to collect him?"

"I hired you to follow Wyatt." Marcus cleared his throat. "Who's this guy who has the baby?"

"He's…" Emily squeezed her eyes closed. "Just some guy. An old friend of Jaycee's."

For some reason, she didn't want to expose Nash Dillon to Marcus Lanier's wrath or even attention. Maybe it was the light in his blue eyes or the way the sun glinted off his sandy-blond hair. Maybe it was because she wanted to protect that handsome face from some serious damage if Marcus thought Nash was standing between him and his son.

Marcus's voice roughened. "I expect a more thorough report on the guy than that when you're through with this job. I'm going to transfer another five thousand dollars into your account. I don't think being a nanny for a few days pays much."

He ended the call before she could thank him. She stashed her phone in a cup holder and took a long drink from her soda. Talking to Marcus always left a bad taste in her mouth.

As far as she knew, he'd made his money on the up-and-up, but she'd heard rumors of some shady connections. And he didn't like law enforcement. That was another reason she'd been vague about Nash's identity. Marcus would probably blow a gasket if he found out a Border Patrol agent had possession of Wyatt.

She pulled out of the grocery store parking lot and headed back to her motel and her laptop. She had a whole lot more research to do on babies before she could convince Nash of her expertise—when in reality, she didn't even like babies.

The following day, Nash Dillon must've done his background checks because he called her cell practically at sunrise. All her fake references had come through like champions.

"It would be great if you could start today. I have to get back to work, so you and Wyatt can get to know each other."

Emily's heart skipped a few beats. Alone with a baby? How hard could that be?

"Give me your address, and I'll be over within an hour."

He obliged, even though she knew damned well where he lived—that vast house on that vast property. His family owned most of the pecan groves in the area and had a large interest in the packing plant. In other words, the Dillon family was loaded. She'd also discovered Jaycee Lemoin hailed from Paradiso and had been friends with Nash's younger sister.

She'd been thrilled to discover that last part. She'd

thought maybe Nash was an old boyfriend or current lover or something. Not that it mattered to her.

When Nash ended the call, Emily darted around the room gathering her purse and a bag of tricks for the baby. She'd taken a drive up to Tucson last night to buy all the latest and greatest toys for Wyatt. She'd come in like a pro.

She drove her rental out to Nash's place, and this time she turned into the gates and circled around the driveway to park behind his truck.

She squeezed the steering wheel with her hands and huffed out a breath. "You can do this, Emily."

Pasting a smile on her face, she hitched the bag of goodies over her shoulder and strode up to the front door. Before she had a chance to ring the bell, Nash opened the door, a crying Wyatt clinging to his side.

The smile froze on her lips before she forced out some words. "Oh, what's wrong with Wyatt this morning? Is someone in a bad mood?"

"Yes." Nash scowled and then his eyes popped open. "Oh, you mean Wyatt. Yeah, I'm not sure what's going on with him."

She jumped back as a Siberian husky nosed his way between Nash's legs and barked at her.

"This is Denali. I guess he wants to get in on the action, too. You're not allergic, are you?" Nash peeled Wyatt from his shirt so that the baby hung in the air between them, his legs dangling just above the dog's head.

She should take him. That was what Nash expected. That was what any self-respecting nanny would do.

"Come here, you little rascal." She placed her hands beneath Nash's on either side of the baby, and Nash released him to her.

She pulled Wyatt against her chest, tucking one arm

beneath his bottom. She couldn't very well hold him out there at arm's length.

He wrapped his hand around a strand of hair from her ponytail that had swung over her shoulder and then put it in his mouth. At least he'd stopped crying.

"Oh, no, you don't, you little—" she swallowed "—rascal." She disentangled her hair from his grubby fist.

"That's the first time he's stopped crying in about thirty minutes. You're a genius." Nash stepped aside and ushered her into the house. "He's had his breakfast. I left you instructions on what he eats when, although you're probably a better judge of that than I am."

Emily bounced Wyatt in her arms as she took a turn around what could only be described as a great room, which led into a huge kitchen completely out of her league. She noted the well-placed and discreet cameras in the corners of the room. She also recognized the type—video, no audio.

Nash may be leaving a new nanny in charge of his friend's baby, but she had no doubt he'd be keeping an eye on her.

"You have my cell phone number already, but I left it and the station number on the counter. I'm not too far, and I'll come home for lunch to check on things."

"Okay, sounds good." She dropped her bag by the couch. "What about Denali?"

"If you don't mind losing some of the AC in the house, you can leave that sliding door open so he can go in and out. He likes running around the pecan groves."

She wandered to the sliding door that led to a covered patio and a sparkling pool and those rows of trees beyond. "Maybe we'll go for a walk. Do you have a stroller?"

"I do." He jerked a thumb over his shoulder at a small

hallway next to the staircase. "I put all the baby stuff in a room down here."

Emily spun around, Wyatt contentedly resting his head on her shoulder, drooling on her blouse. She tapped the list on the granite kitchen island. "I think we'll be fine."

"You are a godsend." Nash put his hands together and bowed his head. "I'll be home for lunch. Call me for anything."

He grabbed a hat, slung a laptop case over his shoulder and waved his way out the front door.

When the door slammed, Wyatt jerked up his head and his mouth puckered.

Emily pinched the list between her fingers and collapsed onto the couch with the baby, positioning him to face her on her lap. "You like Uncle Nash? I do, too, but probably for different reasons than you do."

Emily bit her bottom lip. She probably shouldn't be talking to a baby about how she had the hots for his temporary guardian.

She shook out the list and scanned it. "Food, bottle, diaper. Doesn't say anything about a nap on here. Do you want to sleep?"

As she bounced Wyatt on her knees, he brought his hands together and chuckled. The sound brought a smile to her lips. "You are pretty cute, but does that noise mean you're not interested in a nap? How about some playtime instead?"

Emily had read that babies this age liked to be on the floor to practice their rolling and crawling. She'd been relieved to discover she didn't have to carry him around all day when he wasn't sleeping.

With the baby hitched on one hip, she shooed Denali outside and shut the sliding door after him. No matter how friendly that dog seemed or how much he liked Wyatt, she'd have a lot of explaining to do if Nash came home to a baby with a dog bite.

As Denali scampered past the pool out back, Emily dug through the bag she'd brought and shook out a blanket dotted with clouds and unicorns. She spread it on the floor and placed Wyatt on his back in the middle of the square. He kicked his legs and waved his arms.

She dumped a variety of toys next to him and unfolded a padded arc that had plush cows, pigs and chickens hanging from it. She placed this over Wyatt's body, and he went nuts. He batted the primary-colored animals and gurgled with glee as they swung above him.

Leaning her back against the coffee table, she crossed her legs beneath her and watched the baby play. She'd had limited contact with the babies of a few friends back in Chicago but had never even babysat. Her father, a cop, had been too worried about her going to strangers' homes to watch their kids, so he paid her to clean the house and cook instead.

Generally, babies didn't take to her any more than she took to them, but Wyatt seemed to accept her. Maybe he just missed his mama and she was a better match for Jaycee than Nash.

Jaycee must've crossed the border after dropping Wyatt off with Nash. Was she looking for Brett? Maybe she figured those goons who'd paid her a visit at her place in Phoenix would be tracking her and she wanted to put space between her and Wyatt so they'd believe her story.

What would those guys want with the baby, anyway? Brett must be in some big trouble. If Jaycee really feared for Wyatt's life, why not just drop him off with Marcus? They could work out the paternity and custody issues later. At least Wyatt would be safe with Marcus.

Emily's gaze tracked back to Wyatt, now gnawing on a

set of giant plastic keys with his toothless gums. Maybe she should just take off with Wyatt now and bring him to Marcus. Would any judge blame him for kidnapping the baby to keep him safe from whatever threat those guys posed?

Marcus had explicitly told her not to take Wyatt. He didn't want to do anything that would prejudice a family court judge against him. And she knew more than anyone that the law followed its own protocols.

Marcus hadn't seemed too concerned when she'd reported the visit by the two men. He figured they were looking for Jaycee's boyfriend and that was the end of it. She'd tried to sound the alarm that if those two believed Wyatt was Brett's son, they'd kidnap him to use as a weapon against Brett, but Marcus hadn't seen them as a threat.

Wyatt scooted a few inches and then rocked back and forth in an attempt to roll onto his stomach. She crawled onto the blanket with him and put a toy just out of his reach to the side to encourage him.

When he finally made the big heave-ho and rolled onto his tummy, she clapped and whistled. His brown eyes got big and round when she whistled, so she puckered up and whistled a tune inches from his face. He patted her lips with his hand, and she didn't even mind the stickiness this time.

After more gymnastics on the floor, a bottle and a diaper change, which she managed by holding her breath, Emily wheeled the stroller from the room Nash had pointed out before he left.

"Let's take a walk and give that silly dog some company."

She loaded Wyatt into the stroller and found Denali's leash hanging from the front doorknob. She yelled his name in the back, and Denali emerged from the trees and scampered across the lawn. She patted her thigh. "C'mon, boy. We're going for a walk."

She hooked up the dog and pushed the stroller onto the porch. She eased it down the steps and aimed it onto the circular driveway.

The higher elevation down here made it cooler than Phoenix, although once the temperature reached over a hundred, it didn't make much difference. She crossed the road with baby and dog and steered into the grove of trees, which offered some relief from the blazing sun.

For over thirty minutes, she circled around the trees, smelling the bark and crushing the leaves in her hand. This didn't seem much like the desert.

She checked her phone for the time. "Okay, dog and baby, we need to head home for Nash's lunchtime visit to make sure we're all still alive."

A little chill snaked up her spine, and she shrugged it off as she walked into the blinding sun.

She could definitely do this for a few more days until Jaycee returned. Then wherever Jaycee went with Wyatt, she'd follow, even if it took her away from Nash Dillon.

At the edge of the trees, Emily stopped to adjust Wyatt's hat to keep the sun from his face. When a vehicle roared down the road, she squinted through her sunglasses. Wyatt hadn't given her a chance to make some lunch.

She barreled ahead with the stroller and then tripped to a stop. The engine she'd heard didn't belong to Nash's truck. A black sedan idled outside the gates of Nash's house.

Emily slowed down and stuck close to the tree line as she approached the car. Her heart slammed against her chest as she recognized the dark tinted windows and the round sticker in the back.

The thugs from Jaycee's apartment had tracked Jaycee here to Paradiso—and worse, they had a bead on Wyatt.

Chapter Four

As Nash turned onto his street, a black sedan crept up to the intersection and rolled through the stop sign to make a right. A lot of people came this way before they realized the street came to a dead end, and they couldn't drive through the pecan groves to get to the entrance to the highway. GPS steered them wrong every time, but it wouldn't kill them to stop at the stop sign on their way out.

He pulled into his driveway and dropped his stiff shoulders when he saw Emily's rental car. He knew it was a rental because he'd run the plate. Everything had checked out with Emily O'Brien, but he'd been happy he had Kyle Lewis install some security cameras in the house. He wouldn't want to have to explain to Jaycee that he'd hired a nanny from the grocery store parking lot and she'd kidnapped Wyatt.

He'd been impressed with the way Emily played with Wyatt this morning. The kid obviously knew a good nanny when he saw one. He seemed a lot more content with her than he'd been with Nash.

Had Emily come back from her walk in the time it took him to drive home?

He cut the engine, and as he stepped out of his truck, the gravel crunched behind him and he pivoted.

Emily waved from behind the stroller and dropped Denali's leash. "Hello. You're back sooner than I expected."

Denali trotted up to him, his leash dragging behind him, his tongue lolling out of his mouth in pure joy.

Nash scratched him behind the ear as he studied Wyatt, kicking his legs out in the stroller, a little hat shading his face.

Usually silence and a lonely meal greeted him when he came home from work, not this picture of domesticity. He didn't need the wife and kid, but he should get himself a dog.

He finally shifted his attention to Emily, her fiery hair in a demure braid over her shoulder. The freckles on her nose were pronounced in her pale face, and she stood behind the stroller stiffly, gripping the handle.

Nash cocked his head. "Is everything okay? Did you have a good walk?"

Her smile flashed easily across her face, too easily, and she said, "Great. Our walk was fantastic."

"I hope you're not regretting taking the job. I really need you." Nash cleared his throat. "Need your help."

Emily tossed back her braid. "Not at all. Wyatt and I had a good morning. I just wasn't expecting you back so soon. I was going to make some lunch."

"Don't bother. That wasn't in the job description." He held up the bag of food from Rosita's. "I brought lunch with me. Do you like Mexican food? Of course you do. You're from Phoenix."

"Actually, I live in Phoenix now, but I'm originally from the Midwest. I'm still getting used to some of those hot salsas." She waved her hand in front of her face as if cooling her puckered lips.

He dragged his gaze away from her mouth and pointed

to Wyatt. "I guess our conversation bored him. We put him to sleep."

"Good." She ducked her head into the stroller to remove Wyatt's hat. "What I mean is, he hasn't slept all morning, not even on the walk, so he does need a nap."

Nash made a move toward the porch. "I'll let you get him to bed, and I'll set up lunch."

He held the door wide for Emily to pass through with the stroller. "We can leave that on the porch."

She shook her head so fiercely, her braid whipped back and forth. "No, I don't want to leave it out in the heat."

She skimmed past him, and his hand shot out to pluck a leaf from her hair. When she swiveled her head around, he cupped the leaf in his hand. "Looks like you took a stroll through the pecan groves."

"Are they all yours?"

He closed the door behind them and removed his hat. "They belong to my family. We used to ship them to a processing and packing plant in Texas until some partners convinced us to build one here. A lot of people in Paradiso resent that plant."

"Why should they? It must've brought jobs and a level of prosperity that a lot of these small towns down here must envy." She folded back the canopy on the stroller and slid her hands beneath Wyatt's sleeping form.

"It turned sleepy Paradiso into a real town, and a lot of the locals don't like it. Brings more of everything—more people, more traffic, more crime."

She put a finger to her lips and floated into Wyatt's makeshift nursery with Wyatt fast asleep against her chest.

Nash swung the bag of food onto the counter and got two plates from the cupboard and silverware from the drawer. He set them on the kitchen table next to the sliding doors to the back. He never used the dining room, had never used it once since moving in here after Mom and Dad took off for Florida.

He lifted the containers of food from the bag and placed them on the table.

He jumped as Emily came up behind him. He really wasn't used to having someone else in the house.

"Sorry. I didn't mean to scare you." She lifted her nose in the air and sniffed. "Smells good."

"Chicken burritos." He held up a small container of salsa. "And you can add your own heat."

"Do you like it hot?" Her cheeks sported two spots of color to rival the red of the salsa. "Spicy?"

He raised his eyebrows. So, he wasn't the only one who felt the pull between the two of them. "I do. I grew up in Paradiso, just about spitting distance to the border. Do you want some lemonade? Iced tea?"

"Some lemonade would be great." She pulled out a chair and sat down in front of one of the plates. "You mentioned crime before. Does Paradiso have a lot of crime? I wouldn't think so."

He emerged from the fridge clutching a plastic bottle of lemonade. "It's not fresh or anything."

"I grew up in the Midwest, remember? I don't think I saw a real lemon until I was a teenager." She shook out some chips onto her plate and dipped a corner into the salsa. "Crime?"

He poured the lemonade over ice in two glasses. Was she worried about her safety here in Paradiso in the home of a Border Patrol agent? "We get some crime here— mostly tweekers stealing stuff. Most of the crime happens on the border. We had a case last month…"

"What was the case?" She held her chip suspended in the air and a drop of salsa fell to the table.

"You're eating. I'll tell you later."

"My dad was a cop, homicide detective. I'm accustomed to inappropriate mealtime conversation."

He cut his burrito in half, choosing his words carefully. "We found a body without a head at the border, and then that head showed up on a fellow agent's porch. Then we found a headless body not far from the pecan groves and the second head showed up on another porch."

Emily put a hand to her heart. "Gruesome. I'm assuming those murders and decapitations were part of the drug trade."

"They were. Las Moscas."

"I've heard of them. Brutal." She crunched the chip between her teeth and dabbed the spot of salsa from the table with her napkin.

"Your father's a homicide detective? What department?"

"Retired." She waved her fork in the air. "A couple of different departments. You know what?"

"What?"

"I think my taste buds are acclimating to the cuisine because this is good." She dumped some of the salsa onto the side of her plate and dug into her burrito, running a forkful through the red puddle.

Nash shrugged and sawed off a corner of his burrito. He talked shop enough at work and with his buddy Clay. He didn't need to bring it home.

"You never told me how you came to be in charge of Wyatt. Who are his mother and father?"

Nash gulped down some lemonade. How many of Jaycee's secrets should he keep? If he told a nanny that a mother had left her baby on someone's porch, she might just get it into her head to report Jaycee to DCS. That girl had enough problems if she'd been driven to leave Wyatt with him. She didn't need a social worker on her case.

Nash ran the side of his thumb down the sweating glass. "I don't know who the father is, but the mother is an old friend, local girl, friend of my sister's."

"I suppose that means her family doesn't live here anymore."

"Long gone."

"And your sister?"

"My sister is in New York, pursuing a modeling and acting career."

Emily raised one eyebrow. "Have I seen her in anything?"

"Not unless you pay close attention to commercials."

"That's a tough life."

"She's luckier than most. She has my parents' money as a safety net." He took another bite of his food, relieved the conversation had switched from Jaycee to his sister.

"So, why did Wyatt's mom leave him here?"

Damn. Nash wiped his mouth and took another sip of his drink. "I learned a long time ago not to question Jaycee Lemoin too closely. She asked me to watch her baby for a few days, and I agreed. She's taking longer than expected, and happily I ran into you to help me out until she returns."

"Jaycee didn't let you know she'd be delayed?"

He shook his head. The peaceful domestic scene he'd encountered when he came home had turned into an interrogation. Why hadn't Emily asked him all these questions when he'd first approached her about the job?

"You know, I need to get back to work." He shoved back from the table and grabbed his plate. "Do you need anything before I leave?"

"No. Thanks for the lunch." She curled her fingers around her glass and shook it back and forth, tinkling the ice. "We never really discussed my hours. Do you want me to go back to my hotel when you get home from work, or would you like me to stick around in the evening to help out? You're paying me a generous flat fee, so I'd be more than happy to help in the evenings, too."

"That would be great." He almost suggested she move into the guesthouse, but he didn't want to freak her out. He also didn't want her asking any more questions about Jaycee. Did Jaycee really think she could just drop Wyatt off on his doorstep for a week and it wouldn't seriously impact his life?

He continued. "I'll take care of dinner, too. Any requests? Italian?"

"I can cook something."

"That's not in your job description. Taking care of Wyatt is plenty." He rinsed his plate in the sink and downed the rest of his lemonade. "Maybe he'll sleep for another hour and give you a break."

"He's a good baby." Emily rolled her eyes and blew an errant strand of hair from her face. "Compared to some of the babies I've cared for, Wyatt is an angel."

Nash mumbled under his breath, "Doesn't take after his mother."

"What?"

"Just like his mother." He waved at the door. "Thanks again, and have a good afternoon."

On his way to his truck, he tried Jaycee's number again, and again it went straight to voice mail. He didn't bother leaving a message.

That girl needed to get back to Paradiso and her baby—even if that meant Emily O'Brien would be waltzing out of his life just as smoothly as she'd waltzed into it. And he wasn't ready for that, not at all.

EMILY LIFTED THE edge of the curtain at the front window and watched Nash back his truck out of the driveway. Had the men in the black sedan stayed away because of the truck in the driveway? Would they be back?

Emily scraped the remnants of her burrito from her plate into the sink and ran the disposal. Then she sauntered to where her purse hung on the back of a kitchen chair and unhooked it. She didn't know if Nash could watch her movements from his phone or if he needed his computer to access his cameras' video feed, but she didn't want to take any chances by pulling her weapon out of her purse.

If Nash saw his nanny with a gun with the baby in the house, he'd make a fast U-turn and kick her out, maybe even call the police. But if those guys who'd paid a visit to Jaycee came back here, she wanted to be ready for them.

They must suspect that Brett was Wyatt's father. And kidnapping his son would be a surefire way of getting Brett's cooperation. They'd be disappointed and angry once they discovered Brett probably couldn't care less about his girlfriend's baby with another man. What would they do with Wyatt then?

She shivered as she plopped down on the couch and pulled her purse into her lap, the hard edge of the gun in the side pocket giving her comfort. She cupped her phone in her hand and sent Marcus a text. He hated texting, but Nash might have mics as well as cameras in the room.

She stared at the words on her phone warning Marcus that the same men who'd been around questioning Jaycee were here sniffing around Wyatt. Surely, a mother leaving her baby in dangerous circumstances would be enough to help Marcus's case for custody. Why the wait? He needed to make his move before Jaycee put Wyatt in even more danger.

As if sensing her fear, Wyatt started crying from the other room.

Emily scrambled off the couch and jogged into the

makeshift nursery. Wyatt had pulled himself to his feet and stood gripping the edge of the playpen, rocking back and forth. He had opened his mouth for another howl and then blinked when he saw her and reached out his arms instead.

"I bet you need a clean diaper and a bottle. Do you like to swim? Have you been in a pool yet?"

She'd been a swimmer in high school and paid her way through college by lifeguarding and teaching swim lessons at the campus rec center. She'd taught many a toddler how to jump into the water and paddle to the edge of the pool. Wyatt wasn't exactly toddling yet, but a little pool instruction could never start too early.

Once she'd changed his diaper and given him a snack and a bottle, she tugged off his little onesie and set him on his blanket in the middle of the floor. She hadn't brought a bathing suit with her, but underwear would do in a pinch.

She tugged off her shorts and pulled her blouse over her head, all without looking at the camera. If Nash believed she had no clue about the video setup in his house, he'd trust her even more.

With her bra and panties doubling as a bikini, she scooped up Wyatt from the floor and propped him onto her hip. She hitched her purse over her shoulder and slid open the back door.

She dragged a chair poolside and dropped her purse onto it. She didn't want to be too far from her gun.

Holding Wyatt in front of her, she lowered herself to the edge of the pool and dangled her feet in the water. She put Wyatt between her legs, facing the pool, and dipped his toes in it.

He seemed to enjoy it, so Emily slid off the edge of the pool and put his bottom half in the water up to his waist. His eyes popped open wide when the water enveloped him, and then he grinned. She walked backward, pulling him along with her, and he kicked his legs like a natural.

The time spent with Wyatt passed more quickly than she'd thought possible. Clutching Wyatt to her chest, she lunged for the side of the pool and checked her phone, which she'd left in the shade of the chair. Marcus still hadn't responded to her.

She returned to the house with the baby. The sun and water had done a number on Wyatt, and after fussing for about ten minutes, he dropped off to sleep.

Emily plucked her damp underwear from her body. A few minutes in the sun would be enough to get it bone-dry. Leaving Denali on guard at the sliding door, she grabbed her purse and Nash's laptop, which he'd offered for her use, and headed back outside.

She claimed a chaise lounge on the patio, tipping an umbrella over her face but leaving her bottom half in the sun to dry off. She dragged Nash's computer into her lap on top of a towel and used the password he'd given her to log in.

She surfed the internet, watched a few videos and checked her email. Nash had some folders on his desktop, but they contained innocuous stuff like rodeo competitions and applications. She'd already done her research on him and knew he did the rodeo circuit as a hobby.

She clicked through some pictures of him in rodeo action. Damned hot. Maybe she should email a few of them to herself to drool over later when this job ended.

She launched his email, telling herself she was looking for info about Jaycee Lemoin, but he had a second log-in on his email and the computer password didn't work here.

As part of her PI prep, she'd taken quite a few online classes on computer hacking and had gotten pretty good at it. After several attempts, Nash's email program launched, displaying his inbox.

She scrolled through his messages, which mainly told her he needed to opt out of some of these mailing lists. He had a lot of junk piled up in here. He obviously kept this laptop for personal use and must have a different one for work, but occasionally he sent messages from his work laptop to this one.

These jumped out at her because of the sender's long government official email address. She had no interest in the drug trade across the border, but he'd piqued her interest with the story about the headless bodies.

She double-clicked on a couple of the work emails and scrolled through gibberish about sectors and coordinates and drone capabilities. One email had a spreadsheet attachment called Finances with a list of names.

With the mouse poised over the Close icon in the upper-right corner of the document, she scanned through them. About halfway through the alphabetical list, her gaze stumbled over a familiar name and a breath hitched in her throat.

What was Marcus Lanier's name doing in a Border Patrol agent's spreadsheet about finances?

Chapter Five

Nash put the bag of food from Mario's on the seat beside him and slammed the door of his truck. He clamped his hands on top of the steering wheel and hunched his shoulders. He should probably tell Emily about the cameras in his house.

He'd felt like a voyeur this afternoon when he'd watched her strip down to her underwear to hit the pool with Wyatt. Of course, he could've looked away.

He cranked on the engine and drove home, his mouth watering at the smell of garlic that filled the truck. First the hot salsa and now the garlic. She'd think he was trying to ward her off. Maybe he was.

He pulled in behind her car again and made a mental note to ask her about the rental. He cut the engine and gathered his stuff, the plastic bag hanging from his fingers.

When he pushed open the front door, he stuck his head into the foyer and called out, "Hello?"

Seemed strange to be doing that in his own house, but he wanted to make sure she wasn't dancing around the room in her skivvies…or less.

"We're in the kitchen eating." Emily's singsong voice drew him in with its promise of companionship and comfort. He hadn't even realized he'd been missing those things.

Denali finally tore himself away from Emily feeding

Wyatt in his high chair and trotted up to him, his nails clicking on the hardwood floor.

With his hands full, Nash nudged the dog with his knee. "You're not supposed to eat garlic. I'll feed you in a minute."

"I fed him already." Emily waved Wyatt's spoon in the air. "We had quite an afternoon."

"Yeah, about that." Nash swung his laptop case on top of the opposite end of the kitchen table, where Emily was sitting next to Wyatt's high chair, and put the bag with their dinner on the counter, where a bottle of wine stood uncorked.

"I haven't been secretly drinking away the day. You mentioned Italian, so I found a bottle of red and I'm letting it breathe." She dabbed Wyatt's chin. "Hope that's okay."

"Perfect. I should've thought of that myself." He unpacked the salad and the garlic bread. "I know you aren't a lush because I have the house outfitted with cameras."

She jerked her head toward him and two red spots formed on her cheeks. "Oh. I guess you witnessed our little impromptu swim."

"Sorry. I should've told you about the cameras before."

She wrinkled her nose. "That's okay. I should've figured you had them. I doubt you would've been so quick to leave a relative stranger in your home with your friend's baby. Besides—" she scooped up another spoonful of food from the jar "—it's not like I was skinny-dipping."

Nash swallowed and turned his attention to getting dishes for their dinner. "Wyatt must've liked the water, since you were out there for a while."

"He loved it." She touched the baby's nose. "Didn't you, my little fish?"

"You're so good with him." Nash divided the salad into two bowls and unwrapped the bread from the foil.

"Those cameras, is there audio, also? Just in case I want to break into song. I wanna warn you first."

He sucked some tomato sauce from his thumb. "No audio."

"Good." Emily stood up with the empty jar of baby food in her hand. "Wyatt had a long nap this afternoon, so I doubt he's going to be sleeping through our dinner. I'll leave him in his high chair while we eat as long as he's not fussy."

"Sounds good to me." Nash raised the bottle of wine. "You get Wyatt settled and I'll get everything ready for our dinner."

He took out a couple of place mats from the drawer next to the fridge and put them on the table. He dumped the pasta on two plates and poured the wine.

By the time he placed the silverware next to the plates, Emily was settling Wyatt back into his chair. She scattered an offering of toys on the tray and collapsed next to the high chair.

"I can take the seat of honor next to Wyatt, if you like. I mean, if you need a break." Nash tore off a corner of garlic bread and popped it into his mouth.

"I'm the nanny. I don't need a break." Picking up her wineglass, she swirled it around.

"Even nannies need breaks." He grabbed his own glass and touched it to hers. "Here's to fortuitous meetings in grocery store parking lots and fate."

"Yeah…fate." She clinked his glass and took a gulp of wine.

Nannies didn't need breaks? She guzzled that cab as if her sanity depended on it.

"Whoa, that's good." She placed the glass on the table and stabbed at her salad with a fork. "What does your job entail?"

Nash blinked. "My job?"

"Border Patrol agent. What do you do mostly? Is it people, drugs, both?"

"There are different sectors down here that report to Tucson, and we deal mostly with drug interdiction in Paradiso. That's our main focus. We don't have many illegal border crossings on our end."

"Is there one cartel in particular in this area?"

"We encounter them all, but Las Moscas is the main source of drug smuggling along the border here."

"The decapitated people?"

He nodded. "Las Moscas."

"The cartels have…collaborators on this side of the border? People who finance them? People who move their product?"

"You *are* your father's daughter, aren't you?"

The glass in her hand jerked, and a few droplets of wine stained the tablecloth. "Why do you say that?"

"I don't know. Most women aren't interested in my job." He pushed back from the table and yanked the dish towel from the oven door and ran it under the faucet.

He returned to the table and dabbed at the red spots on the white material.

"I'm sorry. Let me." She made a grab for the dish towel, but he held firm.

"I've got it." He waved the towel at Wyatt. "Besides, I think your charge needs another toy. He's thrown all of his on the floor."

Emily leaned over. "Wyatt, Denali has slobbered over all your toys. Do you think it's okay to give Wyatt a piece of this bread to suck on?"

Nash lifted his shoulders. "You're the nanny. Will he choke?"

"I—I was just wondering how garlicky it was. He might

not even like it." She pulled the soft center from a piece of bread and put it to Wyatt's lips.

The baby sucked the bread into his mouth and then spit it out onto his tray.

"I guess there's your answer—no garlic for dogs or babies." He picked up the bottle of wine. "Do you want a refill?"

Pinging her fingernail against the half-empty glass, she shook her head. "I still have to drive back to my motel, and one glass is my limit for driving."

"Very responsible of you, but then I suppose a cop's daughter would be careful." He splashed another few sips of wine into his own glass. "I'm not driving, so I'll live dangerously and have another half a glass. I somehow don't think babysitting and alcohol mix, do you?"

"Definitely not. I once witnessed a mother smoking weed right in the presence of her baby." Emily reached out and stroked her knuckle across Wyatt's cheek. "A baby about the same age as Wyatt. Don't you think someone like that is an unfit mother?"

"Me?" Nash inclined his head. "I thought you were the expert. Yeah, I suppose anything that alters your capacity to react quickly would interfere with taking care of a kid."

"The courts usually award custody to mothers, but sometimes fathers make a better guardian."

Her words had a lilt at the end, as if she were confirming her beliefs with him. Being a bachelor with not much contact with kids, he'd never given these issues much thought. Once Jaycee came back to get her son, he wouldn't think about them again.

He lifted his shoulders. "I suppose when drugs and alcohol are involved, that changes the situation. Do you want any more to eat? We have leftovers."

"I'm good." She pushed away her plate of half-eaten

pasta. "I'll wrap this up and have it for lunch tomorrow... if I'm still coming."

"I haven't heard from Wyatt's mother yet, so I hope so."

"You can't call her?"

"She doesn't answer, or her phone is turned off."

"You'd think she'd want to hear how Wyatt's doing."

"She trusts me." *If only he could trust Jaycee.*

Emily jumped up from the table. "I'll help you clear the dinner dishes and get Wyatt comfy. He'll need another bottle before he goes to bed. Maybe that'll make him sleepy."

"I hope so. He's been waking up in the middle of the night, and it takes me a while to get him back to sleep." Nash stood up next to Emily and took the plate from her hand. "You go do nanny business and I'll take care of the kitchen."

She plucked Wyatt from his high chair and carried him off to the other room.

Nash put away the leftovers and rinsed the dishes to stack in the dishwasher. He'd feel a lot better if Emily and Wyatt moved into the guesthouse, but he felt selfish for asking. She'd been with the baby all day. Of course, he could offer her more money to stay the night.

If Jaycee spent another full day away, he'd propose the plan to Emily. She was getting suspicious about Jaycee, and he didn't blame her. What kind of mother dropped her baby off with a friend and disappeared, refusing to answer her phone?

And he hadn't even told Emily *how* Jaycee dropped off Wyatt—on his porch like a foundling. Emily would be horrified and might even threaten to call DCS. She'd already been attacking the court system that seemed to favor mothers over fathers, regardless of the circumstances.

Her vehemence surprised him. Had her father the cop told her stories? She didn't seem eager to talk about him, even though she clearly had an interest in law enforcement. Maybe they'd had a falling-out. He knew enough cops to know they could be hell to get along with on the home front.

Border Patrol agents were no picnic, either.

Every woman he'd ever dated had seemed more interested in his family's business than his own. It had made him suspicious, standoffish. His friend April called him superficial.

As Nash swept up the last of the crumbs from the kitchen table, Emily returned, bouncing Wyatt in her arms.

"He's a little frisky, so he might need some playtime before his bottle and bed." She pointed to a blanket folded on top of the coffee table. "I don't know if you saw on your super-duper camera, but I had him out on the blanket on the floor with some toys around him. He practices rolling and getting up on his hands and knees. He can't actually crawl yet, but he rocks back and forth, which is a precursor to crawling."

"We'll give it a try, right, buddy?" Nash poked Wyatt in his belly, which got a laugh out of him.

"I hope his mother doesn't miss any of his firsts in her absence." Emily sucked in her bottom lip. "You'd think she wouldn't want to miss a thing."

"If he starts crawling, I'll capture it on my phone." Nash patted the pocket of his shorts.

Emily seemed determined to attack Jaycee—not that she didn't deserve it.

"I'll leave my toy bag here for tomorrow, and I'll even bring a swimsuit." She winked as she turned Wyatt over to him.

He and Wyatt stood at the front door and waved Emily into her car.

Setting Wyatt in the middle of the blanket on the floor

worked wonders. The little guy got up to all kinds of new tricks on his own, so Nash reached for his laptop and pulled it onto his thighs as he stretched his legs out next to Wyatt's play area.

He entered his password and launched the web browser. He hovered the mouse over the history tab and then said, "Hell, you saw her in her bra and panties. Snooping into her internet searches is nothing."

And it was nothing. She'd watched some music videos and a short documentary on Mount Everest. She'd even checked out a few baby sites. Must want to keep up on all the latest trends in childrearing.

He closed out of her browsing history. The woman deserved a little privacy. Had he been expecting her to read how-to articles on kidnapping or something?

He launched his email. He squinted at the new messages loading and then leaned back against the couch and crossed his arms. The new emails scrolled in from about three o'clock this afternoon even though he hadn't launched his email program since last night.

He sat up. Emily had gotten into his email.

EMILY SWUNG BY a liquor store on her way back to the motel. She pulled into a space in front of the plate glass window and threw the car into Park. She slumped down in the seat, gripping her phone.

Marcus still hadn't responded to her message about the thugs sniffing around Wyatt. She eked out a little sigh of relief. She didn't know what to say to Marcus right now.

Why did a Border Patrol agent have Marcus's name in connection to the cartels? Of course, finances could mean anything. She'd done her research on Marcus Lanier before taking the job, and it hadn't been difficult. Everyone in Phoenix knew about Marcus.

He had his fingers in many pies around the city, and he seemed to have the Midas touch. He made money and he made other people money. And he spent money.

Whatever passed for a social scene in Phoenix, Marcus Lanier took center stage in that scene—he and his perfect wife. Did that perfect wife know he fooled around on the side? Probably. Did she know he'd fathered a baby with his side piece, Jaycee Lemoin? Probably.

If Marcus had hired her to keep tabs on Wyatt and gather evidence against Jaycee to take her to court for custody, Ming Lanier would have to know about her husband's infraction.

But the public didn't necessarily know what the Border Patrol knew. Were all of Marcus's enterprising ventures covers for his real business, drugs?

"Damn." Emily shoved her phone into the side pocket of her purse and flung open the car door. She may be using dirty money.

She stalked into the liquor store and made a beeline for the wine section. Might as well stay with the same poison. After the day she'd had, she needed more than that half glass of wine with dinner. But Nash had been right. Her father had drilled into her the evils of drinking and driving.

She grabbed a bottle of merlot by the neck and charged up to the register. Dad never said anything about drinking and watching TV, though.

She paid for the wine and slid back into her car. She drove to her motel and parked as close to her room as she could get. Paradiso had a limited number of lodging choices, but it was hardly a hot spot for tourism. Bisbee and, of course, Tombstone drew the lion's share of visitors to this area. Paradiso wasn't even near a well-traveled border crossing—at least not a legal one. She'd read that the border here was porous with tunnels used for the trafficking of drugs and even people.

She dug her key card from her purse and then hung her bag over her shoulder. She grabbed the wine and exited her vehicle.

The streets of Paradiso rolled up early. Most of the restaurants and bars still open lined the main drag through town, and this little gem of a motel was definitely off the beaten track.

Pinching her key card between her fingers, she walked toward her room. As she passed the stairs that led to the second floor, a shadow moved across the wall.

Instinctively, she reached for the side pocket of her purse where her gun nestled, but it was too late.

An arm shot out and ripped the purse from her shoulder. She started to wield the bottle of wine like a club. Her attacker grabbed it and dropped it to the patch of grass under the stairs. Then he dragged her toward an open door she hadn't noticed before now and shoved her into a utility room.

A low voice growled in her ear, "Make one noise, and you're dead."

In case she hadn't gotten the message, her assailant jabbed the barrel of a gun beneath her ribs.

Chapter Six

Emily gulped in breaths of air as the man held her from behind, curling one arm around her neck.

"Who is that baby to you?"

"What baby?"

He tightened his hold and she choked. "The baby at the Border Patrol agent's house. Who is the baby to you and who is he to that cop?"

Should she tell him? Should she just blurt out the truth that Marcus Lanier was the baby's father? Wouldn't they leave Wyatt alone once they knew Brett wasn't the father?

She gulped. She had no authority to reveal that information. That was the one thing she'd promised Marcus—she'd never tell a soul Wyatt was his child, not until he was ready to do so. Even to save Wyatt's life?

Marcus should've taken her warnings seriously about the men who'd threatened Jaycee. Did he not believe her?

For now, Wyatt was safe with Nash. That was why this guy had gone after her. They knew Nash Dillon was Border Patrol and they knew better than to mess with the law. That bought her a little time.

He drilled the gun into her side. "Answer me. What do you know?"

She clawed at his arm and he relented a fraction of an inch. She coughed.

"I don't know anything about the baby. The Border Patrol agent is my friend and the baby belongs to his friend who had an emergency. I don't know the mother. I don't know anything."

He released her, giving her a push forward. That didn't fool her for a minute, as she still felt the weapon up close and personal. She eyed her purse on the ground outside the utility room.

The man didn't know she had a gun in there, but she didn't plan to use it unless her life was in imminent jeopardy. If she dove for her purse, yanked out her .22 and shot him between the eyes, she'd have a lot of explaining to do—to everyone.

"I'll tell you what, *pelirroja*. You're gonna help us."

"Me?" Her voice squeaked as much from surprise as the pressure that had recently been applied to her windpipe. That was not what she'd expected from him.

"How am I going to help you? I told you. I don't know anything. If you're the baby's father, I suggest you go through the proper channels to—"

"Shut up." He slugged her in the back and her knees buckled.

"Are you going back there tomorrow?"

"No. I'm leaving Paradiso tomorrow." She gritted her teeth against the throbbing pain right above her kidney.

"You lie, *pelirroja*." His hot breath stirred the hair at the back of her neck, and she shivered. "You're gonna go back there tomorrow, and when the cop goes back to work after lunch, you're gonna take the kid for a walk—away from the cameras at his house. Then you're gonna turn that kid over to us. You got it?"

She nodded. What else could she do at this point? If she refused, he'd inflict more pain on her. She had a feeling he liked administering pain.

"Wh-why do you want him? Are you going to hurt him?"

He shoved her away from him and she stumbled against the wall. "Don't worry about it. And if you get any bright ideas? We will kill that kid. Kill you. Kill the cop. And even kill that mutt. Got it?"

"Yes."

"Stay there against the wall until you hear a car drive by. And if you call the police? Let's just say that goes under the category of bright idea and it'll have the same ending. It might take longer, but we always get our man… and baby, if it comes to it."

Her muscles rigid, Emily froze in place until she heard the sound of an engine roll by. She spun around and flew out of the utility room. Dropping to her knees, she scrabbled for her purse on the ground and pulled out her gun.

She had nobody to shoot, but she wasn't going to go to her room without this baby in her hand. She grabbed the bottle on the grass and pressed it to her chest. Thank goodness it hadn't broken. She needed that wine more than ever right now.

With her knees trembling, she wobbled to her room and slipped inside. She threw the chain and slid to the floor, the bed at her back, pointing her gun at the door.

After several minutes and several deep breaths, she staggered to her feet and placed her weapon on the credenza. She screwed open the bottle and poured the wine all the way to the top of a plastic cup.

She gulped half of it before she sank down at the foot of the bed. Maybe she should kidnap Wyatt tomorrow morning and drive back to Phoenix with him and deposit him with Marcus. She could make a good case to a judge why she felt it was in the baby's best interest to leave Paradiso and bring him to his biological father. No family court judge in their right mind would blame Marcus for doing that after what she'd just been through.

She bounded up from the bed and fished her phone from her purse. Still no message from Marcus. Did he think she was joking? Overreacting? He wouldn't think that once she told him what happened tonight.

She didn't have a plan yet, but she sure as hell wasn't turning Wyatt over to those maniacs.

IN THE MORNING, Nash adjusted the angle of the camera in the corner of the living room, but if Emily took his laptop out to the patio again, he wouldn't catch her in the act of snooping through his email. He couldn't take the laptop with him today. She'd be suspicious. Maybe that would be a good thing, a subtle hint that he knew she'd been into his email.

How'd she get into it, anyway? He'd password protected it. It probably wouldn't take a tech genius to bypass an email password, but Emily was a nanny. Wasn't she?

All her references checked out and she even had an online presence, but if passwords could be hacked, identities could be forged.

Nash ran a hand through his hair. She could just be a nosy nanny.

He grabbed the laptop and stuffed it into his bag. She could think what she wanted. He didn't have any top secret info on his computer, but he didn't like the idea of someone spying on him.

Wyatt crowed from his high chair, and Nash ran a thumb across the baby's soft hair. "I know you like her, buddy, and so do I, but I've had enough duplicitous women in my life to last me—starting with your mama."

The doorbell made him jump, even though he'd been expecting Emily any minute.

Denali got to the door first and barked.

"I know." Nash patted the husky's head. "You like her, too."

He swung open the door, and Emily lifted her hand in a wave. "Reporting for duty, unless Wyatt's mom decided to return and whisk him away."

"Not back yet. I'm sure I'll hear something today." He widened the door and stepped to the side.

As she crossed the threshold, Denali jumped, landing his paws against her side. Emily winced and staggered backward.

"Whoa, boy." Nash placed a hand on Emily's back to steady her. "Are you okay?"

"He just took me by surprise." She grabbed Denali's head and touched her nose to his wet, black one. "How are you, Denali?"

"I fed him already, and I gave Wyatt a bottle and put him in his high chair. I didn't feed him any food, though." He grabbed his bag and hat. He wanted to get out of here so she wouldn't notice the missing laptop.

She dropped a backpack on the kitchen table and leaned in to give Wyatt a kiss on his head. "Hello, big guy. Missed you."

Nash cocked his head as he watched Emily stroke Wyatt's hair. Her voice sounded almost shaky. She really did care about him. "I have to run, Emily. Do you have everything you need? I'll stop by for lunch again."

"We're fine." She jabbed her finger at the backpack. "I even brought a swimsuit today. Wyatt liked the water so much, I'll make a swimmer out of him."

But you won't be surfing the internet and my email after the swim this time.

Nash cleared his throat. "You two have a great morning. If there's anything you need…anything you want to ask me, you have my number."

Emily's head jerked up, her green eyes wide. "L-like what?"

"Like… I don't know. Whatever." He chucked Wyatt under the chin and then strode to the front door with Emily right on his heels.

She stood at the door with her purse still strapped across her body, her hand resting on the outside flap as if ready to leave.

When he got to his truck, he turned and waved.

Emily nodded, but she seemed to be looking over his head at the driveway that wound down to the street.

Knots formed in his gut as he drove away from the house. Emily's smiles and good cheer had seemed forced this morning. Her jumpiness made him second-guess everything. He'd be keeping a close eye on the video feed this morning.

At the office, Nash got ready for an online meeting with a forensic accountant. They were digging into the finances of Las Moscas. They knew there had to be some major money-laundering schemes on this side of the border, and they were investigating several suspects.

Nash brought up the spreadsheet that contained the list and several notes he'd already made on each. While he waited for the meeting to start, he set up his personal laptop next to his work computer. Had Emily noticed it missing yet?

With several taps of the keyboard, he brought up his security system and watched Emily cleaning up Wyatt after breakfast. The kid seemed thrilled with her. That was all that mattered right now. So, she was a snoop. Maybe she wanted to find out more about him. Or was that just wishful thinking on his part?

The two meals they'd shared yesterday felt like dates—except for the presence of Wyatt at dinner. He liked her, liked talking to her, and their attraction was undeniable. Again, wishful thinking?

"Good morning, Agent Dillon. Sorry I'm late."

Nash shifted his attention from his personal computer to his work computer and the face of Special Agent Webb filling his screen. "Good morning, Agent Webb. Right on time."

"My name's Bruce. Can I call you Nash?"

"Absolutely." Nash took a sip of coffee. "I have my list up and can take notes as we talk. Who do you want to discuss first?"

"Probably the guy I got the most hits on. His name is Marcus Lanier. He's a Phoenix businessman, a real mover and shaker. He's married to Ming Lee Hong, daughter of a wealthy entrepreneur in China. We're not sure his father-in-law is on the up-and-up, either."

"Makes sense. The wife went from one criminal family to another. What do you have on the guy?"

While Webb went on about anomalies in Lanier's finances, Nash multitasked. He listened to Webb, made notes in his spreadsheet and kept one eye on Emily and Wyatt.

After about an hour discussing two of the possible Las Moscas contacts, Webb started to wrap up. "I'm going to send you Lanier's and Booker's latest payments and withdrawals for your files. It's not like you're gonna find any payments to drug dealers in there, but they serve to outline and support some of what I've been talking about this morning. We can set up another meeting to discuss a few of our other suspects, but I wanted to get to those two first. I have the file, and you'll have the file. That's it. We're not spreading this info around just yet."

"Sounds good, Webb. You guys are thorough."

"I love numbers, man. What can I say?" Webb chuckled and signed off.

Nash waited a few minutes for Webb's email to come through with the attachment. He clicked on it and saved the file to his computer.

Then he stood up and stretched. Taking another glance at his security feed, Nash turned with his coffee cup in hand to get a refill.

Valdez beat him to it, filling up his commuter mug.

"Leave some for the rest of us. What are you fueling up for?"

Valdez's lips twisted. "You missed it while you were in your meeting, but it looks like we have a body at the border."

"Damn. You going out?"

"Yeah, I'm lead on this one." Valdez swallowed. "It's almost in the next sector, so we'll probably be out all afternoon."

"Decapitation?" Nash grabbed the coffeepot from Valdez's none-too-steady hand.

"Not sure yet. Drone picked it up and I was the lucky one monitoring the drone footage, so it's mine."

"You'll do fine, Valdez." Nash gave the green agent some tips before he set off for the border, and then returned to his much less exciting work on finances.

He had done most of the work on the map of tunnels they'd received from April Archer. Nash had the back-breaking job of investigating most of those tunnels, so it was his turn to sit in the office now and look at numbers. With Wyatt's arrival, it couldn't have happened at a better time.

How did Jaycee know he wouldn't be on the border for days and unable to care for Wyatt? Jaycee didn't think. He'd been happy when his sister, Eve, had gotten the harebrained notion to run off to New York to study acting, just because it had separated her from Jaycee. She'd had their parents' money behind her to explore this whim. Jaycee didn't have a dime. Did she have a husband?

Nash blew out a breath as he sat behind his desk, setting down his coffee cup next to his computer. A quick glance at his laptop showed him all was well with Emily and Wyatt.

He grinned as he watched Wyatt's antics on the floor. Emily was right—if Jaycee didn't return soon, she would miss her son's first attempts at crawling.

Nash cracked his knuckles and opened his folder on Aaron Booker. He dragged the newest financial info from Webb into the folder and then opened it. He scanned through the expenses. This guy definitely lived the high-life, but he had the income to support it—at least on the surface. Webb would dig into the money source and get to the bottom of the pit.

Nash also had a folder on Lanier and repeated the actions he'd performed for Booker. Lanier lived a similar lifestyle. Nash's eye scanned down the expenses and the payees when he stumbled across a familiar name.

Lanier had transferred five thousand dollars into the account of an Emily Lang. But his nanny's last name was O'Brien. Emily wasn't an unusual name.

He shook his head and moved on, but Emily Lang's name popped up again—another five-thousand-dollar transfer. Lanier had made no notes with the transfer. It could be anything, but why the same amount and why two…no, three payments to this Emily Lang?

Webb had delved deeper than a cursory look at finances ever could. Nobody would be able to track these transfers, not the IRS, not Lanier's wife.

Maybe Emily Lang was a high-priced escort.

Nash closed the file and turned to other work, but a persistent feeling of unease had him by the back of the neck.

Why had Emily been looking through his private emails? Why had she turned up in the grocery store parking lot at precisely the moment he needed her? Why would a woman on vacation be willing to work for a few days for a stranger?

Nash dragged his work computer keyboard toward him. With his fingertips buzzing, he launched a search engine and entered *Emily Lang*.

Emilys from around the country popped up—Realtors, city council members. He couldn't go through them all.

He went back to the top of the page and entered *Emily Lang Chicago*. That didn't help. The same amount of Emilys filled his screen.

With his heart thudding, Nash switched gears and accessed the National Crime Information Center database. He wiped his brow with the back of his hand and entered *Emily Lang*.

He held his breath as several Emily Langs populated the display. He looked into each one, but none of them matched the pretty redhead currently at his house.

Okay, she wasn't a felon. That was because she wasn't Emily Lang.

Nash swirled his coffee in the mug and stared into the brown whirlpool. He placed it carefully on the blotter and wiped his hands together. Then he entered *Homicide Detective Lang*.

Several articles popped up and Nash opened the first one. He read aloud, "'Chicago homicide detective Joseph Lang was shot and killed while chasing a suspect in the East Side Strangler investigation.'"

He perused a few more articles on the murder of Detective Lang. The SOB who'd killed him had been shot later in another shoot-out. Good riddance.

Nash clicked to the next page of search results and hovered over another article. Apparently, Lang's daughter had gone into police work, too, and had gotten herself fired. Nash clicked on the article, and his mouth dropped open.

The red hair was shorter and the green eyes sadder, but he'd found Emily Lang, and the disgraced police officer was in his house under false pretenses…alone with Jaycee's baby.

Chapter Seven

Were they watching the house? Emily peeked out the front curtains for the hundredth time that morning. The man last night had seemed so sure she'd be meeting him with Wyatt in hand after lunch. What would they do if she didn't show?

They didn't want to come to Nash's house. If they did, they would've made an attempt already. They wanted to stay off Nash's radar.

If they weren't watching the house, how would they know if she left early this morning with Wyatt? They must be tracking her. If she didn't make the meeting, they'd know where and how to find her.

How had they tracked her to the motel last night? She knew she hadn't been followed from Nash's place to the liquor store. They must be keeping tabs on her the same way they'd followed Jaycee down here and the same way she'd followed Jaycee down here—GPS device on her car.

She'd have to get it off and then make her move. She'd leave a note for Nash so he wouldn't think she was a straight-up kidnapper. She'd keep it vague enough and then contact him when she got Wyatt safely into Marcus's hands.

Not that Nash would believe her or let the abduction of

Wyatt stand. He'd come after her for sure. He'd put an APB on her car, which she would ditch. He'd call in the police.

She'd have to evade law enforcement, the thug from last night and Nash Dillon—all with a baby in tow. Hell, she'd been a cop herself for all of three years. She could handle them all.

With Nash keeping an eye on her via those cameras, she'd have to make her movements look natural. She should've told Nash that she'd planned to take Wyatt to the park today. Leaving with him in his car seat would be the most natural thing ever.

She could always disable those cameras, but he'd probably freak out. He'd taken his personal laptop to work with him today. Either he knew she'd been looking through his stuff or he didn't quite trust her.

She patted Wyatt's back as he slept in the bassinet that she'd had Nash take down from his room upstairs. She'd been gradually loading up Wyatt's toys in her bag throughout the morning.

With her purse over her shoulder and her hand hovering near the weapon zipped inside, she slipped through the front door and sauntered to her car. She ducked down on the side of the car away from the cameras stationed at the front of the house. On her knees, she swept her phone across the undercarriage of the rental.

She got a hit. She reached beneath the car and felt along the wheel well, her fingers dancing along the greasy surface. They stumbled over a round disc, and she peeled it off the car.

She couldn't throw it away or even move it and give away the fact that she'd found the device. She dropped it on the ground and shoved it to the center of the car so she wouldn't roll over it and crush it on her way out.

They had to think she was still here waiting for the afternoon appointment.

Squatting on the gravel driveway, she brushed her fingers together and popped up. She hustled back into the house and opened the sliding door to the back, emitting a high-pitched whistle. "Denali!"

She heard the dog bark in the distance and hung on the door, waiting for him. When he ran up to her, she scratched his head. "You're a good boy. I wish we could take you with us for protection, but I can't kidnap a baby *and* a dog and leave Nash with...nothing."

A little sob bubbled up her throat. Nash would think poorly of her only until she could fully explain. Then he'd understand why she had to get Wyatt away from here.

Denali stood at attention at the foot of the bassinet. If she'd been anyone else trying to remove Wyatt from this house, Denali would've raised a fuss. But he trusted her... just like Nash trusted her.

She bent over the bassinet and scooped up Wyatt. "Do you want to meet your daddy? He may not be ready, but it has to be now."

Marcus still hadn't answered her texts, but he might be avoiding communication with her. Maybe his wife had gotten ahold of his burner phone and he was in damage mode.

She still didn't understand why he was in a Border Patrol spreadsheet, but maybe she'd misunderstood. Maybe those people were donors or fund-raisers or something. She knew Marcus had connections with law enforcement in Phoenix and often contributed to their causes.

With Denali standing guard over Wyatt, she grabbed a piece of junk mail from Nash's counter and scribbled him a note full of apologies and a few explanations. She wanted him to know that she had Wyatt's best interests at heart and was taking him to his father. She placed the note in the center of the counter, held in place with the half-full wine bottle from last night. He couldn't miss it.

She settled a sleepy Wyatt in his car seat and strapped him in. Nash hadn't said she couldn't take Wyatt in the car, so hopefully he wouldn't see anything unusual in her actions. He might not even be watching her right now. He had a job to do. He couldn't stay glued to his security feed all day.

She hitched her bag of goodies over her shoulder and hoisted up the car seat. She smacked a kiss in the air. "Bye, Denali. Be a good boy."

She locked the front door and trudged to her car, Wyatt swinging next to her. Nash had transferred the car seat base from his truck to her car for just this reason—well, not this *exact* reason, but he shouldn't be alarmed that she was taking Wyatt for a drive.

She snapped his car seat into the base in the back seat—facing backward. That had been her in with Nash in that grocery store parking lot. Of course, if it hadn't been advice about the car seat, she would've come up with something else. Nash had been so primed for help, and she'd pounced on his weakness.

She got behind the wheel and swiped a sniffle from her nose as she pulled away from Nash's house, leaving the GPS tracker in the driveway. By the time one o'clock rolled around, she'd be in Phoenix.

Marcus should be able to protect Wyatt when she got to his place and even admit to being the baby's father. Her attacker and his sidekick would have no use for Wyatt at that point. They could get their man another way.

She'd had a feeling even if she'd told the guy last night that Wyatt wasn't Brett's son, he wouldn't have believed her. Or maybe he wouldn't have cared. They'd figured out that Jaycee was lying about Wyatt, so they knew he was *her* son, and if Brett cared anything about Jaycee and her baby, he might be willing to make a deal.

She rolled up to the end of Nash's road and turned right, away from the town. She could take a back road to the freeway and wouldn't have to pass through Paradiso and the Border Patrol office on her way out.

This was going to work.

Emily accelerated, but not too much. She didn't need to get pulled over for a ticket or draw attention to herself in any way. She checked her rearview mirror and her heart did a flip.

A truck, traveling at a high speed, a cloud of dust in its wake, had appeared behind her out of nowhere. Had they been watching and waiting for her instead of depending on the GPS tracker? They had no way of knowing she'd find that device. They didn't know her profession…or former profession.

She applied more pressure to the gas pedal, but she didn't plan to get into a high-speed chase with Wyatt in the back seat of her car. Lodging her tongue in the corner of her mouth, she glanced in her mirror again.

The truck was gaining on her, and then she blinked and adjusted the mirror as if that could change what she saw.

That white truck looked an awful lot like Nash's truck. She couldn't afford to see him right now, either. She could tell him she was taking Wyatt for a drive to calm him down, but then how would she escape?

What was he doing home this early, anyway? He'd told her he would be coming home at lunchtime, and he sure as hell didn't see her leaving on the cameras and drive this far this fast from his office.

Maybe that wasn't even Nash. Lots of people drove white trucks in this town. She squinted in her rearview and swore. No mistaking the aviator sunglasses. That was Nash on her tail.

She'd have to pull over, or he'd know for sure she was absconding with Wyatt. She eased off the pedal and put on her signal. Gripping the steering wheel with sweaty palms, she veered toward the side of the road and shifted into Park without turning off the engine. Not that she could make a quick getaway with Nash standing beside her car.

As he pulled in behind her, she wiped her hands on her skirt and pasted a smile on her face. "You sure you don't want to start crying back there to bolster my story, Wyatt?"

The baby gurgled and burped up some white gunk, clearly not appreciating the seriousness of the situation, although the gunk on his onesie might indicate an upset baby.

She winked at him in the mirror. "Good boy."

Emily buzzed down her window as Nash drew near, his hand hovering over the weapon on his hip. Force of habit? Did Border Patrol agents make traffic stops?

She called out in a singsong voice, "Hey, you. What are you doing home so early?"

"Cut the engine." His tone lashed her, and she jerked her head back from the window.

She also obeyed his command, her fingers fumbling with the keys in the ignition. She left them swinging there. He must be angry that she'd taken Wyatt for a ride without telling him first.

She ran her tongue along her dry teeth. "Wyatt was cranky and restless, so I thought a drive might calm him down."

"Stop with the lies, Emily, and get out of the car. Put your hands where I can see them. You know the drill, Officer Lang."

Her blood ran cold in her veins. Busted. How had he discovered her true identity?

"I—I can explain. I don't mean any harm to Wyatt."

"Stick your hands through the open window and step out, keeping them in front of you, when I open the door."

She swallowed and slid a glance to the side. At least he didn't have his weapon drawn, but that could change if she didn't comply.

She twisted to her left and stuck her hands out the window, wiggling her fingers to show him she didn't have anything.

He stepped toward the door, the leather of his equipment belt creaking. She knew the sound of that belt intimidated suspects—and she understood why.

The doors of her car had automatically unlocked when she turned off the engine, and Nash reached over and opened the door with her arms hanging through the window.

She *did* know the drill—had applied it many times herself before she went rogue. She stepped out of the car with her arms still outstretched, and she looked at her reflection in his sunglasses for a split second before he commanded her to turn around and face the car.

She pulled her arms from the open window and turned toward the car, looking at Wyatt in the back seat kicking his legs in excitement at the sound of Nash's voice.

"Hands on the car, legs apart. Do you have any weapons on you?"

"C'mon, Nash. I'm not kidnapping Wyatt." Well, technically she *was* kidnapping Wyatt, but it was for a greater good. She'd make Nash see that once he stopped this tough-cop routine.

He nudged her leg to the side with his boot and patted her down—not exactly how she'd imagined their first physical contact to go.

"Any weapons in the car?" His voice dismissed any familiarity or...fondness between them.

"In the side pocket of my purse on the passenger seat—a .22 Smith & Wesson."

He sucked in a breath behind her and slammed the driver's-side door shut. "Now you're gonna tell me what the hell you want with Jaycee Lemoin's baby. Then I'm gonna call the police to pick you up for attempted kidnapping."

"Like this?" She lifted one hand from the car. "Can we talk like reasonable people?"

"Are you a reasonable person, Emily? Do reasonable people lie about who they are to get close to...a baby and then take off with that baby? Do reasonable people create identities and references and fake lives?"

"Private investigators do when they're working a case."

"A case? Wyatt is a case?"

"Yes, he is. I'm working for his father. I'm trying to keep him safe because he is in danger, and not just from his flighty mother, whom you seem to have a soft spot for to the extent of protecting her when she doesn't deserve it. Jaycee abandoned her baby, and you know it."

A car sped by in the other direction and honked. Emily jumped. The longer she stood exposed out here with Wyatt in the car, the better the chance the real criminals would move in on them.

"You're working for Wyatt's father?" He prodded her in the back with his knuckle. "Turn around."

With her hands out to her sides, she rolled on the car to face him. "Wyatt's father hired me to keep an eye on Wyatt until he can get his results back from a DNA test and make a move for custody."

"You can drop your hands."

Nash pushed his sunglasses on top of his head, and Emily let out a breath when she finally got to look into those blue eyes. She could make him understand better when he was the Nash she knew instead of the law.

"Is that his story, or are you lying to me…again?"

"Story? It's not anybody's story. A client hired me in Phoenix to follow Jaycee and the baby. When Jaycee split off from the baby, my orders were to stay with Wyatt, which I did."

"Stay with Wyatt until you could kidnap him? What kind of father would do that to the mother of his child?"

"No." She shook her head, and a gust of wind from a passing car whipped her hair across her face. She pushed it out of the way and held it in a ponytail. "The kidnapping was my idea."

Nash's jaw formed a hard line, and one hand clenched into a fist. "At least you're starting to tell the truth now."

"I didn't mean it like that." She waved her hand as if she could dispel all the tension between them—only, it wasn't the sexual kind this time. "Wyatt is in real danger and not from me or his father."

"Yeah, yeah, Jaycee is an unfit mother."

"I'm not even talking about Jaycee." Another car roared past, and a shower of dust peppered her face. "Can we please sit in the car and finish this discussion?"

"With your gun?"

She smacked her palm against her forehead. "Take the damned thing. I told you. It's in my purse. You can even point it at me if it would make you feel better. Wyatt needs the AC."

Nash opened the driver's-side door and motioned her to the back. "Get in the passenger side. I'll take your purse. Do not try anything."

"With Wyatt in the car?" She stalked around the back of the car and dropped into the passenger seat.

Nash had her gun in his hand and was unloading it. He poured the bullets from his palm into the cup holder. Stroking one finger along the barrel, he said, "Nice piece."

"Thank you." She cranked her head around and wiggled her fingers at Wyatt. "Do you even know why Jaycee dropped off Wyatt with you? Did you even ask?"

"I didn't talk to her."

"What?" Her voice squeaked, and she cleared her throat. "Did she just hand off the baby and you took him with no words exchanged?"

"Jaycee left Wyatt on my porch when I wasn't home."

"Oh, that's rich." Emily slapped the dashboard. "She abandoned her baby on your front porch?"

"She knew I was in town. She knew when I was coming home from work, and she timed it perfectly."

"Oh, that makes all the difference in the world. Do you see why his father might be concerned?"

"Do *you* know why she left Wyatt with me?"

"I do. Two men...thugs, paid Jaycee a visit in Phoenix. They were looking for her boyfriend, Brett Fillmore. Do you know him?"

"The name sounds vaguely familiar, but there are a lot of men in Jaycee's orbit."

Was Nash one of them?

Wyatt started fussing in the back seat, and Emily reached over and turned on the engine. "He needs the air-conditioning."

"He needs his toy." Nash reached onto the floor behind him and plucked up a multicolored stuffed caterpillar. He waved it in Wyatt's face and allowed the baby to grab it from his hand.

"Why were these guys looking for Brett, and what makes you think they were criminals?"

Cocking her head, Emily pursed her lips. "You know I was a cop. Give me a little credit here."

"Okay, why Brett?"

"Brett is involved in drugs—taking and selling. He must've crossed these guys or something and then disappeared. They were sniffing around Jaycee to see if they could get a bead on Brett, and they saw the baby."

A muscle twitched in Nash's jaw. "What did Jaycee tell them about Wyatt?"

"That he belonged to her roommate. Your friend might be a flake, but she's street savvy. She knew why they were asking about the baby."

"But if the baby's father is…your client and not Brett, why didn't Jaycee just tell these guys? Get them off the baby's case."

"Probably for the same reason I didn't tell them. If she admits Wyatt is hers, they take him and maybe her, too, to force Brett's hand. Also, Jaycee was a side piece. My client has not admitted his paternity yet, and he's a married man."

"Sounds like a prince." Nash ran a hand across his mouth. "Wait, for the same reason you didn't tell them? You've met these guys? These drug dealers?"

"I've met one of them. He's here in Paradiso…and last night he threatened me."

Chapter Eight

Nash's blood thrummed in his ears. This situation just kept getting worse and worse.

"Threatened you? Where?"

"When I got to my motel last night." Emily rubbed her midsection. "Shoved a gun in my ribs, punched me in the kidney, and told me if I didn't turn over Wyatt today at about one o'clock, he'd kill me, you and Denali."

Nash ground his back teeth together. "He knows where I live? He knows who you are?"

"This is what I figured." Emily held up her hand and ticked off her fingers with each theory. "They followed Jaycee here to Paradiso and your house, just like I did. They were watching the house but didn't want to make a move because they found out you were Border Patrol, and they saw me coming in and out with Wyatt. They put a GPS tracker on my car and followed me to my motel, where the one guy accosted me."

"You're telling me there's a GPS tracker on this car right now?" Nash glanced at the side mirror and the time on the dashboard. They'd be expecting her and Wyatt in just over an hour, unless they saw that she was on the move.

"I took it off and dropped it in your driveway. As far as they know, I'm sitting at your place getting ready to turn over Wyatt."

Nash studied Emily's face, a slight crease between her eyebrows but calm. No wonder she came across as Mary Poppins. The woman had things under control—or thought she did.

"So, you see why I took Wyatt? I was trying to protect him." She folded her hands in her lap and twisted her fingers. "I—I left you a note on the counter explaining things. I wouldn't have just taken off without giving you some kind of…goodbye."

Nash squeezed his eyes closed and pinched the bridge of his nose. "You're not protecting Wyatt, Emily."

"Of course I am. Even though my client isn't expecting me to bring Wyatt to him, once I do, he can keep his son safe." She flicked her fingers in the air. "I'm sure he'll work out some sort of custody arrangement with Jaycee. He's not going to cut her out of Wyatt's life completely."

"Why isn't your client aware of the situation? Why doesn't he know that you're bringing his son to him?" Nash twisted his head to the side and pinned her with a stare.

"He hasn't responded to my texts yet. He's a busy guy, and I'm sure he trusts me to make the right decisions."

She at least had the self-awareness to blush. The reasoning that had been going through her head for the past few days must've sounded even more absurd when she said it out loud in the small confines of the car.

"So, a man who's paying you big money, tens of thousands of dollars, to follow his son and keep him safe is not monitoring or answering texts from you?" He snorted, a restrained sort of sound compared to the screaming in his head. He'd been so impressed with her detective skills up to this point.

"You don't know this guy…" Her voice wavered. "How do you know what he's paying me?"

"I do know this guy, Emily. I just spent quite a bit of

time with his finances this morning." He drummed his fingers on the steering wheel. "How do you think I discovered your real identity? You did a hell of a cover-up job—employment history, references, driver's license, a little social media. Helluva job, Officer Lang."

"Stop—" she held up one hand "—calling me that. You can't possibly believe Marcus Lanier is involved in the drug trade."

He narrowed his eyes. "You *do* know what I'm talking about."

"Okay, look. I hacked into your personal email account and I saw his name listed on some spreadsheet, but I thought maybe he was a donor or something."

"I guess he is—a money donor to you and a sperm donor to Jaycee." He hit his fist on his knee. "That's really what you thought, or is that what you wanted to believe as long as he's throwing the money your way?"

"I had no idea, and I still don't believe it." She plowed her fingers through her hair. "He's an important figure in Phoenix. His wife is on all the charity boards. They're movers and shakers."

"His wife, Ming Lee Hong, is from a criminal family in China. She's no angel."

"Wait, wait. Even if Lanier is involved in the drug trade, and I'm not convinced, how does that cancel out his concern for his son?" Lifting her shoulders, she spread her hands. "Bad guys are fathers, too, concerned fathers."

Nash tapped his head. "You're not connecting the dots, but you weren't a cop long enough to make detective, were you?"

She tossed her hair and shot him a glance from her green eyes that looked almost…predatory. "What dots?"

"Let's for the sake of argument agree that Lanier is involved with the cartels. You don't think it's coincidental that he's following a baby that one of the cartels is following? That his so-called mistress, Jaycee, also happens to be involved with a man, Brett, who has drug associations?"

"Are you saying that Lanier sent me *and* those two thugs after Wyatt? For what? Insurance?"

"I don't know, yet, Emily, but think about it. It's too coincidental. If I didn't know what I do about Marcus Lanier and his connections, your story might make sense." Nash wrapped his fingers around the steering wheel. "I could understand a man wanting to keep tabs on his son if he felt the mother was unreliable or negligent and even waiting to get paternity results before making a move, but Lanier?"

"What possible reason could Marcus Lanier have for hiring a PI to follow a baby that's not even his?" She pressed her fingers to her temples.

"Same reason two members of a drug cartel are after him."

"To get to Brett?" Her eyes popped open, and she took a quick glance at Wyatt in the back seat, gnawing on the corner of his caterpillar. "But why use me to do it if you've got a couple of violent gofers ready to do the deed?"

"For the same reason those violent gofers, which has me picturing rabid, bucktoothed animals, didn't strong-arm their way into my house. How much more civilized and less upsetting for a pretty, young nanny to abscond with the baby. It's still a crime, but not a crime that can be attached to him."

"Until I tell the authorities I was working for Marcus Lanier."

Nash met her wide eyes and then dropped his gaze.

"What?" She grabbed his arm. "What's that look?"

"If Marcus Lanier is who we think he is, he's a very dangerous man. He could be setting you up. He could have plans for you."

She crossed her arms, rubbing her skin. "You're freaking me out."

"We have to get Wyatt to safety." Nash tapped the clock display on the dashboard. "It's almost your meeting time. Your buddy is going to come after you when you don't show up at the appointed time."

"I could've been more than halfway to Phoenix by now."

"Halfway to Marcus Lanier." Nash reached around and tugged on Wyatt's bare foot. "Let's get him out of here. The AC isn't even cold anymore."

"Your truck?" She jerked her thumb over her shoulder.

"Can I trust you not to go speeding off to Phoenix?"

"You can trust me." She held up two fingers. "Scout's honor."

"Let's get back to my place. We can leave your car there and we'll take my truck out of town, just to get some breathing room." He snapped his fingers. "Better yet, we can pick up that GPS tracker in my driveway and attach it back to your car. I can have my buddy drive the car somewhere, down to the border, to buy us some time."

"What about Denali?"

"I'll ask him to take Denali, too. His girlfriend has looked after him before, so the dog will be fine with them."

"Would your friend do all that for you?"

"He owes me a couple of favors." Nash grabbed her purse and pinned it between his arm and body. "I'll take this. Follow me back to my place—and don't even think about ditching me."

"I won't. I think this plan will work…for now."

Leaving the keys in the ignition, Nash exited Emily's vehicle and strode back to his truck. He made a U-turn and watched in his rearview mirror as Emily followed suit.

Did she really not know Lanier's character? Why would she? Nobody else in Phoenix did. He was friendly to law enforcement and donated to fund-raisers and other causes. He had all the trappings of a smooth, sophisticated SOB. Emily couldn't see past that? Nash shook his head. She didn't want to see past it.

She'd been fired from her job with the PD and had moved out west to start fresh. Getting your foothold in as a private investigator in a new city couldn't be easy, and doing a job for Marcus Lanier would look good on her résumé. She'd been willfully blind.

He put on his left turn signal just to make sure she remembered the way to his house. As he made the turn, she followed and he blew out a breath.

He pulled his truck just inside the gate, but not too far, as he didn't want to crush the GPS in the driveway.

Emily parked behind him and went around to the passenger side to collect Wyatt. As she approached him, she held out the baby, legs dangling beneath him. "Take Wyatt. I'll get the tracker."

Wyatt whined in his arms, and Nash patted his back. "I know, buddy, but she's all we got right now."

Emily returned with her hand held out and a black device in the center of her palm. "Here it is. We're putting it back on my car?"

"Let's make a trade." He peeled Wyatt from his shoulder. "Get this one a bottle, and I'll secure the GPS to your rental and call my friend. Then I'll throw a few things in a bag and we'll hit the road."

Emily scurried into the house with Wyatt, and Nash got busy. His friend Kyle, who was in security, was more than happy to take Emily's car out to the desert. He was going to have his girlfriend, Meg, follow him in her car, and they'd abandon Emily's rental near the border.

By the time Emily returned with Wyatt clutching a bottle, Nash had settled everything. "We're good to go. Let me just pack an overnight bag."

He threw some things together, his only thought to get away from Paradiso for a day and make a plan. If Jaycee came back here and he was gone, it would serve her right. If she ever turned her phone back on, he could leave her a voice mail. She had to know these guys were after her, or that someone was after her. She wouldn't have dropped Wyatt on him, literally, if she hadn't known. Did she go off in search of Brett? Was Brett Wyatt's father? Was Lanier? Had Jaycee even had an affair with Lanier? Too many questions, no answers.

He burst from the house, holding his breath until he saw his truck idling at the foot of his driveway, Wyatt strapped in the back. He still didn't completely trust Emily.

He rapped on the window of the driver's side and she powered it down. "Let me drive. I know this area better than you, and I have an idea."

She scrambled from the truck and went around to the passenger side with no argument, and he slid behind the wheel and repositioned the seat. "How's our guy doing back there?"

"Happy with his bottle. I think he's sleepy and probably confused."

"That makes two of us." Nash shifted into gear and pulled away from his house.

Emily turned away from blowing kisses at Wyatt and tucked one leg beneath her. "He really is a good baby, isn't he? He hardly ever cries. That's not normal, is it?"

He lifted one eyebrow. "You really don't know anything about babies, do you?"

"It's amazing what you can learn from online videos, but Wyatt did seem to take to me, didn't he? Babies aren't much different from dogs. Dogs always seem to know exactly who isn't thrilled with their presence and then glom on to that person."

"So, not only do you not know much about babies, you aren't particularly thrilled with them?"

"I wouldn't say I dislike babies." She shook her finger at Wyatt. "Don't listen to this, Wyatt. I've just never been around them much. I don't have siblings, and my dad was too paranoid to allow me to babysit when I was a teen. Only one of my friends has a baby, and I don't see much of her."

Nash placed his hand on her shoulder. "I'm sorry about your father. I read some news articles about his murder."

She blinked and grabbed her sunglasses from the console. "Thanks."

"You got fired from the same department he served?"

"Yeah." She shoved her glasses onto her face. "Where are we going?"

She'd been more forthcoming as Emily O'Brien. Nash cranked up the air-conditioning. "I thought we'd head out to Tombstone, get lost among the tourists. Something tells me you didn't actually do any sightseeing down here."

"You would be correct. In fact, I haven't been to Tombstone since moving out to Arizona, and I always meant to go." She formed her hands into two pistols. "I wanna see the shoot-out at the OK Corral."

"They do a re-creation of that. It's all kinds of kitschy, but they do a good job of recounting the history of the town in all its violent, bloody glory."

"That's for now." Emily pinned her hands between her bouncing knees. "How are we going to shake these guys?"

"We'll figure out something. When Jaycee returns, I'm going to convince her to go to the police—regardless of what happens to Brett. Right now, I'm more interested in finding out what Lanier's stake is in all this. Is he really the father? Has he discovered some paternal instinct for his girlfriend's baby? What's he going to tell his wife?"

"I told you what he told me. He's in the process of getting a paternity test done—thanks to me." She patted her chest. "I was able to get one of Wyatt's bottles for the test."

Nash twisted his lips. "You were spying on and sneaking around Jaycee and Wyatt before you followed her to Paradiso?"

"Y-yes. I was doing surveillance on her for several days before she took off for Paradiso." She crossed her index fingers, one over the other, and held them out. "Don't crucify me. I thought I had an up-and-up job, helping a father protect his son. That may still be my mission. You don't know for certain that Lanier is involved with the cartels."

Nash ran his tongue along his bottom lip. "Question for you. Whose idea was it to collect Wyatt's DNA? Yours or Lanier's?"

"It was his idea. He wants a DNA test done first, and then a more formal paternity test once he makes his claim."

"Is he sure Wyatt is his and not Brett's? How can he be certain?"

"Brett didn't come into the picture until later when Jaycee already had Wyatt."

"Are you sure? You got that info from Lanier, right?"

"Yes. I didn't have any reason to suspect or doubt him— and I still don't. Why in the world would a man like that want a baby?"

"Didn't we just go through this? He could want Wyatt for the same reason those two men want him. He knows he's Brett's child and they want to use him as bait."

She shoved her fingers beneath her sunglasses, covering her eyes. "I don't know. I'm confused, but I can get some clarity if you know people."

"Know people?" He cranked his head to the side. "What kind of people? What kind of clarity?"

She'd been cleaning her sunglasses on the corner of her shirt, and she waved them back at a sleeping Wyatt. "Well, we have his DNA...and I have Lanier's DNA, too."

Chapter Nine

Nash swallowed hard and said, "Not sure I want to know how that happened."

"His straw." She rolled her eyes. "I have a straw he used, and I put it in a plastic bag."

"Does Lanier know that?"

"No."

He glanced at her profile, her chin firm. "Why did you take his DNA? It must've been because you didn't trust him. That's it, isn't it? You got a bad feeling from him." He wiggled his fingers in the air. "It was that cop sense."

"I can't tell you why I did it." She slumped in the seat and wedged one sandal against the glove compartment. "Stop calling me a cop. I'm not a cop. I'm a PI."

"What happened to your career in law enforcement? Your father was a respected homicide detective at the same department."

"I thought you did a dossier on Emily Lang and knew everything about me." Her bottom lip quivered, and he had a strong desire to press his mouth against hers.

He snorted instead. "I know almost nothing about you. I'm assuming most of what you told me was lies. You slipped up by mentioning your father the homicide detective *and* by using your real first name. Seeing Emily Lang in Lanier's financial records wouldn't have even been a blip on my radar if I hadn't just met another Emily."

"And if that other Emily hadn't snooped in your email. You figured that out, didn't you?" She rubbed the tip of her nose.

"I did, but you had me fooled with your act." He clamped his mouth shut, and his lips formed a thin line. She'd fooled him. Used him.

She ran her knuckles down the side of his arm. "It wasn't all an act, Nash. I've really come to care for... Wyatt over these past few days. I'll admit I saw him as a pawn, a piece in a job for a client, but now I'd do anything to protect him—and not just for a paycheck from Lanier."

Puckering his lips, Nash blew out a breath. "What do you plan to do with Lanier's DNA?"

"Ah, this is where your people come into play. Do you have access to Rapid DNA? I'd like to do my own test to find out if Lanier is, in fact, Wyatt's father. If he's not—" she placed a hand over her heart "—then he must want Wyatt for some nefarious purpose, and I'll do anything in my power to stop that."

"Rapid DNA." Nash drummed his thumbs against the steering wheel. "We do use it. We used it in the case of one of the decapitated women last month."

"Having that piece of information about Lanier and Wyatt could tell us a lot." Emily tapped on the glass. "We're getting closer. There's a sign for Boothill."

"Yeah, except Wyatt Earp is buried out in California."

"Wyatt." Emily turned in her seat and ran a finger over Wyatt's chubby thigh. "Do you think Jaycee named her boy after Wyatt Earp?"

"Could be. Jaycee Lemoin moved to Paradiso right before high school, and she and my sister became fast friends. She was always wild and kept dragging my sister into mishaps."

"Were you a little in love with her?" Emily glanced at him out of the corner of her eye, twirling a strand of hair around her finger.

Nash threw back his head and laughed. "God, no. Jaycee was an annoyance just like my sister, but my sister had her head on straight. Jaycee could lead my sister into almost any harebrained scheme, but my sister drew the line at drugs. She put her foot down for that, and she and Jaycee drifted apart because of it."

"Good for your sister." Emily flicked her finger at his phone, which buzzed twice. "Do you want me to look at your texts, or no?"

"That's my personal phone. You can have a look. Unlike some people, I have nothing to hide."

She plucked his phone from the cup holder and swiped. "Password protected."

He held out his hand and she smacked it into his palm. He entered his passcode with his thumb and dropped it in her lap.

She tapped the screen. "Your friend parked my car near the border and drove back to Paradiso with his girlfriend."

"Hopefully, those thugs think you took Wyatt over the border. Can you please text him a thanks back?" He flipped his turn signal. "We'll find a place for tonight. There aren't many hotels in town, but most visitors stay in Tucson or even Phoenix and drive down. I think we should be able to find a room."

She turned in her seat and rested her chin on the headrest. She blew kisses in Wyatt's direction and said, "Who could resist this little guy?"

A smile tugged at Nash's lips. That was one thing he hadn't mistaken about Emily. She did care for Wyatt. "Not all the guests are going to be happy when he breaks into a crying fit in the middle of the night."

"He doesn't do that." She pinched Wyatt's toes. "Do you?"

"Yeah, you've never been with him during the night. He does wake up sometimes, but he'll usually go right back to sleep after a bottle."

"Of course he does." She righted herself in her seat and powered down the window. "Do you think the hotel will have a crib?"

"I hope so." Nash scratched his chin. He hadn't thought about the sleeping arrangements. He hadn't thought about a lot. Just wanted to get Wyatt out of Paradiso and away from the danger. But in what direction did safety lie? Surely not in the direction of Marcus Lanier?

They drove past Boothill and the road curved into Tombstone. The center of town where the tourist attractions and performance groups resided still had wooden sidewalks and dirt roads, but cars didn't venture into the center of town. Horse-drawn buggies ruled the road.

He drove past the town's museum and pulled into the driveway of the one hotel he knew had decent rooms. He ducked into the back of the truck and unlatched Wyatt's car seat from its base. Swinging it beside him, he strode into the small lobby of the hotel with Emily leading the way.

Emily tapped the bell at the front desk and a woman dressed in frontier garb poked her head out of the back and said, "Howdy."

Emily pressed her lips together, suppressing a smile. "Hello. Do you have a room for one night?"

"I'm sorry. I don't. I'm actually surprised because July is not typically a big month for tourists—too hot."

"Oh." Emily turned to Nash, scrunching up her face. "What now? Did you say there were a couple of hotels here?"

The pioneer woman interrupted, "I'm afraid the other hotel is full, also, but my friend has an Airbnb not far from here and she loves babies."

"Do you know if she has a vacancy?" Nash raised his brows at Emily, and she shrugged.

"She does, unless someone booked with her in the past hour. I was just talking to her." The helpful woman raised one finger. "Give me a minute and I'll call her for you."

Nash set Wyatt's car seat on the floor, and Emily crouched before the baby to make faces and grab his feet to bicycle his legs.

The hotel clerk picked up her phone and touched the display. After a few seconds, she said, "Cora? This is Teri. I have a young couple here with a baby, and they're looking for a room. Do you still have one of yours available?"

Young couple with a baby? Not quite. Nash opened his mouth to explain they'd need separate beds, but Teri burst out in her loud voice. "Perfect. I'll send them right over."

Teri ended the call and hunched forward on the counter, folding her hands. "She has one room left, out of three, and she has a crib. You'll have to book the room through the website, but she's holding it for you."

Emily popped up. "Thank you so much, Teri. We've been driving all day, and my husband is a big fan of Wyatt Earp and has been looking forward to visiting Tombstone for a long time."

That fabrication came easily to Emily's lips. Too easily.

Teri's cheeks shone like polished apples as she tucked a strand of gray hair that had escaped from her long braid behind her ear. "So happy to help."

She slid a piece of hotel paper across the counter and scribbled on it. "Here's her Airbnb and the address. You two enjoy."

After Nash had lifted his jaw from the floor, he grabbed

the car seat and exited the hotel while Emily clutched the piece of paper.

When they stepped into the heat, he tapped Emily's arm. "Why did you lie in there? All that stuff about your husband and how I was a Wyatt Earp fan?"

"Why not lie? Why not play the happy couple on vacation with their baby? If someone comes looking for us—now or later—we might as well cover as much as possible. Yes, there was a couple here with a baby, but they were tourists. You know, cover our tracks."

"Is this Private Investigating 101?" He tugged on a lock of her hair, on fire from the sun. "You're a redhead. An unforgettable redhead."

She tilted her head and dragged her sunglasses down her nose, where they perched on the tip. "You think so?"

"I mean—" heat surged across his chest "—not many people have red hair. All anyone has to do is ask if the woman with the baby had red hair."

"You have to at least try. Doesn't hurt to throw a few lies out there."

Nash aimed the key fob at the truck and unlocked it. "Maybe you're in the wrong profession. You lied to me, but you included just enough truth that I discovered your identity. Not that clever."

"Ugh, don't say that. This is my new profession, and I'm going to stick with it." She opened the back door for Wyatt's car seat.

In less than thirty minutes, they had checked into the Airbnb, which was actually a small cottage behind the main house, and secured a crib in the corner.

As Emily crouched next to Wyatt on the floor of the room to change his diaper, Nash eyed the king-size bed. Emily hadn't blinked an eye when their hostess, Cora, had ushered them into the room with the lone bed.

He chugged down half the bottle of complimentary water and then grinned at Wyatt kicking his legs in the air. Wyatt could be their guardian. Parents with babies didn't have sex, did they? That would be too weird, trying to make the moves on Emily with Wyatt across the room in his crib.

Staring at Emily through half-closed eyes, Nash swirled the water in the bottle. Not that Emily wanted his moves. Maybe the undeniable heat was all on his side. Hell, she'd duped him without a second thought and was getting ready to kidnap his friend's baby.

He needed to keep her close.

She glanced up from her diapering duties and her eyebrows shot up. "What? You look like you're ready to interrogate me."

"Would it do any good?"

"What?"

"Never mind."

Emily snapped Wyatt's onesie into place and scooped him up. "Can you feed him while I wash my hands? We might as well do some sightseeing while we're here. I wasn't lying when I said I wanted to explore Tombstone. It'll get our mind off more unpleasant things right now and maybe lead to some fresh ideas later."

"That sounds good, but Wyatt's not the only one who's hungry. I missed lunch, so let's get some food before we see any shows or go to the museum."

"I'm on board for that."

Nash swung Wyatt into the truck and snapped him in place. "You ready to learn about another Wyatt?"

After sharing some pizza at a noisy restaurant, they spent the rest of the afternoon watching a show in a re-created saloon that involved some of the more colorful historical figures from Tombstone and the OK Corral gunfight. A few times, the loud pops from the guns would set Wyatt off, and Nash would rush outside with him to allow Emily to see a show he'd watched plenty of times.

During the last break, Wyatt had made it clear he preferred being outside, so Nash bounced him in his arms as he walked back and forth across the wooden sidewalks.

As the show let out, Emily poked her head outside the saloon and then waved when she saw them.

She practically skipped toward them. "I loved that. So fun. I had someone take my picture with two of the gunslingers in the show."

Wyatt giggled and clapped his hands, and Emily clapped her hands back. "You missed a great show, Wyatt."

Nash poured the baby into her arms and she hugged Wyatt close, burying her face in his hair. "He probably needs a nap. Do you want to go back to the room?"

"Yeah, I want to check my messages. I got a couple of calls from a fellow agent but no voice mails."

They drove back to the Airbnb and nodded to their hostess on the way to their room. Wyatt was half-asleep in Emily's arms by the time she got his bottle ready.

While she sat in a chair by the window, Nash called Valdez and left a message. "Hey, I saw you called a couple of times. I was busy. Hit me up again."

"Shh." Emily held her finger to her lips. "He's out already."

She spread out his blanket on the bottom of the crib and settled Wyatt on top of it.

Nash's phone buzzed in his hand. "Maybe he's got some news about Jaycee."

"Valdez, you must have something important to tell me."

"I do." The young agent coughed. "You know that body at the border I was going out to investigate today?"

"Yeah?" Nash's heart began to gallop in his chest.

"I hate to break it to you, man, but it's someone you know."

Nash's throat closed up and he couldn't even squeeze out another word. His gaze traveled to Emily, hovering over Wyatt in the crib.

"You there?"

This time Nash managed a grunt.

"It's Jaycee Lemoin. She's dead."

Chapter Ten

The color drained from Nash's tanned face and his body stiffened.

"What's wrong?" Emily pushed away from the crib and sat on the foot of the bed, clasping her hands.

Nash ran a hand over his mouth. "Murdered?"

Emily bounced up. "Murdered? Who? Marcus Lanier? God, not your friend and his girlfriend!"

Nash shook his head at her. "Okay, thanks for calling, Valdez. I'll be back tomorrow."

He ended the call and sat still on the bed, cupping the phone between his hands, his eyes closed.

"Nash?" Emily scooted closer to him on the bed and rested her hand on his thigh. "What happened? Who was murdered?"

Without opening his eyes, he said, "Jaycee."

Emily cried out and covered her mouth. Tears sprang to her eyes and spilled over her lids, creating hot trails down her cheeks until they met the edge of her hand.

A lump formed in her throat and she sobbed, covering her face with both hands. Her shoulders shook.

Wyatt's mother—dead. He'd never know her. Never remember her. Maybe Jaycee hadn't been the most careful mother, but she loved her boy. Even Emily could see that, although she herself had never felt that love before.

Jaycee had loved him enough to leave him with a trusted friend when she felt his life—and hers—was in danger.

Nash rested his hand on her shoulder. "They killed her."

She dropped her hands and reached for him. His sister's friend, the childhood nuisance, murdered.

He wrapped his arms around her and nestled his head in the crook of her neck. He grated out in a rough voice, "I should've done something. I should've protected her."

She stroked the back of his head, his thick hair springy beneath her fingers. "You couldn't know. You didn't know until I told you she was in trouble."

"I should've guessed. Why else would she drop her baby off on my porch? I should've seen that as a desperate move." He drilled his fist into the mattress.

"You tried, Nash. You tried to reach her, but she didn't return your calls. If anyone's to blame, it's me." She pulled away from him and smacked her hand twice against her chest. "I was hounding her just as surely as those two men were. I should've demanded that Lanier take action right away."

Nash, his eyes bright with unshed tears, grabbed both of her hands with his. "Why'd they do it, Emily? Why'd they kill her? If they wanted to get to Brett, they should've taken her hostage to give him an ultimatum."

"Maybe Brett didn't care?" She squeezed his hands. "Maybe they had her, gave Brett the option of coming in or losing Jaycee, and he chose his life over hers."

"And the baby? And Wyatt?" His gaze tracked over her shoulder to the crib. "My God, he's just lost his mother and who the hell knows who his father is? Some selfish junkie or a possible drug cartel financier? What the hell kind of choice is that?"

Emily flattened her hand against her belly. "Now that they don't have Jaycee, they'll be coming for Wyatt even harder. Maybe that's why they accosted me last night. They'd already killed Jaycee and knew they needed Wyatt. H-how long has she been dead?"

"I didn't ask." Nash wiped his hand across his brow. "I didn't ask much of anything."

"You were in shock." She cupped his face with both of her hands. "I'm so sorry, and I'm sorry I didn't tell you what was going on as soon as I met you."

"You were working for a client." He encircled her wrists with his fingers. "Don't blame yourself."

"But I knew those men were after her, and Lanier wasn't responding to my texts. I should've figured out something was wrong."

"So, we're both going to sit here and blame ourselves for Jaycee's death when the only people responsible are the ones who killed her. Sure, she made some bad choices, but not one of those choices deserved a death sentence. Now Wyatt—" Nash's voice hitched in his throat "—he's an orphan."

"I'm going to have to call Lanier about this."

"Or you can pretend you don't know anything about Jaycee. We haven't publicized her name yet. That story is not going to be released for at least a day. Sit back and see what Lanier has to say. See if he gives away the fact that he knows Jaycee is gone."

"Lanier?" She dropped her hands to his thighs and curled her fingers into his flesh. "You think he had something to do with Jaycee's murder?"

"I don't know, Emily. If he did, that means you're in danger, too."

"After last night, I already figured that, but I have something Jaycee didn't." She pointed to her purse hanging over a chair with her .22 back in its pocket.

"You have something else she didn't."

She raised her eyebrows at him. "What's that?"

"You have me."

"Thank you." She grabbed his arm. "I feel like I brought this danger to Jaycee."

"Jaycee would've been in danger without you...or without me. At least she had the good sense to separate herself from Wyatt."

"Now she's permanently separated from Wyatt." She glanced over her shoulder to look between the slats of the crib at the sleeping baby, unaware that he'd lost his mother for good. "Do you think she found Brett? That's where she must've gone, right? She didn't give you any hint? She must've left you a note with Wyatt along with all those instructions, right?"

"She did." Nash massaged his right temple. "It was brief. Something along the lines of watch my baby for a few days, and here's the baby manual."

"What are we going to do now, Nash?" She clasped her hands, intertwining her fingers to keep from touching him. She wanted to smooth the lines of worry and sadness from his face. "If you hadn't warned me about Marcus Lanier, I'd be headed to Phoenix right now to deliver his son to him."

He met her gaze, his blue eyes still glistening. "You know I'd never allow you to do that—even if I'd never heard of Marcus Lanier. Babies can't be transported around the country by strangers, delivered to people just because they say they're the parents. You understand that, right?"

She lifted her shoulders to her ears. "You mean you have to follow the law, and in this case that means calling the Department of Child Services."

"You can tell Lanier anything you like and maybe he'll even allow you to keep your retainer."

She sucked in a breath. "Is that what you think I'm worried about? Money?"

"Then you agree that we need to contact the proper authorities now? Wyatt doesn't belong to you, he doesn't belong to me and he sure as hell doesn't belong to Marcus Lanier—at least not yet."

"The *proper authorities* don't always make the best calls." She clenched her teeth. "We'll be turning him over to strangers. He knows us. He belongs with us. We can protect him."

"Emily, it's called kidnapping. We can't do it. If we take off with Wyatt and then he's taken from us by force, that'll be a whole lot worse. Think about it."

"I—I see that." She knew her way only led to trouble down the road. Hadn't it gotten her fired? She stifled a sniffle. "Tomorrow? We'll take him back to Paradiso tomorrow and call DCS."

"I'm going to notify the station that we have Wyatt, and I'll have them call DCS. I think that would be safer." Nash scooted past her off the bed and crept to Wyatt's crib. He leaned over and touched one finger to Wyatt's cheek. "What are you going to do about Lanier, Emily?"

"I'm going to try him again today just to test the waters and to gauge if he knows anything he shouldn't. Then tomorrow—" she swung her legs off the bed "—tomorrow I'm going to let him know that DCS has Wyatt because his mother was murdered and advise him to contact DCS to go through the proper channels if he wants custody of his son. And if he wants his damned money back, he can have it."

"You're going to have to make a statement to the police about the man who threatened you."

She opened her mouth, but Nash held up a hand. "You don't have to tell them everything. After all, the guy who accosted you didn't know you had a connection to Lanier, right? He just thought you were a friend of mine who had access to Wyatt. We decided to take a trip to Tombstone to get out of town and heard the news about Wyatt's mom."

He spread his hands. "No covers blown."

"I can do that." She pressed a palm against her forehead. "I'm going to try calling Lanier again. Wish me luck."

She strolled to the window and placed the call as she looked out on a cactus garden in the back of the house. The phone rang three times and then flipped to a message.

She held the phone in front of her and turned to Nash. "I can't even leave voice mail because his box is full. I don't get it."

"Father of the year, unless they got to him, too." He ran a hand through his hair. "Do you mind if we order food in for dinner? I don't feel much like going out."

"I don't feel much like eating. Whatever you like, but that garden out back looks nice. Wyatt will probably want some fresh air when he wakes up."

"He'd like that." Nash sniffed and wiped his nose with the back of his hand.

Emily shoved her phone into the pocket of her skirt. "What's going to happen to Wyatt?"

"As a cop, you should know the drill. They'll contact Jaycee's next of kin, see if she had a will, which I doubt, and try to place him with her family."

"Unless the father steps up." Emily crossed and gripped her upper arms. With Jaycee out of the picture, Lanier would have a clear path to Wyatt. Had he been responsible for Jaycee's death? Had those two men been working for him, as Nash had suggested at the beginning?

"Who is Jaycee's next of kin? Does she have siblings?"

"She may have half brothers and sisters. I don't know. When she lived in Paradiso, she and her single mom rented a house my family owned. Her mother lived with a couple of guys while they were here, and my parents finally had to give her an ultimatum because the men were using and selling drugs from the house."

"Poor Jaycee. No wonder she fell into that lifestyle so easily." Emily dug her fingers into her biceps. Wyatt shouldn't have to repeat that upbringing. "D-do you think her mother will want custody?"

"I don't know, Emily. I hope to God not."

Wyatt stirred in his crib, making mewling noises in his sleep.

Emily said, "I'll get his bottle ready."

"No, let me do it." Nash smashed his fist into his other hand. "I need to do something before I go off and tear this room apart."

Blinking back tears, Emily nodded. Jaycee's death had deeply affected Nash, probably partly out of guilt and partly from childhood memories, but he hadn't been able to let go. She wanted to tell him it was okay if he wanted to cry and let loose. She'd seen her father cry over particular murder cases where he didn't even know the victims, and he'd always seemed more the man for doing so.

But Nash had to deal how he had to deal, and she let him go through the busywork of mixing up Wyatt's formula and warming it up while she hovered over the baby.

Wyatt uncurled his hands and blinked his eyes. His mouth opened for a big yawn.

Emily reached into the crib and rubbed his back. "Hello, sleepyhead. Are you ready for a bottle?"

His unfocused eyes found her face and a smile touched his lips. He recognized her. He was happy to see her standing there. Her heart swelled. Nobody had been happy to see her in a long time.

She slid her hand beneath his body and lifted him toward her. Still sleepy, he nuzzled his head against her shoulder, and she rested her cheek against his soft hair.

The tears came again, silently sliding down her face and running into Wyatt's hair. She choked back a sob.

In a second, Nash was beside her, holding her and Wyatt both in the circle of his strong arms. He bent his head to hers, and his body shook as he cried.

As Nash held her and this motherless child safe in his comforting embrace, Emily's heart filled with a warmth she hadn't felt since the night her father was murdered.

THAT NIGHT, after tacos outside within feet of the cactus garden, Emily put Wyatt to bed in the crib and joined Nash on the patio for a beer.

She rolled the sweating bottle between her hands. "I saw you texting earlier when I was putting Wyatt down. Any more news about Jaycee's murder?"

"No." Wyatt scratched at the soggy label on his beer with his fingernail. "That was Rob Valdez, one of my co-workers. I told him that I would bring Wyatt into the office tomorrow and to notify DCS."

"So, this is it, our last night with Wyatt." Emily traced her finger around the lip of her bottle. "I hope Jaycee's mother takes care of him. I hope he's happy—no matter who he has for a father."

"I don't think it's Lanier. If he told you a true story, he would've been in touch with you as soon as he found out these other guys were after Wyatt. His silence is telling."

"If he isn't Wyatt's father, his intentions from the start were nefarious…and I played right into his hands." Emily took a gulp of beer. "I'm not much of a PI, am I?"

"Even an investigation you'd run on a client wouldn't have turned up Lanier's shady financial deals. We had a forensic accountant working on Lanier, and he's still not sure about the connection to the cartels." Nash eased out of his chair and knelt before hers, sliding his hands up to her hips. "Don't blame yourself. As soon as you explained yourself to me, I believed you. Call me an idiot. God knows, I have plenty of reasons not to trust women, but I knew."

Leaning over, Emily set her beer bottle on the tile and placed her hands on Nash's shoulders. "I'm sorry I tricked you. I really did think I was doing the right thing for Wyatt. I'd seen those men questioning Jaycee and knew they were trouble—trouble coming for Wyatt."

"You did a good job protecting him. You did a good job taking care of him, especially since everything you know about babies comes from online videos."

Her lips turned up on one side, the first time she'd cracked a smile since finding out about Jaycee. "I did okay, didn't I?"

"You did more than okay. You saved me."

She joined her hands together, entwining her fingers behind his neck. "There's something special about us. I felt it from the beginning."

"So did I." Nash's gaze dropped from her eyes to her mouth as his hands moved up to her waist.

She parted her lips, which had started tingling. That ended when Nash pressed his mouth against hers.

She returned the kiss, inching her hands up his throat. With her fingers laced behind his neck, she pulled him closer and he deepened the kiss, thrusting his tongue into her mouth.

She sighed against the kiss and melted into his embrace. Could they make love with Wyatt in his crib? Was that even legal? If not, she'd be willing to break every law to be with Nash Dillon.

Nash's body jerked, and he pulled away from her.

"I—I agree." She put a hand to her hot cheek. "Bad idea."

"Shh." He rose to his feet and turned toward the sliding door that led to their room.

"What is it?" She touched his back, straining her ears for Wyatt's cry.

Nash lunged forward and charged through the door.

With the adrenaline rushing through her system, Emily stumbled after him. She tripped over the sliding door track and screamed as she saw Nash tackle a man hovering over Wyatt's crib.

Nash threw himself on top of the man's skinny frame, shoving his forearm against the man's throat. The intruder bucked and thrashed beneath him, choking out words and foaming at the mouth.

Nash punched the man's face and blood spurted from his beak-like nose. With one knee pressed into the squirming man's midsection, he turned around and ground out, "He was trying to kidnap Wyatt."

Emily yanked her purse from the chair and whipped out her weapon. "Do not make another move or you're dead."

The would-be kidnapper gasped, "Stop. Stop. I'm Wyatt's father."

Chapter Eleven

Nash cranked his head back to stare into the man's face, the high cheekbones prominent, his bug-eyes wild. "You're not Marcus Lanier."

"I'm Brett Fillmore." He held his hands in front of his face. "No more, man. I can prove it. My wallet's in my back pocket."

Emily, her gun clutched in her hand, approached from the side. She leaned over the man, and her gaze scanned his face. "It's him. It's Brett Fillmore."

Brett blinked. "How do you know who I am? Who the hell are you?"

Nash reached for the man's pocket anyway and patted him down after snatching his wallet and throwing it at Emily's feet. Shoving his fingers into Brett's front pocket, Nash pulled out a knife. "I'll take this."

"Hey, a guy needs protection."

Nash pushed to his feet, using Brett's body for leverage. "You're sure he's Brett Fillmore? You saw him before?"

"I did." Emily swept the wallet from the floor and flipped it open, glancing inside and then showing Nash Brett Fillmore's driver's license. "He was in Jaycee's apartment when I was surveilling it—before she left for the border."

Brett used his elbows to prop himself up. "You were spying on us? On Jaycee?"

Nash narrowed his eyes. "I don't care if he's Santa Claus and Mother Teresa rolled into one. He was trying to kidnap Wyatt."

"You can't kidnap your own son." Brett wiped his arm across his bloody nose. "Can someone help me here?"

Emily responded by leveling her gun at Brett's head. Nash knew there was a reason why he liked this woman.

Her nostrils flared. "How'd you find us here?"

"I know you think Jaycee's a bad mom for leaving Wyatt like that, but she had a good reason and she had every intention of keeping tabs on him." With his eyes on the gun pointed at his head, Brett inched up a little farther to lean against the crib, where Wyatt had awoken and was now crying.

Brett pointed to the car seat in the corner. "Jaycee had put a GPS tracker on the bottom of Wyatt's car seat. Wh-when she didn't show up at our meeting place, I tracked the car seat. I thought maybe I'd find her, too, but when I saw you two instead of Jaycee, I made my move. Can you blame me?"

Nash growled deep in his throat. "Yeah, I can blame you. If you were meeting Jaycee and you knew she was tracking Wyatt, you must've realized who I was."

"Yeah, the great Nash Dillon." Brett hacked up some blood, spit it in his palm and wiped it on the thigh of his jeans. "I told Jaycee it was a bad idea to leave Wyatt with the cops, but she wouldn't listen."

"Why would that be a bad idea if you're so concerned with the safety of your *son*?" Emily sounded like she was interrogating a suspect, but she did ease off on her aim.

"Because of this." Brett waved a bony hand around the room. "Because you're not just gonna let me have Wyatt, are you? You're gonna play by the rules. I warned Jaycee that her old friend would turn on her in a minute if he thought she was breaking the law."

Emily said, "We don't even know if you're the father."

Brett hit the back of his head against the crib. "Can someone shut him up?"

"Your concern for Wyatt is touching." Nash held up his hands. "I'm going to wash my hands and see to Wyatt. Don't take your gun off him."

"Don't worry. I'm on it."

As Nash washed his hands, Brett blabbed on about cops and Jaycee and his son but never once mentioned Jaycee's murder. Did he know?

When Nash returned to the room, he tossed two towels at Brett, a wet one and a dry one. Then he picked up a sniffling Wyatt and rocked him in his arms. "It's okay, buddy."

"Finally." Brett wiped the blood from his face and hands and held the towel against his nose.

Emily threw Nash a side glance and he dipped his chin. She cleared her throat. "Do you know where Jaycee is?"

Brett peered at her over the blood-streaked towel. "No. We were supposed to meet in Mexico, and she never showed up. I tried contacting her on her burner phone, but she never responded. That's when I launched the app and the code she gave me for tracking Wyatt. When I saw him here in Tombstone, I made a move."

Emily lowered her gun. "I hate to tell you this, Brett, but Jaycee is dead."

"What? No." Brett shook his shaggy head back and forth. "She can't be. She was supposed to meet me in Mexico. We were going to come for Wyatt together."

"I'm sorry. It's true." Nash patted Wyatt's back as the baby wriggled in his arms. It was as if Jaycee's son had understood what he said.

"Oh, God." Brett buried his face in the towel and muffled cries escaped from the edges. His head popped up, and he said, "It was Marcus Lanier that killed her. I can guarantee that."

Nash studied Brett's face smeared with dried blood. If he'd been crying real tears, the blood would be running down his face again. "How do you know Jaycee was murdered? Emily didn't say anything about that. It could've been a car accident."

Brett's wild eyes shifted to Emily. "Was it?"

"It was murder." Emily slipped her gun into the side pocket of her purse hanging on her body and crossed her arms. "But what made you think that right away?"

"She was being threatened. She told me two cartel guys came by the apartment. She figured Lanier sent them." Brett hunched his narrow shoulders. "That's why she went on the run, and that's why she left Wyatt with you."

With Wyatt nestled in the crook of his arm, Nash sank to the edge of the bed. "What do you know about Lanier? Why would he be after Jaycee? Why would he want her dead?"

"You should know that." Brett swiveled his head between Nash and Emily. "When I told you I was Wyatt's father to stop your attack, you said I wasn't Marcus Lanier. So, you know Lanier thinks he's Wyatt's father."

"But he's not?" Emily's fingers dug into her flesh.

"*I'm* Wyatt's father."

Emily drilled two fingers into her temple and closed her eyes. "Why would Lanier want to claim paternity for Wyatt? He's a married man. Wouldn't it be much easier for him to give up his parental rights when another man is on the scene claiming his paternity?"

"He *thinks* he's Wyatt's father because Jaycee told him he was. They hooked up several times, so it's possible."

"Let me guess." Nash ground his back teeth together. "Jaycee told Lanier he was the father so she could blackmail him. Am I on the right track? Get some cash out of the guy?"

"That's about right." Brett blew his nose on the towel. "You probably know Jaycee better than I do. She told me how your sister was her best friend in high school, and they'd get into all kinds of trouble."

A muscle throbbed in Nash's jaw. "If that's true, you two were playing a dangerous game."

"If that's true—" Emily strolled to the sliding door to the patio, still standing open in the sultry evening, and then spun around to face Brett "—why not just call off the attack dogs? Why not tell Lanier the truth? If he were coming after Jaycee and Wyatt, it's obvious he wasn't going to pay up."

"I told Jaycee to come clean with him. I told her we weren't going to get anything out of him." Brett bunched the towel in his fists.

"And?" Nash switched a fussy Wyatt from one arm to the other.

"She wouldn't listen to me. She said even if Lanier got a paternity test, she had a couple of their hookups on video and she was going to threaten to go to his wife."

"Wait a minute." Emily paced around the room again. "If you believe the two cartel guys who paid a visit to Jaycee before she fled Phoenix were working for Lanier, why didn't they just kill Jaycee then and snatch Wyatt?"

"Are you a cop, too?"

A blush washed across Emily's face, and she put a hand to her throat. "It doesn't matter what I am. You said two thugs went to Jaycee's apartment, and you implied that these guys worked for Lanier. If that's the case, they already believed Wyatt was their boss's baby. They would've had orders then, but didn't do anything. Instead, they left her and the baby alone and put a tracker on her car, just like Jaycee tracked Wyatt and his car seat."

"I'm supposed to understand the mind of a criminal?" Brett jabbed a thumb at his scrawny chest, which had junkie written all over it.

"In fact—" Emily grabbed a handful of Brett's dirty T-shirt and yanked him to his feet "—those criminals seemed a lot more interested in you than Wyatt. Why is that, Brett?"

Brett's eyes widened to the point that his whites surrounded his dark irises. "How do you know that?"

"I was bugging that apartment. I saw all kinds of things." She drilled her finger into his chest. "Those two guys wanted you."

"I don't know why they'd want me instead of Jaycee." He brushed at his shirt where she'd poked him. "But thanks for the tip. Maybe they figured a mother wouldn't use her kid like that, so they thought I was the mastermind."

"Mastermind." Nash rolled his eyes. "We can go around and around all night with this. We'll let the police do their investigation into Jaycee's murder, and we'll let the Department of Child Safety and the family court decide who is Wyatt's father and where he belongs."

"You're kidding, right?" Brett shoved his hands into the front pockets of his jeans. "You're turning my kid over to the system?"

"I sure as hell am not turning him over to you." Nash cuddled Wyatt closer against his chest.

"It's late and Wyatt needs to get back to sleep." Emily flicked her fingers at Brett. "Get out. If you are Wyatt's father and you want to raise him as your own, you can go through the proper channels."

Brett shoved out his hand. "My knife."

Nash snorted. "Now you're the one who's kidding. Leave, and if you make any more attempts to take Wyatt, I'll kill you."

Brett swallowed hard, his Adam's apple bobbing in his skinny neck. "You'll see. I'm that baby's father and he'll wind up with me—where he belongs."

Emily strode to the front door and flung it open.

Brett backed up through the door, as if he didn't trust them not to jump him. Nash grimaced. The guy wasn't as dumb as he looked.

Emily clicked the door shut after him and locked the dead bolt. "Cora needs a chain on this door. He broke in too easily."

She tiptoed to the bed. "How's our boy?"

"He's almost out. After the commotion, he sensed the tension. It drained him."

"But you calmed him down." She tilted her head. "You're good with him. Do a lot of your friends have babies?"

"Almost none." Nash rose from the bed and settled Wyatt on the crib mattress, holding his breath. "It's kind of like soothing a horse."

"Not quite."

"And you know that how, city girl?"

"He's a baby, not a horse."

"Thanks for that." Nash scratched his chin. "What do you think about Brett's story?"

"I'm going to shut this sliding door before I tell you." She made good on her promise and yanked the drapes across the glass. "He's full of it. Did you notice his crocodile tears over Jaycee?"

"I did. He made a quick recovery. But the story about the blackmail?" He picked up a tortilla chip left over from their dinner and crunched it between his teeth. "That's pure Jaycee."

"Maybe that's why Lanier hired me and then wasn't too upset when I told him those two characters were after Wyatt. He could've even figured out at that point that Wyatt was Brett's son and washed his hands of the whole affair."

"Until Jaycee came back at him with her videos and more demands."

"Until then."

"If that's what went down, then the two cartel guys really were looking for Brett and figured Wyatt was his kid."

"Did they find Jaycee first and try to use her to get Brett to cooperate?"

"If so, that attempt failed. Brett didn't take the bait and they killed Jaycee."

Emily hugged her purse to her chest. "I'm going to sleep with this right next to me in case Brett gets the bright idea to come back."

While he wished Emily would show as much desire to sleep with him as her gun, he crouched before the little safe in the room, where he'd stowed his own weapon. "I've got my bedmate right here."

Emily raised her eyebrows. "You really know how to make a girl feel special."

Placing his gun on the nightstand on the left side of the bed, he chuckled. "I guess that's what happens when you get two cops together."

She opened her mouth, grinned and then snapped it shut. As she unzipped her suitcase, she asked, "What do you think he wanted with Wyatt? He barely looked at him."

"Yeah, I find it hard to believe he has any strong feelings for his son…or his son's mother." He stretched out on the bed and clasped his hands behind his head. "That's a mystery, but I'm sure he's up to no good. You take the bathroom first and I'll put the TV on low."

When Emily retreated to the bathroom, Nash watched images flicker across the TV, but his ears were attuned to every sound from the other room as Emily ran the water and brushed her teeth.

Brett had interrupted a moment between him and Emily that Nash had been anticipating for quite a while, but maybe Brett had provided a warning. Nash and Emily had been so into each other, they'd missed Brett breaking into the room. They had a responsibility to that little boy. They had to get him safely to DCS…and Jaycee's relatives.

Nash kicked off his flip-flops and dragged a pillow into his lap, crushing it against his chest. He remembered Jaycee's mother all too well. That woman had no business raising a child. And the possible fathers? Hell no. Poor kid.

Emily threw open the bathroom door, and he snapped out of his funk. She'd already witnessed one breakdown, and he wanted to exude the confidence now that he could get both her and Wyatt back to Paradiso safely.

He slapped on a grin. "Did you leave me some hot water?"

"There's plenty." She shook out her T-shirt as she walked to her suitcase to lay her clothes across the top. "Are you taking a shower, too?"

"This town is dusty. I feel like I'm crunching dirt between my teeth." He swung his legs off the bed and grabbed a clean T-shirt and a pair of gym shorts from his bag.

"It is dusty, and I don't care if it is kind of corny, I liked it…until we found out about Jaycee."

He bunched his clothes in one hand. "It was a good day until that."

He slipped into the bathroom, took a quick shower

and brushed his teeth. When he returned to the bedroom, Emily was propped up against a pile of pillows watching a comedy.

She patted the bed beside her. "C'mon, I think we can both use a laugh right now."

He dropped his clothes and crawled onto the bed beside her.

She scooted close to him and rested her head on his shoulder. "You're one of the good guys, Nash Dillon."

THE FOLLOWING MORNING, they rose early and had a quick breakfast with Cora before hitting the road back to Paradiso. They left the GPS that had been on Wyatt's car seat in the cactus garden.

Jaycee hadn't been as ditzy as Nash thought. His hands tightened on the steering wheel. She should've taken care of herself as well as Wyatt.

Nash had called in their arrival time to coincide with DCS. They'd hand Wyatt over to a social worker and DCS would find him a foster family until his parentage and Jaycee's wishes could be sorted through.

He was gonna miss the kid...and the kid's nanny.

As they passed Boothill, Nash turned his head toward Emily. "Are you going to contact Lanier as soon as DCS has Wyatt?"

"Yes. If I'm forced to leave a text again, I'll let him know about Jaycee—if it's okay with the police—and that DCS has Wyatt and that he's safe. He can figure out what he wants to do from there, but it's all going to have to be legal and aboveboard."

"Do you think you'll get your final payment, or whatever he owes you?"

"At this point, I don't care. If he turns out to be involved with the cartels, I don't want his dirty money." She slid her sunglasses on and tapped her fingers against her knee, her jaw a hard line.

A good reference from a client like Lanier could've catapulted Emily's PI career into the stratosphere—unless he was a cartel associate and money launderer. What the hell did someone like Lanier want with a baby, even if Wyatt were his son? He must've been trying to foil Jaycee's blackmail attempt.

The drive back to Paradiso went a lot faster than the drive out to Tombstone, no matter how much Nash tried to delay it. When he pulled into the parking lot of the station, he scanned the cars to see if he could figure out which one belonged to the caseworker who'd take Wyatt away. He swallowed hard when he saw a sedan with a rear-facing car seat in the back.

He threw the car into Park and sat still with his hands resting on top of the steering wheel. Emily sat beside him, staring straight ahead, not moving a muscle.

Finally, she shoved her glasses to the top of her head. "Before we go in, I'm going to change his diaper one last time. I—I don't want them to think he was neglected."

"I'll help you." Nash exited the vehicle and opened the passenger door behind the driver's side. He dragged the diaper bag from the floor of the truck while Emily scooped Wyatt out of his seat.

"C'mon, you little bug. You need to look handsome and healthy to meet new people." Emily's voice hitched in her throat.

Nash's own throat was aching by the time she came to his side of the car with Wyatt in her arms.

She placed him on the diaper mat he'd laid out on the seat and changed Wyatt—one last time. Without hesitation, Nash took the dirty diaper from her and tossed it into the trash can on the edge of the parking lot. He'd come a long way in a few days.

When he came back to the truck, Emily had snapped up Wyatt's clothes and plucked a couple of diaper wipes from the dispenser. She waved one at Nash. "Here you go."

He wiped his hands clean, and then they walked into the station as if they were going to face a firing squad.

When they entered the reception area, four heads swiveled around to watch their progress. Nash narrowed his eyes as he, Emily and Wyatt approached the clutch of people, each with a different expression he couldn't begin to fathom. He could read only Valdez's open face, filled with an almost gleeful humor, but he couldn't understand it. What the hell was so funny about a murdered mother leaving a child behind?

He recognized Detective Espinoza from the Pima County Sheriff's Department and a deputy from the same department and figured the woman for the caseworker.

They'd all been huddled around a computer when he and Emily had walked in with Wyatt. Now their attention stayed focused on him.

Nash coughed, more to get rid of the lump in his throat than anything else. "We have Jaycee Lemoin's baby. I hope you're ready to take good care of him."

The woman shifted her gaze from him to Wyatt, happily lounging in Emily's arms, and smiled. "I'm Alice Daniels, the social worker from DCS. Wyatt looks like a happy boy. We'll do our best for him until…"

Alice jerked her head back toward Nash and dropped her gaze.

Nash exchanged a look with Emily, who shrugged. She felt it, too.

Espinoza nodded to Nash as he lifted the laptop to the counter. "Agent Dillon, we have something to show you."

"I figured you might. You're all acting weird."

As Emily started forward, Alice put her hand on her arm. "May I hold Wyatt?"

"Of course." Emily did the handoff and Wyatt seemed happy with the smiling woman.

Emily slipped a finger through Nash's belt loop and they bellied up to the counter together.

Nash rapped his knuckles on the wood surface. "What is going on? What's on that computer?"

Espinoza spun the laptop around to face Nash and Emily, where a still from a video featuring Jaycee filled the screen. "When we found Jaycee's body, she had a phone on her."

Nash got an adrenaline surge. "Did she capture her killer?"

"No such luck, but Jaycee knew she was in trouble for sure and took some precautions." Espinoza's hand hovered over the mouse. "Are you ready?"

Nash licked his lips. "Yeah, go."

Espinoza clicked the play button, and Jaycee started talking in a video she'd taken of herself.

Her breathy voice with the slight Southern accent she'd picked up somewhere came across the computer speakers.

"So, I know I messed up…big-time, but I love my little Wy more than anything, and I want to make sure he's safe in case something happens to me. This is my last will and testament, and I'm hoping it holds up in a court of law even if I didn't write anything down or get it notarized, 'cause I don't want my mom to get Wyatt." Jaycee pushed her blond hair from her face. "She didn't do such a great job with me. Sorry, Mom, but you didn't. So, I, Jaycee Lemoin, being of sound mind and body do hereby…"

She stopped and giggled, and Nash's heart flipped over.

"Anyway, almost sound mind and body—and that's a

joke. What I'm trying to say here is, I want to pick a guardian for my son, Wyatt Lemoin, and I want that guardian to be Nash Dillon."

Chapter Twelve

Nash's mouth dropped open, and he couldn't hear the rest of Jaycee's verbal will over the roaring in his ears. What just happened? Did Jaycee just appoint him, a single man, a carefree bachelor, as guardian for her son?

Emily touched his shoulder. "Are you all right?"

"All right?" He twisted his head to the side and met her gaze. "I'm in shock. I can't… I'm not…"

"You're not locked in or anything, Agent Dillon." Alice the caseworker appeared in his peripheral vision, bouncing a gurgling Wyatt in her arms. "I'm not an attorney, but I've seen a few situations like this. Nobody can force you to take a child, and it's not that easy for one parent to cut out another. If Wyatt's father steps forward, he can fight for custody and a judge will usually go with blood over friendship. Unless…"

Nash snapped his head around. "I'm not Wyatt's father."

Alice asked, "Do you know who is?"

At Alice's question, Emily pinched his side. She didn't have to worry. He didn't plan on getting into the whole sorry mess right now.

"I don't know—for sure." He waved a hand at the laptop, where Jaycee's frozen image beseeched him. "Didn't Jaycee mention the father? Did she give any hints about who was after her or why she was in danger?"

Espinoza shook his head. "Unfortunately, she didn't get into any of that. When I saw that she'd created a video two days ago, I had my hopes up, but all her thoughts were with her son."

Nash braced his hands on the counter, on either side of the laptop, almost nose-to-nose with Jaycee on the monitor. "What happens now?"

"We'll take care of Wyatt." Alice touched her finger to the baby's nose. "Detective Espinoza has already contacted Jaycee's next of kin, and we'll do some research into Wyatt's father. This is all going to have to wend its way through the courts."

"Wend?" Emily stroked Wyatt's leg. "That makes it sound like a long and tortuous process. Wyatt needs his forever home as soon as possible."

"There is a procedure that has to be followed, but we always have the child's best interests at heart. We have many foster families who would take excellent care of Wyatt and treat him as their own."

Emily ducked and picked up Wyatt's diaper bag and kicked her own large duffel on the floor. "These are his things, and we have a car seat in the truck. When are you taking him?"

"Not for a little while yet. I have paperwork to fill out with Detective Espinoza and a few phone calls to make." Alice took the diaper bag from Emily. "He'll be fine here. Agent Dillon, you can decide whether or not you want to take on this responsibility, and then file a petition when we bring Wyatt's case to family court. The mother's wishes on that video and the fact that she left Wyatt with you when she went on the run will both bear strong witness to your claim."

A father? Hell, he never even kept food in the house for himself. Jaycee had dropped off Wyatt with him because she wanted her son protected, not nurtured. Had she believed Wyatt would be in danger even after she died? From whom? What did these people want with a little baby?

Wyatt squirmed in Alice's arms and reached out for Emily.

Emily dropped her head, allowing her hair to create a rosy veil around her face, but Nash spied a teardrop quivering on the end of her chin.

There was no way they could stay here waiting for Alice to take Wyatt away. They might not see him for months. Nash clamped a hand over his mouth. Who was he kidding? Emily would probably never see Wyatt again.

He put an arm around her hunched shoulders. "Maybe we should get some lunch and leave Wyatt with Alice. He'll be fine."

Emily's head shot up and she dashed the back of her hand across her cheek. "A man who claimed to be Wyatt's father tried to kidnap him last night."

Detective Espinoza crossed his arms, resting them on his paunch. "Brett Fillmore?"

"Yeah, has he been around here?" Nash squeezed Emily's shoulder.

"No, but his fingerprints are in Jaycee's car, and we know that because he's in the system. She also has pictures of him on her phone. Let's just say Mr. Fillmore is a person of interest right now. Did he happen to say where he was going after you foiled his kidnapping attempt?"

"No." Nash rubbed his knuckles against his stubble. "He told us he and Jaycee were supposed to meet in Mexico and she never showed. She'd put a GPS tracker on Wyatt's car seat, and Brett followed us to Tombstone."

Espinoza's eyebrows bunched over his nose. "Did he know Jaycee was dead?"

"Said he didn't." Nash shrugged. "I'm not sure why he'd

want to kill her, though. Those two were involved in some scams together. We also need to talk about someone else who may be involved in all this. Let me know when you want to interview me."

"Looks like one of those scams got her killed." Espinoza smacked his hand on the counter. "We'll get to the bottom of this, and that little boy will have a good, safe home, whether it's with you, Dillon, or someone else. I'll be in touch. We're still processing items from the crime scene."

Wyatt started to whimper, and Emily cupped his foot with her hand. "It's okay, big guy. Can I hold him for a minute to say goodbye?"

"Of course." Alice handed Wyatt off to Emily, and she held him close, resting her head against his. "It looks like you two took good care of Wyatt. It's no wonder why Jaycee left him in your care, Agent Dillon."

Emily whispered to Wyatt as she cuddled him, and Nash blinked his eyes.

Emily gave the baby a final kiss on the head and held him out to Alice. "Do you need that car seat?"

"No, I have one in my car." As Alice turned to take Wyatt to the back of the station, Nash skimmed his hand across Wyatt's back.

"Bye, buddy—for now."

Then he grabbed Emily's wrist. "Let's get lunch. Espinoza, call me when you're ready. I have a confusing tale to tell you."

"It'll be sooner rather than later, but we're putting out our feelers for Fillmore right now."

Nash entwined his fingers with Emily's and tugged her hand. "We still need to pick up your car by the border."

Emily shuffled her feet beside him, and when they stepped outside into the dense heat, a sob broke from her throat.

He drew her into his arms and rested his chin on top of her head. "That was tough, huh?"

She wiped her nose. "I can't believe how attached I got to that little boy in such a short time. And he was attached to me, too, wasn't he? I didn't imagine that, did I?"

"You were the highlight of his day." Nash kissed the top of her head. "Do you feel like eating anything?"

"Not really, but I'm not ready to go back to your place without Wyatt. Does your friend still have Denali?"

"Don't start worrying about Denali, too. The dog is fine." He cupped her damp face with his hands, sweeping his thumbs across her tears. "Wyatt will be fine, too."

"Then why am I so worried about him?" She grabbed his wrists. "It's not just leaving him that broke my heart, but the feeling in the pit of my stomach that Wyatt will never be safe unless he's with you. Jaycee felt that way, too."

"Jaycee brought Wyatt to me because he needed a bodyguard, but a bodyguard does not a father make. She was being sentimental. If my sister, Eve, were here, Jaycee would've left Wyatt with her. Jaycee only ever felt safe in the confines of my family."

"You don't think he needs a bodyguard anymore?" Emily bit her bottom lip and hugged herself.

"He'll be safe in the system. A judge is not going to hand over a baby to some junkie or a shady, money-laundering businessman."

"That leaves you." Emily grabbed the front of his shirt. "You have to take him if you can, Nash. I know it's asking a lot of a bachelor, and one with a full-time career and rodeo fetish, but it has to be you."

Nash raised one eyebrow. "Fetish?"

"You know what I mean." She released his shirt and smoothed her hands over his chest. "Jaycee had her wits about her for once when she left Wyatt with you and named you his guardian."

"It's a big responsibility." Nash wiped a bead of sweat from his forehead with the heel of his hand. "I'd have to think long and hard about it. Now, let's get to some AC and have some lunch or at least something cold to drink."

He opened the truck door for her, averting his eyes from the car seat in the back. Could he be a father on his own? Emily's presence in their lives had been the only reason the responsibility for Wyatt had seemed easy the past few days. Could he find another Emily?

Before he shut the door, he pinched a strand of honey-rose hair from Emily's sticky cheek and tucked it behind her ear.

Another Emily? Never.

He drove a short distance to a small café, where he and Emily sat across from each other, both slumped in their seats. They'd ordered iced teas but waved off food for now. His hunger clawed at his stomach, but he didn't want to eat while Emily was still in mourning for Wyatt.

As he stirred some sugar into his tea, he asked, "Nothing from Lanier yet?"

"I'd tell you if there were." She spun her phone on the table. "I laid it all out for him in my last text. I told him Jaycee was murdered, DCS had Wyatt and I was officially off the case."

"His silence is strange."

"And I suppose you haven't gotten any more proof that he is involved with Las Moscas."

"I'd tell you if I had. I'm the only one with his file right now—me and Special Agent Webb." He snatched a plastic menu propped up on the edge of the table. "You need to eat something. I know it's hot out there, but try some soup at least."

She plucked a menu from the stack and ran her finger down the selections. "Tomato bisque."

"Good choice." Nash raised his hand in the air to get the waitress's attention.

When she came over with a refill for their tea, Emily ordered her soup and he asked for a club sandwich and homemade chips.

"Have you contacted your friend about my car and Denali?"

"We texted. He gave me directions to the car, and I'm going to pick up Denali when his girlfriend gets home from work." He covered her hand with his. "Stop worrying about everything. Wyatt is safe and whichever one of those losers is his father, even if he wants Wyatt, isn't going to look too impressive to the family court."

She put her other hand on top of his, creating a stack as big as that club sandwich on the way. "Especially with someone like you in the picture, someone Wyatt's mother named. That has to carry a lot of weight."

Nash avoided the topic of his guardianship. "I'm going to have to tell my sister about Jaycee. Although they weren't close in the end, I know Eve is going to be upset about the news."

"It's hard losing people in your life." Emily gazed into the whirlpool she'd created by stirring the tea with her straw.

"What happened to your father?"

She released her straw and it continued to swirl in the glass. "He was chasing a murder suspect—the East Side Strangler. They'd gone to the guy's apartment, and he slipped out the back. My father gave chase, and the man turned and shot him."

"I'm sorry. Did the police catch the killer?"

"He died in another shoot-out—suicide by cop. That

guy was not going in as a cop killer." Anger flashed from her green eyes, replacing the sadness.

Progress.

"And you followed in your father's footsteps."

"For a while, as you discovered." She pulled back from him as the waitress delivered their food.

As he sliced his sandwich in two and took a big bite, she kicked the toe of his shoe. "You're starving. You didn't have to hold off because of me. Did you think I'd tag you as insensitive if you ate after leaving Wyatt?"

"Exactly." He wiped his mouth with a napkin and pinched a thick chip between his fingers and held it out to her. "Try one."

As she crunched into the chip, he asked the million-dollar question. "What happened to your career as a cop? You got fired, didn't you?"

"For going above and beyond." She shrugged and plunged her spoon into the steaming soup.

"When a cop says he…or she is going above and beyond, that usually means trouble." He pointed a salty finger at her. "Tell me, Officer Lang, what trouble did you cause?"

"The only trouble I caused was for the other suspect in my father's murder who got off scot-free."

"There was another suspect?" Nash pulled a piece of bacon from his sandwich and stuffed it in his mouth.

"He was the guy's cousin. He warned him that my father and my father's partner were coming. He gave the killer an opportunity to get the jump on my father, which in turn led to my father's death."

"He was never charged?"

"No." Emily transferred her whirlpool activity from her tea to her soup, and red waves of bisque slid over the sides of the bowl. "And I was going to remedy that."

"Oh, boy." He put two fingers on her wrist. "Stop making a mess and eat your soup."

She stopped stirring the soup and tapped her spoon on the edge of the bowl. "You see that? You'd make a great dad."

He dug into his sandwich. Why was she pushing fatherhood on him? Did she figure she could visit him...and Wyatt? He wouldn't mind that one bit, and Wyatt would be over the moon, but he couldn't use a baby to get a woman. If he refused to take custody of Wyatt, which he could do, would Emily drift out of his life?

That poor kid had already been used as a pawn—including by his own mother if Brett were to be believed. He didn't want to accept that Jaycee had planned to use Wyatt as a blackmail chip to get money out of Lanier, but as he'd told Emily, that would be a total Jaycee move.

Emily would have to want to see him for him, whether or not he had Wyatt—and his decision to care for Wyatt was too weighty to include an ulterior motive.

If he did take Wyatt, he'd need a nanny—a real one.

Emily waved her spoon in the air. "What are you thinking about?"

"Nannies."

"That's a good sign." She dragged her napkin from her lap and patted her lips all prim and proper as if she were auditioning as a nanny again. "You're right. This soup is delicious. I may even snag a few more of those chips from your plate."

"Be my guest." He shoved his plate toward her. Her depression over Wyatt had lifted either because he'd distracted her by asking about her father's murder...or because she felt confident in seeing Wyatt again when he took custody of him.

Either way, her return to life dispelled his own sadness.

He had to believe Wyatt would be fine—with or without him as his father.

He lightly smacked her hand reaching for another chip. "I didn't know you were going to eat all of them."

She spread her fingers and held them out. "Greasy and salty—my two favorite food groups. I need to hit the ladies' room to wash my hands."

"Go ahead. I'll pay." He swirled his finger in the air. "We'd better wrap this up and go get your car out by the border before it gets dark. We can pick up Denali first, and he can come with us."

"Do you think we might be in danger retrieving that car?" She crumpled a napkin in her fist. "They must've followed their GPS out there, and I'm sure the tops of their heads blew off in unison when they discovered what we'd done."

"That's why I want to go out there before dark, and I'm taking you as my sidekick."

"Wait, maybe you're *my* sidekick."

"I'll be the Doc Holliday to your Wyatt Earp any day, Officer Lang." He saluted.

She didn't even get mad at him this time for calling her Officer Lang. Instead, she gave him a smirk as she scooted out of the booth.

By the time she returned from the restroom, he'd paid the bill and gulped down another refill on his iced tea. "Ready?"

As Emily slid into the truck, she put her hand on his arm. "Do you think Alice has taken Wyatt by now?"

"Probably." He snatched her hand and kissed her fingers. "He'll be fine."

They swung by Kyle's girlfriend Meg's place to pick up Denali, and she handed Nash Emily's keys. "Does this have anything to do with the body found out by the border yesterday?"

"You don't need to know, Meg, but that body?" Knots tightened in Nash's gut. "That was Jaycee Lemoin."

Meg covered her mouth with both hands, her eyes wide in her face. "Oh, my God. Does your sister know yet?"

"Not yet. I'll call her later. I doubt she's going to hear this news in New York first."

"I hate to say it…" Meg shook her head. "No, I'm not going there. No matter what Jaycee was up to, she didn't deserve to get murdered."

"I agree." Nash scratched Denali's head as the dog thumped his tail against his bare leg. "Tell Kyle thanks for me, and I'll catch up with him later."

"Okay. Be careful out there." Meg showed him out and then stepped onto the porch and waved at Emily waiting in the truck. "She's a cute girl. Is this one going to stick around for more than a few weeks?"

"She's not… We're not…you know." Nash bent over to grab Denali's collar so Meg couldn't see the heat wash into his face. He felt like he was back in elementary school.

"Riiight." She slammed the screen door before Nash even made it off the porch.

He let Denali jump into the back seat of his cab, and Nash plopped down behind the wheel.

Denali sniffed the car seat and whined.

Emily twisted in her seat. "I know, boy. We miss him, too."

She undid her seat belt and ducked into the back seat. She popped back up, holding a stuffed caterpillar in her hand. "Oh, no. We forgot Wyatt's caterpillar. It's his favorite."

"I'm sure DCS will have lots of toys for Wyatt."

"Really?" Emily whacked him on the back of the head

with the caterpillar, which squeaked. "It's his favorite, Nash. He's going to an unfamiliar place with unfamiliar people. He needs this caterpillar."

"This is not an excuse to get another glimpse of Wyatt, is it?" He rubbed his head. "I thought a clean break would be better."

"I don't even need to see Wyatt. In fact, I'm not sure I want to, but if we can catch Alice before she heads into Tucson, I'd like to give it a try."

He grabbed his cell phone from the console and made a call to the station. Agent Perez picked up. "Dillon here. Did the caseworker already leave with Wyatt Lemoin? We forgot to give her…something."

"She left about fifteen minutes ago, but you might be able to catch her before she gets to the 10. She asked about a drive-through where she could pick up some food for the road."

"Thanks, Perez." Nash ended the call and dropped the phone in his cup holder. "We'll try to catch up with her before she hits the 10."

Nash navigated to the two-lane road that led to the 10 freeway with a heavy foot. Once Alice got to the freeway, they wouldn't be able to stop her.

He glanced at Emily hugging the caterpillar to her chest, a small smile curving her lips. She'd better not be up to something.

Five minutes of driving and they'd seen just one other car on the road. He took the next curve and eased off the gas pedal as he spotted a white car up ahead. He tapped the windshield. "Does that look like Alice's car?"

Emily hunched forward in her seat and shoved her sunglasses into her hair. "Yeah, maybe, but that car isn't moving, Nash. It's on the side of the road."

"Are you sure?" He squinted through the shimmering

waves that pulsed off the scorching pavement and plucked off his own sunglasses. Dusk in the desert could come on fast and create optical illusions.

They drew closer to the white car, and as it got bigger, he realized Emily was right—it wasn't moving. The hair on the back of his neck quivered. "I think that is the car. Maybe she's changing Wyatt."

"In the middle of the desert." Emily shot forward in her seat. "A DCS worker wouldn't do that."

"Unless he got sick."

Emily's hands clenched as she pressed them against her stomach. "Is it crooked? Does the car look like it's parked at an angle to you?"

"Some." Nash slowed the truck and blew out a breath. "She's in the car."

"What's she doing?" Emily had grabbed the handle of the truck as if ready to jump out now.

Denali barked into the tension radiating throughout the truck's cab.

Nash put on his signal and rolled over the gravel on the side of the road, kicking up dust. His heart hammered against his rib cage. "Why the hell is she sitting there?"

Before the truck came to a complete stop, Emily threw open the door. "Something's wrong."

"Maybe she had some car trouble." Nash cut the engine and made a grab for Emily as she slipped out of the truck. "Wait, Emily."

As he opened his own door, Emily scurried to the driver's side of Alice's car. Emily stumbled back, her hand to her chest, her mouth gaping.

Nash charged out of his vehicle and strode toward Emily, his shoes crunching over glass in the road. When he got to the white car, he stared through the jagged glass at Alice sitting upright behind the wheel—a bullet hole in her head.

Chapter Thirteen

Emily huffed air from her nostrils to expel the sickening metallic taste that seeped down her throat, making her gag. She stumbled past Nash and yanked open the back door of Alice's car.

She blinked at the empty seat and dived into the car, sweeping her hand across the leather as if Wyatt's car seat were just invisible. She flung herself forward and buried her head in her arms. "They took him. They took Wyatt."

Behind her, Nash spoke urgently into his cell phone, his words muffled through the pounding blood in her ears.

His hand stroked the back of her calf. "Emily? I called the Paradiso police and Detective Espinoza. They're on their way. Come on out. You might be compromising the crime scene."

Covering her face, she scooted out of the car backward until her feet touched the ground.

Nash curled an arm around her waist and pulled her out the rest of the way. She barreled into his chest, sobbing against his shoulder.

"I knew it. I knew Wyatt was in danger. As soon as he left us, I've been fearing for his safety."

Nash smoothed her hair back from her hot forehead and set her away from him to look into her eyes. "There's good news here."

"Here?" She flung her arm back at the bloody mess in the front seat and the yawning emptiness of the back. "What could possibly be good?"

"They *took* Wyatt. They didn't kill him."

At the thought of Wyatt's death, her knees buckled, and Nash caught her arm. "Think about it. If they wanted to get rid of Wyatt, they could've done so when they overtook Alice and killed her. They didn't."

She rubbed her eyes and cranked her head around to peer into the back seat again—this time to look for Wyatt's little lifeless body. She nodded jerkily, as if someone were pulling strings to make her move, as her muscles seemed frozen.

"But for what purpose? Why did they take him? What are they going to do with him?"

Nash's voice continued to soothe. "They took his car seat. They took his diaper bag."

"They took *him*. Why?" That one word threatened to turn into a wail, so she clamped a hand over her mouth.

"What has Wyatt always been, even to his own mother? A bargaining chip. Not that I trust Brett any farther than I can drop-kick him, but he made the claim that Jaycee planned to use Wyatt to blackmail Lanier. Like I said before, that sounds like a Jaycee move. And those two thugs wanted Wyatt to force Brett to give himself up to them. Lanier wanted Wyatt for some other reason, and that's why he hired you. Was it to find out if he's the boy's father? Was it a countermove against Jaycee?"

Emily doubled over. "I feel sick that he used me. I sold out Wyatt for money. I'm as bad as all the rest."

"Stop that." His hands pinched her shoulders. "You were the one good person Wyatt had on his side."

"And you." She tipped back her head to search Nash's

face. "But we gave him up. We had him protected, and we handed him off."

"We didn't have a choice, Emily."

"That's where you're wrong." She twisted away from him. "You play by the rules, but I don't. If it were up to me, I never would've handed Wyatt over to DCS."

"That would've gotten you arrested, and I can assure you that would've been a lot worse than getting fired from a PD. Focus." Nash's head jerked to the side as the sound of sirens pierced the darkening sky. "Wyatt's alive, and he's going to stay that way because he's valuable to the person who took him."

"Who did take him, Nash? The way I see it is that we have three suspects or groups of suspects—the drug thugs, Brett and Lanier."

"I agree. You saw the car the two cartel guys were driving, didn't you?"

"Black sedan, Crown Vic, dark tinted windows, white wall tires, antenna, paper plates on the back."

"Good job. You got all that when you saw the car driving by my house?"

"I thought I might need that information later—and here we are." The emergency vehicles came into view, and Emily gritted her teeth against the cacophony of horns, beeps and sirens. She pressed her hands against her cheeks. "Poor Alice. She was just doing her job. Why'd they have to kill her? They could've taken Wyatt from her at gunpoint."

"Maybe she wouldn't let them. It seems Wyatt had someone else on his side."

It was almost ten o'clock by the time they got through questioning at the Border Patrol station. Denali had been napping in an interview room with a bowl of water and someone's leftover steak.

The Pima County Sheriff's Department had put out an APB for Brett Fillmore, using one of his old booking photos. Every patrol unit had an eye out for a black Crown Vic with paper plates. Detective Espinoza had even put a call in to Marcus Lanier when they told him the billionaire might be involved, and discovered he was out of the country.

Emily, her emotions wrung out, slumped in the passenger seat of Nash's truck, holding Wyatt's caterpillar against her chest. Denali whimpered in the back, but Emily couldn't bear to turn around and see the empty car seat.

Wyatt joined her in the truck and clutched the steering wheel with white-knuckled hands. "It's a good start. We'll find him."

She drew in a shaky breath. "I'm exhausted."

"I know you are." He rubbed her leg. "We're going back to my place, right? There's no way I'm dropping you off at that motel to be on your own."

"I wouldn't want to be."

"Good." He started the truck and veered toward the main drag in town. "And we're eating."

She dropped her chin and pulled at the fabric of her grimy blouse. "I'm not going out looking or feeling like this."

"We do have take-out pizza in Paradiso, believe it or not. I'm going to run in to the pizza joint and place an order for delivery." Nash parked in a strip mall boasting a chain pizza place and whistled through his teeth. "Denali, take care of her."

When Nash slammed the door of the truck and locked it with his remote, Emily pulled her purse into her lap with the gun pocket on top and then reached back and scratched

Denali under the chin. "I trust you, boy, but I need extra insurance. Whoever named Paradiso must've been joking."

Nash returned faster than she expected and hopped into the truck. "I ordered us a large with everything on it. They're going to deliver it in about forty minutes."

"I don't think I can eat with Wyatt out there somewhere."

"In one way it's a blessing he's still a baby. He's not going to remember any of this drama when he gets older. We'll have stories to tell." The truck bounced as Nash wheeled out of the parking lot and Emily's stomach bounced with it.

Did this mean Nash was going to accept the conditions of Jaycee's will and adopt Wyatt? If he did... Her thoughts trailed off into some vague, hazy future of Nash raising a son by himself. Where did she fit into that picture?

If Jaycee's mother took Wyatt, Emily would never see him again. If Lanier or Brett got him, God forbid, she'd never know another good night's sleep. It had to be Nash.

They drove through town and made the turn to Nash's place. Emily gripped the sides of her seat. "It seems like we left here so long ago, but it was just yesterday. We thought we were keeping Wyatt safe and we turned him over to danger."

"We didn't know that, Emily. Stop blaming yourself for one minute." He slammed the steering wheel with the heel of his hand. "Stop blaming me."

She grabbed his bicep. "I'm not blaming you. I'm sorry if it seems like I am. I'm just so damned worried about him."

His nostrils flared and he closed his eyes. "We'll get him back. Do you still have that straw with Lanier's spit on it?"

"Yes, why?"

"I wanna know who fathered Wyatt. That can go a long way to tell us motive. If Brett's his father, I can't understand why he'd want to kidnap him. He can't seriously want to be Wyatt's father without Jaycee around to take care of the baby."

"But if Lanier really is the father and Brett took him?" Emily held her breath, her muscles stiff.

"Maybe Brett wants to continue the blackmail scheme he and Jaycee started. Maybe he's going to hold Wyatt over Lanier's head until Lanier coughs up some money." He parked the truck, but neither one of them made a move to get out.

"What if those two goons are the ones who took Wyatt?" She shivered. "They must believe Wyatt is Brett's son. What worries me about that scenario is if that's what happened to Jaycee, then clearly Brett doesn't care about anyone but himself and Wyatt will meet the same fate as his mother once they discover that."

Nash brushed a thumb across her cheek. "Don't go there."

"Are you going to try to pull some strings to test Lanier's DNA against Wyatt's? Because you know the official route will take forever even with a missing baby at stake."

"I'll see what I can do." He jerked his thumb over his shoulder. "Denali is going crazy in here. Let's go inside before the pizza beats us."

When Nash got out of the truck, he had his gun at his waist. Emily strapped her purse across her body ready to be his backup, or his sidekick. Did she want to be more? Was she confusing her feelings for the baby with her feelings for the man who would adopt him?

Nash let Denali have free rein to sniff the porch and the front door as an early warning system. The dog just seemed anxious to get inside.

Nash shoved open the door and stood back, his head held to one side. "I think we're good. Denali's instincts are right on, and right now he just wants to run out back. I've also been checking my security cameras and all has been quiet."

Despite his words, Nash went through the house and kept his gun with him. Satisfied, he slid open the back door for Denali. "Go for it, boy."

Denali scampered out back for a run and Emily collapsed in a deep chair, grabbing the remote for the TV. She clicked it on and immediately regretted it as a picture of Wyatt stared back at her from the local news.

She called to Nash, "They put out an Amber Alert."

"I knew they were going to do that." He took the remote from her stiff fingers. "Let's turn that off and put our heads together. The other possibility we didn't discuss in the car is if Lanier kidnapped the baby and he's the father. Why would he do that?"

A whisper of fear feathered across the back of her neck. "That's the worst possible scenario, Nash. If Lanier's the father and he killed Jaycee and kidnapped Wyatt, it could only be to stop this blackmail attempt. And what better way to stop it than to get rid of the evidence?"

"If that's the case, why not dispose of the evidence right away, at the same time he took care of Alice?"

"If he killed Wyatt right there in his car seat—" she stopped and pressed a hand against her galloping heart "—he'd be leaving the evidence, wouldn't he? Nobody but Jaycee and maybe Brett know Wyatt's true parentage at this point. Espinoza's going to want to find out who Wyatt's father is. If Lanier leaves Wyatt in the car and the detectives find out Lanier is the baby's father, he'll have a lot to answer for."

"Good point, but just because he's the father, it doesn't

mean he'd want to kill the baby." Nash moved into the kitchen and opened the fridge.

Emily snapped her fingers. "He also wouldn't want his wife to know."

"Is that what he told you when he hired you?" Nash held up two bottles of beer in the kitchen. "Beer?"

"Please."

"Glass?"

"No, thanks."

He handed her the bottle and she took a swig before continuing. "When Lanier hired me, he was all concerned parent. Jaycee had told him he might be the father and he wanted to protect Wyatt from her if that were the case. He told me he was hiring an attorney and arranging for a paternity test."

"Touching." Nash raised his bottle and chugged back a few gulps.

"What if that's true, Nash? What if everything Lanier told me is true? What if Brett is lying about the blackmail scheme?"

"If Lanier was being honest, we have one less person to worry about. But that doesn't explain why Brett kidnapped the baby. The only use Wyatt is to Brett is as a bargaining chip, and he wouldn't be much of a chip if Lanier were the happy father."

Emily folded her hands around the bottle. "I wish we would've been more insistent about protection for Wyatt."

The knock on the door saved her from Nash's retort. He snapped his mouth shut and held up his hand. "Food."

Nash returned to the room balancing a pizza box on his palm. "Let's eat and strategize."

She hopped up from the chair and followed him into the kitchen. "Plates?"

He swiped some paper plates from the top of the pizza

box. "I had them include the plates and napkins. All we have to do is eat and throw away the trash."

"That's my kind of meal." She pinned a plate to the counter with her index finger as he dropped two slices of pizza piled with meat and veggies onto it. She carried the plate back to her chair and tore the slices apart.

Nash joined her, taking the couch and plopping his plate on the coffee table. "Brett's not going back to the apartment he shared with Jaycee in Phoenix. He knows the cops are after him now to question him about Jaycee's murder and Wyatt's disappearance. Where would he go?"

"I'm trying to think." She pulled a string of cheese from the top of her slice and sucked it into her mouth. "When the two cartel guys came looking for him at the apartment, Jaycee pretended they'd split up. He'd been gone a few days by the time those men showed up, so he probably knew they were looking for him."

"You were bugging the apartment prior to that, right? While Brett was still there?"

"I was."

"Video?"

"Video and sound."

"You saved it?"

"I have it on my phone. I can download it to your laptop." She licked her fingers, although she hadn't yet managed a bite of pizza. Nervous excitement now fizzed through her veins. "He could've mentioned some place, right? A place where he was going to hide."

"That's what I'm thinking. It worked so well the first time. Those guys never did find him. If he did take Wyatt, maybe he headed back to his safe place."

"Yeah, yeah." She bounced on the chair. "They for sure talked about his plans, but I didn't pay much attention at the time."

"Then that's a good start." He wiped his hands on a clutch of napkins and pushed up from the couch. "Let's do that right now."

Emily retrieved her phone while he set up his laptop on the coffee table, next to their plates.

"We can do the download via the Wi-Fi. Our tech guy in the department showed me how to do a bunch of stuff like this." He tapped the table. "Bring up the videos and put your phone here."

She accessed her video files for the dates before Brett left the apartment and read off the file names to Nash, who entered the information into his laptop.

"Voilà." He waved his hand over his laptop. "Now we have entertainment while we eat."

Emily munched on a piece of pizza while hunched over Nash's computer, her gaze following the figures on his display as they moved in and out of Jaycee's living room.

"Whoa, who's that?" Nash leveled a finger at another woman in the frame.

"That's Jaycee's roommate. Jaycee tried to tell the cartel guys that Wyatt was the roommate's."

"They obviously didn't believe her." Nash shook his head. "Did these two fight all the time like this?"

"Pretty much." Emily felt a smile twist her lips despite herself when Jaycee came into the frame from the back carrying Wyatt. "There's our boy."

"I'm going to turn up the sound, but they probably won't say anything important with the roommate there. We can take turns keeping an eye on it."

"You know what's weird?" Emily held her hands over her plate and brushed the crumbs from her fingers. "If they did have this blackmail plan for Lanier, I never heard it."

Nash lifted a shoulder. "Doesn't seem like they talk about much at all—mostly snipe at each other."

"Jaycee had bad taste in men…except for one." Emily crumpled her napkin and tossed it onto her paper plate with her crusts. "You."

Nash finished off his beer and clinked the bottle onto the coffee table. "I'm no prize. I work too much, I prefer superficial relationships and there's that rodeo fetish."

"It sounds like you're trying to warn me off." Emily scooted to the edge of the chair. "And why do you prefer superficial relationships?"

"Because of this." He swept his arm to the side. "This property, this business. My family has a lot of money, and women seem attracted to that."

"How can you be so sure it's the money and not the man?" She assessed the handsome face in front of her, the pure masculinity emanating from the lanky frame that housed a sinewy strength. Was he fishing for compliments?

"Let's just say I had a couple of bad experiences that made me wary."

"You weren't too wary to hire a nanny on the spot in the supermarket parking lot." She swirled the remaining sips of her beer in the bottle.

"There was something about that freckled face I trusted." He hunched forward, elbows on his knees, a light smoldering in his blue eyes. "And I wasn't wrong."

"Ha!" She slammed her bottle next to his. "You couldn't have been more wrong. I was a nanny under false pretenses, and I almost absconded with Wyatt."

"For what you thought were the right reasons. You turned on a dime when I explained things to you." He had inched closer across the table.

"So did you." She wound a lock of her hair around her finger. "For a distrustful sort, you accepted my story pretty quickly, even inviting me to your side."

"Like I said—" he reached across the coffee table and

cupped her face with one rough hand "—something about that freckled face I trusted."

Emily parted her lips. Her breath came out in short spurts. "I can't imagine why."

"Neither can I." He pulled her close and slanted his mouth across hers, right over their paper plates, greasy napkins and pizza crusts.

The spicy pepperoni on his lips mingled with hers, and she braced a knee on the edge of the table to dive deeper into his kiss.

He rose to his feet, hitching an arm around her waist to take her with him. Their bodies created an arch over the table, and when she wrapped her arms around his shoulders, she took them off balance.

Nash steadied them and broke their connection. Then he took one long step over the coffee table and took her in his arms properly...or very improperly with the way his hands wandered down to her derriere, cupping and lifting her to fit their hips together.

She sighed against his mouth, and he murmured, "Do you want this?"

This time she broke their kiss to gaze into his eyes, the smolder more like a blue flame now. "There's nothing more I want right now, except..."

He placed a finger against her throbbing lips. "We both want Wyatt back, but I need to know you want me, too."

Did she want him without Wyatt? Would she see him again if he refused custody?

Falling against his chest, she entwined her arms around his neck. "I do want you, Nash Dillon. I wanted you the minute I saw you fumbling with that baby in the parking lot."

He pressed his mouth against hers again, and this time it seemed as if a barrier had been lifted between them.

The kiss scorched her lips, branding her somewhere deep inside, taking possession of her soul. If she had doubts before that she could separate the man from the baby, Nash's kiss torched those doubts and turned them to ash.

He turned around with her in his arms and sank to the chair she'd just vacated, pulling her against him.

She bent her knees and wedged her legs on either side of his hips as she straddled him. She plucked at the hem of his T-shirt and yanked it up and over his head.

Running her hands along the hard ridge of muscle on his chest, she planted a kiss on his collarbone. "Mmm, if this body is the result of your rodeo fetish, I wholeheartedly approve."

He lifted one eyebrow in that sexy fashion he had and said, "Let's see if you approve of my other fetishes."

"If one of those is making love in a recliner, again you have my stamp of approval." She ditched her blouse and tossed it over her shoulder.

Nash unhooked her bra with an expertise that gave her pause, but only for a second, as he took one of her nipples between two of his fingers and rolled it slowly.

She gasped and arched her back.

He bent his head and took her other nipple between his lips as she squirmed in his lap. He caught his breath and slammed his head against the back of the chair.

"You're gonna have to stop moving against me like that. I'm only a simple man."

"Nothing simple about you, Nash, but I'm no tease." She pulled at his fly, undoing the buttons at the top and then yanking down his zipper.

He lifted his hips in all eagerness, and she pulled off his shorts and briefs in one motion. She rubbed her bare thighs against his, and he groaned.

He lifted her skirt and ran his hands beneath her panties, caressing her bottom. He grabbed the edge of her underwear, and she awkwardly rose to her knees and tried to disengage one of her legs from between the chair and his thigh.

"Go ahead, rip 'em. I've got others. Better ones."

"I can reimburse you."

"Don't worry. I'll give you an itemized receipt."

Nash chuckled in her ear, gathered her panties in his hand and gave a quick tug. The lacy material ripped, and she lifted her hips and skimmed her tingling flesh along the tight skin of his erection.

The chuckle in her ear turned to a moan, and he dug his fingers into her backside. He positioned her body so that his tip caressed her wet folds.

In a rough voice he said, "We can take it slower later or if we ever make it to a bed, but right now I want you so much it aches."

She whispered. "I feel it, too. I need you to fill...to fill me up."

Did she need to feel whole after losing Wyatt? She didn't want to think right now.

When Nash plunged into her, she stopped thinking altogether. Her body and mind became a mass of feelings and emotions. She moved against him and up and down, bracing her hands on his shoulders.

She rode him just as surely as he rode those bulls in the rodeo.

He slowed his thrusts and shoved his fingers into the crease where their bodies met. He stroked her flesh. "Tell me how. I want you to reach your climax before I explode inside you."

She had no words. Whatever he was doing at this minute was driving her to a pinnacle she'd never reached before.

She just nodded, and he kept caressing her in the same spot, in the same way.

She held her breath as the tension built in her body. She'd stopped moving and her rigid muscles made her feel as if she were ready to shatter.

Then she did shatter. Her climax whipped through her, lashing her over and over. She thrashed her head back and forth, her hair creating a red wave between them as Nash pumped her harder and faster.

Before she even came to her senses, Nash's body stiffened and he drove into her, lifting her to her knees. A red flush spread across his chest and his jaw clenched.

He gave a harsh cry and pulled her in for a kiss as he reached his peak and plunged into her again and again.

She slipped off his lap to the side, one leg still hitched over his leg, her skirt crumpled around her waist, her head on his shoulder. All she could manage was a faint "Oh."

Tracing a finger down her spine, he said, "Maybe we can brush our teeth, bring Denali in and slow this down in the bedroom."

She ran her tongue along her teeth. "I definitely need a toothbrush."

"I'll get the dog." He planted his hands on her bottom and shifted her off his lap. Then he struggled to his feet and crossed the room to the patio door. He stuck his head outside and whistled.

As Emily swept up her tattered undies from the floor, she glanced at the video they'd left running on the laptop. They'd have to backtrack and see what they'd missed while they were otherwise engaged.

The roommate had left and Jaycee and Brett were discussing his departure. Her pulse bumped up a few notches as she pulled the computer closer to the edge of the table and turned up the volume. She listened to their conversation for several seconds, the thumping of her heart almost drowning out their words.

She let out a squeak, and Nash jerked his head up as Denali ran through the door. "What's wrong?"

Jabbing her finger at the laptop, she said, "I know where Brett took Wyatt."

Chapter Fourteen

Nash almost tripped over the dog as he rushed to Emily's side, and he still ended up stubbing his toe on the coffee table. The throbbing pain didn't even faze him. "Whaddya got?"

"Listen to this." Emily dragged the time back on the video and clicked Play.

Nash peered at Jaycee, clutching Wyatt to her chest. "Where will you be?"

Brett winked. "Somewhere no one can find me. One of my mom's husbands had a place in a trailer park. He's dead and gone, but I've used that trailer on and off for years. Nobody knows about it."

"Where is it?"

"Down by the border." He continued giving Jaycee the particulars, but Nash didn't even have to listen.

"I know that trailer park. I wouldn't even call it a trailer park, and it's not official—just a bunch of people who brought their RVs and campers together. These places dot the desert."

Emily bunched her ripped underwear in her fist and pounded her knee. "He must be there now with Wyatt."

"If he has him." Nash stopped the video and shoved the computer back on the coffee table. "We don't even know if Brett has Wyatt."

"He tried to kidnap him from us. That's good enough for me." She swept her bra and blouse from the floor and stuck her arms through the straps.

Still naked, Nash pulled Emily's skirt down around her legs and smoothed the material against her thighs. "Where are you going?"

"We're going to get Wyatt." She grabbed his briefs from the floor and tossed them into the air for him.

Nash caught his underwear and shook them at Emily. "Hold on."

"No, no, no." Emily whipped her head back and forth. "You're not going to tell me that we're turning this information over to the police, are you? Do you think they're going to rush over there immediately and grab Wyatt? They'll need a search warrant at the very least. If they come rolling in with lights and sirens, they'll spook Brett and the other residents."

"Brett Fillmore is a person of interest in a murder and kidnapping. The Pima County Sheriff's Department will do this the right way." His words faltered at the end as he caught sight of Emily's face, her liquid eyes and thin lips conveying both sadness and determination at the same time.

"Please, Nash. We did it the right way when we turned Wyatt over to DCS and look what happened." She grabbed his hands. "Of course, we'll go through proper channels if we find Brett, but let's try it my way this time."

"Your way got you fired from your job." But those shimmering green eyes were already weakening his resolve—and Emily knew it.

"Okay, we'll slow down. I need a shower—" she dangled her lacy panties from her fingertips "—and a change of underwear, and then we're going out there to rescue Wyatt."

They both showered—separately—and changed into

dark clothing. If he hadn't made love with Emily, would he be so quick to chuck all his good sense out the window and rush into the desert to confront Brett? He loaded his weapon and clicked the chamber shut. *Guess you'll never know, Dillon.*

Emily strapped her purse across her body, her hand resting against the gun pocket. "How far is this place?"

"Now you ask?" He hitched a backpack containing all kinds of gadgets over one shoulder. "It's about an hour. We head south and then we veer east toward New Mexico. Let me warn you. The kind of people who inhabit these desert compounds are not big fans of law enforcement. They're not fans of outsiders at all. Brett must be known there to feel comfortable, and the inhabitants wouldn't blink an eye if he showed up with a baby."

"Even more reason for us to contact him on our own without the law."

He cocked his head. "Do you think Brett's going to give up Wyatt without a fight?"

"No." She licked her lips. "But from what I saw of him, he doesn't pose much of a threat."

"Really? If he did take Wyatt, he murdered a DCS worker and kidnapped a baby in broad daylight. Dude may be stupid, but he's got guts and that's a lethal combination for anyone who gets in his way."

Emily widened her stance and crossed her arms. "He has Wyatt, and we're gonna get him back."

He stalked toward her and planted a kiss on her forehead. "I know you mean that, but if I sense you're in any danger, we're pulling out."

"I hear you." She dropped her head to adjust her purse strap, and Nash's gut tightened.

He knew he'd have to physically remove her from rescuing Wyatt in the face of danger, and he wouldn't have it any other way—but he'd be ready.

Nash locked the sliding door to the patio in position with just enough space for Denali to squeeze through it. He set up some dry kibble and water in the kitchen. Scratching the dog behind the ear, he said, "Sorry, boy. Clay is never going to let me dog sit you again when he hears about this."

"But Denali is going to be so happy to have Wyatt back home again." She hugged Denali, burying her face in his fur.

Nash didn't want to ruin the moment by pointing out that even if Brett did have Wyatt and even if they got Wyatt back, they'd still have to turn him over to DCS. Nash was already going out on a limb here. He didn't need to add a charge of kidnapping to the list.

Once he secured the house, he and Emily climbed into the truck. He didn't need the GPS to find the border. He knew every inch of it, and this particular desert outpost wouldn't register, anyway.

He cranked on the engine and said, "We're going to have to hike in. We can't drive a truck up to this site, even after midnight, or *especially* after midnight."

"I'm ready." She wedged a sneaker on the dashboard. "It's a good thing we still have Wyatt's car seat in the truck—not that I'd let a little thing like a car seat stop me from taking him home."

Nash bit the inside of his cheek as he swung around the crescent of his driveway and through the front gate. *Home.* Emily kept using that word. Even if he decided to go through with the custody arrangement, Wyatt couldn't come here right away.

They drove into the night, the silent desert sucking them in after just a few miles, outside of the Paradiso town limit.

Nash flicked on his brights. "Remember, we check for

Wyatt's presence first. If he's not there and Brett is, we call off the mission and contact law enforcement."

"And if he is—" Emily placed her hands on her bouncing knees "—we break in silently."

"If he's sleeping, we slip inside the trailer, I'll hold Brett at gunpoint and you'll get Wyatt." He scratched his chin. "I suppose we can't expect Wyatt to be quiet, which means he'll wake up Brett. If this all goes according to plan, you take Wyatt away and call Espinoza. I'll hold Brett for the authorities."

"And we'll take Wyatt home."

"Until DCS sends out another caseworker."

"But this time, Wyatt needs more security. Even with Brett out of the way, there still could be others after Wyatt. He's not safe until we know the whole story."

"I think after the murder of one of their own, DCS will acknowledge the threat and take it seriously."

"Then we're on the same page."

Nash released a long breath. "That's what I like to hear."

The landscape rushed by, the lights illuminating a saguaro cactus here and there, tall enough to resemble a human shape, and occasionally picking out the glowing eyes of some night critter dodging the roaring mechanical intruder into his habitat.

Nash pointed out the mile marker that indicated their proximity to the trailer park. "We're about a half mile out. Any closer and some night owl's going to spot our headlights once we make that bend."

Emily's eyes widened, and the cords stood out in her delicate throat as she swallowed. "We're walking a half a mile in this? In the dark?"

"Thought you were ready." He gave her a playful punch in the arm.

"Oh, I am as long as you're leading the way."

"We can use the flashlights on our phones to make our way down the road. Nobody is going to see those from that distance." He steered the truck into an outlet and cut the engine. As he stepped from the vehicle, the silence of the desert seemed to wrap him in a warm blanket, muffling his senses. He shook it off. He needed all his wits about him.

As if following the desert code, Emily eased her door shut, closing it with a click. She whispered, "I suppose there are snakes and scorpions out here."

"If we don't bother them, they won't bother us." He touched her arm and she jumped. "Sorry, take my hand and we'll use our flashlights with our other hands."

They stayed on the shoulder of the road, although they could've marched down the center divider as this area didn't have a lot going for it and few people ventured out this way.

Emily stumbled a few times, swore and bumped against him, and then righted herself. After several yards, they got into a rhythm and traversed the distance smoothly.

He put his lips close to her ear as if someone were eavesdropping. "Let's cut our lights. Those rocks up ahead mark the entrance."

"How do you know this place?"

"I've made an arrest or two here."

"Great, so you're not exactly going to be popular."

"Nope, but as we have no clue which ramshackle trailer belonged to Brett's stepfather, we're going to have to check out every one of them until we find him."

"Ugh, I hope nobody's awake." She killed her light and tapped his phone. "Turn your phone off or put it on silent so it doesn't start ringing or buzzing in the middle of the site."

"Glad someone's thinking clearly." He silenced his phone and pocketed it. "Some of these residents may not be outside waiting for us, but my guess is there will be a few of them awake inside their trailers."

He drew his weapon from his shoulder holster and held it pressed against his leg. "You follow me. I don't want you going off on your own."

"That's ridiculous, Nash. We can cover more ground if both of us are looking." She unzipped the pocket of her purse concealing her gun and pulled it out. "I'm a cop, remember? That's what you keep telling me. Now act like you believe it."

"All right." Yeah, he should've never slept with her. "If you run into any trouble, you scream, yell, shoot your gun in the air. Got it? Don't try to be a hero."

"Same goes for you." She smacked his backside with the palm of her hand.

Hunched over, creeping on silent feet, they approached the boulders. Nash squeezed her shoulder and pointed with his gun to the right.

He watched as the darkness enveloped her, and then he veered left.

When he got to the first trailer, he peered through an open window on the side. A fan whirred inside and light from a tablet cast a blue glow over the interior. When his eyes adjusted, he made out a man and a woman on a double futon. The man's long, gray braid snaked over the edge.

Nash slipped away from the trailer and approached the next one about twenty feet away. Voices carried out the open window of this trailer, and he listened for a few minutes to two women arguing in low tones about the excessive alcohol use of one of them.

Nash backed away from the trailer, feeling like an eavesdropper. As he loped toward the next domicile, an old motor home with no wheels, the hair on his arms prickled. He froze and lifted his head, his nostrils quivering like a horse's.

His ears strained to catch the sound he thought he'd heard—a gasp that hung on the air and swirled right through him. He made a half turn and almost stumbled over Emily.

She looked up at him and put her finger to her lips. She tugged on his arm, half dragging him across the open space of the trailer park.

When they approached a trailer at the edge of the site, she thrust out a finger. She plucked at his sleeve and he bent his head to hers.

"That's his place. I recognize the shoes he left out front." She patted her chest. "He made it easy for us."

Nash slipped a knife from a holster on his leg and placed one foot on the porch. He pressed down on the door handle, and it turned.

He nudged Emily. Brett had made it really easy for them by not even locking his door.

Nash yanked on the aluminum door, and it opened with a huff.

Behind him, Emily had her weapon ready.

He eased open the door and stumbled back, gagging. He held out his arm to stop Emily, but she squeezed past him and fell to her knees.

She cranked her head around, her eyes wide above the hand clapped over her mouth. Her muffled words added another element of horror to the scene.

"He's dead."

Chapter Fifteen

An adrenaline rush spiked through Emily's body, and she crawled past Brett's inert form on the floor of the trailer. She lunged toward a basket next to an unmade bed and grabbed the sides, staring down into a jumble of blankets, one of Wyatt's pacifiers discarded in the middle.

She grabbed it and spun around. Holding it out to Nash, who'd stepped over Brett's body. "Wyatt was here. Brett *did* kidnap him and now someone else has him. We're too late."

She scrabbled forward on her hands and knees and bunched up Brett's shirt with both hands, avoiding the bloody exit wound on his head. "Where is he, you SOB? Who has him?"

Crouching beside her, Nash placed a hand on her shoulder. "Careful, Emily. Don't disturb the evidence."

She released Brett's shirt and brushed her hands together. "There's not going to be much evidence. They must've used a silencer on the gun or everyone in the compound here would've come running."

"Get on your phone and call 911."

"How are we going to explain our presence here?" She pulled her phone from her pocket anyway. The sooner the police knew this dirtbag was dead, the sooner they could go after the next suspect—who might not be so willing to keep Wyatt alive.

"*Now* you're asking me that?" Nash glanced at her over his shoulder as his hands moved through Brett's clothing. "Maybe Jaycee mentioned this place to me or—"

"My God. What have you done?"

Emily held her phone out to the man with the long braid, who was pointing an accusatory finger at Nash still hunched over Brett's body, his flashlight giving his face an ancient cast.

"I'm on the phone to 911 now." She rambled off the nature of the emergency and then paused. "Where should I say we are?"

"Let me do it." Nash pushed to his feet, shoving his own phone in his pocket. He took the phone from her and started speaking with the 911 operator.

Emily squeezed past Nash and out to the porch, where the man with the braid was now throwing up over the side. She took several steps away from him and gulped in some fresh air to replace the fetid odor from the trailer.

When the man had wiped his mouth and straightened up, she called to him, "Are you okay?"

"What happened in there?"

"Someone shot Brett in the head, killed him." She added that last part needlessly. "He was wanted for questioning in a murder and kidnapping. Did you see him with a baby?"

The man narrowed his eyes so that they glittered in the dark like one of those night creatures they'd passed on their way here. "We saw the baby. My wife helped him with the little one. He didn't know what he was doing."

"Yeah, because he kidnapped him." Emily clamped a hand on her hip. "Didn't you know he was wanted? Didn't you see his picture on TV?"

The man shrugged. "People come and people go."

Emily clenched her jaw. No wonder Brett knew he'd be safe here—no questions asked, no police.

A few other people wandered from their trailers and motor homes. A woman called out, "What happened, Zeke?"

The Native American, presumably Zeke, spit into the dirt. "That smell left a taste in my mouth."

"That's death."

Zeke nodded to her and turned to answer questions from the residents. A few broke past him and approached Brett's trailer.

Emily took a step forward. "You need to stay back. That's a crime scene. You don't wanna go in there anyway. Trust me."

A man with a buzz cut and bad teeth leered at her. "Trust you? Why should we trust you? Are you a cop?"

Emily almost smiled at the question. *Depends on who you ask.*

But there *was* a cop on the scene. Where the hell was Nash and what the hell was he doing in there?

"She's not, but I am." Nash emerged from the trailer, large and in charge. "Border Patrol, and this man was wanted by the police for questioning in a murder and kidnapping. Why didn't one of you fine citizens call the police?"

"The police? Border Patrol?" The skinhead blew his nose into the dirt. "We don't like your kind around here."

Nash deliberately walked between her and the skinhead, creating a barrier between them, looming over the smaller man.

"Skeeter, give it a rest." Zeke grabbed a handful of Skeeter's grimy shirt and pulled him back. "They already called 911. I heard them. So, if you don't want to be around when the cops get here, I suggest you go back to your domiciles or head out for a while."

The residents grumbled, but several left the scene, including Skeeter, and a few minutes later a couple of motorcycles revved up and took off.

Emily cupped the pacifier between her hands and rested her chin on the tips of her fingers. "When are they going to get here?"

"A patrol car's on the way. It'll take another thirty to forty minutes for Espinoza and the Pima County Sheriff's Department to get out here." Nash circled her wrists with his long fingers. "Are you okay?"

She closed her eyes for a second. "Pretty gruesome in there, but the worst was seeing that empty makeshift crib. At least Brett wanted to keep Wyatt alive for some reason. What do the others want with him?"

"Again, the fact that we didn't find Wyatt dead in that trailer next to Brett is a good sign. Brett didn't kill Wyatt when he shot Alice because the baby served a greater purpose for him. The same applies here."

"Excuse me."

Emily turned toward the soft voice. An older woman with short gray hair and a sleeve of tattoos raised her hand and waved. She'd been standing next to Zeke.

"Yes?" Emily raised her chin. She was done getting attacked here when they were the ones who'd had a dead man in their midst.

The woman tilted her head. "Is the baby okay?"

"You were the one helping Brett with the baby?" Emily pressed a hand to her heart. "The baby's gone. He wasn't in the trailer when we found Brett. Did Brett tell you anything about the baby?"

"Thank the Goddess the baby wasn't hurt." The woman crossed her hands over her chest. "Brett told me the baby was his son and that the baby's mother had died in an accident and they were separated at the time, so he hadn't spent much time with Wyatt."

"The baby's mother was murdered, Brett is a suspect in that murder and we're not even sure he's the baby's father. What's your name?"

"I'm Luna. I didn't believe his story, but out here..."

"I know. People come and people go." Emily thrust out her hand. "I'm Emily. Thanks for helping out with Wyatt. Brett kidnapped him from a DCS caseworker after shooting her."

Luna closed her eyes and pressed her fingers against her temples. "He brought violence and discord with him. I keep telling Zeke we need to move to another location. There's a rough element infiltrating our place."

"Did you see Brett with anyone? Did he tell you anything about someone wanting the baby?"

"He didn't. I'm sorry, but at least the baby is missing instead of dead in that trailer. I had such a foreboding when I followed Zeke outside. I just knew the trouble involved Brett and that little baby. Such a precious little thing—an old soul. I could see it in his eyes."

Emily blinked. She sensed Nash's restless scorn, but she understood Luna completely.

Sirens blared in the distance and it took Emily a few seconds to recognize them for what they were. They seemed so out of place here.

"I know you folks aren't fond of the police out here but if you cooperate with the detectives, it might help bring Wyatt back safely."

"I will do my best." Luna touched Emily's arm. "You were meant to be with that baby."

Luna floated away and Emily glanced at Nash to make sure she hadn't dreamed the whole encounter.

His lips twisted. "Earth mother, but at least she's not hostile like the rest of them."

When the patrol car pulled into the site, bathing the battered residences with red-and-blue lights, the space in front of Brett's trailer cleared out, although Zeke and Luna stood firm.

When the officer exited his vehicle, Nash introduced himself and flashed his badge. Emily stayed outside as Nash led the officer to the trailer. They came out seconds later, the young cop covering his nose and mouth with one hand.

Brett's body couldn't have been there that long, but the heat had accelerated the decomposition process and anyone who'd entered that trailer would be living with the smell for a while.

The officer unfurled the yellow crime scene tape and blocked off the area. Then, notebook in hand, he began to question Zeke and Luna.

They had to wait almost another hour for the Pima County Sheriff's homicide squad, led by Detective Espinoza.

When he strode up to the scene, his cowboy hat creating a big shadow behind him, he nodded once to Nash, not looking at all surprised to see him here.

Several minutes later, Espinoza questioned Emily, and she stuck to their story as closely as possible. She assured him that she and Nash would've called the police, but they didn't really consider this a lead—just an offhand comment by Jaycee to Nash had led them here.

While Espinoza turned to ask Nash some further questions, Luna tugged on Emily's arm. "Come to our place for a cup of tea. We'll sit outside so you can keep an eye on things. I have a blend that'll cleanse the evil aura for you."

"I need that." Emily poked Nash in the side and pointed to Luna.

She followed the older woman to her mobile home, where two chairs sat beneath an awning and a tin of water boiled on the camp stove.

When the tea was ready and steeped, Emily sipped the fragrant brew and tilted her head back to take in the stars, sitting in companionable silence with Luna.

After about thirty minutes, Nash ambled over. "Are you ready?"

"I am." Emily patted Luna's arm. "Thanks for the tea and the company."

As Emily handed the empty cup to Luna, the older woman covered her hand and leaned forward, almost touching her nose to Emily's. "Find that baby."

Nash took Emily's hand and led her back to the police presence. "Sorry I couldn't rescue you sooner."

"Actually, that was just what I needed." She patted her stomach. "That tea had a calming effect. Why are we going back to Brett's trailer?" Emily scuffed her feet in the dirt.

"We're not. Officer Soltis is giving us a ride back to my truck in his squad car."

"Did they find anything? Any clues?"

"None that they shared with me."

"That's it, isn't it? They're not going to share anything with us."

"Shh." Nash squeezed her hand as Officer Soltis trudged toward them.

She and Nash scooted into the back seat of the squad car while Soltis got behind the wheel. "Sorry you both have to ride in back. It's policy."

"Understood, Officer." Nash rapped a knuckle on the wire screen separating back from front. "Thanks for the ride."

A few minutes later, Officer Soltis dropped them off

at Nash's truck, and Nash swung his pack into the back seat. Before taking the wheel, he pulled two phones from his pocket, dropped one on the console and powered up the other.

Emily wrinkled her nose and picked up the other phone. "What's this?"

"That—" Nash turned the ignition "—is Brett's phone that I took from his pocket before the police got there."

Her jaw dropped as she clapped the phone to her chest. "Is that what you were doing in there all that time?"

"I figured once Detective Espinoza arrived on the scene, he'd make everything off-limits to us. So, I took a few liberties." He lifted his shoulders. "We can always give it back and say we took it in the shock and confusion."

"You did that for me, didn't you?" She tapped the phone to wake it up. "I know you never would've taken those… liberties if I hadn't harassed you about leaving Wyatt with DCS."

"Maybe, maybe not. Seemed like the thing to do at the time."

"The battery will be dead in seconds." She picked up a charger plugged into a port in the truck and held it up to her face, squinting at it in the dark cab. "This'll work."

Once she'd plugged in Brett's phone, she folded her hands in her lap, around Wyatt's pacifier. "I'm so scared for Wyatt. Why is that baby so important? Whoever took him can't possibly believe Wyatt is Brett's son, right? Brett is now dead. If those two thugs who were looking for Brett found him and killed him, what interest could they have in Wyatt? They presumably got what they wanted."

"Let's look at the other possibility. Wyatt is Lanier's son and Brett was telling the truth—Jaycee and then Brett were looking to blackmail Lanier with this knowledge."

"I can't believe I ever trusted that man…took money

from him." She leaned her head against the window and bumped it against the glass once. "But if that's the case, Lanier's in the clear with both Jaycee and Brett dead. Why would he need Wyatt? Nobody else is going to blackmail him. Nobody else needs to know Wyatt is his son."

"I don't know what the guy is thinking." Nash poked at the phone charging in the cup holder. "Maybe he told Brett. I think his phone is sufficiently juiced."

Emily pinched the phone between her fingers and tapped it. "We lucked out. He doesn't have a password."

"Check his texts first."

Emily touched her fingertip to the message icon and scanned the sparse numbers. "This must be a burner phone, like Jaycee's was. None of these messages have names associated with them, just numbers, and he has no contacts stored."

"Probably why he didn't bother with a password. Can you figure out who he's texting?"

"He doesn't have many messages and not a lot of history. Either it's a new phone or he's been deleting them." She swiped at a few of the messages. "These texts are pretty cryptic—nothing like 'Let's blackmail Lanier' or 'I'll meet you at the border.'"

"Damn. Thought I'd hit the jackpot with that phone."

"It was a good idea." She tapped the photos, but apparently Brett hadn't been interested in taking any pictures of *his* son. She scanned a few of the standard apps on the phone, her gaze tripping across an unfamiliar icon with footsteps on a blue background.

She opened the app, which launched a map with a red dot positioned on it. With her fingertips buzzing and her heart racing, she enlarged the map on the phone.

She squealed and twisted in her seat, shoving the phone in Nash's face.

He jerked the steering wheel. "Whoa! I'm driving here."

"You did hit the jackpot, Nash. I know exactly where Wyatt is."

Chapter Sixteen

Nash gave Emily a quick glance from the corner of his eye. She'd taken Luna's hippie-dippie, new age pronouncements a little too seriously. "What, you're communing with Wyatt now and he's sending you his location through the airwaves?"

She poked him in the arm with the phone...hard. "Look at my face. Would I be this excited without good, logical reason?"

He peeled his gaze from the dark road ahead and shifted it to her face for a peek at her glowing eyes and smile that practically reached from ear to ear. "You're serious. What did you find on that phone? A clue?"

"Better than a clue. Remember how Brett tracked us to Tombstone?"

"Jaycee had put a GPS tracker on Wyatt's car seat." His fingers flexed on the steering wheel. "But we removed it and Wyatt's not even in the same car seat."

She tapped her head. "You're a little slow tonight, Dillon. I'll put it down to the late hour and the desert driving. Brett obviously thought that was a good idea because he put another tracker on the car seat from DCS."

"You're sure?"

"He has an app on his phone. It's live and it's tracking something heading up north to Phoenix."

"Something." His heart slowed its thudding. "How do you know it's Wyatt's car seat or even Wyatt?"

She twisted her mouth and studied the phone's display. "What else would he be tracking? He used it to find us in Tombstone, and it must've given him the idea to do it again in case someone grabbed Wyatt—he just didn't figure he'd be too dead to make use of it."

"Okay, that makes sense. If the GPS is attached to the car seat, we can lose Wyatt as soon as whoever has him switches car seats." He wagged his finger at the phone. "Can you tell where he is in Phoenix?"

"You mean, can I tell if he's at Lanier's home or office?"

"Exactly."

"He's not at Lanier's office, at least not the one I went to. I'd have to look up his home address to see if he's there, but if he knows the Pima County Sheriffs are looking to talk to him, I doubt he's going to have Wyatt at his home."

"Espinoza said Lanier was out of the country. I wonder if that's even true. He could've had his office lie for him, or he lied to his office."

"But why, why, why?" Emily pounded a fist on her knee with every why. "He could let it all go right now. I'm certainly not going to suggest DCS do a paternity test on Lanier. I don't care whether or not he's Wyatt's father, and I'm certainly not interested in blackmailing him."

"Does he know that?"

"What do you mean?" She tucked her hands between her knees. "You think he sees me as a blackmail threat? He wouldn't have hired me in the first place if he thought that."

"When he hired you, it was under false pretenses. The way he's acted the past few days by not contacting you, he can't keep up the ruse as the concerned father anymore. He realizes by now you're not buying his original motive."

"Your guess is as good as mine. I don't know what he

wants—and that worries me." She ran her finger along the edge of the phone in her lap. "But now we know where he has Wyatt."

"We need to tell the police, Emily. We have to give them this information so that they can formally move in on Lanier."

She grabbed the phone, her lifeline to Wyatt, and hugged it to her chest. "We know this GPS tracking app on Brett's phone is significant, but they don't know that. Do you think the police can get a warrant to search any of Lanier's properties in Phoenix based on a red dot on a phone?"

Nash rubbed his jaw. He'd never considered himself a blind rule follower—until he collided with Emily and her "anything goes" approach to policing. No wonder she got fired from the force. She hadn't even told him the full story of how she tried to nab the accomplice of her father's killer, but he could guess how things went down.

"Look, you have a point, but if things don't go the way we plan them to, we could really screw things up for the police if we go in willy-nilly."

"Me, you—" she pointed to herself and then leveled a finger at him "—we don't do things willy-nilly. We're a good team, Nash."

He reached over and ran a hand down the black, stretchy material of the leggings covering her thighs. "I know you want to rush in with guns blazing to save Wyatt, but we could be putting him in more danger."

She pressed the phone against her cheek. "Does this mean we're not driving up to Phoenix right now and zeroing in on this red dot?"

"Oh, I didn't say that. The closer we are to Wyatt, the better, but we have a few things to do first and it doesn't mean we can't get the police started on what they need to do."

"We have to take care of Denali for one thing."

"Kyle and Meg will take him again, but I do want to swing by my house and grab a bag and a few other things."

Emily practically bounced in her seat. "And then it's on to Phoenix…and Wyatt."

"I don't want you to get your hopes too high, Emily. That red dot—" he pointed at the phone clutched in her hand "—could just be the car seat, probably is the car seat. It doesn't mean Lanier, or whoever has Wyatt, is going to keep him in that car seat."

The light died from her eyes, and her fingers curled even tighter around the phone so that the veins popped out in her wrist. "I know that. I'm trying not to think about it."

"I know, sweets, and I don't want to be the voice of doom and gloom, but I don't want to watch you crash." He thumped his fist against his chest. "That'll rip my heart out."

She covered his clenched knuckles with her hand. "I know, but I have to hold on to something. When my dad was killed, the one thing that kept me going was the belief that I'd track down the guy who could've stopped it. That thought gave me hope, gave me a reason to carry on. I need that now."

The knife that had been embedded in his gut ever since Jaycee's murder twisted a little more. Emily needed Wyatt to feel whole. He couldn't do that for her. If they failed to bring him home safely, what then? She'd forever associate him with that failure.

He lifted her hand to his lips and kissed the soft skin on the back of it.

"Then I guess we'd better find that baby and bring him home."

She nodded and closed her eyes for the rest of the trip

back to his place, her tight grip on that phone the only thing that indicated she wasn't sleeping.

The glow of Paradiso arose from the desert floor like an oasis, and Nash adjusted his speed as his truck approached the turnoff.

When he rolled up to a stop sign and put on the brakes, Emily opened her eyes. "Pack, take care of Denali and get moving, right?"

"That's about the order of things. I don't think we should stay at your place in Phoenix, do you? Lanier may be watching your apartment."

"Maybe, but as far as he knows, I'm off the job and I don't have a clue about him."

"Yeah, I wouldn't bank on that. If he'd contacted you in a normal manner, he could get away with that level of cluelessness, but he must know that you think his response was odd."

"Maybe, but I'm not going to play it like that with him ever."

"Still, it may be a good idea to stay in a hotel in Phoenix."

"I agree."

He pulled into his driveway, beating sunrise by at least an hour.

"I hope Denali isn't going crazy."

"Uh-oh, looks like he got out front." Emily powered down her window and called out, "Hey, boy. It's all right. We're back. Don't run off."

The headlights of the truck picked out the dog as he loped across the front of the house, his tongue lolling from his mouth, his mismatched eyes luminescent in the glare.

"How the hell did he make it to the front of the house?" A tickle ran across Nash's flesh as he glanced at the cameras on his house. He hadn't checked his security footage since their trip to the border. He made a grab for the back of Emily's T-shirt. "Hold on, Emily."

His words came too late. She slipped from his grasp and opened the door of the truck, hopping out onto the driveway, her sneakers crunching the gravel.

Nash clawed at his phone and his gun on the console and burst from the truck. Denali staggered toward him, whimpered and collapsed at his feet.

"Emily!" His gun now cocked and ready, Nash vaulted over the dog and charged toward the back of the truck.

A figure moved out of the darkness and a low growl sounded close to his ear. "Drop it, or she dies now."

Two other shapes stepped into the lights from the back of the truck, and a cold fear gripped Nash as he made out a man, one arm wrapped around Emily and a gun to her head.

Chapter Seventeen

Emily wriggled in the man's grasp, but the cold metal of the gun pressed against her temple stopped her in her tracks...along with the look of rage stamped on Nash's face.

"I'm all right. I'm all right, Nash. Just do as he says."

The man who had accosted her at the motel sneered at Nash. "And I say drop your piece and head inside for some civil conversation."

Nash's eyes flashed once before he dangled his gun from his fingers and let it fall to the ground.

The man scooped it up immediately and waved it at Nash. "Everyone inside."

"The dog?" Nash folded his arms and widened his stance.

Emily's heart jumped. What had they done with Denali? He'd been out here running around and then disappeared on the other side of the truck.

"We just sedated him with a tranquilizer. He's not dead." The man nodded to her captor. "Let's move, Danny."

While her guy, Danny, kept the gun on her at the bottom of the steps, Nash unlocked his front door. The man who now had Nash's weapon prodded him in the back with it, and they both walked inside the house.

She knew and Nash knew, one aggressive move on Nash's part would result in a bullet in her head.

Danny pushed her toward the porch, and she stumbled, bracing her hand on the top step. She could've easily swung around on this goon and disarmed him, but she had no clue what kind of position Nash was in at this point. She didn't want to get him killed.

Grabbing her T-shirt, he pulled her up and shoved her again.

She ground her teeth together. "I can walk myself. Stop pushing me."

"Danny, *basta*. That's enough."

When Emily walked into the house, her gaze flew to Nash, sitting at the kitchen table, his own gun trained on him, his jaw set in a hard line.

"My name is Gustavo." His mild tone made it sound like he were visiting for lunch instead of holding them at gunpoint. With his other hand, he pointed to the chair next to Nash's. "Sit down. We just want answers. Nobody needs to get hurt."

"Yeah, like Jaycee? Like Brett?" Emily plopped down in the kitchen chair. "What do you want now? Both of them are dead. Weren't you after Brett all along? Well, you got him."

"We didn't want that skinny junkie dead…or we didn't care one way or the other." Gustavo narrowed his dark eyes. "He took drugs and money from us, hijacked one of our mules just coming across the border."

Nash ground out between his teeth, "And you were willing to use a baby to get him to turn over your property."

"We use what's at our disposal, Agent Dillon, just like you do."

Nash snorted. "So, what? You killed the poor bastard

when you found out he didn't have your product? What did you do with the baby?"

Emily held her breath and curled her feet around the legs of the chair. Of course she and Nash wouldn't let on that they had an app to track Wyatt. These two would never tell them where they'd sent Wyatt.

The man's bushy eyebrows, incongruous paired with his shaved head, slammed over his nose. "The baby is missing?"

Emily said, "Nice try. You killed Brett and took the baby. We know. We were there in that trailer to see your handiwork."

He stroked his chin. "We didn't kill Fillmore, and we didn't take the brat. We figured someone killed him for our stash of drugs, and we thought you could tell us who."

Nash hunched forward, his hands on his knees. "You're telling me you didn't kill Brett Fillmore and take that baby."

"That's exactly what I'm telling you, amigo. We didn't kill the girl, either."

"You would say that." Emily crossed her arms over her chest and stuck out her legs, crossing them at the ankles. "You're talking to a Border Patrol agent—not a good idea to confess to any crimes."

Gustavo lifted his shoulders. "Think what you want. The junkie killed his girl. Maybe he thought she was gonna rat him out. He killed that social worker, too, and took the baby, and then someone killed him, took the baby and our property."

Danny, still pointing a gun at her, cracked a gap-toothed smile and spoke for the first time. "We want our stash and you want that baby. Looks like we're on the same side."

Nash grunted. "That'll be the day. Why would the

person who killed Fillmore and stole your drugs take the baby?"

Emily had her own theories, which probably matched Nash's, but neither one was going to blurt out anything in front of these two. The farther they kept away from Wyatt, the better. And the more she and Nash kept them talking and thinking they were all in this together, the better.

Gustavo shook his head. "What is it about that baby? I know why we wanted him, but why did Fillmore want him and why did the people who killed Fillmore take him instead of killing him?"

Emily flinched. "Brett wanted him because he was the baby's father. That's obvious. That's why you wanted him—to force Brett's hand."

"Maybe that baby had more value than we realized." Gustavo renewed his grip on Nash's gun. "That's why you're going to tell us where he is and who took him. We'll find our product in the bargain."

"There is no bargain." Nash reached down and scratched his ankle. "We don't know who stole your stuff and we don't care. We want to find the baby."

"And that's—" Gustavo tipped his head toward Danny "—where our worlds collide. You're going to look for the baby, and you're going to keep us informed so we can collect what's ours. We'll even let you have the brat."

"You've been smoking too much of your own product if you think I'm going to help a couple of soldiers for Las Moscas recover the drugs they illegally smuggled across the border."

"You'll help us, *Agent* Dillon, because if you don't, we'll kill this *pelirroja*." Danny flipped her hair with the barrel of his gun.

Emily jerked away, and Danny smacked her across the face with the back of his hand—just in case she'd forgotten they were actually on opposite sides of the law. Tears sprang to her eyes, and through her blurry vision she saw Nash scratch his left ankle again—where he'd removed a knife from a holster outside of Brett's trailer.

"Hey!" Nash shouted. "There's no need for that. You're gonna make me think we can't work together. If you're not gonna take care of her, I'm not gonna help you."

A smile stretched Gustavo's lips. "I like where this is going, Agent. We'll keep *la pelirroja* safe and sound while you use your connections to find that baby—and our drugs. You keep one. We'll take the other."

"Don't I get a say in this?" Was Nash's plan to get the thugs to separate the two of them so they could each go one-on-one? She knew without a doubt Nash had something up his sleeve…or rather up his leg.

She studied Danny's dilated pupils. She could take this guy, but not while Gustavo had a gun on Nash.

She continued. "Nash, do you really believe Las Moscas will allow either of us to live after this? You? A Border Patrol agent?"

"We won't allow either of you to live right now if you don't agree to cooperate, so I guess you take your chances." Gustavo nudged Danny. "Get her out to the car."

"He's right, Emily." Nash tapped his left knee. "Think about the baby. They have no use for the baby once they get their drugs. He can't be a witness. We have to trust that they won't harm him."

Okay, that had to be a signal. There was no way Nash would ever tell a member of Las Moscas that he was right.

"Listen to him, *la pelirroja*. We'll keep you comfortable while he locates the baby. Then we'll release you." Gustavo's eye twitched, and Emily knew he was lying, not that she needed an eyebrow to tell her that.

"Go with him, Emily. Do what he says."

Another signal if she ever heard one. It'd be a cold day in hell before she ever did what this scumbag told her to do.

"All right, but what are you going to do to him?" She leveled a finger at Nash. "Don't hurt him."

"Hurt him? He's going to help us. We're going to work out a few things while you wait in the car, and then I'm going to join you and leave him here so he can get to work." Gustavo spread his hands. "Cooperation, *si*?"

Emily stood up suddenly, and the gun flashed in front of her.

Danny said, "You move when I tell you to."

"Got it." She stared into Nash's face. "You do what you have to do. I can take care of myself."

Danny jabbed her in the back with the gun. "Move."

She walked to the front door, her muscles coiled, ready for anything on one word from Nash.

When they stepped onto the porch, she asked in a loud voice, "Where's your car? We didn't see it when we drove up."

"Shut up." He gave her a shove from behind and she tripped.

A low growl reverberated in the air, making the hair on the back of her neck stand up.

Something scrambled from beneath Nash's truck, and Danny took a step back. A white flash barreled toward him, and as Denali sank his teeth into Danny's leg, he screamed and got off a shot.

While he hopped on one leg, Denali attached himself to the other. Emily sprang up, wrapped her arms around Danny's middle and tackled him.

Two shots popped off in the house, but she closed her mind to what might be happening inside.

Danny's arm flailed at his side as he tried to take aim with the gun, which he'd held on to but in an awkward position.

Still on top of him, Emily kneed Danny in the groin and then lunged for the gun. Their hands twisted into an intricate dance to gain control of the weapon.

She ground her teeth together as the gun began to turn in her direction.

"Hold it, or I'll blow your head off." Nash's voice cut through the life-and-death tension, and the man's body went limp beneath her.

She peeled the gun from his hand and rolled off him, panting in the driveway.

Denali whined and licked her face.

"Nash, are you all right? What happened in there?"

Nash strode toward them, handcuffs clinking as they dangled from his fingers. "When we heard the commotion out here, I made a move for my knife strapped to my leg. I was able to stab Gustavo, get possession of my gun and shoot him. He's dead."

Danny swore, and Denali bared his teeth and stood over him so that the drool from his tongue dripped onto his face.

Emily rose to her hands and knees and then stood up. She held out her hands for the cuffs. "Do you want me to do the honors?"

"Do you remember how?"

"Just like riding a bike." She took the handcuffs from Nash, commanded Danny to roll over and cuffed his hands behind his back. She placed her shoe on his neck. "Stay there."

Nash already had his phone out. "I'm calling the Paradiso PD right now."

"Were you just playing dead, boy?" Emily patted Denali's head. "You came back to life with a vengeance."

"Is that what happened?" Nash tucked his phone in his pocket. "I heard this idiot scream, but I wasn't sure if you did something to him or he did something to himself."

"Neither case." She scratched Denali behind the ears. "When we came out of the house, Danny pushed me one too many times. Denali must've already come out of his unconscious state and immediately went on the attack. When he did, I saw my chance and *I* went on the attack."

"Good job, both of you." He cupped her face and kissed her cheek, which had started throbbing from the slap she'd received inside the house. "I hope you didn't believe I was ever going to allow them to take you away."

"I didn't believe it for a minute. I always knew you had a plan—you were behaving way too meekly." She touched her fingers to her hot cheek.

"You, too." He tapped his own face. "You need ice for that."

"Those two obviously didn't know anything about—"

"Shh." Nash put a finger to his lips and glanced down at Danny, still prone in the gravel with Denali standing guard.

She flipped the gun around in her hand, crouched beside Danny and cracked him on the back of his head with the butt. He passed out with a grunt. "Now we can talk."

Nash raised his eyebrows. "I can see where you would have problems on a PD with your methods."

"I already figured I'm not cut out to be a cop." She handed the gun to Nash. "They didn't know anything about Lanier."

"Didn't appear to, unless they were keeping that piece of info to themselves. We knew they were after Brett, but we finally learned why. He'd stupidly intercepted one of Las Moscas' mules at the border. Did he really think they'd let him get away with that?"

"Maybe that's why he hatched the blackmailing scheme with Jaycee. He planned to return the drugs to Las Moscas."

"They probably would've never let him live after that—

or they'd force him into becoming one of their mules. That's what they do—human fodder." His eyes narrowed as he peered down at Danny. "I'm glad you knocked him out."

"So, Lanier, or whoever works for Lanier, took Wyatt and probably took the drugs, too."

"Lanier isn't doing his own dirty work." He stroked her hair. "Look how he used you."

"I wonder if Lanier knows his flunky stole those drugs." She snapped her fingers. "Maybe we can use that information to get Wyatt. If Lanier's hired killer stole those drugs and didn't tell his boss, he wouldn't want his boss to find out, would he?"

"No, but he wouldn't want his boss to know he helped us find Wyatt, either. And there's one small detail. We don't know who the hit man was."

"Hit man?" Emily snorted. "I think you're elevating the guy's credentials. If the killer stole those drugs, he's probably another junkie like Brett."

For the second time in the past twelve hours, sirens blared through the night.

Denali lifted his head, and his ears quivered.

Nash patted the dog's furry side. "You can go inside, boy. You've done a good job tonight. Wait until I tell Clay."

Emily had transferred Brett's GPS app from his phone to hers, and she dragged her phone out of her back pocket to check on Wyatt...or at least Wyatt's car seat. "Wyatt is still in the same spot. Do we tell the police tonight? Do we tell Espinoza?"

"I think we have to, Emily."

"They don't know Brett's recent history like we do. They won't know the significance of this tracker. They won't have the same urgency."

"Maybe not, so we tell them and then we go to Phoenix

ourselves. We're private citizens, or at least in this capacity I am. We don't need a search warrant or probable cause. We can get the jump on this, and Espinoza can come in later and tie things up with a bow."

She pinched his sleeve. "Do you think that's how this is going to end, tied up with a bow?"

"I'll do my damnedest to make sure of it, and I know you will, too." He nodded toward the emergency vehicles pulling into his driveway. "But first things first."

The Paradiso PD flooded the scene, along with Border Patrol. Danny came around just in time to be arrested and loaded into the back of a police car.

Emily finally followed Nash into the house, where Gustavo's body lay in the kitchen, blood spreading out from beneath his facedown body onto Nash's beautiful hardwood floor. She had more sympathy for the floor. She only regretted not witnessing Nash take him out.

The police had plenty of questions for her and Nash, and they had to confiscate Nash's weapon. The Border Patrol put him on leave immediately, which would save him from taking another vacation or personal day to go up to Phoenix.

By the time Espinoza showed up on the scene, the sun was rising and the medical examiner had loaded Gustavo's body in the van.

The only thing left to do was clean that floor.

As Emily went through the questions and the explanations, she kept her phone cupped in her hand and kept checking on that red dot. With Espinoza here, she knew they'd have to turn that information over to him. Would he make light of it? Perhaps it would be to their advantage if he did. Then they'd be free to pursue the leads without being hampered by protocol.

That was what she'd hated most about police work. Proper procedures always hampered true justice.

Emily's heart fluttered as Nash shook Espinoza's hand and drew him close. She glanced down at her phone again and sucked in a breath.

The first contact from Marcus Lanier since she'd told him she was working as Wyatt's nanny. She swept the message open, and a tingle of fear crept up her back as she read the text.

Her head jerked up, and she zeroed in on Nash and Espinoza.

Then she rushed toward them to stop the conversation at any cost.

Chapter Eighteen

Espinoza shifted his toothpick from one side of his mouth to the other. "Do you believe that these Las Moscas soldiers didn't kill Fillmore? I can see them going in there looking for their drugs, and once they figured Fillmore didn't have them, they killed him. Wyatt was already gone because the person or persons who kidnapped him didn't know about any drugs and left Fillmore alive after they took the baby."

Nash followed the path of the toothpick for a few seconds before he answered. "That could be. Every word that comes out of their mouths is suspect."

"They must've really believed you could get a line on Jaycee's baby to risk coming to a Border Patrol agent's house and kidnapping your...friend. Why is that? Why do they think you know where the baby is?"

Nash scratched the scruff on his chin and opened his mouth.

Emily butted her way between the two of them and clung to Nash's arm. "When are they going to be done here, Nash? I'm still a nervous wreck. I just want to get back to Phoenix and forget this whole thing."

Nash snapped his mouth shut and studied Emily's face. She winked at him.

Was he supposed to know what that meant? If she thought he was about to tell Espinoza about the GPS tracker on Wyatt's car seat, she'd interrupted that moment for a reason. One thing he knew for sure was that Emily Lang was no nervous wreck after cracking Danny in the skull with his own gun.

"I think they're ready to wrap it up, right, Detective?"

"We are. Ms. Lang, do you have any idea why these two men thought you and Nash knew who took the baby?"

She turned toward him, her hand at her throat. "I have no idea. If we knew where Wyatt was, we'd tell you right away. Maybe they thought it was some other drug dealer who Nash had in his sights."

"They'd be wrong." Nash folded his arms with Emily's fingers still digging into his bicep and covered her hand with his.

Espinoza clapped his hat onto his head. "We're almost done. We'll question Danny Trujillo, for all the good it'll do. We'll see if it was his gun that shot Fillmore, so that'll be a start. He does have a silencer on it. Damn shame about that baby. Don't get why the lowlife who killed Fillmore didn't just leave the baby there, but thank God we didn't find the baby dead."

Emily closed her eyes and swooned against Nash's shoulder, but Nash didn't think she was faking it this time.

He shook his head at Espinoza, and the detective grimaced and said, "We'll be out of your way."

"I'll be off duty for a few days and maybe out of town, but not far. Call me if you need anything else." Nash held out his hand to Espinoza to hurry him along.

Ten minutes later, only the crime scene tape hanging limply outside and the bloodstained floorboards inside gave any indication that a man had died here and another had been hauled away.

When Nash finally closed the door, Emily pounced on him.

"Oh, my God. I'm so glad you didn't spill the beans about the GPS on Wyatt." She pulled his arm and dragged him to the couch.

"I gathered that. You stopped me just in time. I was about to reveal all. Now tell me why we didn't."

When they sat down, Emily tapped furiously on her phone and crooked her finger at him to have a look at her display.

"Read this. It's from Marcus Lanier."

Nash took the phone from her and read the text message out loud. "'I have the baby safe and sound. All you need to do to get him back is tell that Border Patrol agent to delete the file Webb sent him and forget about its existence. If you involve the police, the baby will disappear. Let me know when this is done and I'll let you know where to pick up the baby.'"

Nash dropped the phone, his blood thumping hot through his veins. "What the hell is this about?"

"D-do you know what file he's referring to? Who's Webb?"

"I know what file he means and Special Agent Bruce Webb is the guy in finance who sent it to me, but how does he know about Webb and that file?" Nash dug a hand through his hair. "The information in that file has the potential to show his connection to Las Moscas and his money-laundering efforts on their behalf."

"You have to do it, Nash. You have to get rid of it so we can get Wyatt back."

He whipped his head around. "Do you trust Lanier? He lied to you from the beginning. Do you really think he'd release Wyatt unharmed if I destroy evidence of his criminal activity?"

Her green eyes widened, and the freckles stood out on

her pale cheeks. "What's the alternative? Refuse and send Wyatt to his death?"

"Was that what this was about all along?" Nash clasped his hands behind his neck. "It couldn't be. Lanier had no idea Jaycee would leave the baby with me. I doubt he even knew of my existence before this."

Emily held up her hands. "I didn't tell him about you. When I informed him that Jaycee had dropped off the baby with an old friend, I didn't tell him your name or your occupation."

"Why not?"

She lifted and dropped her shoulders quickly. "Just a feeling—a feeling that you were the good guy and Lanier has a lot of money to throw around if he doesn't get his way."

"Well, you got that right." He picked up the phone again and reread the message. "If this opportunity just fell into his lap by coincidence, why was he after Wyatt in the first place?"

"You never did follow through with getting that Rapid DNA test done."

"Like I had time?"

"I'm not criticizing, but what if the story Brett concocted was the actual truth all along? Wyatt is Lanier's baby, but Lanier didn't want that getting out. He didn't want his wife to find out. Or Jaycee was going to blackmail him, so he wanted to…destroy the evidence."

"That could all be true. When Jaycee died, one threat had been eliminated, but Brett knew. He had the baby and he was ready to follow through with Jaycee's plan."

Emily wedged her bare feet on the coffee table and wiggled her toes. "Lanier had Brett killed but, by this time, had figured out who you were and what you could do to him. So when he ordered Brett killed, he also ordered his henchman to take Wyatt as insurance."

"Poor kid." Nash ran a hand beneath his nose. "His whole life he's been nothing more than a bargaining chip."

Emily turned toward him and, taking his face in her hands, said, "That's why we have to rescue him now, Nash. We have to give Lanier what he wants and hope he follows through."

"Listen to yourself." He lightly clinched her wrists. "We're not letting a guy like Lanier get away with his crimes and continue to make money from people's suffering. We're not going to hope that a known liar, thief and killer is going to follow through on his promises."

"I get all of that, but we can't abandon Wyatt." A sob caught in Emily's throat, and tears splashed down her cheeks.

He caught one of her tears with his thumb and sucked it into his mouth. "We're not going to abandon Wyatt. We're going to rescue him without giving Lanier a damned thing except a jail cell in federal prison."

"How are we going to do that?" She swiped a hand across her wet face.

"First of all, I need to find out what Webb knows about all this. How is it Lanier knows the name of the guy responsible for his forensic accounting? Why does Lanier believe he's in the clear once I delete my file?"

"That is weird." Emily scooped up her phone and checked the location of the car seat. "Still there, but with all this work you have to do, we can't get him."

"I want to know what we're walking into." He tapped the phone in her hand. "Lanier didn't mention how we're supposed to know Wyatt is okay. Maybe that's the first thing you text him. Ask for proof that Wyatt is alive and healthy. Tell him I need some time."

"Now?"

"What time did he send that message?"

"Around six this morning—after we took care of Gustavo and Danny." She held her fist out for a bump. "We do make a good team, don't we?"

"I told you. You have the instincts of a cop. Get out of this PI business. You never know what kind of clients you're going to get." He leaned over and kissed the side of her head. "Send that text. I'm going to feed Denali. He deserves a steak."

"Should we take him to the vet today?"

"Does he look like he's suffering any ill effects to you?" He tipped his head toward Denali in the corner, gnawing on a bone.

Emily cupped the phone in her hand, her thumb hovering over the keyboard display. "What should I write?"

"'We're working on it. Send proof that Wyatt is okay.'"

Her thumb darted over the display, and then she held the phone out to him. "How's this?"

"Hit Send."

Emily sent the text, and Nash went into the kitchen to get Denali's food ready. When he opened the fridge, his gaze tripped across one of Wyatt's bottles, filled with formula. He'd talked a bold game with Emily, but fear clawed at his gut when he thought about Lanier with Wyatt. That man had no regard for the child—whether Wyatt was his or not.

And how was Webb involved in all of this? If Lanier knew Webb's name and title, he must know he had the data, too. He wouldn't put it past Lanier to put a hit on Webb, but the file implicating him would still be on Webb's computer.

Emily called from the great room, "He responded."

"Read it to me." Nash grabbed Denali's dish.

"He said he'd have the woman watching Wyatt live chat with me."

"That's good. Do it now. We have to have proof of life right now."

"I just texted him that."

Denali abandoned his bone when Nash carried his dish out to the dining area. "Here you go. Steak later."

Emily waved her phone at him. "I'm waiting for this person to call me."

Two minutes later, Emily's cell rang and she answered with the phone display toward her.

Nash didn't want to have his mug on this call, so he stood just out of view behind Emily on the couch.

Wyatt's face filled the screen, and Nash swallowed the lump in his throat. The woman didn't allow her own face on the display, but she held Wyatt in her lap and said, "You can see. The baby is fine. He's healthy and well cared for, and Mr. Marcus told me to tell you he'll stay that way until Mr. Marcus gets what he wants."

With a catch in her voice, Emily said, "Hello, Wyatt. I miss you, baby boy."

Wyatt gurgled and smiled when he heard Emily's voice.

Emily blew him a few kisses but then addressed the woman. "What's he paying you? Why would you do this to an innocent baby? Bring him to us, and we'll make sure you walk away from this."

The display swung away from Wyatt and captured a room. A gruff voice came over the phone. "Shut up. The kid's fine. That's what you wanted. Just do what you're supposed to do, and we won't harm him."

Emily shouted, "Let me see him again."

Wyatt appeared on the display again and Emily cooed. "It's okay, Wyatt. We'll see you soon. I love you, baby boy."

They ended the call on the other end, and Emily slumped against the couch cushions.

Nash squeezed her shoulders. "You shouldn't have done that. It didn't help."

"Sure it did." She swung around to face him. "We know he's not just with some woman. There's a man there for security, and we got to see some of the room where he's being held. There was a window in that room and a view of the outside. I'm going to go frame by frame and enlarge those images to get a better look at everything."

He bent over and kissed her sassy mouth. "You're a badass, Officer Lang."

"I'm terrified that Lanier has Wyatt, but in a way I almost feel better. He won't do anything to Wyatt until he has proof that you deleted his file." She pressed the phone against her heart as if it had captured Wyatt from that chat. "How are you going to contact Webb if you're off duty?"

"Our sector is low-key. Even though I'm on leave, nobody at the station is going to stop me if I want to come in wearing my civvies to close out a little business before taking off. I'll try to reach Webb then. I hope..." Nash bit the inside of his cheek.

Emily finished his sentence. "You hope he's still alive. They couldn't kill him. He still has Lanier's file on his computer."

"That's right, but he only did the investigation into Lanier. He didn't reach any conclusions." Nash wedged his hip against the back of the couch. "If Webb is dead and I delete my file, nobody will pick up the thread."

"Wouldn't you have heard by now if Webb were murdered?"

"If his body has been discovered. What if nobody knows?"

Emily grabbed a pillow from his couch and hugged it.

"I guess you won't know until tomorrow...or rather later this morning when you call him."

"Lanier's communication and that live chat with Wyatt just bought us some time, and I'm going to use mine to get a few hours of shut-eye, a shower and breakfast—in that order. I suggest you do the same."

Emily stared at the red dot on her phone and then held it up. "We have the advantage, don't we? They'll never see us coming."

"We'll hit 'em like a ton of bricks." Nash brushed Emily's hair to the side, like gathering sunset in his hands, and kissed the nape of her neck.

Just like he'd never seen Emily Lang coming. She'd hit him like a ton of bricks...and he'd never be the same.

LATER, AFTER A few hours of sleep with Emily curled up at his side, Nash dropped off Denali at Meg's place. Meg complained that Clay and her cousin, April, should've left the dog with her when they went on their honeymoon, but she just liked complaining.

Nash and Emily went to breakfast, where he wolfed down eggs, bacon, hash browns, toast, the works, while she played with a bowl of oatmeal. He left her with that cold oatmeal and a hot cup of coffee as he made his way into the station.

Valdez blinked when Nash walked in. "You supposed to be here, bro?"

"Does it look like I'm working?" Nash plucked at his white T-shirt and patted his hip. "I don't even have my weapon."

"What the hell went on last night?" Valdez raised his coffee cup as if in a toast. "Brett Fillmore dead. Some Las Moscas soldier dead. Another soldier in custody."

"Baby still missing."

"Yeah, this is complicated. Do you need any help?"

"Nah." Nash pulled out his chair and waved at his computer. "Just wanna close a few loose ends in case the investigation into the shooting takes a long time. It shouldn't, but you already know how slowly the bureaucracy works."

"I sure do." Valdez slurped some coffee. "Let me know if you need anything."

"I will, thanks." Nash waited until Valdez was on the phone, deep into a call. He scrolled through his contacts on his computer and found Webb.

With a sick flip-flop of his stomach, Nash placed the call. He closed his eyes and blew out a breath when Webb answered on the second ring.

"Nash Dillon."

"That's right. Everything okay there, Bruce?"

Bruce responded, "I was expecting your call, Agent Dillon."

Nash's gut twisted again. Hadn't the guy told him the other day to use his first name? Nash licked his lips. Why did he feel that the *Agent Dillon* held some significance?

Nash lowered his voice. "You know about Marcus Lanier and that file, don't you?"

"Marcus who?"

Chapter Nineteen

Nash's hand curled into a fist. Had Lanier gotten to Webb?

He cleared his throat. "The file you sent me linking Lanier's finances to those of Las Moscas—you have it, I have it and Lanier wants it destroyed."

Webb's voice dropped to almost a whisper. "You're the only one who has that file now, Dillon. I suggest you delete it, and I sincerely hope you didn't make any copies or send it to anyone. That file never sees the light of day. I will deny any knowledge of it and its contents."

"What does he have on you, Webb?"

"Just do it, if you know what's good for you and that baby."

"What's to stop me from duplicating the file or not deleting it at all?"

Webb clicked his tongue. "I put in fail-safes, Dillon. You'll send the file I emailed to you back to me. I'll be able to tell if it's been duplicated or attached to an email. Then I will corrupt the file and send proof to our friend."

"He's no friend of mine... Yours, either, Webb. We can do this together."

Webb laughed and Nash knew he'd lost him. The finance guy who loved numbers had gone over to the dark side.

"He *is* my friend, and while he may never be yours,

you don't want him as your enemy. I'll send you instructions on how to embed certain codes in the file. You do that, send it back to me, and he will cooperate with you. Any recording or reporting of this conversation will have a very bad ending for you, Dillon."

He and Emily would have to fix this on their own. "I've been put on leave for a shooting. I won't be back at work for a few days."

"I know that. We have time. I'll explain it to him."

Time. That was what Nash wanted and what Wyatt needed.

"Send those instructions to my personal email."

Webb got Nash's personal email address to send him the instructions to prepare the file for obliteration. He didn't have to know that Nash had no intention of using them—but he would be obliterating Webb's career.

Nash ended the call with a feeling of dread gnawing at his gut. Lanier's tentacles reached farther than he thought, but he didn't know who he was dealing with. When Lanier had hired Emily to spy on Wyatt, he'd unknowingly unleashed a powerful force of reckoning—a mama bear protecting her cub. Emily would go to any lengths to protect Wyatt…and Nash would go to any lengths to protect both of them.

On his way out of the station, Nash waved to Valdez, talking on the phone. He drove back to Emily, still nursing the same cup of coffee.

She half rose from her seat at the booth when he walked into the restaurant, eyebrows raised in a question—or a hundred questions. She started with two of the most obvious. "Is Webb alive? And if he is, what did he have to say?"

He settled across from her and folded his hands on the wooden tabletop. "He's alive, but he's in league with the devil."

Clinging to the edge of the table, she said, "What does that mean?"

"It means Lanier got to him, and I don't mean in the same way he got to me. Lanier is threatening me. I think he's rewarding Webb."

"Webb's dirty?" She chewed on her bottom lip.

"Yeah, he's dirty." Nash brought his clasped hands to his face, digging his knuckles into his forehead. "My guess is that the guy who loves numbers loves them even more when they appear in his bank account."

Emily whistled. "Does that mean his file on Lanier is already gone?"

"Gone, and he's going to send me instructions to add code to my file so when I email it back to him, he can destroy it."

"Can you copy it first? Send it to me?"

"Webb claims that when I send the file back to him, he'll be able to tell if it's been duplicated or forwarded."

"Do you believe him? That could be a complete lie."

"After the stuff I learned from our IT guy, I don't doubt it. Do you want to take that chance with Wyatt's life?"

"What do you think?" She twisted a strand of hair around her finger. "When are you going to do it, or are you? You seemed to think before that we could have our cake and stuff our faces with it—get Wyatt back and prosecute Lanier."

"I believe that more than ever now." He downed a glass of lukewarm water on the table, probably leftover from his own breakfast. "Webb knows I'm on leave. I can't access the Lanier file while I'm on leave. He's going to pass that information along to Lanier, which buys us time, buys Wyatt time."

She dug her elbows into the table and balanced her chin on her palms. "While Webb and Lanier are waiting for you to get back to work and implant the code to facilitate the destruction of that file, we'll be on our way to Phoenix and Wyatt."

"You—" he tucked her hair behind her ear "—are right."

She spun her phone on the table to face him, and he glanced down at the GPS app that she must've been staring at for the past hour. "Then what are we waiting for?"

"Nightfall, for one. We're not going to charge into some Lanier property in Phoenix to rescue Wyatt in broad daylight."

"We can drive to Phoenix, though. I can't sit around Paradiso knowing Wyatt is with that woman and some guard." She scooped her hands into her hair and grabbed it by the roots. "I'll go crazy."

"With your hair like that, you look a little off balance." He smoothed his hand over her red head. "First, we're going to kill some time by going out to the border and retrieving your rental car."

"I always meant to ask you how you knew I was driving a rental."

He twisted his lips. "C'mon. I ran your plates. You must've taken that into consideration, as the car was rented to Emily O'Brien, not Lang."

"When I rented that car, I didn't even know of your existence. I was creating my identity."

"It wasn't that long ago we met, was it?" He didn't wait for her answer. He didn't want to discuss their relationship right now. "Next, we're going to check you out of that motel."

"Which I barely occupied."

"And we're going to pack a bag of gadgets and disguises and weapons."

She formed her fingers into a pistol and aimed it at him. "Let's not forget the weapons."

They spent the afternoon doing just what Nash planned.

When they finally made it out to the border to get Emily's car, they found a smashed windshield.

Emily wedged her hands on her hips as she surveyed the damage. "Gustavo and Danny must've been really upset when they found this car."

"At least Lanier's paying for it, right? What better way to use dirty money than to pay for dirty deeds."

Once they dropped the car off at the rental company, they started packing. The Border Patrol had confiscated Nash's service revolver, but he had his personal stash and he was bringing most of it.

Emily surveyed his weapons duffel bag with an appreciative spark in her green eyes. "Nice collection. You have only two hands, though. Are you gonna share?"

"I've never dated a woman yet who wanted to share—weapons or anything else." He zipped up the bag, closing it to her acquisitive gaze. "But I can be persuaded."

"That's good because I can be persuasive."

"I'm aware of that." He spread his hands to encompass their gear on the floor. "Do you think I'd be doing this otherwise?"

"It has to be this way, Nash. You saw Lanier's warning—no police. And if he compromised some coolheaded accountant, how many others does he have on the inside? I'm sure his close work with law enforcement in Phoenix has netted him a few very good friends in that department."

He held up his hands. "You can stop. You already convinced me."

"You're just giving yourself an out in case things go south." She huffed out a breath. "You never needed any convincing."

He grabbed her around the waist and kissed her hard on the mouth. "But things aren't going south, are they? We're Wyatt Earp and Doc Holliday, and we're gonna make sure justice is served."

EMILY CLAPPED HER hand on her bouncing knee. She could hardly keep still on the almost two-hour drive to Phoenix. They'd missed rush hour, but some freeway construction had made traffic slow.

She stretched out her fingers, which had become cramped wrapped around her phone while she watched the red dot. What if the people who had Wyatt had already moved him to a different car seat, and this pinpoint location was for an empty car seat sitting on a trash heap?

Licking her lips, she glanced at Nash, silent and thoughtful behind the wheel and behind his disguise of beard and baseball cap. Was he regretting his decision to go rogue already? She'd been impressed by his thoroughness. When the man went rogue, he went all out.

In addition to his disguise, he'd swapped his truck for a rental in case Lanier's people knew his vehicle. He'd insisted she cover her red hair, so she found a dark wig and did him one better and added a pair of clear glasses.

Sensing her regard, he twisted his head to the side. "You printed out those enlargements of the room where you live chatted with Wyatt, right?"

She jerked her thumb toward the back seat. "I have them in a folder."

He asked, "How close are we now?"

Glancing at her phone, she said, "About twenty minutes straight through the city to the west. It's in the desert, not Phoenix proper. Where are we going to hole up before we make our move?"

"Depends on how close we can get to this location without raising suspicions. If it's in some small town on the outskirts of Phoenix, we'll be strangers. Strangers stick out in small towns. Trust me."

After another ten minutes of driving, Emily got her bearings. "The location isn't in a residential community, but it has to be some kind of house and not a warehouse because it definitely has a window."

"Unless—" Nash grabbed her hand "—we're just tracking an empty car seat."

She threaded her fingers through his. "You don't think that notion has been gnawing at me?"

"We need to drive by the GPS location now, before the sun goes down, and make some kind of assessment. We can't go in blindly at night if we're not even sure Wyatt is with the car seat."

"I agree." She tapped the phone. "We're there in two more exits."

They left the center of Phoenix to where the buildings grew sparser and the desert began to take control again. Emily instructed Nash to turn off where a few fast-food restaurants and chain stores hugged the freeway.

She cleared her throat. "So, not completely isolated. We're not going to cause a commotion with our presence."

Nobody who had seen her or Nash before would recognize them in these disguises, and they'd stashed Wyatt's car seat in the trunk to distance themselves from anything baby related. This could work.

She continued to give Nash directions that took them past a few scattered houses, a trailer park and a rodeo rink. She glanced at Nash from the corner of her eye. "Don't get any ideas."

He snorted, but his mouth stayed firm. He was as worried as she was, and her little joke couldn't snap the tension that held them in its grip.

Emily rapped her knuckle on the window. "Up ahead, the next turn."

Hunching over the steering wheel, Nash said, "Looks like some warehouses, but there could be offices in the front with windows."

"Should we look now, even though it's not as dark as you'd like?"

He nodded. "There are a few cars driving around, probably coming and going from work. One more car isn't going to make a difference. Just keep me going in the right direction."

They turned right into a large lot dotted with warehouses, and Emily's stomach knotted. People worked here. How could they keep a baby tucked away in a warehouse without drawing attention to themselves?

She swallowed. "It has to be this warehouse on the right, Nash, but it looks nothing like what I saw out that window during the video chat."

Nash drove slowly past the warehouse and around the corner. When they reached the back of a gray metal structure, Nash pointed to a sliding door raised a few feet, leaving a gap.

Emily hugged herself. "There's no way they would leave that open if they had a kidnapped baby."

As Nash slowed the car, she grabbed the door handle. "I have to see. I have to see now."

"If he's in there, Emily, you'll give us away." But he'd slowed down the car anyway, and she didn't wait for him to stop.

She jumped out and did a little jog to keep from falling. She crept up to the warehouse door and dropped to her knees, tilting her head to listen. Nash's idling car was the only sound she heard.

She crawled toward the opening and ducked her head into the space. The high windows cast a gray light over the concrete floor of the warehouse, which contained a desk, a few chairs, a filing cabinet…and an empty car seat.

Chapter Twenty

Nash had kept the engine of the car running in case some-one came after Emily, but she hadn't moved since she'd crouched in front of that opening to peer into the ware-house.

As he watched her, his heart hammering in his chest, she dropped to the ground, flattening her body against the greasy asphalt.

An animal wailed somewhere, its plaintive cry echo-ing in the night. It took Nash a few seconds to realize that sound was emanating from Emily.

With the car still idling, he jumped out and launched himself at Emily, who was screaming and kicking her legs against the ground. He scooped her up from behind and cradled her against his chest as he collapsed against the side of the building.

He tried to soothe her by stroking her back. "It's all right. We'll find him. We'll get him back. We'll bring him home. We'll make him ours."

He didn't even know what he was saying. The words tumbled from his lips—all his hopes and dreams stripped bare.

She peeled away from him and pointed at the opening with tears streaming down her face. "It's there, Nash. The car seat—the empty car seat with the GPS we've been following. The GPS we've been pinning all our hopes on."

"Shh, shh." He rocked her back and forth in his arms as if she were Wyatt. "As long as we're here, let's take a look around. Crawl inside and I'll turn off the car."

She followed his suggestion robotically, rolling beneath the door.

Nash jumped up and ran to turn off the engine. Then he slithered into the opening to join Emily. His gut rolled when he saw the car seat in the corner.

He dropped down next to her where she sat on the floor, her legs curled beneath her. Draping his arm around her shoulders, he pulled her close. "Let's look at the positives. He was here. They brought him here and then transferred him to another location."

"Another location that could be anywhere." She bunched his shirt in her hand. "We have to go back, Nash. You have to go back to work and prep that file for deletion."

"Hold on. I'm not ready to admit defeat just yet." He lifted his eyes and scanned the room. "Let's search this building."

Immediately, her head popped up, and she peered into the four corners of the warehouse. "Do you see any security cameras?"

Patting her back, he said, "That's my girl. Get back in the zone."

He pushed off the floor and examined the four corners of the room. "The cameras aren't in any obvious places, and I can't see a space like this having hidden cameras. It's just a storage area."

Emily had crawled toward Wyatt's car seat and buried her face in it.

A few seconds later, just when he thought he'd have to search this warehouse by himself, she withdrew her head from the car seat and sprang to her feet. "You look through those boxes in the corner, and I'll search the desk."

He released a breath. He needed Emily's help, had been counting on it. "Right, Chief."

He strode to the boxes piled in the corner and looked in each one. Most were empty except for a few bits of popcorn packing material. He sniffed inside, but no particular odor hit him over the head.

He kicked the empty boxes he'd checked across the room. "You find anything?"

"Office materials, some invoices that have this address on them."

"Invoices for what?" Nash dived into the next stack of boxes. Address labels. He should check those address labels.

"Parts, mostly. Numbered parts for I don't know what."

Nash turned a box over and checked the label. It listed an address in Buckeye, a small town farther west along the 10 freeway—definitely not Lanier's glitzy Phoenix office building or ritzy home in Scottsdale. Why would he have shipments going to Buckeye?

Emily called across the open space, her voice taking on a slight echo. "Something was written on a pad of paper and left an impression on the sheet below."

"Shade it over with a pen." Nash grabbed the next box and read the same Buckeye address. That address appeared on the next box and the next.

"I got it!" Emily shouted. "It's an address, an address in…"

Nash said it with her. "Buckeye."

"That address has to have some significance, right? Lanier's not going to keep a kidnapped baby at his house or his office." Emily had been chattering nonstop on the hour drive to Buckeye, asking the same questions over and over, coming up with the same justifications.

Nash brushed his knuckles down her arm. "I think we're on the right track. Wyatt may not be at this location, either, but we're on his trail."

She jerked her head up and down. "We surveil the place first to make sure it's not a dead end like the warehouse. If Wyatt's there, we plan our infiltration and carry it out tonight."

"That'll work, and if Wyatt's not there—" he put a finger to her pouting lips "—we glean as much information as we can from that location, as we did from the warehouse. If there are people there, we get the information out of them—one way or another."

"I like the sound of that, Doc."

He managed to grin, despite his stiff face muscles. If they had to hop from place to place in some kind of demented scavenger hunt, he'd have to peel Emily off the floor.

"If you blink, you'll miss Buckeye." She scooted forward in the passenger seat, her phone cupped in her hand. "It's the next exit."

Again, a few stores and restaurants marked the entrance to Buckeye. Signs greeted them for a resort and golf course, an aquatics center, a historical museum and the Gillespie Dam Bridge. They drove past a big-box store and most of the main part of town before it led to the desert landscape.

Nash pulled to the side of the road. "How much farther?"

Glancing at the map on her phone, she said, "Just about five minutes."

"What do you see out there?" He tapped the windshield.

She sucked in her bottom lip and squinted at the wavy desert floor. "Not much."

"Exactly. We can't drive up to *not much* and not expect to be noticed."

"We have to readjust our plan." She dipped her chin to her chest and let out a sigh. "We go in at night just like we planned, but we'll have to assume Wyatt is there—whether he is or not."

He wedged a finger beneath her chin and tilted her head up. "We can do it. If someone is there without Wyatt, they'll never hear us. We'll turn around and sneak back out."

"Then what?" She sniffed but held her unshed tears in check.

"We'll formulate a plan B—we just don't know what that is yet." He pinched her chin. "You on board?"

"I'm on board with you, Nash." She grabbed his hand and kissed his knuckles. "I couldn't do any of this without you. Wouldn't want to. Whatever happens with Wyatt, wherever he winds up—whether that's with you or Jaycee's mother or, God forbid, some other father hiding in the woodwork—you're…my person."

"You mean that?" He laced his fingers with hers. "I'm not just Wyatt's guardian to you?"

He held his breath as she blinked at him. There. He'd put it out there—probably not the best time to do so, but he had to know.

Slowly, she brought their clasped hands to her chest and pressed them against her rapidly beating heart. "Is that what you thought? I know I used you to get close to Wyatt at the beginning and I even understand why you might not trust me after that, but you and Wyatt are not some kind of package deal to me."

He lifted one shoulder. "If I don't adopt Wyatt, there's no reason for you to come around."

"There's every reason—if you'll have me, and I don't know why you would. I'm a failed cop, a hothead, a liar and a kidnapper."

He kissed her hard on the mouth to stop the litany of her faults. He whispered against her lips, "I know all of that, and I still want you. What does that say about me?"

"It says, I must be your person, too." She curled a hand around his neck. "Did you have to know all of that before we went in to rescue Wyatt?"

"Maybe, but it wouldn't have made a difference to my resolve to find that baby and keep him safe—whether that's with me or someone else." He kissed her again. "Let's pass the time until nightfall by getting something to eat and packing the gear we'll need to hike through the desert. We have just a few hours until darkness descends out here and those people in the house or mobile home or tent will never see us coming."

THEY SAT IN a fast-food chain for almost an hour and a half, eating their chicken and drinking refills on their soda. Nobody paid any attention to them.

When they finished, they drove to some bathrooms at the head of a hiking trail, grabbed some bags from the trunk of the car and changed into all-black attire.

Emily removed her fake glasses so they wouldn't reflect any light and give them away under the cover of darkness. She pulled a black cap over her brunette wig, and Nash swapped out his baseball cap for a black beanie.

They each strapped a weapon around their waist, and Nash slipped his knife in the leg holster, which had worked so well in taking down Gustavo.

Emily packed their backpacks with extra guns, smoke

bombs, tear gas, burglary tools, GPS devices, small cameras and mics and whatever else she had from her PI stash. "If someone's monitoring the security cameras out here, they might think we're getting ready to take over a small country with this stuff."

Nash cracked a smile. "We have to be ready for anything. We have no idea what we're walking into."

Like their other foray into the desert and the makeshift trailer park, Nash parked the car a half a mile out from where they needed to be. They could see lights in the distance, and he said to Emily, "At least there's more than one house out there."

"Luck is on our side." She rubbed her hands together. "I feel it."

"At least the moon is on our side." He pointed skyward at the waxing crescent sliver hanging above them. It kept the night dark.

Emily held Nash's hand and touched her lips to his ear. "At least there's actually a road out here."

"Memorize the location and then shut off your phone. I have a penlight we can use that shuts off quickly—and doesn't ring or buzz."

She studied the display, the blue light highlighting her face, and then shut down her cell and pocketed it. "Got it."

Nash's nostrils twitched. The residents on the outskirts of Buckeye owned property and horses. He tapped Emily's arm. "I hope Lanier doesn't have horses. They'll sense our presence way before any human could."

She tugged on the strap of his backpack. "That's it."

He gazed across the road at a small house occupying a large lot with one other property behind it, like a mother-in-law quarters. The windows of the house stared out at them blankly, dark and silent, but a soft glow emanated from the small structure behind the main house.

"If they're here, I'm glad they're in the smaller house— easier to storm."

"Don't forget there might be a baby in there." She poked him in the back. "Easy on the storming."

They kept moving past the house and then circled around the side to close in on the cottage with the lights burning.

Nash stuck out a hand and Emily plowed into it, tripping to a stop. He pointed to his eye first and then a pinpoint of light moving up and down outside the front door of the occupied house. "Someone's smoking a cigarette out front."

"The guard?" Emily's breath came out in noisy, short spurts.

They crouched and moved in closer, ducking behind a fence that ringed the front property. Someone had parked a black Jag at a skewed angle in front of the smaller house, and Nash could make out figures moving behind the curtains on the window.

In a low voice, he asked, "Does that look like the window from the video chat?"

"It does. That's it." Emily pulled her gun from the holster around her waist. "He's in there, Nash. I can feel it."

Wrinkling his brow, he said, "What are all these cars? There's a truck around the side, that Jag and a BMW."

"That BMW belongs to Lanier." She tucked her fingers in the back of his waistband. "I'm sure of it. Why would he be out here?"

"And the Jag?"

"I don't have a clue. Seems a little high-end for a bodyguard or a nanny."

"We can't go in with all those people there, and the movement behind the curtain means it's not just the guard who's awake." Nash withdrew his own weapon. His muscles ached with tension.

The guard wouldn't move. As the guy lit another smoke, Nash hunkered down and got comfortable behind the fence post, Emily's quivering body beside his.

They both jumped when the front door of the cottage burst open, and a woman strode outside, her head turned over her shoulder, long, dark hair flying. Her shouting carried through the desert calm.

"I'm sick of it, Marcus. If that kid is yours, we're finished." She jangled a set of keys at the doorway. "No more of your ridiculous stories. How the hell would you be able to kidnap a Border Patrol agent's baby?"

Emily gasped. "Lanier's there. She must be his wife."

"And she's not happy." He pressed his shoulder against hers. "We need to take advantage of this."

Light flooded the front of the house, and a trim, dark-haired man with a distinct widow's peak charged after the woman. "Ming, don't be ridiculous. This opportunity fell into my lap, and I'm going to use it. I don't know anything else about that baby except his father is a Border Patrol agent who thinks he has something on me."

"Thinks?" Ming yanked open the door of the Jag. "I told you to steer clear of Las Moscas. There are easier ways to steal money."

"We have to get in there while they're occupied." Emily shifted away from him and went into a low crouch. "I'm going around the back so I can see who's inside."

"Be careful." Nash placed a hand on her back. "Don't do anything until Ming leaves. You'll hear her car. If Lanier goes after her, we might have a shot."

"We have to take it." Emily blended in with the night as she crept away.

Ming screamed an obscenity at her husband and slammed the car door after her. The Jag peeled away from the house in a cloud of dust.

Nash murmured, "One down. Go after her. C'mon, Lanier. Go after her."

Instead, Lanier turned to the guard and bummed a cigarette from him.

Nash's gaze tracked to the open doorway. Did Emily know Lanier hadn't followed his wife?

Nash dropped to the ground and leveled his weapon in the area of the two men smoking in front of the house. Before Lanier had turned the lights on, Nash couldn't take aim at the guard. Now he raised his weapon as high as he could get it from his position in the dirt. He could probably hit a thigh from here, but then what? He could just make out the bulge in the man's jacket that indicated he had a gun within reach.

And Lanier? A man like that probably never left the house unarmed.

Nash could hit either one, but the other would return gunfire...or worse. Nash didn't know what was going on in the house.

Then Emily decided for him.

A pop sounded from the house and both Lanier and the guard jerked their heads toward the open doorway, the guard reaching for his weapon.

Nash had to go with the man who could do more damage at this point. He jumped to a crouch and pulled the trigger. The report echoed through the night, and the guard fell to his knees, wailing as he clutched his leg, his gun forgotten on the ground beside him.

Nash immediately swung his gun to the left and squeezed off another shot. He missed. Lanier had dived to the ground and was clawing his way back toward the front door.

Could it be Lanier didn't have a gun? Had he even expected to be here?

The guard scrabbled for the weapon he'd dropped in the dirt, and Nash marched forward, leading with his weapon, aiming it at Lanier. On his way, he kicked the gun out of the guard's reach. Then he kicked the guard. Where the hell had Emily gone?

And then like some avenging goddess, Emily appeared in the doorway, both hands clutching a gun, the baby crying in the background.

"Take care of the guard." She aimed her .22 at Lanier, still on his belly. "Stop, or by God I'll shoot you in the dirt."

Nash lunged forward. "Who's behind you in the house, Emily?"

"One dead nanny."

"And Wyatt?"

"Scared but unharmed."

Lanier groaned. "What the hell are you doing here? How'd you know about this place?"

Emily stepped on Lanier's hand. "Does he have a weapon, Nash?"

"If he did, he didn't pull it out. Don't let him out of your sight. I'll take care of this guy."

Nash pocketed the guard's gun and then cuffed him, leaving him on his stomach. Then he rolled Lanier over and winced at the dust covering the man's custom-made suit. That had to hurt. He patted him down.

"He's clean. Can't believe you'd come out to a kidnapping unarmed, Lanier."

"I had no intention of coming out here." He growled. "Someone tipped off my wife."

Nash and Emily exchanged a look, and Emily said, "Not a bad idea, but we didn't think of it."

Not until Nash zip-tied Lanier's hands behind his back did he pull out his phone and dial 911. Once he placed the call, he finally took a breath. "These two aren't going anywhere. Let's see to our boy."

Emily spun around and rushed into the house with Nash hot on her heels.

A woman, the same one from the video chat, was sprawled on the floor, her hand inches from a weapon, blood pooling around her head.

Wyatt, gripping the side of a playpen, his face bright red, screamed when he saw them.

Emily shoved her gun in the waistband of her pants and whipped off her hat and dark wig. "It's all right, Wyatt. It's me. Everything's going to be okay now. You're coming home."

As Emily flashed her red hair, Wyatt blinked and sniffled. His wailing stopped, and he hiccupped once. Then he reached out his arms and babbled, "Mamamamama."

Epilogue

Emily watched as Nash signed the last form with a flourish.

He shook the pen at her. "Don't get too excited. We still have to wait for the family court date."

She threw herself against his chest anyway. "You're going to be the best father ever."

Nash's fellow agent Clay Archer popped a bottle of champagne while his wife, April, held out the first glass.

April squealed as the bubbly frothed over the side of the glass. "I can't believe our carefree bachelor is going to be a father."

"I wouldn't be able to do it without my live-in nanny."

Clay rescued the glass from his wife and handed it to Emily. "She's not going to be a live-in nanny forever. I talked to my buddy at Tucson PD, and while Emily's previous firing will be a blip on her application, it won't necessarily keep her off the force."

Nash accepted a champagne flute from April. "Are you sure you want to go back to being a cop, Emily?"

"I've practically been a cop the past few days. What are you talking about?" She tossed her fiery locks over one shoulder.

Nash rolled his eyes. "What we did? That was not police work."

"Then I guess Tucson PD has a thing or two to learn from me." She winked at Clay.

"To Nash and Wyatt, father and son." April raised her glass and four rims clinked. Then she took a small sip and said, "Who was it that killed Jaycee? I was so sad to hear the news. That girl never got a break."

"Crazy as it sounds—" Nash sat on a chair at the kitchen table "—with Lanier and the drug cartel guys after her, it was Brett that killed her. The cops discovered evidence that proves it. Apparently, she was pulling back on the idea to blackmail Lanier and Brett wouldn't have it."

"Aw, she wasn't such a bad mom after all." April downed the rest of her champagne, her eyes sparkling with tears.

"You and the underdog." Clay shook his head at his new wife. "So, Lanier is Wyatt's father?"

Emily pressed a hand against her stomach. She didn't want to think that a father could put his baby at risk. "Actually, we're not sure. A paternity test hasn't been ordered yet."

Clay grabbed the champagne bottle by the neck and topped off the four glasses. "Brett killed Jaycee, and Lanier's guy killed Brett?"

Nash answered, "Killed Brett, found the drugs Brett had stolen from Las Moscas and took the baby on Lanier's orders. By that time, Lanier had discovered that Jaycee left the baby with a Border Patrol agent and had found out that I also happened to be the one who'd received the financial information from Webb."

Clay shook his head. "I can't believe Webb turned like that."

"He'll lose his job, but he did have second thoughts. He's the one who dropped a dime on Lanier to his wife. I'm not sure what he hoped to accomplish by doing that, but her presence at that house in Buckeye is what gave us our chance to rescue Wyatt."

April drew her brows over her nose. "And who was the woman you...killed, Emily?"

"She was part of Lanier's criminal empire. She did whatever he told her to do—and that meant killing Wyatt instead of giving him up." She ran a hand through her hair. "When I broke in the back door of the house, she was going for a weapon."

Nash rapped on the kitchen table. "Emily's been cleared. It was a righteous shooting."

"As was yours." Clay clapped Nash on the shoulder. "It's good to have you back at work."

Denali came to the screen door and barked, and April lunged forward and hugged the husky. "Oh, I missed you, too—especially after I heard how these two treated you, shuttling you back and forth to Meg's, getting you poisoned."

"That dog is a hero." Emily aimed a kiss in Denali's direction.

April tipped her head. "Come out back with me, Clay. I want to dangle my feet in the pool."

"You didn't get enough water in Hawaii?"

April crooked her finger at him.

Clay shrugged, filled up his champagne glass and set the bottle between Nash and Emily on the table. "I think my wife wants me."

As the two of them wandered toward the pool, hand in hand, with Denali at their side, Emily scooted back her chair and sat in Nash's lap. "You're sure you want to take on the responsibility of a baby?"

"I don't have a choice."

Tilting her head, she traced a finger along his jaw. "I

thought I told you, you're stuck with me with or without Wyatt."

"I know that." He curled an arm around her waist and drew her close. "While I can't live without you, I also discovered I can't live without Wyatt in my life, either."

She cupped his face with her hands and planted a kiss on his lips. "Are you sure *Paradiso* doesn't mean *Paradise* in Spanish?"

"It has no meaning in Spanish, actually, just some gringo's butchered attempt at naming something in Spanish. Why?"

"Because I came out to Paradiso and found a man, a baby and a love I've never felt before. Seems like paradise to me."

Nash kissed her back and proved her point.

* * * * *

BADLANDS
BEWARE

NICOLE HELM

For the family secrets that never get told.

Chapter One

Rachel Knight had endured nightmares about the moment she'd lost the majority of her sight since she'd been that scared, injured three-year-old. The dream was always the same. The mountain lion. The surprising shock and pain of its attack.

Things she knew had happened, because what else could have attacked her? Because that was the truth that everyone believed. She'd somehow toddled out of the house and into the South Dakota ranchland only to have a run-in with a wild animal.

But in the dreams, there was always a voice. Not her father, or her late mother, or anyone who should have been there that night.

The voice of a stranger.

Rachel sucked in a breath as her eyes flew open. Her heart pounded, and her sheets were a sweaty tangle around her.

It was a dream. Nothing more and nothing less, but she couldn't figure out why twenty years after the attack she would still be so plagued by it.

Likely it was just all the danger that her family had been facing lately. As much as she loved the Wyatts, both sturdy Grandma Pauline and her six law enforcement grandsons who owned the ranch next door, their connection to a vicious biker gang meant trouble seemed to follow wherever they went.

And somehow, this year it had also brought her foster sisters into the fold time and again. Putting them in jeopardy along with those Wyatt brothers—and then culminating in true love, against all odds.

All of their tormenters were in jail now, and Rachel wanted that to be the end of it.

But something about the dreams left her feeling edgy, like the next dangerous situation was just around the corner.

And that you'll get thrust into the path of one of the Wyatt boys and end up...

Rachel got out of bed without finishing the thought. Just because four of her five foster sisters had ended up in love with a Wyatt didn't mean she was doomed. Because if she was doomed, so was Sarah. Rachel laughed outright at the thought.

Sarah was too much like Pauline. Independent and prickly. The thought of her falling for *anyone*, let alone a bossy Wyatt, was unfathomable. Which meant it was inconceivable for Rachel, too. She might not be prickly, but she had no designs on ending up tied to a man with a dangerous past and likely even more dangerous secrets.

So, that was that.

Rachel went through her normal routine of showering and getting ready for the day before heading downstairs. She didn't have to tap her clock to hear the time to know it was earlier than she usually woke up.

She was—shudder—becoming a morning person. Maybe she could shed that with the coming winter.

It was full-on autumn now. Twenty-three was creeping closer and while she knew that wasn't old, she was exactly where she'd always been. Would she be stuck here forever? In the same house, on the same ranch, nothing ever changing except the people around her?

Teaching at the reservation offered some respite, but she was so dependent on others. If she moved somewhere with more public transportation, she could be independent.

And yet the thought of leaving South Dakota and her family always just made her sad. This was home. She wanted to be happy here, but there was a feeling of suffocation dogging her.

Maybe *that* was why she kept having those dreams.

Weirdly, that offered some comfort. There was a reason, and it was just feeling a little quarter-life crisis-y. Nothing…ominous.

She held on to that truth as she headed downstairs. Inside the house she never used her cane, even after the fire this summer. They'd fixed the affected sections to be exactly as they had been, which meant she knew it as well as she knew Pauline Reaves's ranch next door, or her classroom, or Cecilia's house on the rez where Rachel stayed when she was teaching.

She wasn't trapped. She had plenty of places to go. As long as she didn't mind overprotective family everywhere she went.

Rachel stopped at the bottom of the stairs, surprised to hear someone in the kitchen. Duke's irritable mutterings alerted her to the fact it was her father before she could make out the shape of him.

Big, dark and the one constant presence in her life, aside from Sarah—who was the opposite of Duke. Small, petite and pale. She couldn't make out the details of a person's appearance, but she could recognize those she loved by the blurry shapes she could see out of her one eye that hadn't been completely blinded.

"Daddy, what are you doing?"

"What are you doing up?" he returned gruffly.

Rachel hesitated. While she often told her father everything that was going on with her, she tended to keep things that might worry him low-key. "I think my body finally got used to waking up early," she said, forcing a cheerfulness over it she didn't feel.

"Speaking of that…" He trailed off, approached her. His hand squeezed her shoulder. "Baby, I know you've got a class session coming up in a few weeks, but I think you should bow out. Too much has been going on."

Rachel opened her mouth, but no sound came out. Not teach at the rez? The art classes she held for a variety of age groups were short sessions and taught through the community rather than the school itself. She only instructed about twenty weeks out of the year, and he wanted her to miss a four-week session? When teaching was the only thing that made her feel like she had a life outside of cooking and cleaning for Dad and Sarah.

"Just this session," Dad added. "Until we know for sure those Wyatt boys are done bringing their trouble around."

It felt like a slap in the face, but she didn't know how to articulate that. Except an unfair rage toward the Wyatts.

Rachel took a deep breath to calm herself. She never let her temper get the better of her. Mom had impressed upon her temper tantrums would never get her what she wanted. "I don't have anything to do with their trouble."

"I might have said the same about Felicity and Cecilia, but look what they endured this summer. It won't do."

"Dad, teaching those classes—"

"I know they mean a lot to you. And I am sorry. Maybe you could do some tutoring out here?"

"I'm an adult."

"You're twenty-two. I know this is a disappointment, but I'm not going to argue about it." His hand slid off her shoulder and she heard the jangle of keys.

Rachel frowned at how strange this all was. Maybe she was still dreaming. "Are you *going* somewhere?"

There was a pregnant pause. "Just into town on some errands."

Her frown deepened. Sarah took care of almost all the errands now that it was just the two of them left living with Duke. Her father almost never ventured into town. And he never gave *her* unreasonable ultimatums.

"What's wrong, Dad?" she asked gravely.

"I want my girls safe," he said, and she heard his retreating footsteps as though that was that.

She fisted her hands on her hips. Oh, no, it was *not*. And she was going to get some answers. If they wouldn't come from her father, they'd just have to come from the source of the trouble.

TUCKER WYATT HAD always loved spending nights at his grandmother's house. Though he kept an apartment in town, he'd much rather spend time with his family at the Reaves ranch.

Until now.

He sighed. Why had he ever thought his current predicament was a good idea? He was *terrible* at keeping secrets.

Case in point, he was about 75 percent sure his brother Brady had figured out that Tucker *accidentally* stumbling into a situation where he could help save Brady's life from one of their father's protégés wasn't so accidental. That it was part of his working beyond his normal job as detective with the Valiant County Sheriff's Department.

And, since their youngest brother had been kicked out of North Star Group just a few months ago, it didn't take a rocket scientist to figure out what group Tucker might also be working for.

He was going to have to quit. The North Star Group had approached him because of his ties to Ace Wyatt, former head of the dangerous Sons of the Badlands, and a few of Tucker's cases that involved other high-ranking officials in the Sons.

Cases Tuck had been sure were private and confidential. But those words didn't mean much to North Star.

They'd wanted him on the Elijah Jones investigation, but then Brady and Cecilia Mills, one of the Knight girls, had gotten in the way.

The only reason Tucker hadn't been kicked out of North Star, as far as he could see, was because the North Star higher-ups didn't know his brother and Cecilia were suspicious of Tucker's involvement.

Which didn't sit right. Surely they didn't think his brother, a police officer, didn't have questions about a mysterious explosion that took Elijah Jones down enough to be restrained, hospitalized and, as of today, transferred to prison.

It had been a mess of a summer all in all, but things would assuredly calm down now. Ace was in maximum-security prison and Elijah was going to jail, along with a variety of his helpers.

But as long as Tucker was part of North Star and their continued efforts to completely and utterly destroy the Sons of the Badlands, he wouldn't feel totally settled *or* calm.

The back door that came into the kitchen swung open—not all that unusual. Grandma Pauline always had people coming and going through this entrance, but Tuck was surprised by the appearance of a *very* angry looking Rachel Knight.

She pointed directly at him, as if he'd done something wrong. "What's going on with my dad?"

Tuck stared at Rachel in confusion. She looked… pissed, which was not her norm. She was probably the most even-keeled of the whole Knight bunch.

While her sisters had all been fostered or adopted by Duke and Eva Knight, Rachel was their lone biological daughter. She didn't look much like her father—more favored her late mother, which always gave Tuck a bit of a pang.

His memories of his own mother weren't pleasant. He'd had Grandma Pauline, who he loved with his whole heart. Her influence on him and his brothers when they'd come to live with her meant the world to him.

But Eva Knight had been a soft, motherly presence in the Reaves-Knight world. Even if she'd been next door and not their mother, she'd treated them like sons. He'd never seen anything that matched it.

Except in her daughter. Tall and slender, Rachel had Eva's sharp nose and high cheekbones and long black hair. The biggest difference were the scars around Rachel's eyes, lines of lighter brown against the darker skin color on the rest of her face.

She could *see*, but not clearly. It always seemed to Tuck that her dark brown eyes were a little too knowing.

At least on *this* he wasn't keeping a secret—and failing at it. He had no idea why she'd demand of him anything about Duke Knight.

"Well?" she demanded as he only sat there like a deer caught in headlights.

"I haven't the slightest idea what's going on with your father. Why would I?"

"I don't know. I only know it has something do with *you*."

By the way she flung her arms in the air, he could only assume she didn't mean him personally but the whole of the Wyatts.

"Why don't we sit down?" He took her elbow gently to lead her to the table. "Back up. Talk about this, you know, calmly."

She tugged her elbow out of his grasp, clearly not wanting to sit. "He doesn't want me teaching this fall. He's worried about our safety. I know it doesn't have to do with *my* family. So, it has to do with yours."

Tucker held himself very still—an old trick he had down to an art these days. Letting his temper get the best of him as a kid had gotten the crap beaten out of him. Routinely.

Ace had told him his emotions would be the death of him if he didn't learn to control them. Hone them.

Tucker refused to *hone* them or be anything like his father. Which meant also never letting his temper boil over. He pictured a blue sky, puffy white clouds and a hawk arcing through both.

When he trusted his voice, he spoke and offered a smile. "I guess that's possible." He didn't allow himself to say what he wanted to. *Your sisters seem to be getting my brothers in trouble plenty on their own.* "I'm not sure specifically what it could be that would have Duke worried about you teaching at the rez. Did something happen? Maybe Cecilia would know."

"What would I know?" Cecilia asked, walking into

the kitchen. She was in her tribal police uniform, likely on her way to work. Though she was still nursing some wounds from her run in with Ace's protege and hadn't been cleared for active duty, she'd started in-house hours this week.

Though Duke and Eva Knight had fostered Cecilia, like Rachel she was a blood relation—Eva's niece. But she had been raised as "one of the Knight girls" as much Rachel's sister as her cousin.

"Has there been any new trouble at the rez that might make Duke nervous about Rach teaching her upcoming session?" Tucker asked.

Rachel scowled at him. "I wasn't going to bring her into it, jerk."

Cecilia's brow puckered. "I haven't heard anything. Dad doesn't want you teaching? Kind of late to have concerns about that, isn't it? Doesn't your session start the first of the month? And why didn't you want to bring me into it?"

Rachel sighed heavily. "Yes, it does, and yes, it's late." She looked pointedly in Tucker's direction, but when she spoke it was to Cecilia. "I wasn't going to bring you into it, because obviously it's not about *you*. I don't think it's about the rez, either. I think it's about the Wyatts."

"Look, Rach, I know the Wyatts are an easy target, no offense, Tuck. But if something bad was going on over here, Brady would have told me."

Because Cecilia and Brady now shared a *room* at his grandmother's house, a simple fact Tucker wasn't used to. Four of his brothers all paired off. And with the Knight girls of all people. It was sudden and weird.

But he just had to keep that to himself. Especially when Brady and Cecilia lived here now. "Well, I'll let you ladies figure this out. I've got a meeting to get to," Tucker said, quickly slipping past Rachel even as she began to protest.

Whatever was going on with Duke and Rachel was not his business, and he had to meet with his boss at North Star to nip this whole mission in the bud. It wasn't for him. He was a detective, and a damn good one, but he would never become adept at lying to his family.

He got in his truck, and drove to the agreed upon location. A small diner in Rapid City. Tucker had never met Granger McMillan, the head of the North Star Group. He'd been approached by field operatives and dealt with them solely.

Until now.

Tucker scanned the diner. Granger had said he'd know who he was, and Tucker had thought that was a little over-the-top cloak-and-dagger, but the large man in a cowboy hat and dark angry eyes sitting in the corner was *quite* familiar.

The man he was sitting across from turned in his seat, looked right at Tucker and gestured him over.

Tucker moved forward feeling a bit like he'd taken a blow to the head. Why was Duke here? What *was* this?

"You two know each other," the man, who could only be Granger McMillan, said. Not a question. A statement. "Have a seat, Wyatt. We have a lot to discuss."

Chapter Two

Rachel didn't get anywhere with Cecilia. Falling in love had certainly colored her vision when it came to the Wyatts. It was a disappointment, but one that was hard to hold on to when Brady had come in and he'd exchanged a casual goodbye kiss with her sister.

She would have never put Brady and Cecilia together, but when they were together, it seemed so *right*. Two pieces clicking together to mellow each other out a bit.

But even if that softened her up, Rachel wasn't ready to give up on being mad at the Wyatt brothers. So, she sought out someone she knew would back her up.

Sarah wiped her brow with the back of her arm. She'd been hefting water buckets into the truck to move them to a different pasture while Rachel laid out her case.

"Yeah, it's weird Dad took off, but what do you want me to do about it? I'm kind of running a ranch single-handedly here while he's doing whatever." Dev Wyatt's dogs raced around Sarah and Rachel. "My biggest concern is why I suddenly have two dogs. I did not consent to these dogs."

Rachel patted Cash on the head. Sarah talked a big game, but Rachel had overheard her just last night loving on the very dogs she was currently irritated over.

With a pang, Rachel missed Minnie, her old service dog. She knew she should start working on getting another one, or maybe even work on training her own, but it just made her sad still.

"What do you need help with?" Rachel asked, feeling guilty about unloading on her sister when she was so busy. The Knight ranch wasn't the biggest operation in South Dakota, but Duke and Sarah had to work really hard to make it profitable, and with all the danger around lately, hiring outside help felt like too big a risk.

"It's fine," Sarah replied, hopping off the truck bed and closing the gate. "Dev's coming over this afternoon to help. Maybe he'll take those stupid mutts back with him."

Even if Sarah could convince the dogs to go back with Dev, Rachel knew Sarah was all talk. She'd be bribing the dogs back over by suppertime.

"Well, I'll go make up some sandwiches for lunch. Want some pasta salad to go with it?"

"Yes, please."

Rachel walked back to the house over the well-worn path along the fence that led her to and from the stables. She moved through her normal chore of preparing lunch for Sarah and Dad, though Dad still wasn't home.

Rachel set the water to boil for pasta salad and frowned. It wasn't like her father to run errands on a ranch morning, even more unlike him to be gone for hours at a time. Cecilia had seemed concerned, but not enough to miss work. Plus, now she was going to tell Brady and he'd talk about it with his brothers and Rachel was fed up with Wyatts interfering.

Ughhh, those Wyatts. Rachel let herself bang around in the kitchen. She supposed Cecilia was a *little* right and Rachel was *maybe* projecting some feelings on them because it was safer than being upset with her father.

But Rachel didn't really care about being fair or balanced in the privacy of her own thoughts. Pasta salad and sandwiches made, she set them in the fridge and went to handling the rest of her normal chores, grumbling to herself the whole way.

Duke and Sarah were terrible housekeepers, so Rachel was often the default cleaner in the house. She didn't mind it, though. Having things to do made her feel useful. She tidied, swept, vacuumed, even dusted. She went upstairs and made the beds. Once she was done, she tapped her clock for the time.

The robotic voice told her it was nearly noon. Still no Sarah and even worse, no Dad. Rachel headed downstairs, wracking her brain for some reason her father would be gone this long without telling her.

She stopped halfway down the stairs. A horrible thought dawned on her. What if he was sick? Like Mom. What if he was at the doctor getting terrible news he wanted to hide?

The thought had tears stinging her eyes. She couldn't do it. She couldn't lose her mom and her dad before she was even twenty-five. Before she found a significant other. Before she had kids. Dad had to be around for that. Mom couldn't, so Dad *had* to be.

Rachel marched toward his room, propelled by fear masked as fury. If something was wrong, she'd find evidence of it there.

She stepped inside. He'd moved down to the main floor with Mom when she had gotten sick. He'd never moved back upstairs. Sometimes Rachel worried about him wallowing in the loss. Now she worried the same fate was waiting for him.

No. I refuse.

She tidied up, deciding it was an easy excuse to poke around his things. Which wasn't out of the norm. When she deep-cleaned the house, she took care of Dad's room. She didn't find anything out of the ordinary, though she wouldn't be able to read any of the medicine bottles to tell if there was something off there— but based on the number and size there didn't seem to be anything more than the usual over-the-counter painkiller and heartburn medicines.

She'd need Sarah to read the labels to be sure, but then she'd have to bring her sister into this and Sarah had enough to worry about with the ranch.

She pondered the dilemma as she made Dad's bed. As she adjusted the pillows, she felt something cool and hard. She reached out and touched her fingers to the object. It was a black blob in her vision, but she quickly realized she was touching a gun.

Rachel stood frozen in place for a good minute, pillow held up in one hand, her other hand grasping the gun. It wasn't that her father didn't have firearms. He had a few hunting rifles, kept in the safe in the basement. He had one hung above the back door because after reading the *Little House* books to her, he'd decided that's where one needed to go.

But this was a small pistol. Like the ones the Wyatt boys carried when on duty. And it was under his pillow. Carefully she picked it up and felt around some more, getting an idea of the gun model before she checked the chamber.

Loaded, which seemed very unsafe in his *bed*. Rachel didn't know what to make of it, but his whole talk about safety sure made it seem like he was worried about some kind of threat.

What on earth kind of threat would Duke be facing?
"Rachel?"

She nearly dropped the gun at Sarah's voice. Luckily, it came from the kitchen, not from right next to her. She quickly slipped the gun back under the pillow, left the bed unmade and tiptoed into the hallway.

"Coming!" she called, trying to steady her beating heart. Sarah didn't need to know about this. Not just yet. First, Rachel had to figure what was going on.

"So, WHAT YOU'RE telling me..." Tucker raked his fingers through his hair, not knowing whether to look at Duke or Granger "...is Knight ranch was a witness protection hideout."

Duke's gaze was patently unfriendly, which was odd coming from a man he'd always looked up to. Tucker had grown up in a biker gang surrounded by nothing but bad. Ever since he'd gotten out, Duke had been there. Grandma Pauline and Eva had been mother figures. Duke had been the father figure.

But Duke clearly didn't want Granger letting Tucker in on his past. His *true* identity. How did Duke Knight of all people have a *true* identity?

"And the girls don't know?"

"Why would they know?" Duke asked, his voice a raspy growl. "I left that old life behind over thirty-five years ago. Met Eva two years later, and we built this family on who I was *now*, not who I was *then*. Then was gone, and has been for a very long time."

"A cop." Duke Knight had been a cop. A cop who, in his first year on duty, had taken down a powerful family of dirty police officers. And then had a bounty put on his head and had to be moved into WITSEC.

A ranch in the middle of nowhere South Dakota sure

made sense, and feeling safe enough to find a wife and build a family here made even more sense. But Tucker didn't know how to accept it.

"Grandma Pauline... She had to know."

Duke shrugged. "Don't know if she did or didn't, but Pauline never asked any questions. Never poked her nose into my business." He looked pointedly at Granger.

Granger, who was here for a current reason. That somehow involved Tucker. "Why would this group want to come after you when thirty-five years have passed? Wouldn't it be water under the bridge?"

"You're Ace Wyatt's son and you really have to ask that question?"

Tuck was chastened enough at that. When fear was currency, the years didn't matter so much. Only proving your strength, your ability to destroy did.

Tucker turned to face Granger across from him at the diner table. "And how does this connect to North Star?"

"We've been working under the assumption Vince MacLean was casing your grandmother's ranch because of the Wyatt connection, which is why we brought you in," Granger said. Facts Tucker was well aware of.

Granger was a tall man, dressed casually. A layperson might not think anything of someone like him, sitting in a diner, having a friendly cup of coffee. But Tucker saw all the signs of someone on alert. The way his gaze swept the establishment. The way he filed away everyone who entered or exited.

"We couldn't quite figure his role out. But the information you've passed along to us, plus what we already had, started to point to the fact there might be a different target." Granger nodded toward Duke. "We started looking into not just who Vince was directly reporting to, but who the people he was reporting to passed information to and so on. What we found is a connection to the Vianni family."

Tucker didn't need to be led to the rest. "Who were the family of dirty cops you took down?"

Duke nodded.

"We started digging into the family, into possible connections, and figured out Duke's. Since he was the target, we brought him in. And now we're bringing you in. The Sons connecting to the Vianni family is an expansion. It gives both groups more reach, and makes them stronger than they were."

"The Sons have been weakened."

"You can keep throwing their leaders in jail, Wyatt, but that doesn't end their infrastructure or ability to regroup."

"What does?" Tucker returned.

Granger's gaze, which had been cool and controlled up to this point, heated with fury. But his voice remained calm as he spoke. "We need Duke to help us. Which means he has to disappear for a little while. Duke's not too keen on leaving his ranch or his daughters."

"Nor should he be," Tucker snapped, his own temper straining. "Have you been paying attention these past few months? Duke being gone doesn't make the threat go away." He turned to Duke, who was sitting next to him in the booth. "You're leaving them to be a new target, that's all. And you—" Tucker faced Granger "—you're caring about your own North Star plots and plans without thinking about innocent lives."

Tucker didn't wilt when Granger lifted his eyebrows regally. "Watch your step, boy. I know more about protecting innocent lives than you could even begin to imagine. But Duke is our key between the Sons and the Viannis, and without him, more innocent people get hurt. A lot more."

Tucker whipped his gaze back to Duke, too angry to be chastened by Granger's words. "You didn't tell any of us? This whole time you knew you were a target and you didn't think to give us a heads-up so we could help?"

"I didn't want to bring you or your brothers into it. I don't want my daughters brought into it, and that's all your brothers seem capable of doing." Duke nodded toward Granger. "His father is the reason I have the ranch I do. The life I do. When Granger here came to me... I might not like it, but I owe the McMillan family, and I owe it to the other people the Viannis have hurt after I bowed out."

Tucker snorted in derision. Maybe he should have felt sorry for Duke, but all he could think about was Rachel already coming to him worried about her father. "You think your girls are going to buy you *leaving*?"

"It'll be your job to convince them," Granger said matter-of-factly, like that was a mission anyone could accomplish. He pushed a manila envelope over to Tucker. "This includes a letter to the daughters from Duke, a packet of fake vacation itinerary. You'll take it to Sarah and Rachel and say you found it—where and how is up to you." Then Granger slid a phone across the table. "You'll also take this. It's been programmed with your cell number, as well as a secret number that will allow contact with someone at North Star directly. We'll reach you through this if we need you. It's also got access to security measures set up around the Reaves and Knight ranches, thanks to your brother. He has no idea you have access to any of this, and no one in your family or Duke's can know, either. Is that understood?"

Tucker looked at the folder and the phone. None of

this made sense, and how on earth was he going to convince Sarah and Rachel—and the rest of either family for that matter—that Duke, who'd barely left the ranch even for errands throughout all their lives, was going on vacation. Suddenly, and without warning. "You can't be serious."

"Oh, I'm deadly serious, Wyatt. And so is this."

Chapter Three

"Something has to be wrong." Rachel stood in Grandma Pauline's kitchen, Sarah next to her. She could hear the dogs whining outside, but Grandma Pauline did not allow dogs in her kitchen.

"If he'd come home before dinner, I wouldn't think *too* much of it. But he still isn't back and he won't answer his cell," Sarah said, wringing her hands together.

"I called Gage," Brady offered. "He's going to head over to Valiant County and see if he can sweet talk them into putting some men on it before the required hours for a missing person. Then he'll look himself. Cecilia said she's going to ask around town after her shift, too. If he's around, one of them will find him."

"What do you mean *if*?" Sarah demanded. "Where else would he go?"

Which echoed the fear growing inside of Rachel. "Do you think something happened to him?" she asked, straight out. Because if Brady Wyatt thought something had happened to him, his instincts were most likely right.

Brady's response was grim. "Duke left the ranch of his own volition, but you were concerned about him being worried about danger. Maybe there's something he wasn't telling us."

The door opened and Tucker entered. Aside from Brady and Gage, Rachel could tell the difference in the Wyatt brothers by general shape. Even though they were all tall and broad, they had a different presence about them.

If she took a lot of time, she could figure out Gage and Brady, but being twins made it a bit more difficult, and she could always tell from their voices.

But Tucker was always a slightly…lighter presence. His hair wasn't so dark, his movements were always a little easier. But something about the way he entered the kitchen now was all wrong.

"Hey, all. What's going on?"

Rachel frowned. He did *not* sound his usual cheerful self. Something was weighing on him, and that was clear as day in his voice.

"Duke's missing," Sarah said plainly.

"Missing?"

"We can't find him. He hasn't come back to the ranch since this morning."

"You're sure he's not out in the fields?" Tucker asked.

"No. I'm worrying everyone because I didn't look around the ranch," Sarah replied sarcastically. "Don't be an ass, Tuck."

"I'm sure there's a rational explanation. If you're all worried, I can—"

"We've already got Gage and Cecilia on it," Brady said.

There was something off about Tucker. Something… odd in the way he delivered his responses.

"Oh, I picked up your mail," he offered as if it he'd just remembered. "It was falling out of the box."

Rachel assumed he put it into Sarah's hands before he moved over to the table. "I didn't have a chance to get dinner. You got any leftovers, Grandma?" He moved farther into the kitchen, still acting…strangely. But no one else seemed to notice, so maybe she was taking her worry about Dad and spreading it around.

There was a thud and the flutter of papers. "There's a letter from Dad," Sarah screeched. The sound of the envelope being ripped open had Rachel moving closer even though she wouldn't be able to read it.

Sarah read aloud. "Dear girls, I know you probably won't be able to believe this, but I've decided it's time for a break. If I don't go right now, I know I never will. I've included my vacation itinerary so you don't worry, but this is something I need to do for myself. Take good care of each other. Love, Dad."

"There's no possible way," Rachel croaked, panic hammering at her throat. "Maybe he wrote that, but not because he wanted to take a vacation. Not of his own volition." Nothing would drag her father away from the ranch, away from his daughters. Not even temporarily.

"And he'd never leave without someone here to help me," Sarah added, her voice uncharacteristically tremulous. "I can't handle the ranch on my own."

"We'll work it out," Dev said gruffly. "Don't worry about the ranch. Brady—"

"We'll tell Gage the latest development," Brady said before Dev could instruct him. "He can—"

"Let me look into it," Tucker said. "I'm the detective. We don't need to get Valiant County involved or have Gage and Cecilia asking around."

"We can *all* look into it," Brady said evenly.

"Yeah, but if we all start looking into it, and something *is* wrong, we've alerted everyone we know. But if I look into it, pretend like I'm just researching one of my cases, we might be able to unearth whatever trouble there actually is without causing suspicion. *If* there's any trouble at all."

"My father did not go on a *vacation*. Period. Let alone without telling us. What kind of trouble would he be in?"

"I don't know, Rach. Let me look into it. If there's trouble, we'll find it."

"Yes, you're very good at finding it," she replied caustically.

"Now, now," Grandma Pauline said, and though the words might have been gentle coming from most grandmothers, from Pauline it was a clear warning.

Rachel blew out a breath.

Tucker's voice was very calm when he spoke, and she could easily imagine him using that tone with a hysterical person on a call. He would promise to take care of everything no matter how upset the person was.

She swallowed at the lump of fear and anxiety in her throat. Tucker could do that because he wanted to help people. She wanted to blame him for all the trouble right now, but deep down she knew it wasn't his fault or his brothers' faults.

The Wyatts were good men who wanted to do the right thing, and she had to stop sniping at them. Division was not going to bring her father home.

"What can we do? While you're looking for him?" she asked of Tuck. "We can't just sit around waiting."

"Unfortunately, I think you *should* sit and wait. If there's danger, and we're not sure there is, we want to know what kind before we go wading in. What we do know is that even if he is in danger, he's alive. He left of his own accord. He's made *some* kind of decision here."

"He could have been threatened to leave," Sarah

pointed out. "Blackmailed. Though over what I don't have a clue."

"Yes," Tucker agreed equitably. "If that's the case, someone wanted him to leave of his own accord. Think how easy it would be to ambush a man like Duke. How often he's out in the fields or barn or stables alone. This is more than Duke being in life-threatening danger. It's deeper and more complicated. *If* it's anything other than a mid-life crisis."

Rachel scoffed simultaneously with Sarah.

"He's not wrong," Grandma Pauline said. "Duke hasn't been himself lately. Wouldn't be unheard of for someone in their late fifties to have a bit of a personal crisis."

Rachel felt like the world had been upended. Why were her and Sarah the only ones freaking out about this? How could Grandma Pauline stand there and say her father was having a *personal crisis*?

"I'll head back into the office right now. Get the ball rolling on an investigation. I'll update you all in the morning."

No one spoke, not to argue with Tucker or demand more answers. Rachel had to believe they were in as much shock as she was. This couldn't actually be happening.

And Tucker wasn't acting right. She couldn't put her finger on what was wrong, just that something *was*. She heard him exit, the normal conversation picking back up. Sarah and Dev discussing ranch concerns, Brady on the phone with Jamison, the oldest Wyatt brother, giving him an update, and Grandma Pauline fussing around the kitchen cleaning up.

Didn't any of them feel it? Didn't any of them... She shook her head and slipped out the kitchen door.

She couldn't make out Tucker's shape in the low light of dusk, but she didn't hear a car engine so he hadn't made it that far yet.

She took a few steps forward until she could make out the shape of him. "What aren't you telling us?"

She could tell he turned to face her, but she didn't have the ability to read his expression. Still there was a lot in that long careful pause.

"If there was anything I could tell you to make sense of this, I would."

She wasn't sure why that made her want to cry instead of yell at him. Which left her unsure of what to say.

He stepped close, then his hands were giving hers a squeeze. "I'm going to do everything I can to bring him home safe, Rach. Whether he's in trouble or not. You believe that, don't you?"

She wasn't sure what she believed in the midst of all this insanity, but in her heart she knew Tucker was a good man and that he loved her father. Maybe none of this made sense, but he wouldn't promise to do everything he could and then not.

"Yeah, I do."

He gave her hands one last squeeze, released them. "Good. I'll have an update in the morning. I promise." Then he left her standing in the cool evening, unsure of how to work through all her emotions, and all her fears.

IT WAS A lot of work. Not looking for Duke, and trying to undo all his brothers had already set in motion. Tucker couldn't very well have the entire Valiant County Sheriff's Department out searching for Duke. Even if North Star hid Duke or used him for whatever their plan was, having people sniffing around just wasn't going to be good.

Tucker scrubbed his hands over his face. Granger hadn't given him much to go on. Just that he had to make sure the Knights thought Duke was on vacation while they did the hard work.

When North Star had first approached Tucker, it had been through a lower operative. The woman had told him they had reason to believe Vince MacLean was gathering intel on the Wyatts, and to do whatever he could to find out who Vince was reporting to.

It had been a simple mission, straightforward and in Tuck's own best interest to help his family. And it had, in fact, helped his family a great deal as his following Vince had led him straight to Brady and Cecilia when they were in trouble.

Tucker locked up his office and headed for his car. He'd have liked to head back to the ranch, but it was two in the morning and he needed to catch a few hours of sleep.

He didn't know how he was going to face Rachel. He hadn't lied to her. He *would* do everything he could to bring Duke safely home. Tucker just didn't know how much of a say he had in things. But the one thing he *did* know? That he was never going to convince her Duke had taken a vacation of his own accord.

He headed for his car. The night was dark, the station mostly deserted. Still, the feeling of being watched had him slowly, carefully resting his hand on the butt of his weapon strapped to his belt.

"No need, Wyatt."

He didn't recognize the female's voice, but when she materialized out of the dark, he recognized her as the woman who'd originally contacted him about North Star.

"What now?" he muttered. Instead of stopping, he kept moving for his car. He wasn't too keen on being accommodating to the North Star crew right now, considering they were making his life unduly complicated. He kept one hand on his gun for good measure.

"There's chatter. Some people know Duke's missing."

"Yeah. Like his entire family? They're worried about him, because no one in their right mind is going to believe Duke Knight left South Dakota to go on *vacation*."

"Like the Sons. From what I've been able to gather, they think the Viannis got him. While they think that, there are certain parties who are going to be interested in friends of the Wyatts being unprotected, so to speak."

Tuck tossed his bag in the passenger side of his car. He was tired and irritable and this wasn't helping. "And who's fault would that be?"

"Look, I'm trying to be friendly here. I know enough about the setup from your brother. Someone needs to keep an eye on the Knight ranch. Just because the Viannis are focused on Duke, doesn't mean the Sons won't focus on a weakness in the Wyatts' armor if they can find one. Last I heard, the Knights are a weakness."

"I'm pretty sure I told your boss to be just as worried about Duke Knight's daughters as he was about Duke. He didn't seem too concerned."

"Yeah, because his concern is the mission."

"And what's your concern?"

She muttered something incomprehensible under her breath. "Watch their backs, huh?"

"Why don't you go talk to my brother about it?"

"Because your brother got kicked out, pal. You, on

the other hand, are in the thick of things. So, grow a pair." She melted back into the dark shadows before he could retort.

Which was for the best. No use taking his nasty mood out on someone who was trying to help.

Especially when she was right. Sarah and Rachel alone in the Knight house, even with Dev's dogs, just wasn't a good idea. He wouldn't be surprised to hear that Cecilia had decided to spend the night over there herself, and she was trained law enforcement.

She'd also been injured not that long ago, and Brady still wasn't on active duty due to his injuries. They'd saved an innocent child from being taken into the Sons, but they hadn't come out unscathed.

So, sending him over there to spend the night with Cecilia wasn't enough of a comfort. Dev would be helping out with ranching duties, but he'd been a cop for all of six months before he'd sustained serious injuries that left him with a limp.

Thanks to dear old Dad.

Jamison and Cody both lived in Bonesteel, and while he knew they'd all pitch in to help, it'd bring Cody's young daughter and Jamison's even younger sister-in-law into the fray and they deserved to be as far from danger as possible after what they'd endured when Ace Wyatt had come after them and their families. The only other option was Gage and Felicity, who both worked almost two hours away. Not to mention, Felicity was pregnant.

Which left him. He didn't mind that. He was happy to protect whomever needed protecting. It was the convincing the women involved they *needed* protecting that was going to be the headache. On top of the one he already had.

Tucker slid into his car. There was no going to his apartment now. Even if it was the middle of the night, he needed to head to the ranches. He had to figure out a way to convince Rachel and Sarah it was best if he stayed with them for a while.

As he drove through the thick of night, he considered just telling everyone the truth. What could the North Star Group do to him? He didn't owe them silence. And with the whole Wyatt clan in on things, wasn't it possible they could help take down the Viannis and the Sons themselves?

The list of reasons not to have his brothers spend the night at the Knight house went through his head. Because for all the same reasons, it didn't feel right to bring them into this. They'd built new lives, survived their own near-death injuries. And what had he done? All this time, all these months of danger and threats from Ace and the Sons, and he'd *investigated*. Between his brothers and their significant others, they'd all been tortured, shot, temporarily blinded and more.

Tucker had fought off a few Sons goons, but had mostly emerged unscathed.

So, no, he couldn't tell them. It was his turn to take on the danger, take on the Sons. His turn to protect his family, and the Knight girls.

Whether they wanted protecting or not.

Chapter Four

Rachel woke up from the nightmare in a cold sweat. The recurrence so soon after the last one made sense. She was stressed and worried. Of course, she'd have terrible dreams to go along with those terrible feelings.

But there'd been no mountain lion in this nightmare. She sat up and rubbed her eyes and then hugged herself against the chill.

The mountain lion had been a man. She could still visualize him. Blue eyes glowing, burn scars all over the side of one face. She could hear his voice in her head, rough and growly with an odd regional American accent she couldn't place.

She shuddered. It was a *dream*. Yeah, a creepy one that was still lodged in her head, but it was fiction. Dreams weren't real.

Though this one had felt particularly, scarily real.

She got out of bed even though it was still dark. She didn't bother to check the time. Too early. She'd just go downstairs and get a drink of water. Hopefully, it would help settle her.

She was safe. Maybe Dad wasn't, but she was. Here in this house, with Cecilia and Sarah down the hall. Though she felt a little guilty that Cecilia had insisted on spending the night since Brady had to stay at Grandma Pauline's due to his leg injury.

She wished she could say her and Sarah could handle it, but while they could manage anything around the ranch, they weren't trained law enforcement, and they didn't have any background or experience in fighting off bad guys.

Cecilia did. In fact, *everyone* else did. Rachel blew out a breath as she tiptoed downstairs. She stopped at the bottom, frowning at the odd sound. Like the scrape of a chair against the floor.

Her breath caught, pulse going wild as panic filled her. Someone was in the kitchen. Someone was—

"What are you doing up?"

Tucker's voice. Coming from the kitchen table. The *Knight* kitchen table. Long before sunrise.

"What are you doing here? It's…dark still."

"Honestly? I got a little tip that I shouldn't be letting you two be here alone. A friendly tip, but still. I thought it was better if I headed over here rather than stayed the night in my apartment."

"You didn't need to do that. Cecilia's here. We have our law enforcement contingent."

"Good." But he made no excuses to leave. Instead, they stood there, together in the dark.

"Which means you don't have to stay," she continued. She wasn't sure why she'd said that. It was a nice thing he was doing, and she should be thanking him. But she was braless in her pajamas and Tucker Wyatt was in her kitchen. She crossed her arms over her chest.

"Unfortunately, I don't agree."

She scowled in his general direction, whether he could see it or not. "A penis is not the protector of womankind, Tucker."

He sighed heavily. "I never said it was, but Cecilia is still recovering from her injuries. It's good she's here. She'll be able to notice and address a threat, but will she be able to neutralize it? No one heard me pick the lock, did they?"

"You picked the lock?" she screeched.

He immediately shushed her, which did not do anything to make her feel better about the situation. "It's just a precaution. Regardless of what's going on with Duke, the Sons know he's missing. We don't want them looking at you as easy pickings."

"Because I'm blind," she said flatly.

"Because we don't know where this threat is coming from, if it's coming. I don't think Sarah should be out in the fields alone, and I don't think you should be in this house alone. And before you lecture me about sexism, it isn't about your gender, it's about numbers. When there's danger, two is better than one."

"Then I can accompany Sarah out in the fields, and *you* aren't needed."

"What do you have against me, Rach?" His voice was soft. Not sad exactly, but there was a thread of…hurt in his voice. "I thought we were friends, but you seem to have something very specifically against *me* right now."

"I don't."

"You're sure acting like you do."

"I…" She felt like an absolute jerk, which wasn't fair. She wasn't acting like she had anything against Tucker. He was just…

She felt him approach and his hands rested on her shoulders. "I know it's a tough time. I'm not trying to make it tougher. I'm honestly just trying to help. Can you let me do that?"

There was no way to say no and maintain that she

was a reasonable human being, which she *was*. Plus, he was giving her shoulders a squeeze—a kind, reassuring gesture. He smelled like stale coffee and she wondered if he'd been up all night worrying over Duke and his girls.

It made her heart pinch. Here he was, doing all he could to find out what was going on with her father, and she was taking out her fear and anxiety on him. She sighed. "Of course I can," she said gently. "I'm not trying to be difficult. I'm just scared."

He gave her a light peck on the temple. It was something he'd always done. Tuck was the sweet Wyatt brother, if you could call any of them sweet. He had an easy affectionate streak, and he often comforted with a hug or a casual, friendly kiss.

But his hands lingered, even if his lips didn't. Rachel didn't know why she noticed…why she felt something odd skitter along her skin.

Then he cleared his throat, his hands dropping as he stepped away, and she didn't have to think about it any longer.

"I think it'd be best if I stay here," he reiterated. His voice had an odd note to it that disappeared as he continued to speak. "It'll help my investigation, and after the fire, we can't be too careful about threats that can get through Cody's safety measures. Everything I've found points to Duke leaving of his own accord."

Before Rachel could object to that, Tucker rolled right on.

"I'm not saying he left because he wanted to. I'm just saying he did it on his own two feet. No one dragged him away. Even if he didn't take a vacation like he's saying, there might be a reason. One that doesn't mean he's in immediate danger. It could be he's trying to protect you girls."

"You don't really think that."

"Actually, so far? It's exactly what I think. You don't have to agree with me, Rach. You just have to give me some space to stay here and keep an eye on things, and maybe go through Duke's room."

"And if I say no?"

"Well, I'll go through the rest of your sisters until someone agrees."

She huffed out an irritated breath. Of course he would, and one of her sisters would. But he could have barged in there and done it without any permission, so she would have to give him points for that. "I guess you could stay in his room, and if you poke around, it wouldn't be any of my business."

"Great," he said, sounding a mixture of pleased and relieved. "Hey, you should go back to bed. It's three in the morning."

"Yeah, I just came to get a glass of water."

"Here, I'll get it for you."

"I'm perfectly capable of getting my own water, Tucker."

"I know you are, but there's nothing wrong with letting someone who's closer to the glasses and the sink do something for you, Rach."

Rachel didn't know what to say to that, even when he handed her the glass of water. So she could only take it, and head back upstairs, with those words turning over in her head.

TUCK WAS NOT in a great mood. Usually when he felt this edgy, he kept himself far away from his family. He wouldn't take his temper out on anyone. Ace Wyatt might be his father, but he didn't have to be like the man. He got to choose who he was and how he treated people.

He was very afraid he wouldn't treat anyone very nicely in this mood, and quite unfortunately he had to deal with Wyatts and Knights all day long.

Tuck hated lying to his brothers. He didn't relish lying to the Knights, either, and last night with Rachel he'd felt like a jerk. She was afraid for Duke and Tucker knew he was fine, but couldn't tell her.

Then there was that odd reaction to touching her bare shoulders and inappropriately noticing that Rachel's pajamas were not exactly *modest*…

Nope. He wasn't thinking about that. Rachel was and always had been off-limits. Him and Brady had always felt like any attraction to a Knight girl was disrespectful to Duke. A good, upstanding man, great rancher, excellent, loving father, helpful and compassionate neighbor. Next to Jamison, Duke had been the Wyatt brothers' paragon of what a man should be.

Of course, Brady had broken that personal rule. Now here he was, in love with Cecilia. Planning a future together once they were healed.

Tucker shook his head. Brady might be the most strict rule follower Tucker knew, but that didn't mean Brady slipping up on one personal tenant meant Tucker would. Or could.

He focused on the fact Brady was coming up to the Knight house, which no doubt meant Tucker was in store for a lecture from his older brother.

"You look rough," Brady commented, limping toward the porch where Tucker was standing, trying to get his temper under control.

"Yeah, you, too," he replied, then immediately

winced. Brady had been shot in the leg just last month. He'd made great strides—this wound healing a lot quicker than his previous gunshot wound had.

Because Brady had been beaten to hell and back over the course of this dangerous summer, and what had Tucker done? Not a damn thing. "I updated Cody."

"I'm not here for an update." He took the stairs with the help of his cane. "I'm here to see Cecilia before she heads in to the rez."

"Shouldn't she be going to you?"

"Walking is part of my physical therapy, Tuck," Brady replied mildly, standing in front of him and putting all his weight on one leg. "What crawled up your butt?"

Tucker scraped his hands over his face. "Running on no sleep. Sorry. Dev's out with Sarah, but I've got to stick close for Rachel. Making me a little antsy."

"How are you going to stick around when you've got work?"

"I've got a call with the sheriff this morning about doing some remote work, and leaving field work to Bligh for the time being."

His brother frowned. "I can help out around here. Just because of the bum leg doesn't mean I can't be of some use."

Tucker could easily read Brady's frustration with being out of commission. He couldn't imagine the feelings of futility, especially since Brady had been dealing with months of healing, not just weeks. "A lot of it's just research and following leads from the computer. Once I've got a decent thread to tug on, I'll share it with you." Which ignored the fact his brother could help with the watching out around the ranch, but Tuck didn't want to go there.

Brady nodded, then studied him a little too closely for Tuck's comfort. "I'm trusting you, Tuck." He nodded toward the house. "I always have. It hasn't changed."

Tucker shoved his hands in his pockets. He knew Brady was referencing last month when Tucker had called in backup to get Brady and Cecilia out of a dangerous situation. There'd been some aspects of that rescue mission that Tucker had had to lie about to keep his involvement with North Star a secret, and he knew Cecilia hadn't trusted him at all. But when push had come to shove, Brady had. It meant a lot. "Well, good. You should."

"I haven't said anything, and I won't. But maybe you could talk to Cody…"

Tucker couldn't let him finish his sentence, since he had a feeling it was about North Star. "This is my thing, Brady. Let it go."

Brady opened his mouth to say something, but the door behind them swung open.

"I thought I heard you." Cecilia came out in her tribal police uniform, smiling at Brady. She crossed to Brady first, gave him a kiss.

Tucker looked away from the easy affection. It wasn't that it bothered him. His brothers deserved that kind of good in their lives, and if they were happy, Tuck didn't have any problem with their choice of significant other.

He just didn't really want to…*watch* it. It caused some uncomfortable itch. At first when Jamison and Cody had hooked up with their ex-girlfriends, both Knight fosters, he hadn't felt it. But something about Gage and Brady falling for Felicity and Cecilia respectively made things…weird.

Rachel stepped out onto the porch, and Tucker's gut tightened with discomfort. Something he *refused* to acknowledge when it came to Duke's daughter who was a good eight years younger than him.

"Who all needs breakfast? I'm making omelets."

"I got fifteen minutes before I need to head out," Cecilia said. She patted Brady's stomach. "Don't tell me you actually snuck away from Grandma Pauline without getting stuffed full of breakfast."

"Mak was doing his crawling demonstration. Grandma was distracted, so I made a run for it." He had his arm casually wrapped around Cecilia's waist. An easy unit where one hadn't been before. They'd helped Cecilia's friend keep her infant son, Mak, safe, and now both lived at Grandma Pauline's, as well.

"All right. Tucker, since you're our sudden houseguest, you can come help me with setting the table." Rachel smiled sunnily, then turned back into the house.

Cecilia and Brady's gazes were on him, a steady, disapproving unit.

"Whatever is going on, she needs to stay far, far away from it," Cecilia said solemnly. "I'll give you the space to handle it, Tuck, because it seems that whatever's going on needs that, but I'm holding you personally responsible if anything happens to Rachel."

"She's not so helpless as all that," Tucker replied, trying not to let his discomfort, or the weight of those words, show.

"You know what I mean, whether you admit you do or not. Now you better get in there and help out."

Tucker had a few things to say in response, but he'd get nowhere against these two hardheads. Better to just save his breath. He had enough of a fight ahead of him—he'd just avoid the ones that were pointless.

He stepped into the kitchen as Rachel sprinkled a ham, cheese and pepper mixture into a pan.

"Let me guess, Cecilia was saying how you need to watch out for me or she's going to leave you in the middle of the Badlands chained to a rock with no water."

Tucker couldn't help but smile—at both the colorful specificity and how well she understood Cecilia. "It was a little less violent than all that, but the general gist."

"I don't need to be babied."

"Believe it or not, that's what I told her."

Rachel made a considering sound and said nothing else, so Tucker set out plates and silverware. He couldn't understand why she was cooking for everyone. "Why do you go to all this trouble?"

"It isn't any trouble to make breakfast."

"You and Grandma Pauline. Cereal isn't good enough. A frozen pizza is an affront. I happen to subsist just fine off of both when I'm at my apartment."

"That's because you have us to come home to."

Come home to. He didn't know why those words struck him as poignant. Of course, Grandma Pauline's was home. It was the place he'd grown up after escaping the Sons. It was the first place he'd been safe and loved.

"I guess you're right."

"Grandma Pauline taught me that you can't solve anyone's problems, but you can make them comfortable while they solve their own."

"What about when *you* have problems?"

She paused, then expertly flipped an omelet onto a plate next to her. "We aren't the ones out fighting the bad guys," Rachel said, and he could tell she was picking her words carefully.

"That doesn't mean you're without problems."

She inhaled sharply, working on the next omelet with ease and skill, but she didn't say anything to that.

Like Grandma Pauline, she was so often at the stove

it seemed a part of her. Yet she'd been blinded at the age of three, lost her mother at the age of seven. Maybe she hadn't survived a ruthless biker gang like he had, but she had been scarred. Now he had to stay under the same roof as her and *lie*.

Not just to protect her, though. He was also protecting Duke, and the life he'd built. As long as North Star brought him back in one piece, did the lies matter?

Still, he stood frozen, watching her finish up the omelets, as Cecilia and Brady strolled in, still with their arms around each other. A few moments later, Sarah and Dev came in from the fields, bickering with the dogs weaving between them.

The North Star worked in secrets, in following the mission regardless of feelings, and he'd made a promise when he'd signed on with them. He wouldn't break it.

But it was a promise to be here, to be part of these families, too. He couldn't break that, either.

So he had to find a compromise.

Chapter Five

Conversation around the breakfast table flowed the way it always did when Wyatts and Knights got together. Rapid-fire subject changes, people talking over each other, Sarah and Dev constantly disagreeing with each other.

They avoided the topic of Duke, though it hung over them like a black cloud. Still, Rachel appreciated how hard they all tried to make it seem as though this were normal. In a way it was. They'd eaten hundreds of meals together over the years. Usually not in her kitchen, though.

"You going to eat that, Tuck?" Sarah asked through a mouthful of omelet.

Rachel frowned. Why wouldn't Tucker be eating? "I can make you a different kind if you'd like."

"No, it's fine."

She heard the scrape of fork on plate and was sure Tucker had just taken a large bite. He needed to eat. He hadn't slept, that much she'd known when she'd woken up and there'd been coffee before Sarah had even come down.

"I'm just thinking," he continued. "Something about this whole Duke thing doesn't...match."

Whatever chatter had been going on around the table

faded into silence at the mention of her father. Rachel's appetite disappeared and she set down her fork.

"Duke left of his own accord," Tucker continued. "Maybe he's being blackmailed in some way, but he left on his own two feet. With everything that's happened this summer, I'd assume it has to do with the Sons, but there's no evidence that it does."

"What else could it have to do with?" Cecilia demanded.

"That's what doesn't jive. Maybe there's something in Duke's background we're missing."

Dad's *background*. "Just what exactly are you suggesting about my father?"

"Nothing bad, Rach. Just that there's more to the story than we've got."

"I don't see how we can rule out the Sons," Cecilia returned. "Not when four of Duke's foster daughters are hooked up with four of Ace's sons."

"I'm not saying rule it out. You can never rule out the Sons. I'm saying, look beyond them, too. Look at *Duke*. Not just where he's gone, but why. He wasn't taken. His house wasn't set on fire. This is different than the times the Knights have been caught in the crossfire of the Sons."

Rachel heard the voice from her nightmare echo in her head. Silly. It was just a dream, and it had nothing to do with what Tucker was talking about.

"What could Duke be hiding? We've been underfoot forever," Sarah said. "Wouldn't we know if he had some deep dark secret?"

Secrets always hurt the innocent.

Rachel squeezed her eyes shut, trying to push the dream out of her head. It had no bearing on the actual real conversation in front of her. That voice was made up, born of stress and worry and an overactive imagination.

She stood and pushed away from the table, abruptly taking her plate to the sink.

"Rach—" But Cecilia was cut off by someone's phone going off.

Cecilia muttered a curse. "I have to get to work."

There was the scraping of chairs, Dev and Sarah arguing over what work they had to get back to, Brady offering thanks for the breakfast as he left with Cecilia. The voices faded away, punctuated by the squeak and slap of the screen door.

And though he didn't make any noise, Rachel knew Tucker was still there. Likely watching her as she cleaned up the breakfast mess.

"Do you have something to say?" she demanded irritably, which wasn't like her. Nothing about the past week or so felt like *her*. She wanted to yell and rage and punch somebody and make her life go back to the way it was.

Weren't you just complaining about your life staying forever the same?

Rachel stopped washing the pan she'd used to cook the omelets and let out a pained breath. She'd wanted change, yes, but on her terms. Not the kind of change that put her father in danger.

"Did something I say upset you?" Tucker asked carefully. Like she was fragile and needed careful tiptoeing around.

"Do you assume everything is about you? That's pretty self-centered of you."

He was quiet for a long time, then she could hear him stacking dishes and placing them next to her so she could finish loading the dishwasher.

"It's just a theory, that this has something to do with Duke and not the Sons. It's not the only theory. I'm just struggling to find any evidence that ties to the Sons."

"I'm sure that struggle has nothing to do with how little you want to tie your father's gang to my father's disappearance."

"Don't be a child, Rachel," he snapped, with enough force to make her jolt. And to feel shamed.

"I wasn't—"

"I'm more aware of everything my father has done than you'll ever know. He's also in maximum-security prison because my brothers put their lives on the line to make it so. And so did some of your sisters. Let's not pretend I'm under any delusion that I could ever erase the effect my father has had on your family, through no fault of your family's."

The shame dug deeper, infusing her face with heat. "I'm sorry. I didn't mean—"

"You meant to slap at me, and I get it. You want to take out your fear and your frustration on me and I'm usually a pretty good target. But not today. So back off."

Fully chastened, Rachel reached out. She found his arm and gave it a squeeze. "I am sorry."

She could hear him sigh as he patted her hand. "I am, too. I didn't sleep worth a darn, and I'm not handling it well."

Silence settled over them, her fingers still wrapped around his arm, his big hand resting over hers. It was warm and rough. Despite being a detective, Tucker helped out at the ranch as much as he could, which was probably where he'd gotten the callouses. The big hands were just a family trait. All the Wyatts were big. She was a tall woman, but Tucker's hands still dwarfed hers. If she flipped her hand over, so they were palm to palm—

Why was she thinking about that? She pulled her hand away from under his, and only the fact she was at the sink kept her from backing away. She had dishes to finish, so she turned back to them, ignoring the way her body was all…jittery all of a sudden.

"My theory about Duke seemed to upset you," he said, in a tone she would have considered his detective voice. Deceivingly casual as he tried to get deeper information on a topic. "Do you know something about what's going on? About Duke's past?"

She laughed, with a bitterness she couldn't seem to shove away. "No, I don't know anything."

"You're acting like you do."

She blew out a breath. Mr. Detective wasn't letting it go, so she had to be honest with him even if it was embarrassing. "I had one of those nightmares last night that felt real. I can't seem to shake it."

"Why don't you tell it to me?"

She shook her head. How embarrassing to lay out her silly, childish dreams for him to hear. He'd tell her they were natural. She'd had a traumatic experience as a young child and her brain was still dealing with it and blah, blah, blah.

"Grandma Pauline always said if you explain your nightmare, it takes away its power."

She couldn't help but smile at that. Grandma Pauline had something to say about everything, and wasn't that a comfort? "Did that work?"

He was quiet for a minute. "With the things that weren't real."

The word *real* lodged in her chest like a pickax. Sharp. Painful. Both because Tuck probably had plenty of real nightmares after almost eight years raised in a terrible biker gang, and because hers wasn't real. No matter how much it felt that way. "It wasn't real," she insisted.

"Then lay it on me."

TUCKER HAD NEVER seen Rachel quite so…wound up. He understood this situation was stressful, but they'd been in stressful situations all summer, and she'd kept her cool.

Did she know something? Was the dream some kind of distraction? Something wasn't adding up.

He'd brought up Duke's past because it was a possible answer. If Brady or Cecilia stumbled upon those facts on their own, without him telling them specifically what, then he wouldn't have betrayed his promise to North Star.

They probably wouldn't see it that way, but the more he felt the need to comfort Rachel as she came slowly unraveled, the less he cared about North Star's approval.

They'd put him in an impossible situation. All because he wanted to do what was right. Well, getting some of his own answers was right.

Rachel hesitated as she did the dishes. Finally, she shrugged. "It's silly. I just… I've always had nightmares about the night I was attacked by that mountain lion."

"That makes sense."

"It does. Usually they're few and far between. Especially as I've grown up. But something about the last few weeks has made them an almost nightly occurrence, and they're morphing from memory into fiction. But the fiction feels more real than the memory." She frowned, eyebrows drawing together and a line appearing across her forehead.

She really was beautiful in her own right. Much as she could remind him of Eva, the older she got, the more she was just… Rachel. He knew her sisters sometimes saw her as the baby of the family, the sweet girl with no grit, but that was her power. A softer Grandma Pauline, she held everyone together. Not with a wooden spoon, but with her calm, caring demeanor.

And *why* was he thinking about that? He should be thinking about what she was saying. "Well, what's different? Between the real dream and the fiction dream?"

She took a deep breath and let it out slowly. She looked so troubled that he wanted to reach out and hold her hand. He curled his fingers into his palm instead. Touching seemed…dangerous lately.

"Instead of a mountain lion, there's a man. He has blue eyes, and half his face is scarred. Not like mine. Not lines, but all over. Like a burn, sort of. He's carrying me. We're…" Her eyebrows drew together again, like she was struggling to remember. "It was the hills in one of the pastures. I don't know which one, but that's where the mountain lion attack happened. Outside one of the pastures."

"Do you remember if that's where the mountain lion attack happened or is that just what you've been told?"

She stopped rinsing a plate. "What does it matter?"

"For the purpose of your dream. Is that part real— what you actually remember when you're awake. Or is it what you've been told so that's what your subconscious shows you?"

"I… I guess I'm not sure." She put the plate in the dishwasher then turned to him.

He'd hoped getting it off her chest would ease her mind some, but she seemed just as twisted up. Like the more she talked about it, the more it didn't add up.

"Mom and Dad didn't like to talk about it, but I remember sometimes they'd mention something and it didn't…match with what I thought had happened. But I was only three. Their memory would be more accurate."

"Okay, so in your dream the mountain lion usually takes you somewhere?"

"No. I'm already there. He jumps out of nowhere. I see the glint of something sharp and then I wake up before it swipes at me. But…the dream last night was more involved. I was being carried away. The man's talking. And the thing glinting in the moonlight isn't claws. It's some kind of knife."

She whirled away abruptly. "It's a *nightmare*, Tuck. It's happening when I'm asleep. It's nothing and I'm tired of it making me feel so unsettled."

He watched her agitated pacing, decided to hold his tongue and let her get it out. Maybe she needed a full-on breakdown to be able to find that center of calm that was so inherent to her.

"But I can't get that *fictional* man's voice out of my head. The way he talks. There's an accent. Like New York or Boston. Why is that so clear to me? What can't I shake this stupid dream?"

She raked her fingers through her hair, and Tucker desperately wanted to offer her some soothing words and a hug, but over the past day any physical offers of comfort had gone a little weird. He needed to keep his hands to himself.

"Secrets always hurt the innocent." She dropped her hands, wrapping them around her body instead. "I keep hearing this voice say that. *Secrets always hurt the innocent. Curtis Washington is going to learn that the hard way.*"

Tucker's entire body went cold. He didn't know that

name, but having a specific name, a specific voice in her dreams...

Dread skittered up his spine.

"Who's Curtis Washington?"

"I don't know. I've never heard that name before. It's just in my head."

Tucker had to work to keep his breathing even. To maintain control and a neutral expression rather than let all his theories run away from him in a jumble of worry.

She gestured toward him. "Say something."

He had to be careful about his words. About how he approached this horrible possibility. "Mountain lions aren't particularly aggressive."

"No, but I was three. Who knew what I was doing."

"You were three. Why were you so far from your parents? Duke and Eva weren't exactly hands-off parents."

"They...they didn't like to talk about it. I probably wandered off. Accidentally. Not because they weren't paying attention. You know how toddlers are. It's possible... It just happened."

She didn't seem so sure.

"This voice...this man..."

"It's stupid. All my life the dream has been a mountain lion. The man is a recent change, Tuck. It's a new morph on the old nightmare. If something else happened that night, why would I only dream about it now?"

Because Duke was in trouble, in danger. And this was his WITSEC life. Which meant he had another name.

Could it be the name in Rachel's dream?

Chapter Six

Tucker made himself scarce after Rachel had told him her dream. She could hardly blame him. Why was she coming so unglued over a nightmare? It made no sense, and if it was irritating to her—she could only imagine how annoying it was to the people around her.

She wouldn't bring it up ever again. Not to Tucker, not to anyone. Her dreams were her problem.

She went through the rest of the day without seeing him, though she knew he was there. Then he popped in for dinner, chatting cheerfully though she could tell he was distracted. He helped clean up after dinner, then he disappeared into Dad's room.

Door shut.

She had to admit, she didn't feel babysat, even though that's why he was here. Still, it helped that he wasn't hovering. Which meant she had the space inside herself to recognize Sarah's irritation simmering off her in its usual fraught waves.

Rachel had never been to the ocean, but she always associated Sarah's moods with the slapping waves and whipping winds of a hurricane.

While Sarah's moods were often operatic in nature, Rachel couldn't blame her right now. She was carrying the entire ranch on her shoulders, even with Dev's help.

"How about an ice-cream sundae?"

"I'm not a child, Rach," Sarah replied grumpily. But Rachel heard her plop herself at the kitchen table.

Rachel got out all the fixings for a sundae. Her conversation with Tucker from breakfast repeated in her mind.

Grandma Pauline taught me that you can't solve anyone's problems, but you can make them comfortable while they solve their own.

What about when you have problems?

She supposed her comfort was making other people food, and she supposed she'd gotten that from Grandma Pauline. She'd never fully realized how much she'd adopted the older woman's response to stress or fear, or wondered why before.

It wasn't hard to put together, though. Grandma Pauline was the last word around here. You didn't cross her, but everyone loved and respected her. They spoke about Grandma Pauline with reverence or loving humor.

"What do you think about what Tucker said?" Sarah asked.

Rachel blinked, remembering she was supposed to be making a sundae. Heck, she'd make one for herself, too. "Which part?"

"This being more about Dad than the Sons?"

Rachel scooped the ice cream, poured on chocolate syrup and sprayed on some whipped cream. She set one bowl in front of Sarah, then took her seat at the table with her own bowl.

They were the two youngest Knight girls, often sheltered from danger. Not just because they were the youngest or because Rachel was blind, but because they hadn't come from the dire circumstances their sisters had. Rachel had been born happy and healthy to Duke and Eva, their miracle baby. Sarah had been adopted at birth, so Sarah didn't remember or know anything about her birth parents.

Neither Rachel nor Sarah had ever left home. No tribal police or park ranger jobs for them. Rachel's part-time job as an art teacher was a challenge, and Sarah being a rancher was definitely hard work, but they were home. Still sheltered from so much of the *bad* in the world.

So, if Rachel could be honest with anyone, it was Sarah, because more than everyone else they were especially in this together. "I really don't know what to think of it."

"He's a detective," Sarah said.

"It doesn't make him infallible."

"No, but it gives him some experience in putting clues together. He also knows the Sons, and much as I hate to agree with Dev, he's right. The Sons have left Duke alone for all this time." Her sister released a breath. "So why would they start poking at him now? Especially with Ace in jail. Ace is the one with the vendetta against the Wyatts, not the Sons in general."

"I don't imagine they feel kindly toward the boys who escaped, or the men who put their leader in jail."

"Maybe not. I'm not saying it can't possibly be the Sons. God knows almost all our problems this summer have come from that corner of the scummy world. But... Dad never talks about his parents."

Rachel frowned at that. Surely that wasn't true. But no, she couldn't remember any stories about Dad's parents.

"It never really dawned on me that it was weird since we had Grandma and Grandpa Mills. And I always *assumed* this ranch was passed down, Knight to Knight, because Dad's so proud of it, but…wouldn't there be stories? Heirlooms?"

"What are you trying to say?" Rachel demanded, panic clutching at her.

"We don't actually know anything about Dad, and we never asked. As far as stories I've heard, and just being around Dad, his life started when he met Mom. And that can't be true."

Rachel couldn't eat another bite of ice cream. What was there curdled in her stomach. Sarah was right. She couldn't think of a thing Dad had ever told her about his life before he'd met her mother.

"So, you think he's running from something in his past?"

"Or running *to* something in his past."

Rachel thought of the gun under his pillow. About Dad not wanting her teaching. "He didn't want me to teach this session. He blamed it on the trouble with the Wyatts, but I taught all summer through all that danger."

"So, he was afraid. Something was *making* him afraid. I can't imagine Dad leaving us if he thought we were in danger. Unless…"

"Unless what?" Rachel demanded.

"What if he did something wrong? What if there isn't danger so much as… I mean, he could have run away from something bad."

"Dad would never. He wouldn't… No, I don't believe that."

"He wouldn't have left us in danger, Rachel. So one of these things he would never do *has* to be what he's done."

What a horrible, horrible thought. Maybe it was true, and maybe she was naive, but she refused to believe it of the father she loved. This man who had been a shining example of goodness and hard-working truth. "What if he thought only he was in danger? Just like Cecilia and Brady when they were trying to save Mak. They thought staying here would bring trouble to our doorstep, so they took off trying to draw the danger with them."

Sarah didn't respond to that. They sat in silence for ticking minutes.

"We have to tell Tucker he was right," her sister finally said. "That we don't know anything about his life before Mom. The answer is somewhere in there, and Tuck can find it. He's a detective. He has to be able to find it."

Rachel wasn't so sure. If her father had kept this secret for over thirty years, maybe no one could find it.

"Rach." Sarah's hand grasped hers across the table. "We have to help in whatever way we can. We're always swept off to the sidelines. But who put out that fire last month? We did. Who always holds down the fort? Us. And we're damn good at it. But Dad's gone. He can't protect us like he's always trying to do. Whether he's running away or hiding or *whatever*, it's just us. We have to step up to the plate."

Rachel knew Sarah was right, and she didn't understand the bone-deep reticence inside of her. It felt like they were stirring up trouble that would change *everything*, and she didn't want everything to change. Maybe she'd wanted a *little* change, but not her whole world.

"I can talk to Tucker myself. If you don't want to—"

"No...you're right. It's just us. We have to work together. It's the only way to make sure Dad's safe."

"He's a tough old bird," Sarah said firmly, and Rachel knew she was comforting herself as much as trying to comfort Rachel.

"He is. And we'll bring him home."

TUCKER CALLED EVERY North Star number he had in his arsenal over the course of the day, and no one would answer. He was too annoyed to be worried that was a bad sign. He needed to know if Curtis Washington was Duke's real name.

It would change things. For North Star, too. He barked out another irritable message into Granger's voice mail, then threw his phone on the bed in disgust.

He'd searched Duke's room, too. No hints to a secret past. There'd been plenty of guns secreted throughout the room, which led Tucker to believe Duke was a man who'd known his past would catch up with him eventually.

No. He'd fostered five girls, raised one daughter of his own. Duke had been certain he'd left that old life behind. Something must have recently happened to lead him to believe he was in danger.

And it tied to the Sons. It shouldn't make Tucker feel guilty. Just because he'd been born into the Sons didn't make him part of them. His life had nothing to do with Duke's secret past.

But the guilt settled inside of him anyway. Luckily, a knock sounded at the door and he could pretend he didn't feel it.

"Come in," he offered.

Sarah poked her head in. "Hey, can we talk to you in the kitchen for a second?"

"Uh, sure."

He followed her out of the room and down the hall. Rachel was already in the kitchen, washing out some bowls. He wondered if she ever stepped away from that constant need to cook and clean for everyone. He wondered if anyone offered a hand, and doubted it very much. He knew from experience how little kitchen work held appeal after a long day ranching.

Maybe that explained it. This was her way of helping her family, the ranch. It was how she felt useful.

When she heard them enter, she turned and smiled. "Did you want some dessert?"

"No, thanks. What did you want to talk about?"

Rachel took a seat at the table, but Sarah paced, wringing her hands together. "We were thinking about what you said. About Duke's life, and the truth is…" She looked at Rachel, so Tucker did, too.

Her expression was carefully blank, calm, which told him all he needed to know. Inside, she was anything but.

"We don't know anything about his life before he married Mom," Sarah continued. "He never talked about parents or siblings. Where he was born or if this ranch was passed on. We just…assumed. And we had so much family, and everything with losing Mom, and Liza and Nina disappearing and… Well, you know. It just didn't come up. Until now."

Liza's stay with the Knights had been brief, but her returning to the Sons had hurt all of the Knights, and Jamison. Liza and Jamison had since patched things up after saving Liza's half sister, but it had taken a long time.

Nina's disappearing had been the only time in Tucker's life where he thought Duke might actually cut all ties with the Wyatts. He'd personally blamed Tucker's youngest brother Cody, Nina's boyfriend at the time. It had taken a long time for Duke to get past it. When Nina had returned—injured and with her daughter in tow—Tucker had been sure Duke would be furious all over again, but the reconciliation of Cody and Nina had soothed some of his anger.

Some.

There was the guilt again, darker this time. Tucker *knew* Duke had a secret life. He'd put the idea in their heads. Now he was going to lie to them as if he didn't know what it was.

Where does your loyalty lie? North Star or your friends?

Two very different women stared at him. Rachel, dark hair, eyes and skin. Tall and slender. Sarah, petite, curvy, with baby blues and flyaway blond hair.

He wanted to tell them the truth. He couldn't think of a good reason not to, except Granger had told him not to. Duke hadn't argued with it. There might be a very good reason Sarah and Rachel should be kept in the dark.

What might they do if they knew the truth?

"I'm…looking into it. His past, that is. Best I can. To see if it connects to anything that's going on." He did his best not to cringe, not to show how utterly slimy he felt for the flat-out lies. "I haven't gotten very far because I don't have a lot to go on. I don't suppose you have any ideas?"

Sarah shook her head sadly. "That's just it. Who *never* talks about their parents? Or where they're from. Dad's got to be from South Dakota. How else would he end up with all this?"

Tucker really hated that he knew the answer to that question. He forced himself to smile reassuringly. "I'll keep digging. I—"

He was interrupted by his phone going off. It wasn't his regular ringtone. He frowned at the screen. It must be a North Star number. "I have to take this," he said, pushing away from the table.

Both women looked at him with frowns, but he lifted

the phone to his ear and stepped out of the kitchen. "Wy—"

Granger was barking out questions before Tucker even got his last name out of his mouth. "Where'd you get that name?"

Tucker felt shattered, and he didn't even fully understand why. He looked back at the kitchen. No one had followed, but he still slid into Duke's room and closed the door. "So, it's true. That's his real name."

Why was Rachel dreaming about Duke's real name? A man instead of a mountain lion?

"I asked where you got the name, Wyatt."

Tucker hesitated. He had the sinking suspicion if he mentioned it was in Rachel's dream, she'd be dragged into this. Maybe North Star would keep her safe. Maybe they even needed to know that she knew something. But...

He couldn't bring himself to utter her name. It felt wrong, and beyond that, he doubted very much Duke wanted his daughter dragged into this even if she did know something.

And his loyalty *was* to his friends over the North Star Group. Even if they were doing something good in trying to take down the Sons, and that *was* important. But so was safeguarding Rachel.

So, he lied instead. "I did some research on dirty cops in Chicago. You did give me enough information to go on to make an educated guess."

"Wyatt. Your job is to keep your families from getting suspicious while we handle the real threat. I don't need any misdirected people wading into this. Keep your side out of it. No more digging. Do you understand me?"

Tucker wanted to say *or what*, but he had a feeling

Granger McMillan was dangerous enough to make *or what* hurt. "All right, but it seems to me it'd be more helpful if I knew the whole story."

"I don't need your help. I need you to keep your families out of it. That's it. If you can't do that, I'll bring in someone who can, and you will be dealt with accordingly."

Tucker opened his mouth to tell Granger to jump off a cliff, but the line went dead.

Probably for the best. He let out a long breath.

Rachel knew her father's real name without knowing that's what it was. Which meant, she'd had *some* encounter with *someone* who'd been a part of Duke's previous life.

If that someone was still out there, if that someone was behind this connection to the Sons, it meant Rachel was as much of a target as Duke.

Chapter Seven

Rachel didn't have the dream. She woke up feeling rested for the first time in days. It might have put her in a good mood, but as long as her father was missing, there was no real good mood to have.

Tucker had promised to look into Duke's past, but she had to wonder if it wouldn't end up being…catastrophic somehow. She didn't want to believe her father was involved in something bad, but how could she ignore facts?

He'd left of his own accord, sort of. She still believed he'd been forced to leave, but he hadn't been carted off or held at gunpoint. His little disappearing act and fake vacation *had* to be born out of threats, or something like that.

Rachel got dressed, trying to remind herself there wasn't anything she could do about it. She had to trust Tucker and the Wyatts to look into her father's disappearance. And Cecilia. Cecilia wouldn't sit idly by. None of her sisters would. Sarah would ranch, Nina and Liza were busy with their children but would probably help Cody and Jamison in whatever ways they could. Felicity should be concentrating on growing her baby, but she would likely discuss with Gage what was going on.

And Rachel would be left to cook and clean. She tried not to be disgusted with herself. After all, if it was good enough for Grandma Pauline, it was good enough for her.

But Grandma Pauline was eighty. Rachel also had no doubt she'd pick up that big rifle she kept hidden in the pantry and take care of whatever intruders might deign to invade her ranch.

What could Rachel do? Scream?

No. That really wasn't good enough. She needed to learn some basics about getting away or fighting back.

She'd insist Tucker teach her. If he had to be underfoot, the least he could do was be useful. She headed downstairs and to her normal routine of making breakfast, but she stopped short at the entrance to the kitchen.

Tucker was in her kitchen. She couldn't tell what he was doing, but she could make out his outline. She could hear the sounds of…cooking.

"What are you doing?" she demanded, maybe a little too accusatorially to be fair.

"Thought I could take breakfast duty since I'm staying here," he replied, continuing to move around *her* kitchen as if she were just some sort of…bystander.

"But… I always make breakfast."

"Don't tell me you've completely morphed into Grandma Pauline and can't stand someone else carrying some weight?"

"That isn't…" She had to trail off because it was silly to be upset someone had beaten her to breakfast. She'd been complaining for years that Duke and Sarah never even tried to figure out their way around the kitchen.

She should be grateful someone was lending a hand, even if it was Tucker. But mostly she felt incredibly superfluous and useless. "I guess I'll—"

"Have a seat. It's almost ready. I don't want you picking up after me. I can do my own laundry, keep Duke's room tidy and all that. I'm not your houseguest, so you don't need to treat me like one. I'm here to help. That's all."

"Being here to help does technically make you a guest," Rachel muttered irritably.

"Well, this guest can take care of himself." As if to prove it, he slid a plate in front of her. "All I did was bake some of Grandma's cinnamon rolls you had in the freezer and cut up a melon. Hardly putting myself out."

"But what if your coffee sucks?" she asked, trying to make light of how small that made her feel. When did she get so pathetic that she needed to make a meal to feel worthy of her spot here?

He slid the mug in front of her. "It doesn't. And, I already doctored it. You're welcome."

The coffee didn't suck. She might have made it a little stronger for Sarah, but he had indeed put in cream and sugar just how she liked it. She wanted to make a joke about keeping him around, but it sat uncomfortably on her chest so she couldn't form the words.

It was a little too easy to picture. She knew it would be…difficult to find a significant other. Not so much because of her scarring and lack of sight, but because she just didn't get around much and lived in a rural area. But she'd always had that little dream of a husband and kids in this kitchen.

To even picture Tucker filling that role was *embarrassing*. So she shoved a bite of cinnamon roll in her mouth instead. Even after being frozen, Grandma Pauline's cinnamon rolls were like a dream.

"You know, Sarah and Duke would mess up even reheating frozen rolls," she offered, trying to think of anything else than what was currently occupying her brain.

He took the seat next to her, presumably with his own plate of food and mug of coffee. "If that's what you want to tell yourself, Rach, but I don't think you give them much space to figure out how."

She frowned at that.

"I'm sorry," he said. "I wasn't trying to be a jerk. Maybe you're right and they can't."

But she could tell he didn't think so, and worse she knew he was right. She complained about how little they did, while never ever giving them even an inch to do it for themselves.

She ate her feelings via one too many cinnamon rolls, then started on the fruit. She could wallow in…well, everything, or she could do something. She could act. She could *change*.

"Tuck, I want you to teach me how to fight."

"Huh?"

"I can't shoot. But I could fight." She pushed the plate away, ignoring the last few bites of melon. "I want to be able to defend myself. Maybe nothing bad happens here, but I want to be ready if it does."

"Rach, you don't have to worry about that. We're all—"

"Tucker." She reached across the table, found his arm. She needed that connection to make sure he understood this was more than just…a suggestion. She needed it. Needed to feel like she could contribute or at least not make a situation worse. "I could fight. I want to be able to fight." She gave his arm a squeeze.

He hesitated, but he didn't immediately shoot her down again. "I'm sure Cecilia—"

"Isn't here. You are. Didn't you teach some self-defense class at the Y for a while?"

She could hear him shift in his chair, a sense of embarrassment almost. "Well, yeah, but—"

"But what? What's different about that and this?"

After a long beat of silence, he finally spoke. "I guess there really isn't one."

"Exactly. So, you'll do it." She didn't phrase it as a question, because she wasn't taking no for an answer.

"I guess I could teach you and Sarah a few things." He didn't sound enthused about it, but she'd take agreement with or without excitement.

Rachel heard Sarah stepping into the kitchen, and then her small bright form entered Rachel's blurry vision.

"What things are you teaching me?"

"Self-defense. Rachel wants to learn how to fight."

Rachel noted that, while he didn't sound sure of teaching her anything, he didn't seem dismissive or disapproving. Maybe he didn't like teaching was all.

Well, he'd have to suck it up.

"Good idea," Sarah said around a mouthful of food. "But I can shoot a gun. And kick your butt, if I had to."

"Kick *my* butt?" Tucker replied incredulously. "You're five foot nothing. If that."

"I also wrestle stubborner cows than you, Wyatt. I could take you down right here, right now."

"All right." There was the scrape of the chair against the floor. "You're on."

"Oh, you don't want to mess with me."

Rachel could see the outlines of them circling each other. "You aren't really going to…"

There was the sound of a grunt, a thud and then laughter. It was a nice sound. Comforting. Like having her family home. Except Dad wasn't here, and they were pretending to fight.

"All right. Sarah gets a pass," Tucker conceded. "Though I maintain you did not kick my butt."

"Whatever you gotta tell yourself, Tuck," Sarah replied cheerfully. "Dev's truck is already out there." The cheer died out of her voice. "I could wring his neck. I told him to wait for me. Leave me a cinnamon roll to heat up," she called, already halfway out the door.

The door slammed.

"Did you let her win?" Rachel asked.

"It wasn't about winning. I just wanted to see what she's got. Good instincts and a nice jab. She's scrappy and mean, which is good in a real fight. Besides, she's right. She can shoot."

"Are you saying I'm not scrappy and mean?"

Tucker laughed. "I wasn't saying that, but we both know you're not. Which is why I'll teach you a few self-defense moves, if it'll make you feel better."

"It will. When do we start?"

AUTUMN IN SOUTH DAKOTA meant anything could happen. A nice sunny day. A sudden blizzard. Today was a pleasant morning, thank God. The yard in front of the Knight house would be as good a place as any to teach Rachel a few moves.

Rachel had changed from jeans and a T-shirt to something…he couldn't think too much about. It was all stretchy and formfitting, so he kept his gaze firmly on the world around him and not on her.

"Shouldn't we have padding or something? I don't want to hurt you."

The fact she wasn't joking was somehow endearing. Before he'd moved to detective, he'd been on the road.

Fought off the occasional person too high on drugs to feel pain, quite a few men larger and meaner than him, and more than one criminal with a weapon.

"We're just doing a few lessons. Learn a few rules and moves. You're not going to be beating me up quite yet."

"But shouldn't I be able to?"

"Sure. But we'll have to work up to it. You can't learn everything there is to know about self-defense in a day."

She wrinkled her nose. "Is it *that* complicated?"

"It's not about being complicated. It's just…something you practice, so it becomes second nature. So you're ready to do it. But listen, Rach. You're not going to need to, because I'm here and—"

She shook her head. "I don't want to feel like the weak link. Like the person everyone has to protect. Maybe it isn't much, but I just want to be able to land a punch or get away from someone if I need to. That's all."

She more than deserved that. He just wished he didn't have to be the one to teach her. It would involve touching and guiding, and she was… Hell, exercise leggings and a stretchy top were not *fair*. He was *human*.

Human and better than his baser—and completely unacceptable—urges. Because he'd shaped himself into a good, honorable man. One who did not take advantage of a young woman who meant a lot to his family.

And to you.

Because what he could forget when he didn't spend too much time one-on-one with Rachel was that they had a lot in common. What she'd said inside about wanting to feel useful echoed inside of him. Her surprise and irritation that he'd help out around the house made him want to do it all the more.

Take care of her and—

He cleared his throat, forced himself to focus. To treat this like any other lesson. "Rule number one. Always go for the crotch."

She made an odd sound. Like a strangled laugh. "I'm not going for your crotch, Tucker."

Jesus. He could *not* think about that. "Thanks for that. I just meant, in real life, that's your target. Crotch. Eyes. The most vulnerable points." He hated the thought of her needing to do *any* of that.

"Okay."

"You have to be mean."

She fisted her hands on her hips. "I know how to be mean."

"*Really* mean. Channel your inner Sarah."

"I'm going to channel my inner Grandma Pauline and whack you with a rolling pin."

Tucker laughed. "All right, killer. Show me how you'd punch."

He walked her through the proper form for a punch. Tried to talk her through aiming even though her sight was compromised. He instructed about grabbing anything she could make into a weapon. How to kick with the most effect.

Her form wasn't bad, and it got better the more she practiced. He offered to quit or take a break at least five times, but she kept wanting to go on. Even as they both ended up breathing heavily.

"The problem is I'm not going to be in a boxing ring. If *I'm* going to be in a fight, it's probably going to be because someone's trying to hurt me or someone I love. But they'd underestimate me. Either by ignoring me or just grabbing me."

"Maybe, but you have to learn the basics."

"But I can practice punching and kicking form on

my own. We need to practice like…how to get away if someone grabs me. I know you don't want to hurt me, and I don't want to hurt you, but it has to feel more like an actual fight."

"You don't have to worry about hurting me."

"Because I'm that weak?" she demanded.

"No, because I'm a professional at dodging a punch, Rach. I've been a cop for almost nine years. I've been learning to not get hit my whole life." He hadn't really meant to say that last part, or wouldn't have if he'd known she'd get that…sympathetic look on her face.

Nothing to be sympathetic about. He'd survived eight years of Ace Wyatt and the Sons of the Badlands. All his brothers, except Cody, had survived more time than him. Jamison hadn't gotten out until eighteen, after working hard to get Cody out before his seventh birthday. Tucker had followed not much later when he'd been eight. Gage and Brady had been eleven, and Dev twelve.

Tucker had gotten off easy, like he usually did.

She opened her mouth to say something—likely something he didn't want to hear, so he spoke first. "Come on then. If I'm coming at you, land a punch."

She got in the stance he'd taught her, made a good fist. As he moved forward, she swung out. He easily pivoted so she didn't land it.

"That's good."

"I didn't hit you!"

Tucker laughed. "Don't sound so disappointed." He took her still-clenched hand by the wrist and held it up. "This is your dominant hand, so you want it to do the big work." He took her other hand and brought it up. "But this one needs to do the work, too. Make a fist."

He walked her through using both hands to punch. Using her arms to block. He let her land a few punches.

She wasn't going to ward off any attackers with her fists—she'd have better luck kicking a vulnerable area or grabbing something to use as a weapon. Still, if it made her feel as though she was more prepared, that was what mattered.

It wasn't so bad all in all. It felt good to teach her something useful. A little *uncomfortable* teaching her to break holds by holding on to her against her will—but an important skill nonetheless.

Until he had the bright idea to teach her how to get away from someone who grabbed her from behind. Which necessitated…grabbing *her* from behind.

They went through the drill a few times. Slow, with pointers, and he tried very hard not to think about anything related to his body. He told her how to position her hands, how to maneuver her body. All while pretending his was made of…ice. Or plastic. Whatever kind of material that was not moved by a woman's body.

She was…lithe. Graceful.

Hot.

That was a really, really unacceptable thought when it came to Duke's daughter. Duke's daughter who's safety he was being entrusted with.

The strangest part was he'd scuffled with Sarah just this morning, and it hadn't felt any different than wrestling with his brothers. Familial. Funny.

But this was *none* of those things and he hadn't the slightest idea why.

"Do that again."

"I don't think—"

"Do it again," she insisted. "Come at me from behind."

He allowed himself to curse to his heart's content silently in his head. Rachel turned her back to him.

He just needed to enact a quick, meaningless grab around the waist.

The problem was he didn't like putting himself in the mind-set of an attacker. And he didn't like staying in his own mind-set, which was way too aware of how the exercise clothes she wore molded to every slender curve.

But who else could he be?

He gritted his teeth and tried to think about times tables as he wrapped his arm around her waist. She lifted her right hand to keep it from being held down by his grab, but he used his free hand to ensnare her arm.

She mimicked a kick to the insole and twisted in his grasp. He gave a little, as if stepping away from her kick. It gave her room, but kept his arm slightly around her, palm pressed to her stomach.

He wanted to tell her to pull her arm down in the way he'd shown her earlier, but he was afraid his voice wouldn't come out even. Or that he could manage to unclamp his jaw.

But she paused there, in this awkward position. His hand was on her abdomen, the fingers of his other hand curled around her wrist. He could feel the rise and fall of her breathing because her back was against him, her butt nestled way too close to a part of him he could *not* think about right now.

She tilted her head, and though he knew she couldn't see out of one eye and only general shapes out of the other, it felt as though she were studying him.

And then there was her mouth. Full and tempting. She wasn't trying to get out of his grasp, and she definitely wasn't putting any distance between their bodies.

She smelled like a meadow, and everything they were doing faded away. There were two aches inside of him—one he fully understood, and one that didn't make any sense. They both grew, expanded until there was only his heartbeat and the exhale of her breath across his cheek.

The sound of people arguing interrupted the buzzing in his head. He dropped her abruptly, moving away clumsily.

"Tucker…"

He didn't like the soft way she spoke, or the way her breath shuddered in and out, or that look in her eye, which he could not in any circumstances think about or consider.

"Hey, there's Sarah and Dev. We've been at this a while, huh? How about a break? I'm starved, you know?"

Sweet hell he was *babbling*. He cleared his throat. He was a grown man. A grown man with an inappropriate attraction, but that just meant he knew what to do with it. Scurrying away and babbling were not it. Getting himself together and *handling* it was what he needed to do. Would do. Absolutely. *Obviously.*

The dogs raced over first, so Tucker focused on them, squatting to scratch them both behind their ears. He spoke to them in soothing tones and tried his damnedest to get that *ache* coursing around inside of him to dissipate.

"How goes the self-defense?" Sarah asked.

"Great," Tucker said, far too loudly. "Going to take a break now."

"Yeah, us, too."

When Tucker looked up, Dev was frowning at him, but Tucker reminded himself that his brother's resting face was frowning disapproval. That was all.

Besides, he had enough frowning disapproval for himself. He didn't need anyone else's.

Chapter Eight

Rachel went through the rest of the day with an odd... buzz along her skin. Like the precursor to getting poison ivy. It was uncomfortable. Not quite so painful as a rash, but uncomfortable. Definitely.

She knew it was all Tucker's fault. Though she couldn't figure out why. Had he read her mind? He had been horrified that she'd kind of enjoyed him manhandling her. Or, had he enjoyed manhandling her and was horrified?

Either way, there was some horror. And then locking it all away and acting his usual genial self.

Except that he avoided her at all costs.

Which was probably for the best. Or was it? She got ready for bed, edgy and worked up. There was just too much going on. Her father was missing. She was having recurring nightmares. She was apparently attracted to a man she'd always looked at as family. Sort of. And worse than being attracted to *him* was the wondering if he was attracted to her right back. Or oblivious.

She groaned and flopped onto her bed. She needed to talk to someone. With most problems, she confided in Sarah or Cecilia. Sarah would be no help with this one, and Cecilia... She'd be too blunt. Too...forthright.

Rachel needed someone with a softer touch. So she called Felicity.

"Hey, Rach. Everything okay?"

"Yeah. Nothing new to report on our end."

Felicity sighed. "I really hate all this waiting. Gage keeps fluttering around me, trying to distract me from my stress, but all he is doing is stressing me out even more."

Rachel smiled. That was sweet. And also the perfect segue. "How did you end up involved with Gage?"

"What kind of question is that?"

"Not a mean one. I just… I wondered." Rachel rolled her eyes at herself. She sounded like an idiot. A transparent one. But at least of all her sisters, Felicity would never call her on it.

"Is this about Tucker?"

Rachel forced out a laugh. She was afraid it sounded more like a deranged array of squeaks. "What? No."

"You're a terrible liar. And even if you weren't, this is completely transparent."

Rachel pouted in spite of herself. "Of course it is. But you weren't supposed to call me out on it!"

Felicity laughed. "Sorry. Normally I wouldn't, but you're strung tight. I know Dad's whole disappearing act is scary, but you're usually calm in the midst of a crisis."

"I'm calm." Aside from the dreams. Aside from Tucker *touching* her. "Tucker believes Dad left of his own accord. Whatever prompted it, he doesn't think he's in any immediate danger and I have to believe that."

"I do, too. And so does Gage for that matter." Felicity paused. "So…why are you wound up?"

Rachel could blame it on the dreams. Some of it *was* the dreams, and the possibility of Dad being…far more complicated than she wanted him to be. But she didn't want to lay either of those things at Felicity's feet, where she'd worry needlessly.

"I think there was a moment. With Tucker. When he was teaching me some self-defense moves."

"Define *moment*."

"I don't know. Like…like…an awareness of each other. As a man and a woman. Not…family friends. As people who…"

"Might want to have sex?"

Rachel squeaked, her face getting hot, even though she was alone in her room and no one but her sister had heard that word. "Oh my *God*, Felicity."

"Sorry. It's just that's what moments usually lead to with the Wyatt boys."

"Why? I don't get it. I don't get why we're falling like dominoes for that lot of…"

"Really good guys who also happen to be hot and smart and caring? Who want to protect you, not because they think you're weak or need protecting, but because it's just who they are. On a cellular level."

Rachel expelled a breath. "I don't… I'm twenty-two."

"Is that commentary on the age difference or on being too young to have a serious relationship?"

"Neither. Both. I don't know! Why are we talking about relationships? It was like a moment of…lust. Fleeting lust. Very fleeting."

"Let me tell you this, Rach, lust over a Wyatt is never fleeting. I wasn't exactly planning on doing this whole baby thing yet. But then Gage came along and…boom, lust. And love."

Love. That was *terrifying*. "Just because you four did it, doesn't mean I will."

"Of course it doesn't. You're your own person, and

so is Tucker. I'm just trying to say it's normal to be attracted, and to be confused by it since you haven't always had those feelings. Danger and worry has a way of…stripping away our normal walls. When it does that, we can see someone as they actually are instead of how we've always perceived them to be."

"I don't have any walls."

Felicity was quiet for a few seconds. "Okay." She did *not* sound like she agreed. "But Tucker does. Even knowing how awful that childhood before Pauline must have been, I don't think I fully understood it until I saw Gage in that cave with Ace. Knowing Ace would have killed him and felt…justified. It isn't just viciousness and abuse they were raised with, it was…well, insanity."

Felicity paused, and Rachel shuddered. She hated to think about what Gage would have gone through. As a child and as a man. Tucker seemed so…not as afflicted as the others. She knew the older ones had spent longer being at the mercy of Ace Wyatt, but Tucker's eight years were nothing to ignore.

"The point is, being scared churns things up," Felicity continued. "That's okay. It doesn't mean you're weird. It doesn't mean you're not worried about Dad. It just means you're human. And Tucker is hot."

That shocked a laugh out of her. "Aren't you supposed to only have eyes for Gage?"

"Heart and soul for Gage. Eyes for anyone else. Things will be clearer when this is over, and Tucker and the rest of them are working hard to figure out what's going on so Dad can come home."

Rachel wanted to believe her. More than belief, though, she heard something in her sister's voice she wasn't sure she fully ever had before. Felicity had grown up nervous and shy, and she'd slowly come into her own the past few years. But Gage and this pregnancy had really given her an even bigger strength that she'd been afraid to believe in growing up. "You sound happy, Felicity."

"I am. And I'm mad ai Dad that he's adding worry to my happy, but that's life. Happy and worry and even attraction can all pile up on each other in the same moment. I'm learning to accept that. I think the the thing is…we were raised right. We've got good instincts. Don't question your instincts."

Rachel let that settle through her. Wasn't that what she'd been doing? Or maybe she'd been questioning her worth or usefulness but it all kind of added up to the same thing. "Thanks, Felicity. This helped."

"I'm glad. Try to get some rest, Rach."

"You and baby, too."

They said their goodbyes and Rachel climbed into bed. She didn't feel any more clear on the whole Tucker thing, but she felt…more settled.

Don't question your instincts.

She'd be thinking about that a lot over the next few days.

She fell asleep, hopeful for another restful, uninterrupted night. But in the shadows of night came the noise. The rustle. The unearthly glow of cat eyes.

Were they cat eyes? They weren't human but…

Secrets always hurt the innocent. Curtis Washington is going to learn that the hard way.

He had her. He was holding her too tight and she couldn't wiggle away. The eyes weren't his, but they followed. Animal.

The human who had her was someone entirely different. She could hear the hum and scuttle of night life. Could see the moon shining bright from above. But she couldn't see the shadow who carried her too quickly and too easily away from everything she loved.

She squirmed and tried to scream, but she was squeezed too tight—both by the man's grip and her own fear.

When he stopped, it was worse. He wasn't squeezing so tight, but she couldn't breathe at all as he lifted the thing he always lifted, glinting silver in the moonlight. Some kind of…pronged knife. Slashing down at her face.

Run. Wake up.

She always did. Until now.

This time she felt the searing pain of the knife. But a growl, and a thud kept the knife from scoring too deep. It was painful. So painful she thought she might die. She was bleeding and her eyes felt like they were on fire, but the man didn't have her anymore.

TUCKER TOOK THE stairs two at a time, the safety already off on his gun. Rachel's blood-curdling scream had woken him from a fitful sleep, and he'd immediately jumped out of bed and run upstairs.

"Tucker." Sarah stood in the hall in her pajamas, holding a baseball bat.

"Go back to your room," Tucker hissed at her. The screaming had stopped. He inched toward Rachel's room, keeping his footsteps light. He controlled his breathing, pushed all the fear away and focused on the task at hand.

Save her. Now.

He could bust the door open, which was his first instinct. But he didn't know who was behind it, and if he could go for stealthy, he had to. Carefully, he reached out and placed his hand on the door. He willed the slight tremor away with sheer force.

He couldn't afford to be emotional right now. He had a mission. Slowly, carefully, he turned the knob and eased the door open inch by inch.

The room was bathed in light. Rachel sat in the middle of her bed, head in her hands, but Tucker didn't see anyone else.

He immediately swept the room. "Where is he?"

"Tucker." She wrapped the blanket around herself. "What are you doing?"

"I… You screamed." He slowly lowered the gun, belatedly realizing she wasn't in trouble at all. All the fear drained out of him until his knees nearly buckled. "Hell, Rach. That scream could have woken the dead."

"I'm sorry. I'm…" She inhaled shakily and he finally realized she'd been crying. Tears tracked down her cheeks even as she spoke calmly. "I had a bad dream, that's all. I didn't mean to scare you. I…" She shook her head. "Did Sarah wake up?"

"Yeah, but—"

She picked her phone up off the nightstand. "Text Sarah. I'm okay. Bad dream." She dropped her phone, and Sarah burst into the room a few seconds later.

"Oh my God. Rach. How awful. What do you need?"

"Noth—" She seemed to think better of it. "I think I could use a drink."

"I'll be right back." Sarah scurried away.

Tucker studied Rachel. She was shaking, and though she made no noise, fresh tears leaked out of her eyes.

"I'm sorry to have woken you up. I—"

"Stop apologizing," he said, and he knew his voice was too harsh when she winced. But he felt…ripped open. That scream and all the most terrible scenarios that had gone through his mind even as he'd shoved them away to do what needed to be done had taken years off his life.

He let out his own shaky breath. She was okay. Well, not okay. She was crying. Upset. He moved for her bed. "Are they all like this?"

She shook her head, pulling the blanket up to her chin. "No. Usually I wake up before…" She took a steadying breath and he just couldn't take the fear still in her eyes, in her voice. He sat on the very edge of the bed, putting his hand on her shoulder.

She took a deep gulping breath. "It's just I usually wake up before he hurts me. But tonight the knives slashed across my face."

He rubbed his hand up and down her arm. She seemed to need to talk about it, and he had some suspicions now about these dreams. "Knives?"

"A man. He had me. He had this knife or knives with multiple points. He…" She couldn't seem to swallow down a hiccupped sob. She shuddered, so he pulled her closer until she leaned into him.

She let out a little sigh, and some of the shaking subsided. "I could feel it. The pain. The blood. I don't know if it was a memory or made up, but it felt real. And I was small. I had my adult brain, but he could cart me around easily. It was a man, but there was also an animal. I don't think it was a mountain lion. It was more… doglike. And he jumped on the man when he hurt me. That animal saved me, I think."

She shook her head. "It doesn't make sense. I don't want it to make sense." She buried her head in his shoulder. "I want the dreams to go away and I want Dad to be home."

"Of course you do, sweetheart." He rubbed his hand

up and down her back. "So do I." He tried to keep the grimness out of his voice. But this situation was grim. The more she explained the dream, the more he had to wonder if Rachel knew more than she understood.

And he had to wonder if *Duke* knew that. If that was half of why he'd agreed to disappear with North Star on such short notice. To keep Rachel out of it.

"I heard that name again. Curtis Washington. Do you think that's a real person?" She pulled back from him, her gaze meeting his. Her complexion was a little gray, and the faded pink of her scars seemed more pronounced against the brown of her skin. She looked at him earnestly, even though he knew she couldn't see him clearly. "Why am I dreaming this name? I've never thought my dreams were real, but..."

"It keeps repeating. And getting worse."

She nodded. Her face was close to his. Their noses would touch if he leaned just an inch forward. His arm was still around her and she was leaning into him.

In her bed.

Tucker let his arm slip away from her, though he stayed seated at the edge of her bed. He inched even closer to that edge so that, though he was close, their bodies were not in danger of touching, and berated himself for even the second of inappropriate thought that gripped him.

She was shaking, crying and scared.

And very close to a truth he wasn't supposed to let her know about.

"I think we need to look into that name. Don't you? Maybe it has something to do with Dad. Maybe—"

Sarah bustled into the room carrying a tray full of glasses. "I didn't know what kind of drink so I just kind of brought..."

"Everything." Rachel smiled indulgently. "Thank you. I think I'll take the water."

Tucker slid off her bed. He needed to let Sarah take care of this. Comfort her. He needed to escape before she asked him to do what he wasn't supposed to do.

He eyed Sarah's tray, took the shot glass off it and downed the whiskey. He put the glass back, then tried to disappear.

"Tuck, I want to look into the name. I think we have to."

How could he say no to her? "I'll see what I can do."

Chapter Nine

Rachel knew that Tucker would look into the name Curtis Washington, and he was a detective so he'd be able to do far more than her. Still, that didn't mean she couldn't aid him in his search.

If the name connected to everything that was going on, that meant it connected to Dad. And if the dream connected to everything that was going on…

She didn't know what it would mean.

It scared her. That it might be terrible. That it might be buried deep in her subconscious…

"There's a lot of junk up here, Rach. I don't know how we're going to go through it all," Sarah said.

Rachel could tell Sarah was antsy to get outside, to do her work on the ranch, even if it was a rainy, dreary day. But when Rachel had mentioned going up to the attic, Sarah had insisted on helping.

"I know it's overwhelming, but I can't sit around waiting for Tuck to figure it out. I know it was a dream. This is probably insane, but—"

"Look, that's some dream. Maybe normally I'd brush it off, but everything is off right now. Dev is being *nice* to me." The horror in her tone had Rachel smiling.

"That's sweet of him."

"It's creepy as hell." Sarah moved through the attic,

and Rachel figured she was doing what she had asked—reading labels of boxes and pulling out anything that seemed relevant. "Speaking of creepy, Tuck was totally checking you out last night."

Rachel nearly stumbled over what she assumed was a box. *"What?"*

"One hundred percent checking out your rack, sis."

Rachel sputtered, and she could feel heat creeping up her face. "Geez, Sarah…"

"I can tell him to knock it off if you want."

"What? No. Oh my God, don't do that!"

"Why not?"

Rachel tried to work through this insane turn in the conversation. "Because that's embarrassing and weird."

"So, not because you'd *like* Tucker to be checking you out. Tucker Wyatt."

"I know who Tucker is," Rachel replied, all too shrilly.

"That doesn't answer my question."

"Did you actually have one?"

"Yeah. Are you creeped out Tuck was looking at your boobs, or do you like it?"

Rachel opened her mouth but no sound came out. She wasn't creeped out, but she wasn't sure if she liked it, either. She was just… "I don't know."

"I mean, in fairness it wasn't like super creeper ogling. It was like…noticing. Your boobs."

"I need this conversation to be over," Rachel muttered. Her face was hot, her heart was hammering and they had way more important concerns at hand. "Whatever we're looking for, it's not going to be in a box. If it's such a secret that Dad had to disappear, it's going to be somewhere…like in the wall. Or out in the stables or something. It'd be hidden."

"But who would go through all this stuff? Wouldn't hiding it in plain sight work just as well?" Sarah asked, thankfully moving away from the subject of Tucker.

"Not if you expected someone to go looking for your secret stuff. If Dad *had* secret stuff—the kind you run away from so your children aren't in the middle of it—it'd be hidden somewhere. Which means there's not going to be a box labeled *secret stuff*. It's going to be harder than that. Sneakier than that."

Sarah blew out a loud breath. "I really hate this."

"Yeah, me, too."

They worked in silence for a while. Sarah went through reading labels on boxes and checking the contents of those unlabeled. Rachel went around the attic perimeter feeling the walls, trying to determine if there was any place that could be hiding something.

She was about to give up when her hands landed on something metal in the corner by the door. It was some kind of box, but instead of cardboard or plastic, it was a heavy metal.

"What's this?"

"Huh." Sarah stepped closer. "It's a locked cashbox type deal, but there's a little piece of masking tape on it that says *buttons*."

"Who would lock up buttons?"

"Mom loved collecting buttons, but I don't think there'd be any reason to lock them up. Here, give it to me."

"If it's locked, how will you—" Rachel began.

There was a squeaking sound and then a crash—like tiny buttons falling across the floor.

"Oops," Sarah said. "Lock was a little easier to break than I thought. But it is just…buttons. Everywhere now. Here, take the box so I can pick up the ones that fell."

Rachel took the box back. She let her fingers trail over the buttons. Mom had loved to collect them. Old grief welled inside of her, though it had been enough years now that she knew how to push it away.

Still, touching something of her mother's had her eyes and nose stinging with unshed tears. She blinked them back as she dug her fingers into the buttons— and touched something with a sharp edge. She cradled the box in her elbow and pulled the item out of the buttons. Using both hands, she felt around the edge of it. Much bigger than a button. Maybe an oddly shaped belt buckle?

"Sarah?"

"Wh— Oh my God."

"What? What is it?"

"It's a police badge." It was snatched out of Rachel's hand. "It says *Officer. Chicago Police.*"

"Chicago? Why would there be a Chicago police badge in a box full of buttons?"

"A *locked* box full of buttons," Sarah pointed out. "If we're looking for secrets, I think we might have found one."

"Are you guys up in the attic?" Tuck's voice called from below.

Rachel felt Sarah press the badge back into her palm. "Your call. You want to hide it, I will. You want to tell him, I'll be right behind you."

"Why are you leaving it up to me? He's your father, too."

"They're your dreams, Rach. And Tucker seems to be your thing. Let's face it, you're the calm, rational one between the two of us. Whatever you want to do is what we should do."

Tucker's form appeared in the doorway. "Hey. Dev's looking for you, Sarah. What are you two doing up here?"

Sarah didn't answer him. Because she'd put it all on Rachel.

"We wanted to poke around and see if we could find something of Dad's. Get some idea of what he might be keeping a secret." She held the badge behind her back, the box of buttons in the crook of her arm. What else might be in there?

And did she want Tuck to know about it?

"I'll go find Dev. See what he wants."

Rachel heard Sarah's retreat as she let her fingers trace the outline of the badge. Chicago Police? Could she picture her father as a police officer?

Or had he had some kind of run in with a police officer? Was this darker? More awful? Should she *want* to hide it from everyone so they never knew?

But how could she bring her father home without help? Without *Tucker's* help. Why wouldn't she trust Tucker Wyatt with everything she found? He was…a Wyatt. He was a good person. He didn't lie. He was a detective who searched for the truth, who's father's sins weighed on him even when they shouldn't.

He was a good man.

Tucker was totally checking you out last night.

"You okay?"

She nodded and cleared her throat. "We found a box of my mom's buttons."

His hand was on her shoulder, giving her a friendly squeeze. "That's a nice thing to have. Even if it makes you sad."

She nodded, because she agreed. Because she knew he didn't have anything from his mother, whatever complicated feelings he might have had about her. And he wouldn't want anything from his father. She had two good, supportive, loving parents who hadn't just loved *her* but had fostered or adopted five other girls over the years and made them all a family.

"I miss her most around this time of year," Tuck said, his voice gentle. "She was always rounding us up, trying to help Grandma Pauline get us ready for school rather than show up the first day looking like feral dogs."

"She used to say you boys needed love, education and a hardheaded woman to keep you on the straight and narrow."

He laughed. "Grandma Pauline did all three. So did your mom."

It was strange to talk to Tucker about her mom. She knew Eva Knight had considered the Wyatt boys part of her own brood. She'd helped Grandma Pauline corral them as much as she could. Mom had loved them. She'd cared about people who needed help, and love, and she'd given hope to those in the darkest places.

Rachel didn't have any dark places. Not really. Even her dreams were just dreams—even if they were pointing to *something*. She wasn't like Liza and Jamison who had survived the Sons, or Felicity who'd survived an abusive father both as a child and then as a woman. She wasn't any of the Wyatt boys with the horror they'd grown up with and escaped.

She'd had a good, mostly easy life. So, Mom had always tasked her with helping, providing for, being the hope.

If there was any hope in this situation with Dad, it was that they could get him home. Secrets wouldn't do that. Being suspicious of Tucker wouldn't do that.

Rachel took a deep breath, feeling around the edge

of the badge one more time. Then she held it forward. "I found this in the box of buttons."

TUCKER STARED AT the badge held out in Rachel's hand. Chicago PD. He didn't know how to react. He knew, of course, that it was Duke's, though Rachel probably didn't. Wouldn't.

He wanted to tell her. Not just about her father's past but about everything. North Star and where Duke was.

An equal part of him wanted to laugh it off, stop her from probing into this, from entwining herself in trouble. He wanted to wrap her up in a safe bubble so she didn't have to worry about all this.

But he remembered all too well that terrifying scream that had woken him in the middle of the night. Some of this mystery and danger was inside her subconscious somewhere. No matter what he did—he couldn't protect her from that.

"It's a police badge," he said, his voice a shade too rough.

"Yes. Sarah told me it says *Chicago Police*." She pressed it into his palm. "It has to mean something."

Boy, did it. "Did you check the rest of the box?"

"I haven't had the chance. We'd just found this when you came up."

He frowned over that. "Why didn't Sarah say anything?"

"She said she'd give me the choice whether to tell you or not."

"Why wouldn't you tell me?"

Rachel shrugged. "I did tell you, though."

He wasn't sure that was much of a comfort, but he supposed it had nothing to do with the issue at hand. He set the badge aside, then took the box of buttons from her. He found an empty mason jar to dump the buttons into. As he poured them into it, he let the buttons fall over his fingers. There was nothing else big, but as he came to the end of the buttons, a key fell into his fingers.

He held it up, looking at it on both sides. "Nothing else in there except a key."

"A key to what?"

"I don't have a clue. It's just a key."

"It can't *just* be a key."

"Well, no. It was in with the buttons and the badge so it has to be something, but there aren't any hints as to what." Tucker examined the box. It was a rusted out cashbox, nothing special about it. No space for any kind of false bottom.

"A badge and a key. A missing father. Dreams that feel way too close to real." She blew out a breath. "Anything else life wants to throw at me?"

"Please don't go taunting the universe like that."

Her mouth curved. "You don't honestly believe in curses and jinxes?"

"*Believe* might be a strong word. Let's say I have a healthy respect for the possibility."

Rachel shook her head, though she was still smiling. A beam of sunlight shone in front of her, making dust motes dance around her face. He'd always *known* she was pretty, but something about doing all this made him *feel* it.

Maybe he wholeheartedly believed in curses and jinxes, because his sudden attraction for Rachel felt like both.

She frowned. "Did you hear that?"

He hadn't heard much of anything except his own stupidity. "What?"

"I'm not sure. Like an engine, but…" She trailed off and he strained to hear what she heard. Everything was silent, but he felt the need to hold himself still, and continue to strain to hear long after the moment had passed.

Creak.

Rachel's frown deepened, and she opened her mouth, presumably to say something, but Tucker laid his hand gently over her mouth.

She'd heard an engine. He'd heard the creak of a floorboard under the weight of someone. If it was any Wyatt or Knight, they would have announced themselves—or they'd know which boards to avoid.

Tucker scanned the attic. Maneuvering Rachel to hide her would make noise. Everything would make noise, and whoever or whatever had creaked the floorboard had gone silent again. He was too far from the tiny window letting in the light to see through it and scan the surroundings.

He didn't wear his gun around the house because he was afraid it would make Sarah and Rachel nervous, and now he mentally kicked himself for caring more about feelings than safety.

He'd have to fight off whoever was at that door. He'd need the element of surprise. And to do it all while keeping Rachel out of the way.

There was only one way to do it, since once the attic door opened it would open this way and give whoever was on the stairs clear sight of Rachel.

But if he hid on the other side of the door, he could come at whoever it was from behind. They might know he was up here, but Rachel would be a momentary distraction he'd use.

He pressed his mouth as close to her ear as he could. Spoke as softly as humanly possible. "You're going to stay right here. Don't move unless I tell you to. Squeeze my hand if you understand."

When she squeezed, he squeezed right back. He was loathe to let go of her, to do what he knew he needed to do. He wanted to promise her things would be okay. He wanted to be a human shield between her and hurt.

But he had to stop doing what was most comfortable, and start doing what was the safest. He moved in absolute silence to the opposite side of the door.

He waited, counting his heartbeats, keeping his breathing even. Rachel's life rested in his hands, so he could not focus on panic or worry or that heavy responsibility. He could only focus on eradicating the threat.

The door squeaked, the narrow opening slowly growing. He saw the barrel of a gun first. It was pointed down at the ground, but he couldn't take any chances.

He waited until he actually saw an arm, then pushed the door as hard as he could. The gun didn't clatter to the ground as he'd hoped, but the intruder had stumbled back onto the stair.

"Get down, Rach," he commanded, moving through the door and closing it behind him. A figure in all black was on the stairs. The figure didn't raise the gun, but that didn't mean it wasn't dangerous.

The figure struck out, and Tucker managed to block most of the blow. They grappled, exchanging punches and elbows and kicks. Eventually they both stumbled, crashing down the first flight of stairs and onto the landing that would go down to the second floor.

Tucker banged up his elbow pretty good, and he'd landed on the side with his phone in his pocket so not only did a shooting pain go through his hip, but he was pretty sure the phone was crushed.

He swore, and so did the figure. Tuck frowned. It

was a woman. He noticed blond hair had escaped the black ski mask she wore. He scrambled to his feet, recognizing her as the woman who'd first approached him on behalf of North Star, then again outside his office.

"You." Why was the woman from North Star sneaking through the house? Pointing a gun and fighting with him?

The woman glared up at him, then landed a kick to his stomach, and he cursed himself for being caught off guard. She made a run for it to go up the stairs, but Tucker got his breath back quickly enough to grab her by the foot. He heard her let out a curse as she crashed into the stairs.

"Why are Wyatts always ruining my life?" she demanded, kicking back at him.

"What the hell are you doing? North Star is supposed to be the good guys."

She stopped kicking and fighting him off and gave a derisive snort before rolling onto her back. Tucker had the sense she could easily kick him down the stairs and there wouldn't be much he could do about it.

"I have my orders, from those *good* guys." The woman jerked her chin toward the attic "She knows something. She needs to come with me or our mission is compromised. Granger knew you'd be difficult about it."

"How do you know she knows something?" Tucker demanded. How on earth could they know about Rachel's dreams?

The woman gave him a withering glare. "We know everything, Wyatt. Haven't you caught on?"

It didn't matter. It couldn't. "Screw your mission. She's got nothing to do with it and you know it. You're going to drag an innocent into the midst of this? Via kidnapping?"

The woman's expression went grim, but Tucker thought he saw a flash of conscience. "I have my orders," she repeated.

Which told Tucker she didn't particularly want to follow those orders.

"Excuse me?" Both he and the woman he'd fought looked up at the top of the stairs. Rachel stood with her arms over her chest, expression furious. "Maybe one of you could tell me what's going on and I, the woman in question, can decide for myself?"

Chapter Ten

Rachel was shaking, but she'd wrapped her arms around herself to keep it from showing. She was at the top of the stairs and from what she could tell, Tucker and...some woman he knew were on the landing in the middle of the stairs having an argument about her.

"Rach."

"No, I don't think I want you to tell me," she said, holding on to her composure by a very thin thread. Tucker had been lying to her, that much was clear.

"Listen. My name is Shay. I'm with the North Star Group. Tucker and Cody Wyatt have worked for us. Your father's past connected to ours, so we're helping him out. If you come with me—"

"What a load of bull. You're not helping him. You're using him," Tucker said disgustedly. "If you're taking her against her will, you're not in this to protect anyone."

"No one said it was against my will, Tucker."

She heard him take a few stairs. "She was damn well going to, Rachel. She snuck in here, and she fought me—"

"You started that," Shay interrupted.

"She was going to kidnap you. Because you know things about your father's past. Not because she wants to protect you or Duke, but because they'll do anything to bring down the Sons. Including letting innocent people get hurt."

There was a heavy, poignant silence.

"Don't have anything to say to that?" Tucker said scathingly to the woman.

Who still didn't say anything. Rachel didn't understand any of this, but she understood one thing. "You have my father."

"We're helping your father," this Shay person said. "It's what we do."

"What does this have to do with the Sons?" she asked. Because of course it did. Tucker had lied to her and her father was in danger because of the Sons of the Badlands.

What else was new?

"Rachel, listen to me—"

"You knew where he was, who he was being protected by and *why*, but you didn't think to share that with me?" Her throat closed with every word, until the last one was a squeak.

"Rach." He sounded pained, hurt.

But she couldn't have any sympathy for him. He'd lied to her. Let her worry and fear and… He'd used her. Even if he was right about this North Star Group using Dad instead of helping him, Tucker had used her. Knowing…everything.

"If I go with you, what happens?" she said, addressing Shay.

"I'd take you to your father."

"Oh, that's low," Tucker said sourly. "She would not. They would interrogate you about your dreams until they got the information they wanted. If you give them what they want, they *might* let you see Duke, but considering they're using him as bait, I don't think that's happening anytime soon. They need him. They need the information they think you might have. What they don't need is a father–daughter reunion. And who knows, they might use you as bait, too. You can't go with her, Rachel."

"She's coming with me. Whether she does it willingly or not, my mission is to bring her back. So I will."

But Rachel noted they were standing in the attic staircase having this conversation. Shay wasn't making a move to fight Tucker anymore. She hadn't yet attempted to take Rachel against her will like she was saying she would.

"Can you promise my father will be okay if I go with you willingly?"

There was a hesitation. "I…can't promise that. Your father's in a dangerous situation."

"Think, Rachel," Tuck implored her. "I know you're mad at me. Maybe you'll never forgive me. I get it. But think about your father. What would he want you to do?"

"I don't care as much about what he'd want me to do as what I can do to protect him."

"They'd use whatever you gave them to complete their mission. You and Duke would be collateral damage." Tucker sounded so…desperate. So intent. It wasn't his usual self.

But his usual self had been lying to her. Should she have seen it? There had been hints. Hesitations. A carefulness.

The woman was suspiciously silent at Tucker's accusation. "Is that true?" Rachel asked quietly.

There was a long silence. "It's not…untrue."

"So, you're both liars who don't care about anyone?"

"Your father wanted you safe," Tucker said, and while he was being contrite, so to speak, there was a thread of steel in his words. "You and Sarah. Why do you think I'm here? He—"

"You saw him. Before he disappeared. You saw him and you lied to all of us."

She couldn't see his expression, but she knew all those accusations landed like blows. Unless he was a completely different man than she'd always believed. Which maybe he was.

"He wanted you and Sarah protected," Tucker repeated, and his voice was rough. She wanted to believe that was emotion. Guilt.

She just didn't know what to believe about him anymore. He'd seen her father. He'd let her worry.

He'd comforted her after her dreams. Stepped in and made meals, cleaned up. He'd taught her self-defense and…maybe he'd tried to ease some of her fears. She thought of the badge, the key.

"Were you lying about looking into the name?"

Tucker was silent for ticking awful seconds where she wanted to curl into herself and cry. Just…disappear from this world where the man she trusted was such a liar.

"I wasn't lying. I looked into it. I was told to leave it be."

"In fairness, he didn't leave it be," Shay said. "Which is why I'm here."

"You guys are keeping some kind of tabs on me?" Tucker growled as if he was both surprised and disgusted by the information. "What the hell is this?"

"It's business, Wyatt. The business of taking down the Sons."

"I'm so tired of people trying to take down the Sons,"

Rachel said, her voice growing louder with every word. "I'm so tired of people getting hurt because of the *Sons*. My father and I have nothing to do with them. Why can't you leave us alone?"

"Listen, you can dismiss me and all, but neither of you actually have a say. If I don't take you, they'll send someone else. You're a part of North Star's mission now. They won't just take no for an answer. It'd be easier if you just came with me."

Rachel didn't know why that was the straw that broke the camel's back. "And I am really done doing what's *easier* for everyone else."

TUCKER HAD TO ignore the searing pain in his chest. The slick black weight of guilt. He had to focus on getting Rachel out of this mess. Once she was safe… Well, he could self-flagellate and she could hate him forever.

He rubbed at his chest.

"If you don't come with me of your own volition," Shay said in a careful, emotionless voice, "I'll take you by force."

Tucker had already positioned himself between Shay and Rachel. He was ready to fight. He didn't think Shay would use the gun against him. At least he hoped not.

"She is an innocent bystander. Whatever she knows is wrapped up in nightmares she can't untangle." He thought about the badge, the key he'd slid into his pocket. He could give that to Shay as a peace offering. It might even help Duke, and it wasn't that he thought North Star was evil—they just didn't care about people. They cared about their mission.

As for him, he cared about too many people involved to let this go so far as to touch Rachel. The key might be some kind of insurance if he kept it. So, he had to.

Tucker turned to Rachel. She held herself impossibly still, her expression mostly blank. Except her eyes. They were hurt. Betrayed.

And he'd done the betraying.

He had to get her out of this. Maybe she'd never forgive him, but if he could get her out of this, maybe he could forgive himself.

"Your father wanted me to protect you from this. Keep you separate."

"But I'm *not* separate. If they're here about my dreams, there's something real in them." Her eyebrows drew together. "It has to be real."

"That doesn't mean you have to put yourself in danger. It doesn't mean you have to go with this group who doesn't care about you."

"This group has my father."

"You going there doesn't help him. It helps *them*." He wouldn't let her go. Even if she wanted to. But maybe he could assuage at least some of his guilt if she'd just understand the truth here. A truth he hadn't fully understood until now.

Maybe North Star wanted to take down the Sons, but they didn't care enough about the innocent collateral damage involved.

"Oh, just someone punch me," Shay said with no small amount of exasperation.

"What?" Tucker demanded, turning from Rachel to face her.

"In the face." She pointed to her nose. "Make it good, too."

"What are you talking about?"

"I can't go back to Granger unscathed *and* with you having gotten away. You need to make it look like you beat me. Literally and figuratively."

Finally, what Shay was saying got through. She was…letting them go. "I… I can't punch a woman."

She rolled her eyes. "I can punch you first if it gets you going."

"That's not—"

"I'll do it," Rachel said, walking down the stairs. She stopped on the stair right above Shay.

"No offense, but—"

Rachel squared like he'd taught her, curled her fist and landed a blow right to Shay's face.

Swearing in time with Rachel, Shay gingerly placed her palm on her jaw, working it back and forth. Rachel shook out her hand, then cradled it.

"Well, that'll work," Shay said. "Hell."

"You really think one punch is going to convince them?"

"I can handle the rest, but I couldn't punch my own self in the face." She gave Rachel a once-over. "Not half bad. Keep working on that and you might be one hell of a fighter." She moved as if to leave, but Tucker stepped in front of her on the stairs.

"I should take your gun."

She grimaced, clearly loathing the idea of losing her weapon.

"They can't think you got back in one piece still armed, can they?"

"Yeah, yeah, yeah." She handed over the weapon.

Still, Tucker couldn't move out of her way. "Will they kick you out?"

She shrugged. "Not if I quit first."

"Why would you do that?"

"Because you're right, Wyatt. I'm not in the business of hurting innocent people for the sake of a mission. North Star didn't start out that way, but lately…

Doesn't matter. It's getting old and maybe this is my last straw. You're going to need to run, though. Whether I get kicked out or quit—they'll keep coming for her. She knows stuff." Shay let out a sigh. "That phone Granger gave you?"

Tucker pulled it out of his pocket. It was in a couple pieces after his fall down the stairs.

Shay nodded. "That's good. Leave it here."

It dawned on Tucker that meant Granger had been tracking him, maybe listening to him. He'd know about everything up to the fight on the stairs. He nodded grimly at Shay, tossing the phone onto the ground. He smashed it once more under his heel for good measure.

Shay looked back at Rachel, then leaned close to whisper to Tucker. "Get her out of here ASAP. Whatever she knows, they'll use it. Not to help or protect Knight, but to get the Sons. I want the Sons destroyed as much as anybody, and I imagine you do, too, but good people shouldn't be used as bait to take them down."

"If you don't quit, if you don't get kicked out, you could help keep Duke safe. From the inside."

She smiled wryly. "That's a lot of ifs."

"Like you said, we both want to bring down the Sons. We just don't want innocent people hurt in the process. We could work together on this."

She shook her head. "You and your brother. Two peas in a dumb, naive pod."

"Is that a yes?"

She blew out a breath. "Look, I'll do what I can. That does *not* mean we're working together. Be clear on that."

He wasn't sure he believed her, and when he held out a hand for a shake, she shook her head. "We are *not* partners. Be best for you both if you get out of here before I do."

Tucker nodded and looked up at Rachel. Her expression was grim. But Shay was right, they had to get out of here. He didn't know where yet, but he'd figure it out.

What he wasn't so sure he was going to figure out was how to live with what he'd done.

Chapter Eleven

Tucker stole a horse.

Maybe it was harsh for Rachel to consider it stealing, considering it was *her* horse, and she was one of the people riding it, but it felt like stealing. It felt like lying and scaring the people she loved by disappearing.

Like Dad did?

She didn't even have time to wallow in the betrayal of it all because Shay was absolutely telling the truth, no doubt about it. Someone else would come for her, because her dreams were true.

True.

They rode Buttercup away from the ranch—in the opposite direction of the pasture Dev and Sarah were working in this afternoon. It felt really stupid to be riding a horse named Buttercup when trying to escape a group that was trying to bring down the Sons—which was what she wanted.

How could two groups of people want the same thing and disagree so fundamentally on how to get there?

She didn't speak as Tucker explained everything from the beginning. His helping out North Star. Being ready to quit before he walked into a diner with the North Star guy and her father.

Her father. Who'd brought down dirty cops as a

young man and was somehow paying for it over thirty years later.

Her father wasn't who she'd thought. Tucker wasn't who she'd thought.

Oh, that probably wasn't fair. In fact, it was really quite *Wyatt* of Tucker to want to save the day without telling her. Still, no matter how justified, the fact he'd lied to her and she'd bought it hook, line and sinker… It hurt.

Maybe his deception was necessary, but how easily he'd fooled her made her feel stupid. And weak. Now she was riding a horse, with Tucker's hard body directly behind her, through the rolling hills of southeastern South Dakota like she was some kidnapped bride on the prairie.

Rachel didn't say anything as they rode, and after he'd told the whole story, neither did Tucker. She didn't know how many hours they rode in silence, how many miles they covered. She didn't know where they were going and she didn't ask.

Because she was too afraid he'd offer another lie, and she'd believe it as gospel.

"Sun's going down," Tucker said, his voice rusty with disuse. "We should camp."

"Camp," Rachel echoed. Up to this point, she hadn't been afraid, not really. In the moments Tucker had been fighting Shay, yes, but after that there'd been too many other feelings. Sadness, fury, hurt and the ache in her hand from punching Shay had taken up too much space to be truly afraid.

But now the idea of camping had those beats of panic starting in her chest.

"I'm sorry. It's the only way," Tucker said gently.

He brought the horse to a halt and he got off. Since she couldn't see the ground, she had to let him help her dismount.

Rachel immediately pulled away from his grasp, though she kept her feet in the same place since she couldn't be sure she wouldn't trip and fall.

"So, what's the plan?" she asked flatly.

He handed her something. Her cane. It took her a moment to register that and to take it. They'd left in such a hurry, but he'd thought to grab her probing cane.

After lying to you about everything.

"Right now? The plan is to keep you away from North Star."

"For how long?" she asked.

"As long as we need to."

"We're just going to camp in the hills until someone magically alerts us to the fact North Star no longer needs me?"

"You still have your phone," he reminded her.

"It doesn't have service out here." She was completely alone in the wilderness with a man who…who she'd trusted and who'd lied to her. About the most important things. "Sarah is going to be worried sick."

"She would be worried sick if you'd stayed—because Shay would have taken you, or someone else would have come and finished the job. At least she'll know you're with me."

It was true, but that didn't make it comforting. Maybe because she knew Tucker would have stood up for her. He would have fought and protected her against all the people North Star sent. Liar that he was. "I don't camp."

"I know," he said, with enough weight that she figured he understood it was because it reminded her of that night. Of her memories or dreams. She'd been alone in the wilderness when the mountain lion had attacked, or at least that's what she'd believed until lately.

"I'm sorry this has touched you, Rachel. I wish I could make it not."

She wanted to ask him if that was another lie, but she understood in that statement that while Tucker had lied to her about facts, he'd never lied to her about feelings. He'd promised to try to keep her father safe—and he had been working to do that. He'd promised her father to keep her out of it.

He'd failed, and likely was busy heaping all sorts of guilt on himself. She wished that made her feel better, but it actually deflated some of her anger.

"He's my father. It was always going to touch me no matter what you did, Tucker."

He didn't respond, and she could hear the sounds of him making camp. He'd gotten her out of the house so quickly she didn't know how he'd had time to gather supplies, but he seemed to have enough.

"I know you don't want to camp. I wish there was another way," he finally said, so grave and… It wasn't fair. She couldn't be mad at him when he was beating himself up.

"You know, the same thing would have happened even if you'd told us the truth from the beginning. Didn't Shay basically say that phone North Star gave you was tracking everything?"

"Maybe if I'd been a better liar, you'd be just fine at home."

"Is that what you want? To be a better liar?"

He expelled a loud breath. "No."

"That's why you were going to quit. Well, Dad threw a wrench in your plans, and so did my dreams."

"That sounds a lot like absolution. And misplaced blame."

"It's neither. You did what you had to do. And I can't control my dreams."

"You should be mad at me."

"Oh, I am," she told him. "I'm mad at you. I'm irritated with myself. I'm downright furious with Dad. I don't want to camp. I don't want to run. I don't want any of this."

"I'm sor—"

"I don't want your apologies, either. I want the lies to end. And I want Dad back in one piece. So, we have to figure out how we're going to do that. We can't wait. We can't play the hide-Rachel-away-in-a-safe-corner game. We have to fight. For my father. We have to help him. However we can."

RACHEL SOUNDED FIERCE, and looked it, standing there in the fading daylight, probing cane grasped in one hand, the other clenched in a fist. Her expression was hard and determined.

He wished he could agree. Immediately support her. "If I knew how to do that, I would have already done it."

It was humbling to admit. He'd seen no real way to help Duke except protect Rachel and he'd failed. He'd brought her more into the fold by not suspecting McMillan might be listening in.

The bastard had listened in on private conversations. Rachel's dream aftermath. Talking about her mother and the buttons.

He fingered the key in his pocket. Duke already knew his past. There were no secrets to be uncovered.

Whatever the key unlocked, Duke knew about it. Had locked something up. It wouldn't help him now. In fact, it was probably best if it stayed buried.

"Dad's being threatened by this Vianni family, through the Sons, according to North Star."

"It's not just North Star's story. Your father was there when McMillan told me about it. It's true."

She nodded sharply. "Okay. It's true. North Star is supposed to keep him safe, but both you and Shay acted like they're trying to use Dad as some kind of bait to get enough evidence on the Sons. But to what end? To arrest them all? Kill them all?"

"I'm not privy to North Star's plans."

"No, but Shay said that it's gotten too mission focused. They're not caring about people. I don't want Dad to be collateral damage."

"I don't either, Rachel."

"I know you don't." She moved forward using her cane to avoid the dips and bumps in the ground.

Tucker had found the flattest, most even ground he could, but he'd wanted to stay in the hills and trees as much as possible.

"But North Star knows everything about Dad, and presumably they know a lot about the Viannis and the Sons. They don't *need* him there."

"They're protecting him."

"Are they?" she returned. "Or did they say that to you, maybe even to him, but what they really meant is they're using him?"

It was a horrible thought. Even if he didn't agree with everything North Star had done, he believed in their mission. "Your Dad went to them willingly. He had some connection to their leader. Or the leader's dad. Something about him being the reason he had this

WITSEC life here. He had to believe they were going to…fix things or he wouldn't have gone."

"But I don't. I don't believe that at all. When one of their own, a woman sent to take me, let's us go instead… Something is very, very wrong. I want my father out. Screw their mission. *You* said that."

"I did. And I meant it in regard to Shay's particular mission of kidnapping you. But I don't want to sabotage North Star. Even if I don't approve of their methods, I approve of what they're doing. I *support* what they're doing." How had this gotten so messed up? "Bringing down the Sons is important."

"It is. Should my father die for it?"

"I don't think North Star would let that happen." But their attempted kidnapping of Rachel made him uncomfortably concerned.

"You don't *think*."

Tucker raked his hands through his hair. "People are after him. Dangerous people. Regardless of the Sons or North Star, your father was a target."

"Because he did something right. Don't you know what that's like?"

It snapped something in him. That leash on his temper and his emotions he fought so hard to keep tethered. "Yeah, I do. I know it's living your life in fear, wondering when it shows up to take you down. I know it's watching your brothers get hurt over and over again by this thing you escaped, while you can't do a damn thing about it. Knowing you don't even rate to be a target because apparently you're not that much of a threat to their kind of evil. I know what it's all like, Rachel, and I'm telling you, *we* can't do anything about it."

She blinked. "Tuck—"

He was so horrified by his torrent of words that had

nothing to do with her or this situation, he turned his back on her. "No. It's not about me. It's about Duke."

"Tucker—"

"I said no. I won't steal your father out of the North Star's hands, not with you. I can't protect you both from all the different forces after you. I got you out of there so they can't use you, can't use your dreams. Because Duke would have wanted me to keep you safe and because it's the right thing." Because the thought of putting her in any more danger just about ripped him in two.

He had to stop this…*emotion*. It was weak. It was…

Wasn't that what Ace told you? Emotion is weak? Caring is weak?

"Would you do it without me?" Rachel asked firmly, breaking through those old memories of his father.

He'd promised to not let himself lose control. The whole tirade about the Sons and his brothers was bad enough. He wouldn't say anything else stupid. But how could she say that? How could she think he'd leave her behind? To think he'd ever, *ever* let her be a target.

He moved to her, telling himself to keep it locked down. He didn't lose his temper. He didn't lose control. Not because emotions were weak as Ace had always said, but because he had to handle this.

But he wanted to grab her by the arms and shake her. He wanted to do all manner of impossible, disastrously ill-advised things.

Instead, he stood in front of her, maybe a few inches too close, and kept his voice ruthlessly controlled. "Let's make one thing very, very clear. There is not a damn thing I will do without you right now."

She stood very still. The sun had disappeared behind the hills, though there was enough light to still make her out. She wouldn't be able to see anything, even shapes in this light. Still, she moved unerringly into him, wrapping her arms around him.

A hug. A comfort.

He couldn't return it. He couldn't push her away. He could only stand there still as a statue, her arms around him and her cheek pressed to his chest.

"Hell, Rach. Be mad at me. Hate me. I can't stand you being nice to me right now."

"I guess it's too bad for you, because I can't stand to be mad at you right now." She pulled back, tilted her head up toward his. "If you told me right now, promised me right now, that you won't lie again, I'll believe you."

Even knowing he shouldn't't, he placed his palm on her cheek. "I'm sorry. I can't do that."

Chapter Twelve

Rachel didn't move away from his hand, even though Tucker's words were…not what she'd expected. At all. She liked the warmth of his calloused palm on her cheek, and she liked how close he was as night descended around them.

She shouldn't be concerning herself with warmth. Or how nice it felt. When he was telling her that he wouldn't promise not to lie.

"Why not?" she asked, and the fact it came out a breathy whisper surprised her, as much as the fact he didn't remove his hand. Instead, his thumb brushed back and forth over her cheekbone.

A sparkling heat shimmered underneath her skin, in her blood. She didn't understand it. Not when it was Tucker touching her, but she could hardly deny it existed. The feeling was too big and real and potent.

His voice was low and rough when he spoke. "I can't promise to never lie. I lied to Brady and Cecilia last month. It was one of the hardest things I've ever done— to lie to my brother like that. Knowing they were both suspicious of me. But I'd do it all over again. I'd have to. Because I was trying to accomplish something good and right. If I had to lie to protect you, Rachel, I would. Any of you. Your sisters. My brothers. Your father. Anyone."

She might not have believed him, except she knew from Cecilia he had definitely lied to Brady. His own brother. Even when Cecilia had been convinced he'd been turned into a Sons member, Brady had trusted him. Even with the lies.

If his own brother could—did—how could she not?

"Okay." She didn't dare nod because he might take his hand away. "Okay."

"We'll camp tonight, and maybe in the morning we'll have a clearer idea of what to do. I managed to grab enough supplies for a day or two for us and Buttercup. This is temporary. Until we figure out how to fix this."

She had no idea how they were going to do that, but it didn't feel so impossible with Tucker touching her. Despite everything, she believed in him. He'd gotten them this far. He'd fought off Shay. Convinced her to let them go.

"I want my dad to be safe. I don't want this awful thing to come back and hurt him. He did the right thing, and he had to give up his whole life. It isn't right that he managed to build a new one and they want to take it away from him."

"No, it isn't. If I knew what to do... If I had any clue, I'd do it. *That* I can promise you."

She nodded, the scrape of his rough hand against her cheek a lovely, sparkling distraction from the fear and confusion roiling inside of her.

He didn't need to promise her anything, but of course he would. She had a plethora of *good* men in her life, and it often insulated her to the fact that bad people like Ace Wyatt and whoever was after her father existed. She so seldom remembered what an enormous miracle it was that Tucker and his brothers had escaped the Sons and become...them.

Good men, determined to do good in the world. Maybe not perfectly. He had his issues. That whole spiel about not being worth the Sons' notice because he wasn't a threat.

If anything underscored all her hurt, it was *that*. Tucker put on a face for the world that he was perfectly adjusted, a good detective, brother, man. And he was those things.

But he didn't think he was.

She didn't know how to make him believe he was all the things *she* thought he was. She could only lean into his hand, lean into *him* and this feeling.

She still didn't know how she felt about being attracted to Tucker, about the possibility he felt the same way. She didn't want to be a domino of Knight girls falling in a line for the Wyatt boys.

But everything swirled inside of her obscuring what she didn't want. She could only think of what she did.

"If they don't think you're a threat, they don't understand you. Caring about people isn't a weakness, Tucker." She placed her hand on his chest when the moment didn't evaporate like she'd been afraid it would. "You don't need to be in North Star or putting yourself in mortal danger to be as strong as your brothers, as important. You solve problems. You take *care* of people. That's just as important as putting your life on the line."

He inhaled sharply, but his hand was still on her face. He was so close, their bodies brushing in the increasing darkness around them. "Rach, I don't know what to say to all that."

His voice was as rough as his hand. He was as strong as she'd said, standing there so close. She couldn't resist tipping her mouth up…wishing for something she'd promised herself she couldn't possibly want.

Then his mouth touched hers. Featherlight. No one had ever kissed her before, and she'd always figured it would take some miracle—getting off the ranch, away from her overprotective father and sisters, into a life that was independent and hers, and when would *that* ever happen.

But it was Tucker Wyatt. She didn't need to convince him she was independent—even when he was protecting her, it was only because that's what he *did*.

It ended far too quickly. The kiss. His hand on her cheek. The sound his footsteps made had her thinking he stumbled back and away, as if he'd realized whom he'd kissed.

"We should get some sleep," he said, his voice tight.

She barked out a laugh, couldn't seem to help the reaction. He'd *kissed* her and he was talking about going to sleep. He was ignoring it. Coward. "You kissed me."

"Forget it. It was… Just forget that."

"Forget it? Why would I?"

"Wrong place. Wrong time. Wrong everything."

She frowned at that. Intellectually, he was probably right. Wrong time certainly, which went along with place. But… "It didn't feel so wrong."

"Well, it was," he said firmly.

So firmly that she thought maybe she was missing something. "Why?"

"*Why?* Because…"

She waited impatiently for him to come up with this reason she was missing. "Because?" she demanded when he was just silent.

"Because you're…you're like a sister to me."

She snorted. It was such a pathetic grasping at straws. "Then you're a pervert, Tucker. You don't check out your sister's boobs and then kiss her."

"I didn't! I never…"

"Sarah said you did."

"I…"

"Maybe you can't promise to lie to me, but if you lie to me about *this*, I won't forgive you. Period."

He was quiet for a long stretched-out moment. "I don't know what you want me to say."

"Why did you kiss me?"

"You want the truth? Here and now of all places? Fine. Maybe I owe that to you after all this. Yeah, I'm attracted to you. I don't have a clue as to why…why *now*. I just am. It's just there. Then you had to go say all that stuff, looking up at me like you meant it."

"I can't see," she pointed out, hoping to lighten the moment.

"You know what I mean," he replied gruffly.

"Yeah, I think I do." Unfortunately that made her all the more gooey-hearted when they had much more important things to deal with. Still, truth for truth was only fair. "I meant it, Tuck. I did. And I…guess I'm attracted to you, too."

"You guess," he muttered disgustedly.

Which almost made her smile. "I'm still working through all that. I haven't exactly had a lot of experience with this."

He groaned. "Please God, tell me that wasn't your first kiss."

"Okay, I won't tell you."

He swore a few times, and she had no idea why that made her want to laugh.

"Look. We need to…go to sleep. Tomorrow, we'll come up with a plan. No more of…this stuff."

"This *stuff*?"

"Whatever this is, we'll figure it out when we're not

camping in the South Dakota wilderness, with absolutely no plan on how we're going to accomplish what we want. For now, we get some rest and focus on the important things."

She nodded as though she agreed with him, and let him lead her into the tent.

TUCKER WOKE UP in his own personal nightmare. He had to come up with a plan to save Duke, to keep Rachel safe. To outwit North Star, the Sons and some other group of people out for blood.

All knowing he'd kissed Rachel. And now she was curled up next to him. Because he'd only had time to grab the pack out of his truck—which was outfitted for one person. A tiny tent and *one* sleeping bag.

It was edging far enough into fall that nights were cold, so he'd had to let her cozy up next to him and fall asleep. All while pretending that kiss had never happened.

It was the only way to survive this. Put a brick wall around his own personal slip-up. Seal it off and forget it.

But he'd never in a million years be able to forget the feel of his lips on hers. Simple kisses weren't supposed to…do that. Make you forget who you were and what was important: safety. Hers most of all.

But he'd forgotten everything except her for those humming seconds—not just the kiss, but her talking to him like she understood him. When it felt like no one did.

He knew his brothers saw him as an equal. They couldn't understand that he didn't *feel* like one.

Right now in this warm tent, Rachel's hair curling against his cheek, the soft rise and fall of her chest matching time with his… Well, he supposed Rachel seeing through his issues was a better line of thought than how good she felt here against him.

She shifted, yawned, her eyes slowly blinking open. Even though she wouldn't be able to see in the dim light of the tent, he could see. The sleep slowly lift. Realization and understanding dawning.

And the way she definitely did not try to slide away or disengage from him, but seemed perfectly content to cuddle closer.

There was a very large part of him that wanted to test it out, too. To see what it would be like to relax into her. To touch her face again. To recognize the soft curves of her body as they pressed to his. To kiss her and—

No. Not possible.

Carefully, he disengaged from her arms and scooted away from her as best he could in the tiny tent.

"Maybe we should go back. I've got nothing. My brothers might have some ideas. They're better at this than I am."

She was quiet for a while as she pushed herself up into a sitting position. "Are they better at it, or were they just put in a position you weren't?"

"You don't need to keep defending me. I don't have low self-esteem. I—"

"You've got issues, Tuck. Good news is, we all do. Better news, you have someone around who's not going to let you believe the crap you tell yourself. So…" She yawned. "I don't suppose you have any coffee?"

He didn't know how to stay in this tiny tent with her looking sleepy and rumpled and gorgeous, talking about how everyone had issues. "I've got some instant. I'll go warm up some water." He didn't *dive* for the tent opening, but he got outside in record time.

The sun was just beginning to rise and the grass held

the tiniest hint of frost. It was cold, made colder by the fact that the tent had been so warm. He shivered against the chill as he zipped the tent back up.

A piece of paper fluttered to the ground next to him. Tuck whirled around, scanning the area. But there was nothing except the soft whisper of the wind against the rolling hills of ranch land.

He crouched down, studied the note on the grass. It was wet from the dew, and all he could figure was that it had been left on the tent, and opening the flap had knocked it off.

He looked around, scanning all he could see for any sign of human life or movement. But the world was quiet, with only the interruption of birdsong.

He picked the paper up and opened the fold. Water had smudged the first word, but Tucker could figure it out and read the rest clearly.

Rachel knows the key and the lock.

Tucker flipped the paper over. Nothing on the back. Nothing else on the front. Just one sentence. That didn't make any sense.

The key and the lock? He thought of the key in his pocket. But what did it unlock? And Rachel definitely didn't act like she had any idea what the key was to.

"Rach." He unzipped the flap again and stuck his head in. She was crouched over, rolling up the sleeping bag. He could tell she'd already tidied what few things were inside. "I found something."

She yawned again. "I take it not coffee." She sighed. "What is it?"

"A note. I… I think this is Duke's handwriting." He frowned, studied it. He wasn't a handwriting expert, and he'd never spent much time scrutinizing Duke's writing, but it certainly looked like his typical slanted scratch.

Tuck looked around the campsite again. He hadn't heard anyone so it was near impossible Duke had left the note for them. He was a big man, and even if he'd been a cop in a former life, stealth was not Duke's current skill. "It was on the tent, then when I opened the flap it fell to the ground."

The only one who knew enough, and had enough access to Duke to get a message to them, was Shay. "Shay must have gotten it to us. She must have."

"Is there any way it's a trap or a trick?" Rachel asked.

"It wasn't addressed to us. There's no signature. It's written in *some* kind of code. So, it might not be from your father, but it's Duke's handwriting." He cleared his throat. "As of yesterday, North Star still had Duke. It could be from North Star. They could have made him write it, but I have to believe if they went through the trouble to track us down, they would have just taken us. You especially. Or written a more specific note."

"Here. Let me see it."

He handed her the paper, though he wasn't sure what she was going to do with it. She felt the corner of the paper. "It's Dad. And not like someone made him write it, either. That's an actual note from him."

"How can you tell?"

"We developed a little system when I was in school. If he had to sign something and he'd done it, he'd poke a little hole in the corner. If there was no hole, I knew I needed to ask him again." She held up the paper, and sure enough there was a small hole in the corner. "What does it say?"

"Rachel knows the key and the lock."

Her eyebrows drew together. *"Me?"* She shook her head. "I don't know anything about that key we found. Let alone what it would unlock."

They were silent for the next few minutes, Rachel frowning as if searching her mind for an answer. Tucker studied the note again, wondering if there was more to it. Something he wasn't seeing. Something more... abstract.

He looked up at Rachel. She'd gone back to tidying up the tent. It was less smooth than how she did it at home since she was going by feel rather than lifelong knowledge of a place. Still, she had the inside of the tent all packed up in no time.

Duke thought she knew what he was talking about, Tucker assumed. Rachel didn't think she knew anything about the key or its lock.

"Maybe it's about your dream. If you know, but you don't actually *know*, maybe the answer is in your subconscious."

Chapter Thirteen

Her dream. Rachel's arms broke out in goose bumps. As much as she was slowly coming around to the idea her dream might be more reality and memory than fiction, she wasn't comfortable with her subconscious knowing something she couldn't access.

Especially when it came to this.

"Dad doesn't know anything about my dreams changing. He still thinks they're about a mountain lion."

"Did you tell him about your dreams?"

"When I was a kid. When I first started having them. He…" An uncomfortable memory had her chest tightening, like she couldn't breathe.

Tucker was immediately at her side. He rubbed a hand up and down her back. "Hey, breathe. It's all right, sweetheart. Take a deep breath."

She managed, barely. The panic had been so swift, so all encompassing, it was hard to move beyond. "I don't know if this was the first time I had the dream, but I remember being little. I still… I may have even still had the bandages on my face. Dad would sleep on the floor of my room. Mom would try to get him to come to bed, but he would insist. He said he was afraid I'd wander away again."

Tucker kept rubbing her back, and it gave her some

modicum of comfort as her body seemed to chill from the inside out.

"I remember telling him about the nightmare and he told me not to tell Mom. That whenever I had nightmares or felt scared, I should tell him. Only him. He said so Mom wouldn't worry, but..."

"If your mother didn't know..."

"How...how could she have not known? How could he have lied to her? How could he have had *me* lie to her?"

"He was in WITSEC, Rach. I'm not saying it was the right thing to do, but you're supposed to leave your old life behind. Entirely."

"It's his story. The mountain lion. He made that up." The horror of that almost made her knees weak. He'd pushed her into the mountain lion story, made sure he convinced her the dreams were of that.

Even when they weren't.

"Are you sure?" Tucker asked gently.

"No. How can I be sure?" Her throat closed up and she refused to cry, but how was she expected to have an answer from a dream? "Everything is wrapped up in a dream that suddenly changed on me!"

"Hey. Maybe it's not about your dream. Maybe I've got this all wrong."

She shook her head. "You know you don't. You're a detective. You know how to piece things together." She wrapped her arms around herself. "What else would I know that I don't think I know? You're right. It's something about my dream, but I don't know *what*."

"Okay, then let's work through this like I'd work through any case. We start at the beginning. What's the very first part of your dream you remember?"

"Do you really think the answer is in my dream?" she asked.

"I don't know. I really don't. But it might help. To lay it all out."

Rachel didn't think that was possible. She'd spent most of her life knowing this dream might pop up. Except the dream had morphed. From what Dad had pointed her to—to the truth? It was impossible to know for sure.

Maybe she'd never get rid of the nightmares, but maybe she could find the truth in the way it had changed… Maybe.

"I'm not sure I know where to start," she said, her voice rough and her chest tight.

Tucker's arm came around her shoulders and he gave her an affectionate squeeze. "Sit. No use crouching around."

"No, no. I need to…to move. To be doing something."

"Okay, so we'll go out and break down the tent while you talk. Sound good?"

She nodded. He helped lead her outside, then led her to the first stake.

"Do you mind if I do it myself?"

"Whatever you need, Rach."

She nodded once and pulled out the stake. Then she felt around the tent, slowly taking it apart. She didn't like to camp, but she and Sarah had often put tents up and down around the ranch as forts or playhouses, so she was familiar with the process of breaking down the tent even without her sight.

Tucker didn't push. He didn't ask questions. Nor did he jump in to help take down the tent. He waited until she started to speak herself. "I'm not sure I know exactly where it starts. When I wake up, when I try to remember, it's just that I'm suddenly aware I'm being carried away."

"Carried away from where?"

"Home. I don't see home, but I know he's taking me away from home." Even knowing she was safe with Tucker, the fear and panic clawed at her. She focused on the tent. "He's taking me away from…lights. I think there's a light behind us and he's going into the dark."

"Lights on in the house maybe?"

"I think so." Even though it was silly since she couldn't see anyway, she closed her eyes. She tried to bring the nightmare back to her. She'd seen for the first three years of her life. There were things she could remember, and this dream had always been one of them.

"Or maybe it's the stables." She opened her eyes, frowning. She could tell light was beginning to dawn in the here and now, but she still couldn't fully make out Tucker's shape. "It isn't windows. It isn't a glow like if it was home at dark. It's more one lone beam of light. I think it's the light outside the stables."

"So, he's taking you away from the stables," Tucker said. His voice was calm and serious and believing. He took everything she said at face value and put it into the puzzle they were trying to work out. "The light on the stables is on the north side. If you're moving straight away from it, that's heading into the north pasture."

"Or toward the highway." She felt how *right* it was, more than saw or knew. Going away from one lone light, heading for the dark of the highway. "The new dream, the changed dream, he's holding me so tight I can barely breathe. I'm too scared to scream. He's talking, but I can't make sense of the words. In my head, they're just a jumble. I just want my mom."

Tears welled up because she still just wanted Mom

and couldn't have her. Couldn't find comfort in her. She'd been gone for so many years now. Rachel folded the tent poles and blinked back tears, fought to make her voice steady. She appreciated that Tucker didn't rush her.

"At some point I notice eyes watching us. They glow a little."

"Mountain lion?"

"At first, that's what I thought. As me. Adult me." She frowned. "I think Dad convinced me that's what I was seeing when I told him about the dream. But when I think about how I saw the eyes move, how it jumps out… I think it was a dog. We used to have dogs then. Lots of them."

"Yeah, four or five, right?"

Rachel nodded. "If this is all real—if it isn't my three-year-old brain getting things mixed up, or dreams mixing with reality, I think it was one of the dogs."

"And it just follows you while the man is carrying you away?"

"Yes. I'm not scared of the eyes. I'm scared of the man. He's holding me too tight, and he has…" She trailed off. This was where she didn't want to go, even knowing she had to.

"Last time, you said he had some kind of knife."

Rachel nodded, folding the tent with shaking hands. "It's either a knife with prongs, or multiple knives. It's sharp, and it keeps flashing in the moonlight." She brought a hand to her scars, and could feel the smooth lines. "It could have made this. Not claws, but this special knife he's carrying." Her breath whooshed out of her. "How is it possible?" she whispered. "And what does any of that tell us about a key?"

"I don't know yet, but let's focus on what you do remember. On the dream."

"That's all I remember. The last one I had, the one where he actually cut me? That's the first time I remember getting that far. Even when I was a kid, he never hurt me in my dream. I woke up before. But in this one, the dog jumps out. The man slashes the knife down and it cuts into me. I can feel the pain and the blood, and hear the dog—barking and snarling. But the dog isn't the one hurting me."

Tucker collected the tent and the poles. She could hear him wrapping it all up and putting it into his backpack. He said nothing.

"Thank you for letting me take down the tent."

"Thank you?"

"Most people can't stand to watch me do something myself, at a slower pace than they would go. They have to jump in to help to speed things up."

"We've got all the time in the world right now, Rach."

But Tucker didn't understand that time didn't always matter. People's compulsion with accomplishing tasks made it hard for them to step back. So, she'd just appreciated that he hadn't needed to do that.

He didn't press about the key, or if she remembered any more of her dream. He simply gave her the space to work through it.

"Do you know where my father is? Where they're keeping him or hiding him or whatever?"

"No."

"Would Cody know?"

Tucker hesitated. "It's possible."

"I don't have the answer to this, Tuck. And Dad clearly wants me to, or thinks I do. He sent us a message, and if Shay was the messenger, it probably wasn't sanctioned by your group."

"No, probably not."

"I need to talk to him. It's the only way."

TUCKER COULDN'T LET his own personal feelings or issues, as she'd call them, rule his thoughts or actions. Though it was hard to ignore how much it hurt, he couldn't do this without bringing his brother into the fold.

His brother who'd actually fought the Sons. On multiple levels. And won. Beat Ace. Beat those who would have hurt Cody and his daughter.

Cody. His *baby* brother.

"Tucker?"

"Sorry. I'm just trying to figure out how that would work. We'd have to get to a place that has cell service, and we don't know for sure that North Star doesn't have ways of tracking your phone, too."

"Maybe we should head back to the ranch. Surely North Star doesn't think we'll go back. They'll think we're on the run. We go back. Get word to someone without phones, and have Cody meet us somewhere? We could hide on the ranch. That's smart, don't you think?"

Tucker had to pause and work very hard to keep the bitterness out of his voice. "Yeah, smart."

"Unless you have a better plan?"

"No, Rachel. I don't." How could he?

He continued to clean up the campsite, leaving Rachel standing there with her cane. She ran her fingers over her horse's mane.

She made quite a picture there, dark hand moving through the cream-colored mane of the horse. Her hair was a mess, but it haloed her face. The sun was rising behind her, making the rolling hills sparkle like some kind of fairyland. Her, the reigning queen of it all.

She made a face. "I can tell you're staring at me."

"Maybe I'm staring at the scenery."

"Maybe. But I don't think you are. Why are you staring at me, Tuck?"

"Maybe I think you're pretty, Rach." Which wasn't what he should have said, even if he meant it. Even if her looking pretty was something akin to a punch in the gut. There wasn't room for this—not just because of the current situation—but because of the *always* situation.

"You could kiss me again," she said, very seriously.

She had no idea what it cost him to sound unaffected. "I could, but I don't think that's such a good idea."

"Why not?"

"I can't imagine what Duke would say if I happened to mention it took us so long to help him because I was busy making out with his daughter after spending the night in a tent together."

"After keeping me from being taken by this North Star Group, who are supposedly good guys but condone kidnapping." She huffed out a breath. "I don't understand why you joined them in the first place. Why you worked for people who made you lie."

"Sometimes lies aren't the worst thing in the world."

"I suppose not, but you're not comfortable with them. The weight of that guilt weighs a little heavier on you."

She was right, somehow always seeing right through him. Which meant it seemed honesty was the only option—especially if it kept him from talking about kissing.

"I've been working with them because… I thought I could do something. My father never thought much of me. Not as a threat or as a successor, and mostly

I've been grateful for that. But I thought I could do something, like Cody and Jamison did. Like Gage and Brady did. Hell, even Dev stood up to him." He scowled. It hadn't ended well for Dev at all, but he'd tried. "I've done nothing. I thought I could be a piece of what brought my father down, so I did what North Star asked even though it hurt."

She dropped her hand from the horse, used her probing cane to move forward until she was close to him. Too close. "Until they wanted to take me." She looked up at him, her eyes dark except where they were damaged.

To think it had been a man not a mountain lion made it all worse somehow. The end result was the same, but someone had done that to her on purpose. When she'd only been three. All because her father had done the right thing decades ago.

"You didn't deserve to be dragged into this."

"No. I'm not sure you did, either." She reached out, resting her hand on his arm.

He wanted to touch her hair, her face. He wanted to somehow take those scars away from her, which was a stupid want. This was the life they had. He could only make the right decisions now.

Which meant he had to keep his hands off her. "The Sons connect to me. They connect to this. Don't they always?"

"Only if you let them." She moved onto her toes, leaned into him. She brushed her lips across his jaw, though he imagined she'd been going for his cheek or mouth. Still, it rippled through him. No matter how he told himself to block it away.

"Dev'd probably be a better option for all this," he

said, voice tight. She'd be good for Dev. All light and hope to his dark and hopeless.

She wrinkled her nose and fell back onto her flat feet. "Dev's even older than *you*. And so grouchy. Dev is better suited for a life of inherent bachelorhood. Grandma Pauline told me once all her uncles were bachelors, and she wouldn't be surprised if the lot of you ended up just like them."

"Did she now. Well, four out of six proved her wrong, didn't they?"

"You won't be a perennial bachelor, Tucker. You're too sweet."

"Gee. Thanks."

"You think that's some kind of slight, but it's a compliment. It's a miracle, actually. The way you were brought up. To have any sweet. I think that's pretty amazing."

She almost made him believe it.

"We should get back. Time isn't on our side. The North Star Group has a lot of skills, technology and reach. We can only avoid them for so long, even with Shay's help."

"All right, but you're not getting out of this so easy."

No, he didn't think he was.

Chapter Fourteen

The ride back to the ranch was quiet. Not tense, exactly. There was a certain comfort to just riding Buttercup, Tucker's strong body behind her. A companionable silence as they both thought through what was next.

She had to believe Cody would know enough about North Star to figure out where they'd be keeping her father or what they'd be doing with him. She had to believe he'd give them the location, Tucker would find Dad, and they'd get him away.

Then what?

Well, the key. Dad would know what the key opened and maybe it would…end everything.

Of course, she thought if it would end everything Dad would have handed it over to North Star, told *them* about the key and the lock. But maybe he just didn't trust them. Maybe he could only trust her.

Rachel wished she had any idea what the key was for. There was nothing to unlock in her dream. There was only darkness and fear. Pain and relief all mixed into one powerful, messy, emotional experience.

Tucker zigzagged through rolling hills. "I'm going to head up along the north pasture, come down to the stables that way. Maybe the route will remind you of something."

"I can't see, Tucker."

"I know, Rachel," he said with an endless patience that dug at her. "But I'll tell you where we are, what I see. It can't hurt to try to reenact the moment. And if it doesn't jog your memory, all we've done is add a little time I would have probably added anyway to make sure we aren't being followed."

She didn't say anything to that. Going through the dream once already had left her emotionally drained. Then there was the fact Tucker had refused to kiss her.

Though she wasn't convinced it was because he didn't *want* to. She figured there was something more about honor or loving her dad or something twisted up. Because he watched her. She couldn't see and she could *tell* he looked at her in ways he hadn't before.

She could feel the tension in him when she'd touched him. That quick little sigh of breath he'd tried to hide when she'd tried to kiss his mouth and ended up just touching her lips to his jaw.

Maybe she'd missed, but that had been nice, too. The rough whiskers against her lips. There had been an exciting friction in that.

Tucker Wyatt and exciting friction. She might have laughed at the thought of those two things going together, but it just seemed…right, when it never had before.

"We're on the hill outside the north pasture gate. I can see the top of the stable. From here I can see the light. If it was dark and the light was on, it'd be visible this whole stretch."

Even though she didn't want to, she brought to mind her dream. The light. "Where's the highway in relation to where we are?"

"We're facing south. The highway is due east."

"And how far would you be able to see the light in that direction?"

He clicked to the horse, and they moved. "Let's see. If you were headed for the highway, but looking back toward the house or stables..." He trailed off and the horse moved in a gently swaying motion beneath them. "Most of the way. The main gate is just coming into view and I can see the very top of it. Which means if the light was on, I'd be able to see it clearer."

The main gate led to a gravel road, which led to the highway, but it all made sense. The light had gotten smaller as the man had taken her. Like it was slowly being enveloped—or in this case, hidden by distance, direction and hills.

"I think that's where he was taking me."

"On foot, right? So, probably heading for a vehicle. Then the dog saves you."

Rachel brought a hand up to her scars. Her mother had never let her feel much self-pity over the loss of sight, over the scars. Rachel supposed her age helped with that. She didn't remember all that much before, so it wasn't a comparison or ruminating over what she'd lost.

But the dog *saving* her felt like too strong a word. She hadn't been saved fully. She'd lost something that night.

"Tuck..." She swallowed at the sudden emotion clogging her throat. "Why do you think he did it? Lied to me. To my mom. Made us think something had happened when it hadn't. I know he had to keep his former life a secret, but... I love him, I do. Nothing changes that, but I'm having a really hard time not being mad at him for warping my nightmares to keep this secret."

"Can you imagine how he feels? He did something right. *One right thing.* He did his job, and he had to leave his entire life. Then he starts a new one and this right thing he did not only haunts him, it hurts and permanently injures his daughter. I lied to you, Rach. Because I thought it would protect you. You and Sarah and… everyone. I can't imagine his lies were any different."

"But they are. He made me think something completely different happened than actually did. It wasn't just a lie of omission or hiding something. He *warped* something I actually experienced."

"What's worse? Believing a random act of Mother Nature hurt you, or that your father's past was out there, just waiting? I know what that's like. To know at any point your past could pop up and ruin your life. I mean, Grandma Pauline gave us a good life, a good childhood once we got out of the Sons. But we always knew Ace could pop up—hurt us, hurt her. We always knew Jamison sacrificed eighteen years to get us out of there. It's a hard, heavy weight."

Rachel didn't know what to say to that. She certainly couldn't argue with it, and as much as it hurt that her father had lied to her in such a devious way, she understood that Tucker thought Duke had given her a gift. Maybe he had. What would life have been like if she'd always been afraid?

Tucker had come through it okay, but she was realizing he had deeper scars than he ever let on.

Tucker's body went suddenly tense, not just behind her but his arms holding the reins around her. Everything in him was iron and she was encompassed in all that strength. "We're going to get off the horse."

"What? Why? What's happened?"

"There's a man watching us." He'd slowed down Buttercup, but they were still moving. "We have to do this quickly. I'm going to swing you off with me. I'll point you in the right direction. Then you run for the stables. I'll send Buttercup off as a distraction, and I'll run for him. Three different directions, and he'll either focus on the horse or me."

"Is it North Star?"

Tucker was quiet for a long moment. "I want you to run to the stables. Hide in there. That's it."

"But—"

"I need you to do it, Rach. If I need help, I'll yell, okay?"

He wouldn't. She knew he wouldn't. But he couldn't protect himself, or her, if she didn't listen to him. He'd try to play the hero even more than he already was.

If he wasn't answering her question about North Star, well, that was worse. So, she'd run. If she made it to the stables, she could make it to the house. She could call for help. She didn't have her cane, but once she got to the stables she'd know where she was. She'd be able to move around the ranch without it.

As long as she didn't fall on her run to the stables.

"On my count. One, two, three." She let him swing her off the horse, and he helped her land a lot more gracefully than she might have alone. He turned her by the shoulders in the right direction.

Then, she ran.

TUCKER POINTED RACHEL in the right direction, gave Buttercup's reins a flick, then ran himself. There was no cover until he got a lot closer, so he couldn't pretend like he was doing anything but going after the man behind the fence.

Who had a gun. If it was North Star, he wouldn't shoot.

If it wasn't...well...

The sound of the gunshot had him hitting the ground. When nothing hit him, he took a chance to look toward Rachel. She was still running, as was Buttercup, so no one had been struck.

Tucker got back to his feet, went back to running toward the man, but this time in a zigzag pattern. If he could get to the copse of trees that followed the creek, he could use some cover to get closer.

Another gunshot. Tucker didn't dive for the ground this time. Based on the angle of the gun, he was almost certain the man was shooting at him, not the horse or Rachel. He didn't have time to pause and look, though. He had to keep going.

He reached the cluster of trees and pulled his gun out of its holster. Clicking the safety off, he gave himself a moment to hide behind a tree and steady his breathing. His chest burned with effort, his heart pounded with fear and adrenaline.

The creek was nearly dry, but the trees were thick and old. When the third gunshot went off, it hit a tree way too close to Tucker for comfort.

The fence the man had been crouched behind was due east of the tree Tucker was behind. Still, moving enough to see and shoot would put him at risk.

It was only a gut feeling, not fact, but Tucker sincerely doubted the man was part of North Star. As much as they might prioritize mission over innocent life, they weren't the type to shoot first and ask questions later.

That was more Sons territory. But what would they be doing just lurking around waiting for Tucker and Rachel to appear? How would they know they'd disappeared in the first place?

Unless it was coincidence.

Tucker couldn't mull it over much longer. He had to

act so whoever the gunman was didn't get it in his head to go after Rachel.

He slid from one tree to another, working the angles to keep as much distance between him and the shooter as possible.

Another shot went off, but it was way more off target than the last one. Tucker got the glimpse of movement out of the corner of his eye, quickly changed direction to get behind a tree. The gunman was coming toward him just as Tucker tried to move toward the gunman.

He was somewhat hesitant to shoot someone not knowing where they came from or why they were shooting at him, but when the next bullet hit the tree he was standing behind, he figured it was time to do what needed to be done.

Tucker used the tree as cover, listened for the man's movements, then when he thought he had a clear idea of where the man was, stuck his arm out to shoot. He didn't need it to hit, just needed to catch the man off guard.

Immediately after the first shot, he peeked out from behind the tree. The shooter had ducked behind a bush, but as he slowly rose again, gun aimed, Tucker managed to get off a shot first.

The man stumbled backward. Tucker immediately charged. He didn't think he'd hit anything vital, which meant he had to get the gun away from him.

The assailant had lost his gun—a long high-powered looking model—after Tucker had shot him, but he was curling his fingers around the barrel as Tucker approached. He had to lunge to get to it before the man could lift it.

It was narrow timing, but Tucker managed to grab a hold of the handle. They grappled, pulling and jerking like a life-or-death game of tug-of-war. Which gave

Tucker the idea to take the dangerous chance of letting the gun go.

Since he'd been pulling hard, the attacker fell backward, the gun winging out of his grasp as Tucker had hoped. Tucker immediately leaped on him.

Even with the gunshot wound, the man fought hard. The bullet must have only glanced his side, even with the amount of blood staining his shirt. Tucker had to fight dirty to win, so he landed the hardest blow he could at the spot with the most blood.

The man howled, grabbing the injured section and rolling away. Tucker managed to pin him, face down, hands pulled behind his back. With pressure on the injured side to keep the man from fighting back, Tucker looked around for something to tie the man's hands.

Which was when he noticed the man was wearing a utility belt. Tucker went through the pockets, found a phone and tossed it as far into the creek bed as he could. Next he discovered a plastic bottle of some kind of clear liquid wrapped in a cloth—he disposed of that in the same way—and then happened upon the perfect answer to his problems. Zip ties. He quickly got them on the man's wrists, then had to fight to get another one around the man's legs.

The man swore and spit and kicked, but there wasn't much he could do with his arms tied behind his back and his legs bound together. Tucker got to his feet and rolled the man over onto his back.

Tucker didn't recognize him—not that he'd recognize every Sons goon. Still, there was something different about him. About the way he dressed and held himself, as though he wasn't quite used to the rough terrain.

Sons members were too local, too used to living in the elements and outside of society. This man didn't even have a knife on him. Just the high-powered gun, some zip ties, the phone and a tiny bottle of something Tucker assumed was a knockout drug.

All the tools for kidnapping.

Tucker's stomach roiled, but he didn't let it show. He sneered down at the man.

"I assume you're with Vianni."

The man spit at him.

Tucker didn't flinch, didn't jump away, as the spit missed him entirely. He kept his sole focus on the assailant. "Who are you here for?"

"Not you."

"I guess I could just leave you here, all tied up, and never let anyone know." Tucker looked up at the sky. "Might be fall, but sunny day like this? Going to get pretty hot."

"Bud, so much worse is coming for you if you don't let me go. I don't even care *what* you do."

Tucker leaned in, smiled. "Oh, you're going to care."

Chapter Fifteen

The gunshots had Rachel pulling out her phone. She was afraid to speak too loudly, but her phone was having trouble picking up her voice with her shaky whisper. "Call Cody," she finally said with enough force.

"Rachel? Where are you?"

There was a sharp command in his voice that calmed her. Because he would know what to do when she didn't.

"I'm in the stables at our ranch. Tucker saw someone and went after them. There's been gunshots. I know you're in Bonesteel—"

"I'm going to get off the line and call Brady. He's right next door."

"No! Listen. I mean, you can call Brady, but you have to know North Star is mixed up in this somehow. They have Dad. Tucker was working for them. Then this woman helped us—helped *me* not get taken by North Star and... I don't understand what's going on."

There was a brief pause. "I'm calling Brady to help Tuck. As for North Star..." Another pause that had Rachel holding her breath. "The woman? Was her name Shay?"

"Yes."

"All right. You stay put. I'll get back to you on the North Star thing." The connection clicked off and Rachel slipped her phone back into her pocket. Sure, Brady could maybe take care of things, but he was hurt, too. Likely Dev was out in the pasture somewhere with Sarah.

Would they have heard the gunshots? Surely, they'd have had to. Wouldn't they come running? Call their own reinforcements?

She couldn't just stand here, though. Tuck could have been the one shot.

She heard the door creak open and she pressed herself against the corner.

"Rach?"

"Tuck." She raced forward too quickly and tripped, but arms grabbed her before she could fall face-first. She was too relieved he was okay to be embarrassed. She held on to him as he helped her back to her feet. "You're okay."

"Yeah. We have to get out of here."

"No, it's okay. I phoned Cody. He was calling Brady and figuring out the North Star thing and—"

"What did you do that for?" he demanded, his voice sharp and unforgiving. He released her and she stood in the middle of the stable, feeling unaccountably chastened.

"What do you mean, what did I do that for? A man was out there. I heard gunshots. What was I supposed to do?"

"Just hide here like I told you to."

"You don't get to boss me around, Tuck. Certainly not when there are *guns* going off. We agreed to talk to Cody about—"

"About where your dad might be. Not drag my brothers into a lethal situation."

"Why not? You got dragged into Brady's thing.

Brady was dragged into Felicity's. It's what we do. Get dragged into each other's dangerous run-ins. And it always goes a little better with help, doesn't it?"

He was silent.

"Besides, it's too late. Cody is calling Brady and he's going to look into the North Star thing. He knows Shay."

"Well, he used to work for them."

"But he knew who she was even before I said her name."

"Sit tight," Tucker said, like he was about to leave her alone again. *Oh, no. Not going to happen.* She lunged forward and managed to grab his shirt.

"You will stop this right now." He tried to tug her hand off his shirt, but she only held on tighter. "I don't know what the damn key unlocks, Tucker. I don't understand anything Dad said in that letter. Now there's a man after us. Don't brush me off. Don't tell me to sit tight, and don't act like a child because we need help. I can't even do the *one thing* Dad seems to think I can." Emotion rose up in her throat, making her words squeak when it was the last thing she wanted. "If we need help, it's because of me. Not you."

"Rach." Instead of tugging her hand away again, he drew her close and smoothed a hand over her hair. "None of this is your fault."

Wouldn't that be nice? She leaned into Tucker, wondering if she'd ever fully believe that when the letter had said she was the key. It helped that he'd said it, though. That he'd take the time to give her a hug.

Someone cleared their throat from over by the door. "Uh, sorry to interrupt but I was just wondering if I should ask why there's a guy in zip ties lying next to the creek?" Dev said.

"What are you doing here?" Tucker demanded, releasing her abruptly.

"What am I doing here? You know how sound travels, right? Gunshots ring out while I'm tending to my cattle, and I'm left figuring out who the hell is shooting things. I sent Sarah over to Grandma's to round up help."

"Tucker's being very childish about help."

Dev made a sound that *might* have been a laugh, if he wasn't perpetually grumpy Dev who almost never laughed. At least not without a sarcastic edge. "Yeah, we Wyatts get that way sometimes. Should I leave the guy where he is?"

"Yes," Tucker said.

"And there aren't others?"

"Not yet."

"Who is he?" Rachel demanded.

There was a pause and Rachel didn't have to see to know *something* passed between brothers.

"I guess I'll go head over and stop Sarah and Brady and whoever else off at the pass."

"Have Brady call local police—ones he'd trust to keep it as quiet as possible—to pick up the guy."

Dev didn't say anything to that, but she heard him retreating so she assumed it was some kind of assent.

"What exactly are we going to do?"

"We're going to follow the original plan. Sort of. The next step is getting Cody to see what he might be able to tell us about North Star and Duke, but I want to keep the rest of the family out of it as much as we can. Not because I need to do this on my own, but because the more people we drag into this, the more targets they have. The wider it gets, the harder it is to fight."

She supposed that made sense. A gunman had been

waiting on the ranch. What if Sarah had happened to drive by on her way to town? Or what if Dev had come that way instead of across the pasture where Knight land butted up against Reaves land?

If she and Tucker went off on their own, maybe they'd be able to keep the focus on them, not their families.

"So, we're heading to Bonesteel on Buttercup?"

"Not exactly. The guy has to have a car around here somewhere. And it just so happens, I grabbed his keys."

TUCKER LED RACHEL toward the front gate. He imagined Vianni's man had hidden the car somewhere on the gravel road. There weren't very many places to hide a car, so it should be easy enough to find.

"It still doesn't make sense," Rachel said, one arm hooked with his as he helped her walk. Though this ground was a little more familiar than not, she didn't spend a lot of time walking this far past the main buildings.

"What doesn't?"

"Dad's note. I've gone over and over my dream. There's never been anything about a key. Or a lock. Not in old dreams and not in the new ones. Dad wouldn't even know about the new ones. I never mentioned it to anyone until you. In fact, the more I think about it, the more I don't think he knew I still had the nightmares. I didn't tell him. I didn't wake up screaming. For all he knew, they went away."

It made Tucker's chest ache that she'd continued to be tormented by the dreams and hadn't told Duke, or anyone else. Just dealt with them. As they slowly morphed into something real.

"What else could it be?"

She shook her head as they walked. "I don't know,

but we've only focused on my dream. Maybe it's something else..."

"Okay, so the note said you know the key and the lock. We've been focusing on the key, since we found that. Maybe we should think about locks. Are there any locks in your dream?"

She shook her head. "No keys. No locks. Nothing even symbolic of a key or a lock."

"So let's think about Duke. Do you remember anything about keys and locks you specifically associate with him?"

They reached the gate and Tucker looked down the gravel lane. He wanted to get out of here before the police arrived. Avoid answering any questions they'd have so he and Rachel could move on to the next step.

He wasn't looking forward to bringing Cody into this, but there didn't seem to be another option. Brady was involved now. Dev as well, to an extent.

It ate at him that he'd failed so spectacularly at keeping them out of it. He'd wanted to let them heal and protect their families and instead...

"Wait." Rachel stopped abruptly. "Key and lock. It wouldn't have to be...literal, would it?"

"I mean, we have a key. That's pretty literal."

"Or it's not. It's not about the dream. It's not about the key. It's about Dad. Take me to the cemetery."

"I'm sorry...*what*?"

"The cemetery. Where Mom's buried. It's not far from here. Dad always said... Mom was the key to his lock. Like, always. It was one of his favorite sayings before she died. He doesn't say it much anymore. But he used to. Key and lock."

"Okay," Tucker said gently. "But..."

"Maybe it's nothing. I know it sounds crazy. But Dad

wrote that letter and it says, *Rachel knows the key and the lock*. Well, if he's the lock—she's the key."

Tucker couldn't imagine what might be hiding at the cemetery, let alone at Eva Knight's grave, but it was hard to refuse her request. Even knowing it was beyond a long shot.

"We have to find the car first." He opened the gate and led Rachel through. The Knight ranch was the last turn off on the gravel road. If Tucker had been trying to hide a car, he'd have gone past the gate, then tried to hide the car in a ditch.

They walked down the side, Tucker keeping an eye and ear out for any cars that might be coming.

Just as he'd predicted, he found the car just a ways down, half in a ditch. You'd only see it if you passed the gate and likely their little spy had been counting on no one going that far.

Tucker helped Rachel into the car, then slid into the driver's seat himself, adjusting the seat. It smelled a little too much like cigarettes and cheap cologne, so he rolled down the windows.

Keeping his eye out for a police cruiser, he took the backroads to the cemetery where Eva Knight was buried. The parking lot was empty, which was good. "We can't spend too much time here."

"I know. I just need to… I don't know. If she's the key…"

"I get it." He thought it was too symbolic and metaphorical, but she had to look. Hell, even he had to look or he'd wonder if he'd missed something. He got out of the car, then went over to Rachel's side and helped her out, leading her through the archway of the cemetery entrance.

He didn't have to lead her any farther than that. She'd

clearly been here plenty, since she walked around the other graves with unerring accuracy, before stopping in front of her mother's.

Eva Knight. Loving wife and mother to all her girls. 1970–2006.

She'd been more than that little epitaph. She'd been the only calm, gentle presence across the Knight and Wyatt ranches. Until Rachel had taken on that mantle, and maybe Tucker had tried to be some of that as much as he could.

"I miss her," Rachel said softly.

"Me too." Missed her, and felt suddenly ashamed he'd let Rachel get so involved in this. Eva would have expected him to keep her safe. Keep *all* the girls safe. "She'd want you to be safe. At home."

"No. No, she wouldn't." Rachel smiled at him, and though there were tears in her eyes, they didn't fall. "She wanted everyone to treat me like an equal. Even if it hadn't been for the blindness, I was their only biological daughter and she never wanted the other girls to feel less. She was careful. So careful to treat me like everyone else. To give me the same responsibilities and expectations. Honestly, I think that's why… Well, Dad and Sarah, they kind of treat me like a maid. They don't mean to. It's just, I was always supposed to pull my weight. Mom wanted me on equal footing." She took a deep shaky breath. "I *am* on equal footing. Maybe you have the eyes and the police skills, but I know the key and the lock. What do you see?"

"Just the grave. Just the grass around it. There are some flowers in the holder."

"Fresh?"

"Yeah, they're drooping a bit. Maybe been here a few days, but fresh enough."

"So, Dad's been here recently. Before he left."

"It could have been one of your sisters."

She shook her head. "No. They always tell me if they're going so I can go, too. It had to be Dad. And it was in the last few days. The key *has* to be here."

Tucker didn't remind her that technically they had a key, and they were essentially just searching for a lock. Still, he would do it for her because… Well, his leads were nonexistent. He went around the grave, looking for anything. He even pulled out the flowers and looked into the water holder. He laid his hands over the stone, and it was only as he moved his palm over the side of the grave that he felt something odd under his foot.

Unsure, he stood. "Wait. This is…" Tucker toed the grass with his boot. A whole section of it moved, like a square of sod had been placed down over dirt. Coincidence, no doubt. Still he let go of Rachel and crouched down. He pulled up the square of sod. Underneath was freshly unpacked dirt. Tucker poked his finger into it. Not far beneath the crumbles of dirt was something hard.

"What is it?" Rachel demanded.

He began to dig in earnest. It was just a tiny metal tube, but it had a lid and Tucker screwed it off. He pulled out a slip of paper. It only had numbers on it, but it was clear what they were. "I found a piece of paper buried in the ground. There are numbers on it. It's a combination. Like to a safe."

"The only safe I know of is…"

"Grandma Pauline's," they finished together.

Chapter Sixteen

They drove to Reaves ranch in silence. Rachel felt a little raw as she always did after visiting her mother's grave. She'd only been seven when Mom had died, but she had worked so hard to live up to that memory that it felt like her mom had been around longer.

Which was nice.

It was also strange that Tucker had said Eva would have expected him to keep her safe, and suddenly she understood her place in her family a little better. Mom had done her best to make her an equal for two very different reasons—biology and her blindness—and both had worked. She was an independent, equal individual in her family.

If she'd felt trapped before this all started, or scared her future was never going to change, maybe that was just normal adulthood stuff—not the result of her blindness.

"What are we going to do?" Tucker muttered. "Just barge in and demand Grandma Pauline let us open her safe?"

Rachel didn't think he was actually asking her, but she answered anyway. "She knows something, Tuck. If this leads to *her* safe, Dad certainly didn't hide it there without her knowing."

She could sense his frustration. She wasn't sure exactly what it was toward, so she reached over and rested her hand on his arm. It was tense, and she imagined he was gripping the steering wheel hard enough to break it.

"If Grandma hid something about this, you should be angry with her," he told her.

"I'll save my anger for when I know what actually happened. You're only angry because you're scared."

"Scared?" he demanded.

"Your brothers can take care of themselves, even if they're injured or have kids to protect. You have a certain comfort in knowing they're all law enforcement and know how to deal with these issues. But your grandmother?"

"Raised the six of us, put the fear of God into Ace so he never came after her, and taught us all how to shoot way better than any law enforcement training. I'm not scared for her."

Rachel wasn't so sure. Sometimes you could know someone was strong and good, like her father, and still worry something had changed. Or something had been there that you'd never known.

She sighed as Tucker slowed the car. "How are we going to play this?"

"We're going to go in and tell her we're going to open the safe."

"You've met your grandmother, right? You go in there demanding things, she's going to knock you out with that wooden spoon."

Tucker didn't say anything to that, so she opened the car door and slid out. "You let me handle it," she said decisively. She closed the car door and started striding for the house. Tucker hadn't parked in his normal spot, so once she reached the house she had to feel around for the door.

She didn't knock. She stepped inside, and she could hear Tucker striding quickly behind her as if he meant to beat her to the house and take over.

No. Not on this. "Grandma Pauline?"

"What on earth are you doing here?" Pauline demanded.

Rachel could make out her form over by the sink or oven. "We need to get into the safe."

Tucker closed the door behind her, and she could feel him standing next to her. She couldn't see Grandma Pauline's expression, but she could feel the hesitation in the silence.

Rachel nodded toward Tucker. "We have the combination. Because Dad gave us a clue. He wants us to get into the safe."

Grandma Pauline sighed. "All right, then. Follow me."

"That wasn't exactly asking nicely," Tucker muttered into her ear. He took her arm as if he meant to lead her, and though she didn't need it in this house, she didn't mind her arm in his hand.

"I can say things like that to her. *You* can't," Rachel whispered back as Grandma Pauline led them down into the basement.

Rachel had to trust Grandma Pauline and Tucker to open the safe. To tell her what was inside. She knew from hearing everyone talk about it that it was a giant safe. The boys used to joke it was where Grandma Pauline hid dead bodies.

Rachel shuddered at the thought.

"Bottom shelf there. That's Duke's," Grandma Pauline said in her no-nonsense way.

Tucker let go of her elbow. There was the sound of shuffling and scraping. "It's another safe," Tucker said, sounding wholly baffled. "Not small, either. What on earth is happening here?"

"Is it another combination?"

"No. This one has a lock. I'm assuming that's what the key you found is for."

"Well, open it," she urged. Surely this safe wouldn't lead to yet another. *Surely* this was the last step.

Rachel had to wait more interminable seconds. She could hear Tucker fitting the key into the hole on the lock. The click. A squeak as the safe opened.

Tucker swore. Not angrily but more shock. More… fear. Rachel even heard Grandma Pauline's sharp inhale of surprise.

"What is it?" Rachel demanded when no one spoke.

"Rachel…"

"Tell me," she insisted. "*Now.*"

Tucker sighed. "It looks like… It looks like the knife you described in your dream. And there's…there's old blood on it."

Rachel couldn't even make sense of that. "I don't understand."

"He kept the weapon that injured you. Kept it locked away." There was a ribbon of hurt in Tucker's voice that finally made the words sink in.

Except, how…

"He kept the knife. That hurt me. On purpose."

"You knew," Tucker accused, and Rachel understood he was talking to Grandma Pauline.

"No. Not in the way you think," Grandma Pauline replied. Though she didn't betray any emotion, she didn't speak with her usual verve. "After the accident, Duke was distraught. He needed… Well, he felt alone.

Guilty. Responsible. Now, you've both dealt with the Sons enough to know that it wasn't his fault. It was those awful people's fault."

It was an admonition disguised as fact—Grandma Pauline's specialty. It didn't make Rachel feel any better about anything, though.

"He asked me to hide something for him and not to ask questions. I didn't. He called it insurance. That's all I know about it. Timing-wise, I knew it connected to what happened to Rachel, but not how or what."

"It doesn't make sense. If he had what hurt me, he would have taken it to the police. He would have used it." She turned toward Tucker's form. "Why wouldn't he have used what he could to put them in jail with this when it happened?"

"I don't know, Rach."

He sounded immeasurably sad, which of course made her feel worse. Dad had kept a weapon that had blinded her at the age of three. Locked it up like he was protecting the people who'd hurt her.

"I know it's hard, but let's not jump to conclusions."

"Not jump to conclusions?" Rachel couldn't tell where Grandma Pauline was standing in the dark with her own heart beating so loud in her ears. "I was blinded by a man with that knife when I was *three years old.* I might have been killed. I'll jump to every damn conclusion I want."

And because all she wanted to do was cry, she marched back the way she'd come and up the stairs.

"WELL, DON'T JUST stand there, boy. Go follow her."

"Grandma…" Tucker couldn't wrap his head around it. He didn't know how this could have gotten so much worse. "This is…"

"You don't know *what* it is. And before you get all high and mighty on me, I don't know what it is, either. I took the safe and put it in my own because a friend asked me to. I didn't ask any questions, because I'd been around enough to understand some things are better left alone."

"He made her believe—and all of us believe—she'd been mauled by an animal."

"Any person who'd use that knife on a child *is* an animal. That's the truth of it. You don't know Duke's truth or what he's done or escaped or how this might have been him protecting her. Don't you think I've done some shady things to protect you and your brothers?"

It was a horrible thought. She'd raised them to do what was right. To uphold the law after watching their father break it, try to destroy it for the entirety of their childhoods. And she was admitting to *shady* things to keep them safe.

"Rachel's hurting. She feels betrayed. Fair enough. But you're protecting her, which means you've got to think beyond her hurt. Duke's a good man. You know it and I know it."

"Maybe he's not as good as we think he is."

"Or maybe, good isn't as simple as you want it to be. Now, go after her."

Tucker did as he was told, in part because it was habit and in part because he was worried what Rachel would do next. *He* knew what it was like to feel like you could never understand or believe in your father, but she never had.

She wasn't in the kitchen and the door was ajar, so he stepped outside. She was pacing the yard. He had a feeling that constant movement was what kept her from losing the battle with tears.

"We need to keep moving. Stay on plan."

She shook her head. "The plan? To save him from those people when he…" She just kept shaking her head as if she could negate the truth. "He shouldn't have that. I can't think of one good reason he'd have it locked up."

"Then let's go find out the reason," Tucker said gently. "We find your father. We have our answers."

"What if the answers are… What if he's…"

She couldn't get the words out, so he supplied them for her. "Not the man you thought he was?"

Her lips trembled, but she gave a sharp nod.

"Nothing he's done changes two very simple facts. One, we know he helped bring down dirty cops. Whatever he's done, he fought for the right thing and probably out of a need to protect his family. Two, he's been a great father and a good man for as long as I've known him. If he made a mistake, it might have been for the right reasons. Or maybe it's forgivable. Or maybe, it wasn't a mistake at all. We don't know until we talk to him." He took her by the shoulders, trying to give her a certainty he didn't fully believe. "He gave you the clue. You figured it out. No matter what…we have to see this through. If only so you can have some answers."

"Answers. What possible answer could make this not awful?"

"I don't know. But that doesn't mean there isn't one."

She leaned into him. They didn't have the time, and yet he couldn't rush her. Not when she was grappling with what he knew too well was… He hated his father. Always had. Yet even with all that hate, it was complicated knowing he was related to someone so awful.

Duke wasn't awful. Grandma had that right. Whatever mistake he might have made, it wouldn't have been done out of cruelty. Tucker had to believe that, and with answers, they'd all be able to move forward.

"Come on. Let's head over to Bonesteel. We'll meet with Cody and come up with a plan to get to Duke. He wanted us to find this, Rach. Maybe it's useful. Important."

"Should we leave it with Grandma Pauline if it's so important?"

"She'll keep it safe. That's why it's here in the first place."

"Tucker…" She pulled away, and tilted her head toward him. Her eyebrows drew together and she opened her mouth but didn't say anything, as if she was struggling to come up with the words.

She needed reassurance, and Tucker didn't feel very sure, but he wanted to give that to her. Wanted her to be able to believe in Duke and trust that they were doing the right thing trying to save him from North Star, the Viannis *and* the Sons. "It'll be okay. I'm not saying it will be easy, but it'll be okay. I know it."

It had to be.

Chapter Seventeen

Tucker had to lead Rachel to Cody and Nina's door. Rachel had been to their house in Bonesteel a few times, but most family get-togethers were at one of the ranches. She didn't know her way around very many other places.

Tucker had explained he was parking around back, so she knew she was being led to the back door, which opened into a kitchen. Since it was the middle of the day, Nina was probably teaching her seven-year-old Brianna and Liza's half sister, the just-turned-five Gigi. Her and Liza traded off homeschool-teaching duties.

The door squeaked open. Immediately Nina went, "Oh," as if she knew exactly what was going on.

Then Rachel was quickly being ushered inside and greeted by her enthusiastic niece.

"Aunt Rachel! I didn't know you were coming over. Are you good at adding?"

"Brianna," Nina said in that warning tone moms always seemed to have. "No having Rachel or Tuck do your math while I go get your father."

"Where's Gigi?" Rachel asked as she heard Nina retreat.

"She's sick. I heard Aunt Liza say she threw up *everywhere*," Brianna said with some glee. "If you had three hundred and twenty-four…um, apples. And then Uncle Tuck brought you fifty-seven more—"

"Brianna!" Nina yelled from somewhere deeper in the house.

Brianna humphed. "Why are you guys visiting in the middle of the day?" Brianna seemed to suddenly realize it was odd timing. "Is there trouble again?"

Poor girl. She was way too intimately acquainted with trouble. Rachel forced a reassuring smile. "Just a little, but it's a problem for Uncle Tuck and me. Nothing for you to worry about."

"You need Daddy's help?"

"Only for a few minutes," Tucker interjected. "He won't even have to leave home."

Brianna sighed with some relief. "So are you guys going to get married then?"

Tucker seemed to choke on his own spit, and Rachel found herself utterly speechless.

"What now?" Tuck finally managed, though his voice sounded croaky at best.

"Well, when Mommy and Daddy were in trouble, they ended up getting married. And same with Aunt Liza and Uncle Jamison. Then Uncle Gage and Aunt Felicity are getting married and having a baby. Uncle Brady and Aunt Cecilia aren't getting married yet, but I heard Mom say that it was *inevitable*. Now you two are in trouble. So…"

"No, sweetheart, that's not…how it works…exactly." Tucker sounded so pained it was almost funny.

There was the sound of footsteps and low murmurs. Then Nina's voice. "Get your math book, Bri. We'll go finish up in the living room."

There was a long suffering sigh and the shuffle of books, papers and feet.

"Say goodbye to your aunt and uncle."

"Aren't they going to stay for dinner? We could order pizza." Nina must have given her a significant mom look because Brianna groaned and stomped away.

Rachel felt Nina's slim hand on her arm. "I'm sure Cody and Tucker can take care of whatever this is."

Rachel slid her arm away. "Don't do that to me. You didn't let Cody and Jamison handle your thing."

"Rach, I'm just saying… You're not a part of this. You could go home and—"

"I *am* a part of this. I'm the only reason we've gotten this far. Isn't that right, Tucker?"

There was a hesitation, like he might refute her so Nina could whisk her away and keep her safe. But there was no safety here. Whether she helped get Dad away from North Star or these other groups or not, Dad had still lied to her—to all of them.

She wanted to believe there was a reason for it. Maybe she had to do this so she could actually…see it. If someone just told her, even Dad, that it was for her own good…

She'd never be able to forgive him.

"Rachel's right," Tucker finally said. "We wouldn't be this far without her. If we're going to get Duke away from North Star—"

"Woah, woah, woah," Cody's voice interrupted Tucker. "What makes you think you're getting *anyone* away from North Star?"

"They tried to kidnap me," Rachel said.

"Rach, if they tried, you'd be kidnapped."

"No, she's right," Tucker told him. "They sent this woman named Shay to take her. They must have been listening in somehow and knew she was getting clues about everything from her dreams. Shay and I fought—"

"No offense, Tuck, but Shay'd take you down in a heartbeat."

"You know her that well?"

There was a pause. "I worked with her quite a bit. She's helped me out of a few jams."

"I have to go help Bri," Nina said softly. "Just…be careful. Both of you." Rachel felt arms wrap around her and squeeze, then heard the sounds of Nina exiting the room.

"I pointed out to Shay that kidnapping an innocent bystander wasn't necessary," Tucker said. "That I wouldn't let anyone put a mission above her life. Eventually, she agreed with me."

"So, she let you go."

"Yeah. Because she knew I was right. She knew that what North Star has been doing isn't what I signed up for."

"What *you* signed up for?"

Tucker huffed out a breath. "What? You don't believe they'd tap me for some help? I'm not North Star material?"

"I didn't say that," Cody said evenly.

Rachel wanted to defend Tucker, but it wouldn't change the fact he felt slighted by his baby brother. Still, she understood a little too well what it was like to be overlooked. Underestimated. To not fully realize it until the crap hit the fan.

I'm sure Cody and Tucker can take care of whatever this is. Nina meant well, because she loved her. Because they were sisters. But it still hurt.

Silence remained. Tucker and Cody were likely having some nonverbal conversation she'd never be privy to.

Rachel could be mad about that, and pout, or she

could take matters into her own hands. "After we ran from Shay, after she let us, Dad sent us a note, through Shay. It led us to the weapon that did this to me." She pointed at her face. "We could hand that over to North Star, but what would they do with it?"

Cody didn't answer for a few seconds. "I couldn't say."

"But you know as well as I do that it wouldn't be used to save my dad or keep me safe. It would be used to take someone down."

"Taking those people down *would* be keeping you safe."

"Would it? Because Ace is in jail. So is Elijah and Andy Jay and all the Sons members who've come after you all this year. They're all in *jail*. Am I safe, Cody? Are you?"

Cody didn't have anything to say to that, either.

"Dad sent me this note in secret. He wanted me to get that evidence without North Star knowing. What does that tell you about what North Star is doing? Shay let us go and she *works* for North Star."

"Look, you avoided getting kidnapped because Shay let you. Maybe you're right and North Star can get a lit-tle…people blind. Regardless, you can't get into North Star and get Duke out. You just can't. They're too well organized."

"You know where he's being held?" Tucker asked.

"I have an idea. You wouldn't make it within fifty yards without them picking you up. Then they'd have Rachel like they wanted in the first place. And you're right, mission comes first. It has to or they can't do what they do."

"I don't care what they do, Cody. I care about my fa-ther. I care about the fact someone did this to me when

I was *three*, and I won't let them do anything else to my family. Maybe I'm not a detective or a secret operative, but I sure as hell am in the middle of this thing."

"She's right," Tucker said softly. "She remembers things. She knows Duke. North Star wanted to kidnap her. She's smack dab in the middle of this."

"Why are you, Tuck?"

"Because North Star asked me to be. But they've taken a wrong turn, and I won't let that hurt Duke. They asked me to keep his daughters safe—so that's what I'm going to do."

"If I tell you where Duke probably is, like I said, it's not going to go well. I can't tell you how to sneak in. They'll know you're coming a mile away. I can't help you get in there. I'm not part of North Star anymore, and as much as I know, they know I know it. They'd have protections against it if they wanted to keep me— or someone related to me—out."

"You know how to get in touch with Shay."

When Cody spoke, his voice was firm. "I won't get her kicked out."

"She didn't sound like she was in it for the long run," Rachel said. "She got us the note. Surely you can get in touch with her and give her the option of helping us."

"That won't be necessary."

It was a woman's voice, and Rachel could only assume it was Shay herself.

"So, you'll help us?" Rachel demanded.

"Yeah, but you're not going to like how."

TUCKER HAD TO blink to make sure that was indeed Shay entering the room from where Nina and Brianna had disappeared earlier. "How…"

"I figured you'd hit up Cody once you figured out

Duke's note. The weapon that did that, huh?" Shay said, nodding toward Rachel's face.

Tucker glared at Cody. "You didn't tell me she was there," he gritted out.

"He didn't know," Shay said with a grin. "Nina's the one who gave me the heads-up."

"I never should have let you two become friends," Cody muttered. "You'll get kicked out. This would be the last straw."

"I've been saying that for months now. Apparently, Granger loves me. Also, you didn't *let* me become friends with your wife."

"What aren't we going to like?" Tucker demanded, wanting to keep the focus on what needed to be done.

"My brother do that?" Cody asked with some surprise as he noticed Shay's bruised cheek.

Shay shook her head. "He wouldn't hit a woman," she said as if that was a *bad* thing. "Rachel did it."

Cody let out a low whistle. "Nice work, Rach."

"Can we focus?" Tucker demanded.

"So, all you Wyatts are wound that tight, eh?" Shay said to Cody, earning a frown from both Wyatts in question. "Duke's not going to talk to me. Even if I said I was in cahoots with you. Why do you think that letter I smuggled out was in code? We need to get Rachel to him."

"Or we need to get Duke to Rachel."

Shay shook her head. She was still dressed all in black, but no mask or hat. Her blond hair was pulled back in a tight ponytail and she stood there, legs spread, arms folded across her chest like some kind of special ops soldier.

In a way, Tucker supposed she was.

"We're not getting Duke out of there. It's not possible

unless they're distracted by something they need more than Duke's knowledge of the Viannis and the Sons." Shay looked meaningfully at Rachel.

Even though it didn't change what she'd said, Tucker moved in between Shay and Rachel. "No."

"Don't say no," Rachel told him. "Not *for* me. You'll tell me what you mean, and *I'll* say no if I see fit."

"She wants to use you as bait," Tucker said disgustedly.

"And what's wrong with that?" Rachel returned.

He, of course, couldn't answer that. What he thought was wrong with that wouldn't be appreciated.

"How would we do it?" Rachel asked calmly.

Tucker didn't know how she could be calm. Maybe because she hadn't actually seen that knife that had been used to take away her eyesight, sitting there grotesquely in a box. Maybe because she didn't fully grasp what the Sons could do on their own, let alone with another dangerous group of criminals.

Or maybe she was calm because she lived that night over and over again in her dreams and she had no control over that. This…she felt like she could act on.

How could he not support that?

"I take you to headquarters," Shay began. "I'll say I tracked you down and convinced you to ditch Tucker. You'll say you want to help your father in whatever way you can. Which is all true."

"Except it's sending her into the lion's den."

"Only one, and the less dangerous of the three," Shay returned. "While they're focused on getting information from Rachel, it'll give me a chance to slip out and grab Tucker. We'll work together to get Duke out."

"Except Rachel is stuck in there then."

"It might not matter," Rachel said. "Depending on what the full truth is."

"No, it'll matter," Shay corrected. "The whole point of me going against the group I've dedicated six years of my life to is to help keep you and your father from being caught in a crossfire that's got nothing to do with you, and only a little to do with your father. Tucker will take Duke. I'll go back in and get Rachel."

"It'll be your last hurrah. You take people out of North Star custody, no amount of Granger liking you keeps you in North Star," Cody said gravely.

"I'm okay with that. I wasn't at first. But this whole thing… It's been different since you left, Cody. Since Ace has been in jail. It should have made it easier, but we're going at it harder and caring less and less who gets caught in the middle. I won't be party to it any longer."

"All right, what do you need from me?" Cody asked.

Cody and Shay discussed some technical stuff to do with the North Star security systems and Tucker turned to Rachel. She had her chin set stubbornly. It was stupid to try to convince her to back out of this, but…

"You're risking your life. I want you to understand that."

"Duke already risked it," Rachel replied. "Risked Sarah and me, all of us. Didn't he? By going with them."

"North Star brought me in because he wanted you protected. I was there to make sure you weren't brought into the thick of things."

"Maybe, but we're here. In the thick of things. I won't be swept into a corner. Maybe what we found in the safe hurts my feelings. It…hurts. Even if my father has a good reason, to know that's there is painful. But you were the one who told me it doesn't change the fact he's a good man who's always been a good father. He loved my mother. He loved me and my sisters. He raised us when she died, and all the while…" She blew out a breath. "You've all lived with terrible things. Now, I'm living with mine. I won't back down. You wouldn't. None of my sisters would. None of your brothers would, and I know my father wouldn't. So. Why should you expect me to?"

"It's not that I expect you to, Rach. It's that I care about you and I want you to be safe." Which he would have said before kissing her. Of course, he cared about her—about all the Knights. But it felt heavier in his chest, even in this kitchen with his brother and a North Star operative a few feet away.

She reached out and he took her hand. She squeezed it and smiled at him. "We're all doing this because we care about each other."

Which wasn't exactly what he'd meant or felt. He'd meant *her* in a very uncomfortably specific way.

"It's a risk, but it's not like I'm walking into Sons territory. I'm walking into a group who wants to take down two very bad groups of people. It's the lowest risk I could take. You're taking a bigger one trying to get Dad out." Her hand slid up his arm, shoulder, until her palm cupped his cheek. "So, we both have to support each other taking risks to end all this danger. I'd like to have my life back. I'm sorry I ever wanted something different. It was perfectly nice. Well, mostly." Her thumb moved across his jaw, then she dropped her hand as if she remembered there were other people in the room.

"We should move immediately, right?" she asked.

"Right," Shay agreed. She gave Tucker a considering look but crossed to Rachel. "I'm going to give you a panic button of sorts. It's tiny and easy to lose, so I'm going to sew it into the sleeve of your shirt. Okay?"

Rachel nodded and held out her arm to Shay. Shay worked on sewing the tiny button into the inside of Rachel's sleeve, and Tucker was not at all surprised his brother pulled him away from Rachel and into the hallway.

"It's not really going to go down like this."

"What isn't?" Tucker muttered.

"You and Rachel? Don't think I didn't notice that little moment. That's five for five."

Tucker shrugged uncomfortably. "It's not like that… exactly."

"Yeah, *exactly*." Then Cody laughed. Loud and hard. "Jesus. Dev and Sarah."

"Not in a million years," Tucker said, managing a small laugh of his own. "They'd eat each other alive first."

Cody shook his head. "Don't bet against it."

Chapter Eighteen

Rachel did her best not to act nervous. She knew Tucker didn't approve of this plan, but he was going through with it because of her.

So she had to be brave. She had to be sure. Too bad she was wholly terrified.

Shay had sewn a *panic button* into her shirt, instructing her that it had to be pressed three times to send a signal. Which would go to Cody, who would no doubt send the whole Wyatt clan after her.

After *her*, because she was going to be the distraction. The bait. She was going to walk into North Star and demand to see her father.

Shay warned her they wouldn't let that happen. That they'd likely put her in an interrogation room, holding the carrot of seeing her father over her head until she answered all their questions.

She was supposed to refuse. Give them bits and pieces to keep their attention, but mostly be difficult, and lie if necessary. So that all eyes were on her while Shay and Tucker snuck in to get Duke out.

It was a lot of pressure, and while her family treated her as an equal more often than not, no one had actually ever put *pressure* on her. The hardest thing she'd ever done up to this point was demand to teach art classes at the rez. There had been some pressure to succeed so no one pitied her for failing, but not like this.

"Okay, you'll drop us here," Shay instructed Tucker.

The car came to a halt. Rachel was seated in the back. She hadn't realized until this moment she was going to have to trust Shay implicitly, not just to be telling the truth but to guide her through a completely unknown setting.

When the door next to her opened, Rachel had to fight the desire to lean away. To refuse to get out. She stepped into the autumn afternoon instead.

"Don't be afraid to speak up if I'm walking too fast or something. Better to get there in one piece than worry about hurting my feelings or whatever."

The no-nonsense way Shay took her arm and said those words had Rachel's shoulders relaxing. Maybe it was scary, but at least Shay wasn't going to be all weird about her being blind.

"Let me talk to her for a minute," Tucker said briskly.

"All right," Shay said. She let Rachel's arm go and Tuck's hands closed over her shoulders. He gave them a squeeze.

"You be smart. Take care of yourself first. I couldn't…" He let out a ragged breath. "I don't want you hurt, Rach."

"Tuck…" She didn't know what to say. There wasn't time to say anything. So, she could only give him what he'd given her. "I don't want you hurt, either."

"Then we'll stick to the plan, and everything will be okay."

"You don't actually believe that," she said, both because she didn't and because she could hear it in his voice that he didn't, either. "We'll stick to the plan, and hope for the best. And if the best blows up in our face, we'll just have to fight like hell."

He chuckled softly. "Yeah, you got that right."

Then, before she could say anything else, he kissed her. It wasn't sweet or light. It was firm, a little fierce and had her heart beating for an entirely new reason aside from fear. "Stay safe, Rach."

He released her, and she was passed off to Shay. It was disorienting for a lot of reasons, but the whole being shuttled between people in foreign settings certainly undercut the happy buzz of that kiss.

"They all like that?" Shay asked, leading her forward.

"Like what?"

"Like...gentlemen, but not wimps about it. Think of women as equals, and aren't too keen on using them as a punching bag. Kiss like that and then walk away to save your butt—while you're also busy saving your own butt."

Rachel had to smile. "Pretty much."

Shay didn't say anything else to that, just kept leading Rachel forward.

"Can you describe it to me? Give me some kind of idea of where they're going to take me and how to get out?"

"Good idea." Shay explained that it looked like a hunting cabin from the outside. Inside, they had different holding rooms, a medical center and a tech center. She explained the layout, which room Duke was in and what room they'd probably take her into.

"So, if for whatever reason you want to run, they're going to be able to track you until you get off the property. Not much use in it. But, to get out the door, you'd just need to remember how to get to the hallway."

Rachel filed all that away, tried to bring her own picture to her mind. It would help if she found herself needing to escape.

Shay brought her to a stop. "All right. Here we go."

Rachel expected her to knock or buzz in or something, but the sound of the door opening was the first thing she heard once they stopped.

"This is an interesting turn of events," a male voice said. "Where's the guard dog who gave you that shiner?"

"I got to her without Wyatt," Shay returned. She spoke differently to the man. Sharp. All business. Any hint of the woman who'd asked if the Wyatts were all like that was gone.

"How?"

"Everyone has to take a bathroom break now and again, Parker. Now are you going to step aside or what?"

The man grumbled, but Rachel was being led forward so he'd clearly allowed entrance. "Wait here for McMillan."

Rachel listened as the footsteps quieted.

"McMillan is my supervisor," Shay said in a whisper. "He's all bark and mostly no bite. I imagine since he's been handling Duke, he's going to be the one who questions you. If not? Be as difficult as possible until they bring McMillan in."

"All right."

"Shay."

Rachel had assumed Shay was the woman's first name all this time. But the way her superior barked it out, Rachel had to wonder if it was actually her last name.

"Sir. A little late, but better late than never."

"How'd you manage what you failed at earlier?" He

emphasized the word fail as though failure was the absolute worst thing a person could do.

"Followed them. They were on the run, off their home territory. Wyatt let his guard down and I convinced Rachel to talk to us. She's willing, if you let her see her father."

"Dymon!" the man yelled.

More footsteps, a few hushed words, then someone took her other arm. Shay's grip tightened and Rachel felt a bit like she was in the middle of a tug-of-war.

"Who's that?" Shay asked, suspicion threading through her voice.

"Your replacement," McMillan said, his voice so chilly Rachel thought to shiver. "Shay. You're done here."

"Sir, I think a woman should—"

"I said you're done here," McMillan said, and this was no bark or yell. It was cold, a succinct *or-else* order.

Shay slowly released her arm, and Rachel was being led away. The grip on her other arm was unnecessarily rough. She remembered what Shay said about being difficult. "You're hurting me," she said, trying to tug her arm away from the too-tight grasp.

"Oh, you have no idea what's in store for you, little girl," the voice hissed.

Rachel's entire body went cold. She recognized that voice.

It was the voice from her dream.

"Something isn't right."

Tucker whirled, gun in hand. It was only Shay, but she'd snuck up on him soundlessly. Still, he didn't have time to worry about that. "*What* isn't right?"

"New guy. McMillan isn't in the habit of hiring new guys."

"He hired me."

"Not the same. You're not an operative. You're like a…liaison. This guy I've *never seen* is in the South Dakota headquarters of North Star, and I've never heard his name or even heard whispers of a new guy." She rubbed a hand over the back of her neck. "Something isn't right."

"You left Rachel in there? When something wasn't right?"

"Calm down," Shay said sharply. She pulled her phone to her ear. "Wyatt? Yeah, I need you to do some spying for me." She sighed heavily. "Yeah, yeah, yeah, you ask your wife if she thinks you should stay out of it when her sister is in North Star headquarters with a stranger." Another pause. "Yup, that's what I thought. Someone named Dymon. Get me anything you've got on him." She hung up, shoved her phone in her pocket.

"Are you sure they're not tracking you through that?" he asked.

"Do you think I'm dumb? I had your brother take care of all the tracking devices when we were there."

"It never occurred to you that a group that tracked your every move might not be on the up and up?"

"Look. You don't know anything about North Star, or McMillan for that matter," she snapped. "Like that your father was responsible for his wife's death."

Tucker didn't say anything because he hadn't known that. At all.

"Grief does funny things to people. He's not a bad guy, and whatever is going on doesn't make him one. It makes him…human. And, hell, aren't we all?"

Tucker didn't want to think about how human they

all were. Not when being human meant making mistakes, and they couldn't make any with Rachel inside North Star.

"Let's move. The less time she has to be in there, the better."

Shay nodded. "On that, we can agree."

It was Shay's plan since she knew the headquarters—what from the outside looked like an upscale hunting cabin. They bypassed the front, and Shay would occasionally pause to do something on her phone that allegedly moved the cameras or turned off security or whatever else North Star had in place.

"You sure you know all of those?"

"I installed them. I sure as hell should." They finally got to the back door, which was next to a garage of sorts. "I'm going in. I imagine everyone knows I got the boot, but I've got stuff in there. So, I'm going in to collect my stuff. When no one's watching, I'll open this garage and the door inside. You'll head straight for it. If I don't have Duke waiting, you move back into the garage. Check at five-minute intervals. Once he's there, you sneak him out the garage, go in the direct route we came and get to the car. Once you're there, you'll give me fifteen minutes. If I don't show up with Rachel, you get Duke out. I'll contact you or your brother with the next step once I've got Rachel. And whatever you do, don't go all Wyatt on me."

"What does that mean?"

"Don't play the hero. You may hear or see something you don't like, but you focus on Duke. You're going to want to barge back in here and get Rachel, but I've got it handled. You trust me and I trust you."

"That's asking a lot."

"Yeah, it is," she agreed. "For both of us. You up for the challenge?"

He didn't want to be. Trusting someone he barely knew was like tossing a coin with Rachel's life on the line, but hadn't he already done that? Besides, Shay didn't strike him as a stupid woman and she was putting at least some of her safety in *his* hands. It was a risk they both had to take.

"How long do I wait until I open the door?"

"Minute the garage opens you're in. You hear a whistle—I don't mean a sharp whistle, I mean like me whistling a tune—you go back and hide in the garage. We'll keep trying till it's clear."

Tucker nodded. "All right."

Shay nodded in return, then she slid in the back door. Tucker stood in the corner next to the garage, doing his best to hide his body in the way Shay had instructed. When the garage door opened, almost soundlessly, he slipped inside. Then immediately located the door inside and headed for it.

He turned the knob, eased it open and himself inside. He was in a basement that bizarrely looked like any house's basement might. A TV room in a little finished alcove, a laundry area on the opposite side. The hallway was dark.

Tucker remembered what Shay had said and went back to the garage, waited the aforementioned five minutes, then went inside again. He kept his mind blank. Thought of it like detective work—often boring and tedious…until it wasn't.

Fifteen minutes had passed, and finally Duke appeared. Duke studied him there at the end of the hallway and didn't budge. That was when Tucker realized Shay was standing behind him, with a gun to his back, and he only moved forward toward Tuck when she poked it into his back again.

"He's being difficult," she hissed. "Fix it. I've got maybe ten minutes before Parker comes back. Maybe."

Fix Duke Knight's hard head? Yeah, in what world? Still, Tucker moved forward. "We have to get you out."

"Why should I trust you? I trusted Granger and look what happened. Now I've got two North Star operatives trying to sneak me out? That smells like a setup, boy."

"We're trying to help you. It's because of *you*, and what they want to do with your family, that we're turning our back on North Star."

Duke didn't respond to that. "Who's watching the girls?"

Tucker hesitated. "We're all doing what we should be doing," he said carefully, already knowing that wouldn't fly. His hesitation spoke volumes.

Duke narrowed his eyes. "You've always been a crap liar. Where's Rachel?"

"She's…" Tucker couldn't tell Duke under any circumstances. If he knew Rachel was upstairs, he'd charge up there like an angry bull.

"She's upstairs keeping them busy," Shay said.

Tucker nearly groaned, but he had to leap in front of Duke as he charged for the stairs. Though Tucker was taller, Duke was thicker, and he'd been a cowboy for thirty some years so he was no slouch. Still, Tucker had been trained to deal with threats bigger than him.

Tucker managed to shove him a step back. "You don't know what will happen to her or you if you barge in there. Trust that we've got this under control."

"That's my daughter you're risking," Duke said, and though his voice was ruthlessly controlled in volume, his eyes bulged and the tendons in his neck stood out like he was about to explode.

Tucker couldn't blame him if he did.

"She risked herself, buddy. For you. So maybe you make it easy on us so I can get her out without causing a storm where someone gets hurt," Shay said with absolutely *no* finesse.

Which was apparently what Duke needed to hear. He moved forward, though his scowl was still in place. Tucker passed him up to get to the door first. As he did, Duke he full-on sneered.

"I'm holding you personally responsible."

"As if I'm not," Tucker muttered. He glanced back at Shay.

"Take him out, just like we said. I'll go get her."

Tucker nodded. He led Duke into the garage quietly. Then out. Tucker had to hope Shay remembered to close it.

"Shay will bring Rachel to us," Tucker told him, moving in the same direction they'd come. Shay had disabled the cameras, but they could have come back on. Still, he had to trust she'd handle it.

"I can't believe you'd be this stupid," Duke muttered, though he followed behind Tucker.

Tucker looked over his shoulder and raised an eyebrow. "That's really how you want to play this? When we found the weapon that blinded your daughter in Grandma Pauline's safe? I had to beg your daughter to understand that you *must* have had a good reason for that. So—"

Tucker's phone vibrated. He shook his head and kept walking. When it vibrated again, he swore under his breath and pulled the phone out of his pocket. They were finally in some tree cover, but not to the car yet. Tucker saw it was Cody calling and answered.

"Cody—"

"Shay didn't answer, but this is important. I got into North Star's system to look up this Dymon guy. I managed a quick glimpse into the files before they figured out I was hacking in and kicked me right back out. This guy's got connections to Vianni. I suppose he could be a double agent—helping out North Star. Sort of like us."

"Except we never worked for the Sons or our father." Tucker thought about everything Shay had told him. About this whole lead up. "He's working for Vianni. They're so hung up on taking down the Sons, they don't care who they go to bed with."

"Maybe," Cody replied gravely. "Either way? I'd get Rachel out of there ASAP."

Chapter Nineteen

Fear paralyzed Rachel, but all the man from her nightmares had done was drag her deeper into the building and then shove her into a chair. He was almost immediately followed by someone else, and once that person spoke, she knew it was the head guy. What had Shay called him? McMillan?

At least she wasn't alone with her nightmare—but would this man be just as bad?

It didn't matter. As long as she was in this building, she had a chance of survival. Dad was here. Shay was here. Tuck was here. She would survive.

Rachel studied what she could of the room. She reached out and felt the table in front of her. So she was sitting on an uncomfortable chair at a table. The man across from her was McMillan. He had a big dark presence and he appeared to move in such a way that she figured it meant he was sitting down at the table, too. The other man was dressed all in dark colors, too, but not as broad as McMillan. Not as…still.

She remembered that about him from her dream. A need to move. He stood next to McMillan, a vibrating presence. In the vague way she saw things, they appeared to be a unit.

Did McMillan know? Was North Star actually in bed

with Vianni? It was a horrible thought. If they were, she was dead. Shay and Tucker were likely dead, too, and God knew her father was already dead.

Except he wasn't. They'd gone to rescue him. So, surely North Star didn't know.

Unless they needed that knife, and that was the only reason her father was still alive.

Rachel swallowed. "I just want to see my father," she said through a too-tight throat, terror making her feel like lead all the way through. But she couldn't just lie down and die.

She had to figure out a way to fight.

"That's understandable, Ms. Knight. Your father is here under our protection. Just how much do you know about that?"

She didn't let her eyes drift to the man standing. He had to know she knew who he was. Didn't he? Or would he assume because she was blind that she didn't? But he had to have felt how afraid she was. Her reaction to his voice.

He had to know she knew.

"Miss?"

Rachel sucked in an audible breath. McMillan had asked her a question. "I'm sorry. I… I don't know. I know Shay tried to kidnap me at the ranch. She and Tucker fought and Tucker got me away from her. She followed us, I guess. She…" Rachel had never been a good liar, but she let the genuine fear she felt consume her. Her voice shook. She shook. They'd believe it was a result of fear of the situation, not her lies. "She found me later. While Tucker was… Anyway, she said I could see and talk to my father if I came with her. That everything would be explained if I came with her."

"Our operative was sent to retrieve you because of the dream you've been having. Can you tell us about that?"

"I…" Rachel trailed off. They likely knew everything at this point. God knew the man from her nightmare did. If they'd been listening to Tucker before Shay's arrival, they had the full account of how her dream had morphed.

"It was just a nightmare. Just a…memory of what happened to me." She gestured at her face. "I don't see what it has to do with anything."

"You never dream past the moment you were hurt?" McMillan asked.

He made it all sound so clinical, but he couldn't see the nightmare, the reality in his mind like she could. "I was three. A madman slashed my face up and I was saved by a dog. What more would I know than that?"

"What about the knife?" It was the other man's voice. The voice from that dream, and she couldn't help but flinch at it.

"What knife?" she managed to whisper.

"Dymon." It was a warning from the man. "You're not involved in the questioning. If you can't remember that, you can step outside."

She could all but *feel* the tamped-down energy humming off the nightmare man. Still, he didn't say anything else.

But he wanted to know about the knife. The knife in Grandma Pauline's safe. One thing she knew for certain, she couldn't tell them about that.

"I don't know what you're talking about. I told you about my dream, now I want to see my father."

"What do you know about your father's past?"

"None of your business," Rachel snapped. She wouldn't play the cowering victim anymore. Not when she couldn't decide if the man in front of her was good or bad or some mix of the two. But, regardless, she didn't have to be nice to him.

"The group who's after your father has aligned themselves with the Sons. You've got quite a few in-laws who are former Sons members, don't you?"

"If you think being held in that gang as a child against your will is being a *former member*, you're a monster."

The man sighed, like a disappointed teacher or parent.

"Miss, it'd be easier on you if you simply answer our questions. Once you tell us the truth, we'll take you to your father. I understand you're not part of this, but Duke Knight is in a very dangerous situation. He's trying to protect you, but it's not getting us anywhere. It seems this knife might be the answer to some of our... *problems.* I'm sure you want to help him, don't you?"

She thought about what one of her more smart-mouthed sisters might say in this situation. She managed a sneer and did her best impersonation of Liza. "Go to hell."

She thought about laying her cards out on the table. Lifting her chin and saying, *Is that why you've got someone associated with the Viannis in this room with us? To protect him and help him?*

But her father had gone willingly with this group. Shay and Cody, both people who'd helped her and other people, had worked for North Star believing in its mission. Tucker had helped them. Surely, they weren't evil. They couldn't be evil and fool so many good people.

But the Viannis and the Sons *were.* Didn't that mean someone could have infiltrated North Star without them knowing? Maybe North Star was smart, even good at helping people, but they hadn't brought down the Sons fully yet—and how long had it taken them to put Ace in jail?

They'd needed Jamison *and* Cody to do that. So it was plausible, especially by partnering with the Viannis who were more of an unknown, that the Viannis had in turn tricked North Star.

She wanted to believe that—needed to—because the alternative was too bleak to bear.

Rachel hitched in a breath. She had to find a way to tell the man across from her that the man standing beside him had been her would-be kidnapper—the man who'd blinded her. But she couldn't write a note. And she couldn't just come out and *say* it either, because if the man across from her truly didn't know, he'd likely be killed, no matter what kind of operative he was.

"Why don't I go get you some water? Give you some time to think about what direction you want to go in. Dymon here will watch you until you're ready to talk."

It wasn't threatening exactly. Nor was it friendly. A mission. It was all about the mission.

She could hear his chair scrape back as if he was going to get to his feet. As if he was about to leave her with her nightmare. She reached forward in a desperate attempt to grab him. She managed to do just that, both her hands clasping McMillan's arm before he fully stood.

"Please, wait."

Cody had taught her Morse code when they'd been in middle school. She'd been feeling bad about something—she couldn't even remember what it was now. But he'd cheered her up by teaching her Morse code. They'd made a game of it that summer.

She didn't remember it all, and there wasn't time to stumble. Still, she had to try. She *had* to.

"Miss. Let go of my arm," McMillan said, not totally unkindly.

It gave her an awful hope, that glimmer of kindness.

So she tapped what she could think of, in the most succinct terms she could manage.

Danger.

My face.

Him.

He didn't say anything, but he also didn't pull his arm away. He didn't tell her to let go, so she tapped out the code again. The same code. The same words.

He withdrew his arm, but instead of getting up or doing something dismissive, he laid his hand on top of hers and gave it a reassuring pat. "All right," he said, his voice low and controlled. "Dymon, why don't you go get the water? I'll stay here with Ms. Knight."

"I'm sure you've got better things to do, boss."

"You're still new. I wouldn't push your luck," McMillan warned.

"I did pass all your tests. You hired me. You have to trust me to do this stuff when you've got more important things to do."

Rachel held her breath, but the one thing that steadied her the most was McMillan's hand over hers. A reassuring weight that he'd gotten her message, and wasn't going to leave her alone with this man.

"You told me you hadn't had any personal experience with the Knights," McMillan said quietly. "That you were too low on the Vianni totem pole to know more than a few stories about Curtis Washington and his new life in South Dakota."

"That's right," the nightmare man agreed.

"Is that the story you want to stick to right here and right now?"

There was a long tense silence. McMillan's hand was still atop hers, and he began to tap. It took Rachel the second time through to figure it out.

Duck.

And then a gunshot went off.

There was a scuffle, a moan and then Rachel's arm was jerked as she was pulled out from under the table. "Wrong move, little girl."

Her nightmare had her again.

But this time—she would fight.

TUCKER SLID THE phone back into his pocket. He had to remain calm, because Duke was there and Duke wouldn't remain any kind of calm.

They had to head back to the house and get Rachel the hell out of there, even if he had to fight the entirety of North Star to do it.

"How familiar are you with the area?" Tucker asked, careful to keep his voice calm.

"Who was that on the phone?"

"I need you to get to the car. It's parked—"

"Oh, hell no," Duke snarled. "If you're going back in for my daughter, I'm going with you."

"We can't go in guns blazing. We can't—"

"I was a cop before you were born. I know a thing or two about what needs to be done, and I know what I'd do to keep my daughter safe."

At the end of his rope with indecision, Tucker snapped. "Like when a man tried to kidnap her and blinded her in the process?"

"He would have killed her," Duke said flatly. "But she's alive, because of me. She was hurt because of me,

I get it. I don't know how to go back and change my life. I did what I thought was right, always. You perfect?"

No, he couldn't pretend to be that.

"Now, you got another one of those?" Duke asked, nodding at the gun in his hand.

"No." Tucker considered giving it to Duke. Tucker could fight better with his hands than Duke would be able to. It would—

The muffled echo of a *crack* interrupted the picturesque quiet. *Gunshot.* Tucker was off running before he'd even thought it through. He looked back at Duke once. He was running, too, but at a much slower pace.

"Go!" Duke shouted.

Which was all the encouragement Tucker needed to run at full speed back to the house. He'd break down the front door if he had to. He'd—

The explosion was so loud and powerful, it knocked Tucker back. He managed to stay on his feet, but for a horrible second he watched the entire house go up in flames as the sound of glass shattering and debris thundering surrounded him.

Then, after that split second, he ran toward it. What other option was there? People were inside. Rachel. Shay. But as he headed for the door, flames and smoke already enshrouding it, people came pouring out.

Tucker didn't see Shay. He didn't know if that was good or bad. The people were bloody, burned, coughing. He tried to find someone who looked remotely communicative, but they were all in various shapes of injury and couldn't answer his demands as the fire roared around them.

Two figures emerged then, one dragging the other. It was Shay. He couldn't tell whom she was dragging, but it wasn't Rachel. It was a large man. Tucker ran to her.

"Sorry," she rasped. She let go of the man she'd been hauling as people rushed forward to help him.

"He'd been shot," Shay rasped. "I went to the questioning room and he'd been shot. I couldn't find Rachel or the new guy. The Dymon guy. He had to have taken her out the back." She swayed but Tucker managed to catch her before she fell in a heap. "The explosion went off before I managed to do anything. Got emergency services coming," she continued as Tucker helped her into a sitting position on the ground. "But I don't think I'm going to be much help with Rachel."

"Give me your gun," Tucker managed, though terror pounded through him. When she did, he handed it to Duke who huffed up to them. "Shay thinks Rachel got out—or was taken out with someone. I'm going to find the trail. You do the same," he instructed to Duke.

Much as it pained him to leave this misery in his wake, he had to find Rachel before she met a worse fate. He had to make a wide circle around the flames to get to the back. He didn't worry about how close Duke was. He only worried about getting to Rachel.

Debris had flown more back here, which made Tucker think the explosives had been detonated from the back. If whoever had Rachel had detonated the explosives by hand rather than remotely, it made sense. He'd have dragged Rachel out, then set off the bomb before he dragged her away.

Why drag her away and keep her alive, though? Why not let her die in the explosion?

But the guy hadn't. He'd taken her away, and regardless of the reason, Tucker had to believe that's what happened. Believe it and save her from this.

The yard was wooded. Tucker ruthlessly tamped down the panic gripping him. He had to think like a cop. Like the person he'd trained to be. Like his brothers. Calm in the face of crisis. In the face of someone he loved being taken.

He moved to the trees, looking for signs of tracks or struggle. There was nothing, but this was the only way the man could have gone. Tucker scoured the ground. He heard Duke's approach, though they didn't speak. They moved and they looked.

Tucker couldn't let himself think of Rachel being dragged out of that house by some Vianni thug. He couldn't think about the very real possibility that a Sons member was waiting to help—

"Wait." Tucker stopped. The rational thing to do was head for the trees and cover. Unless there was help waiting somewhere else. He tried to orient himself—the house—where it would be in relation to the Sons. The Sons current headquarters was a few hours away, *but* if they were meeting someone with a car, they'd need a road. It wouldn't have been the road Shay had instructed him to use, because that was the main thoroughfare and would be too obvious.

"Go back to the house. Get a car. Anyone you can find," Tucker instructed, already moving north instead of his original west. "Once you've got a car, start driving for Flynn via Route 5. But be careful. The Sons might be involved."

With no time to spare, Tucker took off for Route 5. It meant running through open land, and that was dangerous, but if he could get to Rachel before they got her into a car, he didn't care what they did to him.

Chapter Twenty

Rachel slowly came to. Someone was dragging her, swearing. She could feel the ground beneath her, tell it was still daylight as the sun beat down on her face.

"Stupid plan," the man muttered.

It was like her dream. The fear and his muttering, but she was bigger. She was a woman now. She'd tried to fight him back in that room, but then everything had gone black.

Now, everything hurt, and her head pounded with excruciating pain. He must have knocked her out. She tried to kick out, but her ankles were tied together. So were her hands. She wanted to sob, but she knew instinctively if he didn't know she was awake, she was better off.

She wasn't going to be able to escape him with her hands and feet tied, and she couldn't use the button Shay had sewn into her sleeve. But she was alive. She supposed that was the silver lining. She wasn't dead.

At three years old, she'd survived being cut in the face and losing her sight. She could survive this. She *would* survive this.

The dragging stopped and he dropped her without warning. She couldn't hold back the sharp groan of pain.

"You awake?"

Dymon nudged her with his foot, and she kept her eyes closed. She let her head loll as she made another soft groaning noise, trying to pretend she was still unconscious. Or just coming to.

He muttered something. There was shuffling, the methodical plodding of feet like he was pacing the hard ground beneath them. "I need help. You can't expect me to make it all the way to the road. Yeah, yeah, yeah. Had to shoot McMillan. No, I didn't check. I had to get her out. Yeah, I know no casualties but things went sideways."

Rachel realized he was on the phone, talking to someone about getting her to the road. And if he got her to the road, she'd be put into a car. There'd be more people.

How would anyone find her if she was in a car? Wasn't there something about not ever letting anyone take you to a second location? Better to be killed than make it to that second location.

She swallowed down the fear. Somehow, someway, she had to fight. There was no waiting for Tucker or Shay to find her if there was a car waiting. Once she got in that car, she was as good as dead.

Dymon continued to grumble, and she slowly realized he was done with his phone conversation and was instead just talking to himself. Nothing important or telling, just complaints about being the only one with the balls to do the dirty work.

Rachel continued to pretend as though she were unconscious as she tried to figure out how on earth she was going to get out of this. She couldn't get out of the bonds on her wrists and ankles—they were too tight—but there had to be *something* she could do.

Back in the room, this man had wanted to know

about her dream. About the knife. So…maybe she had to give that to him to keep him occupied, to buy herself time.

Hopefully enough time for Tucker to intercept her before the man got her to the car waiting for him.

She groaned some more, started to move, thrashed a bit against her bonds for effect. She blinked her eyes open.

Dymon grunted. "Thought I knocked you out better than that." He sighed heavily. "Guess I'll have to do a better job this time. Maybe just fix the problem altogether."

He was going to kill her. Here and now. No getting to the road. No second location, just death.

"No. No. Please—please don't." She swallowed at the fear and the bile rising in her throat. She had to be braver than this. "I know where it is," she blurted out. He'd mentioned the knife. She knew which one he was referring to. "I know who you are. I know what you did. And most importantly, I know where the knife you want is."

"So does your father."

"But you have me. Not him."

Dymon made a dismissive noise, and Rachel didn't know if it was agreement or refusal. She had no idea what he planned to do. He was simply a shadowy figure above her and she had no means to fight.

But no matter what was against her, she did not have to die without *trying* to survive. She knew what side of her the man was standing on, and she knew she was on a little bit of an incline. She could roll. And scream. Maybe someone would be able to save her.

If not? At least she'd tried.

She tested the incline, the placement of her own body

and rocked back and forth a little. If he noticed, he didn't say anything. She counted inwardly and then did her best to use momentum to move into a roll—screaming as loud as she could while she started to gain speed down the incline.

Dymon swore at her viciously, and there was the sound of hard footsteps and a stumble and more swearing. Then her rolling was stopped as she knocked into what she was assuming was him.

"You idiot," he yelled.

She had the impression of him getting ready to strike. She could only brace for impact, but instead of pain—a new voice yelled.

"Don't move."

Rachel almost cried out at the sound of Tucker's voice, but the sound caught in her throat as cold steel was pressed to her forehead.

She didn't know where he was, or if he could see her. She only knew there was a gun pressed to her head. She tried to see. Willed her eyes to work.

She could make out Dymon crouched above her, the gun pressed to her forehead. If she kicked out... He might shoot, but he might fall instead. They *were* on a hill. She just needed to place the kick in the right spot. Somehow.

"Rachel," Tucker's voice was very calm, and closer than it had been. "Do you remember what I told you about fighting?"

"She can't fight," the man said disgustedly. "I'm going to put a bullet through her brain. Then yours. Drop the gun."

"She's the only one who knows where it is," Tucker said, his voice so calm and...lethal. She might have shivered in fear if he weren't the only one who could help her survive this. "The evidence you're after. She's the only one."

Rachel thought about what Tucker had said about fighting. He'd told her to always go for the crotch. She just needed to kick the man in the crotch. She could figure out that general area, as long as she could position her body accordingly, she could do it.

"Curtis knows where it's at. I could kill her and—"

"I'm sorry, Rach. I know I promised never to lie to you again. So I won't. Duke died in the explosion."

Rachel jerked. It was a physical pain, even as she worked through what he'd *actually* said. He'd never promised not to lie to her. In fact, he had promised the opposite. So, Tuck was lying now? He had to be. He was supposed to get Dad out. There was no way Dad was dead. No way.

Please, God.

She didn't focus on the words. On what Dymon and Tucker continued to argue about. She focused on the shadowy outline of the man. Where best to kick. Her aim just had to be right.

Or she was dead. And so was Tucker.

TUCKER COULD SEE Rachel trying to figure out the angle. Slowly, he began to crouch, acting as if he were going to put his gun down. He held one hand up in mock surrender, slowly inching his gun closer and closer to the ground.

He needed Rachel to kick, just one kick even if it wasn't in line would push the guy back. The hill would help with momentum, the gun would go up and Tucker could get a shot off.

All as long as the other guy didn't pull that trigger first.

"That explosion shouldn't have killed anyone," the man finally said after a long tense silence.

Tucker had seen enough of the wreckage to understand where the explosives had detonated. So he had to lie and hope for the best. "Only if everyone was in the front of the house. The basement is another story, and I had a man in there getting Duke out. They're both dead."

He hoped the lies would give Rachel some comfort that Duke wasn't actually dead. That no one was.

Unless McMillan had died of his gunshot wound.

"What's the point of an explosion that doesn't kill anyone, anyway? And you clearly had an in with North Star. Why not take Duke and get what you're after?"

"I could have," the man agreed with a sickening sneer. "But that doesn't finish the job from twenty years ago, does it?"

"This does, though."

All three of them jerked at the sound of Duke's voice, but it didn't last long, since Duke immediately fired a shot that had the man falling to the ground. Lifeless.

"Dad?" Rachel asked tremulously.

Tucker was already halfway to her, but since Duke had come up from the direction of the road, he was closer. He was murmuring to Rachel and untying the bonds on her hands so Tucker took the ones on her feet.

"Dad." They wrapped their arms around each other, so Tucker gave them a moment by making sure the other man was dead.

Tucker couldn't find a pulse, but he still pulled the gun out of his hand and the knife out of his boot. They weren't out of the woods yet, even if they'd managed to end one threat.

"We have to get out of here," Tucker said reluctantly,

since Rachel was still clinging to Duke. "I can't imagine he was working alone."

"He's not. He was talking to someone about dragging me to the car. Is everyone at North Star all right? He shot McMillan. I…" Her hands were shaking, but Duke took them in his. Rachel kept talking. "When Shay took me in, they had this guy. Dymon is his name. He… I recognized his voice, from my dream."

"*He's* the guy?" Tucker looked at Duke for confirmation, and got a slight nod.

Tucker swore. She'd been kidnapped twice by the same man.

"I had to tell McMillan. I didn't think he understood how dangerous he was. So I tapped Morse code into his palm. Then he…this Dymon guy, he shot McMillan. It was so close and McMillan has to be dead, doesn't he?" Rachel asked, trying to wipe at her face, wet with tears. Tucker crouched next to her and used the hem of his shirt to wipe the rest of them away and clean her up a bit. She gave him a small smile.

Tucker could feel Duke's disapproving gaze, but they didn't have time for *that*.

"Shay dragged him out. They were getting him medical attention. He might make it." Probably a bit overly optimistic, but Tucker was willing to give her that in this moment. She'd used Morse code and… God, she was a wonder, but they had to get out of here. "Is there a car down at the road?"

"Yes. Not too far. I didn't see anyone else." Duke helped Rachel to her feet. Tucker flanked her on the other side. The ground was hilly, uneven, and helping Rachel toward the road was no easy task. She stumbled a few times, but they both held her up.

Through the trees, Tucker could begin to make out the road, but it wasn't as deserted as it should have been.

"Get down," Tucker hissed, pulling Rachel to the ground as he ducked for cover behind a swell of earth.

"What is it?" Rachel asked.

"Three men and another car aside from the one Duke drove." Tucker moved so he could get another glimpse. Two men were circling the car Duke had parked in the ditch, and one of them was on his phone. "I need a better look."

Rachel's grip on his arm tightened. "No. You're not going anywhere. Let's just head back to North Star. I know I was unconscious, but it can't be that far."

Tucker didn't want to tell her there wasn't much of North Star left, but more importantly he wanted the opportunity to capture these men who were clearly in on the explosion and kidnapping attempt. The last thing anyone needed was them roaming free—to come after Duke or Rachel again, or whatever else was in their plans.

"Just give me five minutes. Stay put right here." He tugged his arm out of Rachel's grasp and had to trust Duke to keep her there and quiet.

He moved in silence, using trees and rocks and swells of land as cover, until he was close enough to see the three men. Tuck could hear them talking, but couldn't make out what they were saying. He considered getting closer, but with Duke and Rachel not that far away, it wasn't worth the risk.

Knowing he had to get them out of harm's way first, he carefully climbed his way back toward Duke and Rachel.

"Just the three men, but definitely waiting for their guy here to show up with Rachel."

"Vianni," Duke said disgustedly.

"No, they aren't Vianni men. Those are Sons men."

"You recognize them?" Duke asked.

"Got files on all three. The one on the right got off on a rape case because of a technicality. The one in the middle is my suspect on a murder case, but I don't have anything beyond circumstantial evidence and the prosecutor won't issue a warrant. The third has been in and out of jail for dealing drugs, armed robbery, you name it."

"Gotta love the legal system," Duke muttered. "What do we do, then? Pick them off?"

Tucker shook his head. "Too risky. They've got three guys, and three more high-powered weapons than we've got. Even if I use that guy's gun." Tucker glanced at Rachel. She wouldn't agree to this plan, but he didn't feel right trying to make it behind her back either. "Take her back."

"I will not—"

Duke spoke right over her. "What are you going to do?"

"They're accessory to kidnapping, possibly that explosion. I can arrest them."

"On your own, boy? Three against one isn't the best odds."

Tucker pulled out his phone. "I'll even the odds, then."

Duke's expression went even more granite. "And which of your brothers' lives are you willing to risk?"

It was a jab, but somewhere between that explosion and here he'd figured out what he hadn't fully understood until this moment. Yeah, four of his brothers were in love with Duke's foster daughters. Three of them had kids or babies on the way to support and protect.

They had lives, and they shouldn't be taking unnecessary risks.

But they had. Over and over again this summer. Why?

Because nothing was ever going to be truly *good* until the Sons were gone. Truly taken out. The more of them they arrested, the more they had a chance of someone giving that last piece of evidence that brought the entire group to its knees.

"All of them, Duke. All of them."

Chapter Twenty-One

"I will not be carted off while you do something dangerous," Rachel said. She was careful to keep her voice quiet like they were doing, but what she really wanted to do was yell.

Her father's grip was tight on her arm and she wanted to shake it off and rage at him for even *considering* the fact they would go off and leave Tucker to do this, other Wyatt boys or no.

"Give me a second," Tucker said, and then she was being passed off and it was so *infuriating* because she couldn't exactly walk away, could she? Not in this foreign territory she didn't know.

"Listen. I'm not going to do anything stupid. My brothers, law enforcement agents who can also arrest these guys, are going to come and be backup. Maybe get some information that helps us land an even bigger blow to the Sons. I have to do this, and I'm sorry, I can't do it with you here."

Emotion clogged her throat. To get this far and then be relegated to…dead weight. Swept off by her father.

"It isn't right. I didn't *do* anything," she said, feeling raw and cracked open. She *couldn't* do anything. She understood she was a liability in the here and now and it was an awful, awful feeling.

Tucker's hands cupped her cheeks. "Yeah, figuring out where the evidence was, punching Shay in the face, using *Morse* code to tell McMillan his double agent was really a double agent, getting abducted and dragged through the woods but being smart enough to stay alive—nothing at all."

It should have been patronizing, but instead it was soothing. Because Tucker sounded…awestruck. Not in an *oh-poor-little-Rachel-managed-to-do-something* way, but like she was strong and all that stuff had mattered.

And it had. What might have happened if she hadn't gotten the message to McMillan? Yes, he might not have been shot, but Dymon could have gotten away with a lot more, and done a lot more damage.

"The Vianni part of this is over. Now, it's the Sons part. Let your father take you back to North Star. You've contributed, and probably have the concussion to prove it. Now, it's my turn. Okay?"

It wasn't *okay*, but she understood he had to do this. For himself. For his brothers. She moved her hands to his on her face, then slid her palms down the length of his arms, over his shoulders and up to his face.

"Okay," she said, and then pressed her mouth to his. He stiffened, likely because her father was around, but she didn't care. Not when he was going off into danger, and she was letting him.

But he relaxed into it, kissing her back in a way that felt like some kind of promise. He pulled back, taking her hands off his face.

"Be safe, and don't do a thing until your brothers are here." The kiss had felt like a promise, but she needed the words. "Promise me."

There was a pause, and he squeezed her hands in

his. "I promise. Now, let your Dad take you back to North Star. You've got a hell of a bump on your head. I'm completely unscathed."

But he wouldn't stay that way necessarily. Still, there was nothing she could do about that. She'd only be in his way if she tried to convince him to take her along. Rachel knew she'd achieved some important things throughout this whole mess. Now her role was to step back and let him take the next step.

Hadn't she been harping at him to take help from his brothers—no matter what they'd been through and what he wanted to protect them from? Now, she had to take her own advice. Let him get the help he needed.

It didn't make it easy, but it also didn't make her a failure.

"Be safe," she repeated, giving his hands another squeeze before letting him pass her back to her father.

It was hard walking away, but as her father led her, the adrenaline began to fade into something heavier. Her head ached. Her body hurt. She felt nauseous.

"I don't know what you think you're doing kissing that boy," Dad grumbled, once they'd put some distance between them and Tucker. "I hope it doesn't mean what I think it means."

If she'd had any energy, she might have smiled. She was still so relieved he was alive, she couldn't muster any anger toward him. "If all of your daughters end up with a Wyatt, is that really so bad?"

"It is when they have to be dragged through pain and danger to arrive at that conclusion."

She frowned. *Dragged?* "It's your fault I'm even here. That Tucker is even here. This all begins with you."

"If this is all my fault, then the Sons are all those boys' faults."

She opened her mouth to argue, because of course that wasn't true. So, maybe it was true it wasn't her father's fault the Viannis were after him. But… "You had that knife. The one that hurt me. You lied to me, and made me doubt myself."

He was quiet for a few seconds as they walked. She could smell the acrid tinge of smoke on the air and knew they were close to getting to North Star.

"I did what I thought was right at the time. I'm sorry it hurt you, baby. You'll never know… I wanted you all safe. I'd been at the ranch in WITSEC for almost eight years when they found me again. I'd built a life. A better life than the one I'd grown up in, a better life than I'd had on the force. I had your mother, and I had you and the other girls. I could have run, but I wasn't going to give up this life I loved for some lowlife crime group. I needed something stronger than WITSEC, and evidence seemed the best way to keep them gone. An insurance policy."

"So, you let him go?"

"I didn't have him. I had to get you to the hospital. I couldn't go after him. But I could collect what he left behind. I could use it as my own threat. And it worked."

"Until now. Why now?"

"That's why I went to Granger McMillan. When I got a few veiled threats earlier this month, I went to his father. He'd been in charge of WITSEC when they moved me and we'd become friends. He recommended his son's organization to help get to the bottom of it. Because as far as I knew, the Viannis were all dead or in prison. Granger started looking into it, and when he found some connections between the Vianni group and the Sons, he brought me in."

"Of your own volition," she said.

"More or less. I wanted to protect you girls. Getting out of the way seemed the only option. Besides, I had the evidence. I knew I could use it if I needed to, and I thought McMillan could help me get it into the right hands, but I had to be sure I could trust him. I wasn't sure. I'm still not sure."

"He got shot. By this Dymon man. I told him he was the man from my dreams, more or less. He was going to help, but Dymon shot him first."

"Not Dymon. Vianni. The man who blinded you was Vianni's son," Duke explained. "McMillan told me he'd hired a Vianni underling in the hopes he'd be a double agent. He named some low level thug I hadn't ever had contact with, and I didn't recognize him. He must have had plastic surgery, taken on this new identity, because he was supposed to be dead. I was told a hit had taken him out right after your attack. I figured it was because he'd failed. You recognizing his voice is the only reason I put two and two together."

"So, you killed the man who was after you?"

"Appears so. I'm not saying that will end the Vianni group, but the family I put behind bars is mostly dead. It should be over."

"Except Tucker is still out there, trying to take down the Sons."

"He's a Wyatt, Rachel. They can put on a good show, but they can't let it go. Not while the Sons still exist, not while Ace lives, even if he's in prison. You get wrapped up in a Wyatt, that's what you're getting wrapped up in."

He didn't say it like it was some failing, only like it was fact. Which, no doubt, it was.

"You couldn't let injustice go when you saw it. You wouldn't run away when that came back to haunt you."

She inhaled. "I know you love them like sons, and I understand why you'd be protective of your daughters. But you gave us the example. Doesn't it make sense that we'd all see that in you, even if we didn't know the details, and admire it in others?"

Duke was quiet for a long while, though instead of holding her arm he slid his arm around her shoulders and led her that way.

"I want that head of yours checked out," he said, planting a gentle kiss near the place her head hurt the worst.

"Because of Tucker or just in general?"

Duke chuckled. "Both."

Something inside of her eased. She was still scared, worried for Tucker and all the Wyatts. Worried for McMillan and if he'd survived the gunshot wound. But her father was safe and here with her. One arm of this whole complicated thing had been taken care of.

Now Tucker needed to take care of his, and come back to her in one piece.

TUCKER WAS INTENT on keeping his promise. There was just one little problem. The three men on the road weren't staying there. Apparently, they'd grown tired of waiting for the dead man.

Jamison and Cody were close enough that they'd be here in the next ten to twenty minutes, if they rushed, which they likely would. The other three were much farther away, and Brady and Dev were physically compromised in that group.

But Cody had messaged them all.

Tucker wouldn't hide from the men walking up the side of the hill. He'd promised Rachel he wouldn't do anything until his brothers were here, but he could hardly help it when two of the three men were coming for him—one staying behind and poking through the car Duke had left.

Still, Tucker remained still. He kept his gun ready, and he listened.

"These Vianni morons. Soft city idiots. I'm already tired of cleaning up their messes."

"You can't say no to that kind of cash, though. Not with everything falling apart. I've been thinking of heading to Chicago myself."

The other man offered an anatomically impossible alternative and they both chuckled good-naturedly.

Tucker might have been swayed by the fact they sounded like any two men shooting the breeze. But he had files on these guys and he knew what they were capable of. Monsters could walk and talk and laugh, but what they were willing to *do* was what made them monsters.

They were coming up on him. Whatever happened, his brothers were on their way.

"What a lazy SOB. Couldn't even drag her this far?"

"Oh, he got this far," Tucker said companionably.

They whirled on him, one with a gun and the other with a knife. The one Tucker knew from his files as Justin Hollie sneered.

"A Wyatt." He flipped the knife in his hand. "Your free pass is over. We don't have to worry about hurting Ace's kids anymore."

Which wasn't what Tucker had expected anyone to say, let alone so gleefully. "Oh, yeah? Why's that?"

The man snorted. "Guess you're the last to hear. Ace is dead. No need to come after us anymore. He can't do crap." He spread his arms wide. "Now, I'm a reasonable guy. I let you go, you leave us alone."

"Jail isn't dead."

"He died in jail. Crossed the wrong guy." Hollie snapped his fingers. "Boom. Gone. I heard it was even on the news."

Tucker couldn't process that. It couldn't possibly be true. "I don't believe you."

He shrugged. "No skin off my nose. Just telling you there's no beef here anymore."

"Of course, if you want one, we can give you one," the other man said. Travis Clyne, Tucker was pretty sure. The rapist who'd gotten off because the prosecutor hadn't thought the case was tight enough.

Tucker pushed away the thought of his father being dead. It just wasn't possible Ace Wyatt, the black cloud over his entire life, had just been…killed in jail like a common criminal, instead of the evil incarnate that he was.

Because there were two men who'd done plenty of evil right in front of him. "It turns out I've got a beef with kidnapping, explosions, killing people." He turned his gaze from Hollie to Clyne. "Rape."

"Your funeral." Clyne lifted his gun, but before he'd even gotten close to aiming, a shot rang out. It didn't appear to hit anyone, but Cody and Jamison appeared on either side of the Sons members.

The one with the knife whirled out toward Jamison, but Tucker shot, causing Hollie to stumble with a scream of pain. Cody punched Clyne before he could get a shot off at Tucker.

The third man came charging up, likely hearing the commotion. He stopped abruptly when all three Wyatts pointed guns at him. Looking at his friends writhing on the ground, then the guns, the man dropped his own.

"On your knees," Tucker ordered.

"Here. Tie him up." Cody tossed him some zip ties.

"Jeez. Do you always have these on you?" Tucker asked, quickly putting them to use.

"Never leave home without them," Cody returned, using more to tie up the man he'd punched. Jamison was doing the same.

They all stood at the same time.

"Unscathed again," Cody said with the shake of a head. "You've got the touch, Tuck."

Tuck let out a breath, almost a laugh. "Yeah, I felt bad about that for a while. I don't think I do so much anymore."

"I'll call county to pick these guys up. They've already got some guys collecting evidence on the explosives," Jamison said.

"There's also the car down on the road."

Jamison nodded. He quickly called all the information in. When he hung up, Tucker knew he had to broach the topic he didn't really want to understand.

"They said Ace is dead."

Jamison and Cody exchanged a glance. "We heard that too. Gage was getting everything confirmed when you messaged. We told him to stay put, we had this."

"Do you think he actually listened?"

Jamison smiled wryly. "The county guys will pass it along if he started heading this way."

"Do you think it's true?"

Both brothers sobered. Cody shrugged helplessly, and Jamison ran a hand over his neck.

"I don't know what to think," Jamison said. "So, let's focus on the here and now. Waiting for some guys to cart these morons away. Making sure Duke and Rachel are really safe."

Tucker turned to Cody. "North Star is beat up pretty good."

He nodded grimly. "They're all getting transported to the hospital. Liza's got the girls so Nina could drive over and pick up Duke and Rachel."

"She needs a doctor."

"I'm sure Nina will see to it."

Tucker nodded, but the possibility that Ace was dead overshadowed everything. "If he's dead, that means… it's over."

"We're law enforcement, Tuck," Jamison said, ever the cop. "As long as they're out there hurting people, it isn't over."

"No… But he is. Ace existing, linking us to it. The emotional aspect. It's over." He rubbed at his chest. "He can't be the boogeyman if he's dead."

Cody nodded. "So, we'll hope he is. Dead just the way he deserved. Broken and in jail with absolutely no fanfare."

Tucker let that settle through him. It seemed impossible, but it *would* be fitting. No standoff. No showy end. Nothing that could be described as godlike or awe-inspiring to the wrong kind. Ace's worst nightmare. To have a boring death no one remembered.

Tucker smiled at his brothers. Yeah, that's what he'd hope for.

Epilogue

There was fanfare.

No one said they were celebrating Ace Wyatt's death. They were celebrating Duke being okay. They were celebrating Brady healing and Felicity finding out she was having a girl. They were celebrating life and joy.

But Rachel knew that at least some of that joy was in knowing the man who'd caused them such pain and fear was well and truly gone.

Grandma Pauline had made a feast fit for royalty. They'd shoved everyone around the table as they always did. Even Dev was smiling. It was the best dinner in Rachel's memory.

Dad was safe. Everyone was safe. The men Tucker and his brothers had arrested had even agreed to talk, which had led to more arrests and a complete federal raid on the Sons compound. They hadn't been eradicated, but they had been taken down quite a few pegs.

And Ace Wyatt was dead. All the Wyatt men seemed…lighter. A little out of sorts, but lighter. After dinner, no one was quick to leave. Even Dad and Sarah who had ranch chores to see to lingered.

"Why don't you go on out to the porch," Grandma Pauline said quietly into her ear.

Rachel frowned. "Why?"

"Just go on now."

Confused, Rachel did as she was told, stepping out into the quickly cooling off night.

"Rach? You're not headed back on your own are you?"

Tucker. She should have known. He must have snuck out, and Grandma Pauline had sent her to find out why.

"No." She moved toward his voice. "What are you doing out here all by yourself?"

He was quiet for a moment. "I'm not sure. Everyone's so happy. I'm happy. But... It's weird. I don't know how to feel about... I'm happy for all of them. Happy Ace isn't a shadow on our lives anymore, but I always assumed there'd be some big standoff. And now he's just gone. I'm happy, but it's...complicated."

"I think that's fair. I think you get to have whatever feelings on the matter you need to."

"Yeah, I guess so."

His arm came around her shoulders, so she wrapped hers around his waist. She sighed and relaxed into him. A good man, with a good heart. "I'm glad you weren't hurt."

"It seems we all managed to make it through okay. McMillan's going to be released from the hospital tomorrow."

"And Shay didn't lose her job, according to Nina."

"So, all's well that ends well, I guess."

Rachel thought on that. "It's not an ending, though. It's just life. We endured some bad parts. Now, we get to enjoy some good parts."

"Good parts," he echoed. He wound a strand of her hair around her finger. "You know one good part we seemed to have missed? I've never taken you out."

"Taken me out. Like…a date?"

"Yeah, like a date."

She grinned. There hadn't been time to talk much about the things that had transpired between them on a personal level. She'd been nervous to bring it up. Unsure. But he was asking her on a date. "I guess you should probably do that."

"Tomorrow night?"

"I'll see if I can clear my schedule."

They stood in the quiet for a long while. It was a nice moment. A settling moment. He was an honorable man, who'd take her out on a date, and take things slow. But he'd take them seriously, too. She liked to think it was what they both needed after this horrible year.

She turned in his arms, wrapping hers around his neck. "You're a good man, Tucker Wyatt. You're all good men. Whether Ace is dead or alive. That's always been true. Whether you got hurt fighting him or managed to escape unscathed. Who you are doesn't change. I hope you know that."

"I'm getting there. It helps to hear."

"I think you'll find the Knight women are very good at telling you all that."

"I guess it's good I found me one, then."

"Yeah, it is." She moved onto her toes and kissed him. Without fear, without stress. Just the two of them.

His grip tightened, but the kiss remained gentle. Explorative. Because that's exactly what they had ahead of them.

They'd found each other, and somehow ended years of fear. Of worry. Of dark shadows.

Now, they didn't have to worry anymore. They could

get to know each other as something more than friends, find a way to have a life together. With their family.

Happily-ever-after.

* * * * *

COMING SOON!

We really hope you enjoyed reading this book. If you're looking for more romance, be sure to head to the shops when new books are available on

Thursday 9th July

To see which titles are coming soon, please visit

millsandboon.co.uk/nextmonth

LET'S TALK
Romance

For exclusive extracts, competitions
and special offers, find us online:

f facebook.com/millsandboon

🐦 @MillsandBoon

📷 @MillsandBoonUK

Get in touch on 01413 063232

For all the latest titles coming soon, visit
millsandboon.co.uk/nextmonth

JOIN US ON SOCIAL MEDIA!

Stay up to date with our latest releases, author news and gossip, special offers and discounts, and all the behind-the-scenes action from Mills & Boon...

 millsandboon

 millsandboonuk

 millsandboon

It might just be true love...

MILLS & BOON
MEDICAL
Pulse-Racing Passion

Set your pulse racing with dedicated, delectable doctors in the high-pressure world of medicine, where emotions run high and passion, comfort and love are the best medicine.

MILLS & BOON
Desire

Indulge in secrets and scandal, intense drama and plenty of sizzling hot action with powerful and passionate heroes who have it all: wealth, status, good looks… everything but the right woman.